TOO CLOSE TO THE WIND

A NOVEL

RICHARD ATTREE

To my wife, Nikki, with whom I've shared more than half my life, and without whom this novel would not have been written.

CONTENTS

PART I

THE ATLANTIC

"To live is to suffer, to survive is to find some meaning in the suffering."
(Friedrich Nietzsche)

1

A GHOST IN EL MÉDANO

The Atlantic. Monday, October 26, 2015, 07:50. I'm surprised to find myself still alive as the first streaks of light distinguish sky from sea. At least I hope I am, but it's far from certain.

After drifting on my board for twenty-four hours there's not much left of my sanity. Perceptions and thoughts are floating around but it's not clear whose they are. Voices crowd my head, competing for ownership. There's also a whole heap of pain, but who's feeling it? Where the hell am I and how did I get here?

Then I notice something that persuades me I'm either dreaming, hallucinating, or dead. As the sun climbs out of the sea a shape emerges with it. At first it's just a dot, then a mysterious blob travelling towards me on a collision course.

I rub my salt-encrusted eyes, trying to focus on the mirage, expecting it to disappear. Instead, it gets bigger, coming straight out of the sun, backlit like some epic Hollywood vision of an alien spaceship. From somewhere there's a hideous cackle of ironic laughter, possibly mine.

"Mate, this is ridiculous!" a voice-in-my-head sneers. "You really think your story deserves such a blockbuster ending?"

The apparition is a hundred metres away and still heading

straight at me. Pure white, glistening in the dawn, perfectly reflected in the mirror-flat sea. I've never believed in a supernatural being but now I'm not so sure that God is dead. If this is the kind of show he puts on to welcome a soul into the After Life then he can count me in. "Hallelujah, I'm a believer!" my voices sing, like a demented gospel choir.

The previous day—the day I should have drowned, started well enough ... when I opened my eyes it was blowing a hoolie! Of course, the *sangría* and *cerveza* had been flowing in the bar where I worked and Saturday night had already become Sunday morning before I staggered back to my apartment. I woke with a hangover, as usual ... but my friend, the wind, was rattling the shutters, urging me to get out of bed even before the sun hit my window.

Looking out, the mountains were caught in that unnaturally pink light. The sky is immense here and every dawn is a performance. The beach was still in shadow, deserted, but white horses were dancing towards the bay, driven on by *Los Alisios*, the northeast trade-winds. Now I was awake, the hangover forgotten, and the day had a purpose.

The wind, waves and my windsurfing board had been my *only* friends lately, the only reasons to get out of bed voluntarily. My life had fallen apart and I'd been existing as a recluse, a ghost in El Médano, the small Canarian surf town where I'd been living for the past few months—although to call it 'living' would be to flatter my existence. I avoided people, so I had no other friends and I'd made no enemies. I was neither liked nor hated, just ignored.

For a while, after that Sunday I was the talk of the town—much better known as a missing person than as the sad loner who nobody would miss. There was even a mention in the local newspaper, *La Opinión*. When no body turned up most people assumed I was at the bottom of the Atlantic or in some lucky shark's stomach. The story died and I was soon just a ghost again.

· · ·

So, the day was a disaster but it started promisingly ... Conditions looked exceptional and I had a new friend. Stepping onto a brand new board for the first time is always a special moment for a wind-surfer—like launching a ship. We might not smash open a bottle of champagne but she'd been well toasted the previous night. Now I was gagging to ride her—perhaps that's why it all went pear-shaped.

The wind was perfect for a 4.7 metre sail—every wave-sailor's favourite size and the swell had been building all night. The waves on the reef looked *perfecto*—decent size in the sets, peeling cleanly. I'd have them to myself for at least the next hour if I got my act together —that's how early it was. A few tourists were having breakfast in the cafe on the boardwalk but the surf shops weren't open yet. There was still nobody on the beach and I was the only windsurfer rigging up.

I grabbed my new board and ran my hands over her flowing lines. It was a little ritual I had—a pause before I entered the fray, a moment to be inspired by the craftsmanship I held in my hands. She was made by the local shaper: Rick, of 'WHY Custom Wave Boards'— a classic, elegant shape with minimal but effective graphics. I'd asked Rick to make me a pure white board with just his logo in bold black 3-D letters. I told him I wanted something unique, a one-off, so I requested that he add a question mark and I specified that my board should be the only one ever produced with this.

I gazed at the board and the customised graphics confronted me with a simple, stark question: "WHY?" I took a moment to consider my answer. From now on this would be part of the ritual—a moment to remind myself why I spent so much time and resources on this obsessive activity; remind myself how lucky I was to be able to escape gravity and surf the wind. To anyone else she was just a chunk of foam, fibreglass, carbon and epoxy but I was about to trust her with my life. Her logo was a reminder: never take this for granted.

My moment of reflection observed, I threw the equipment together, working on autopilot. My brain didn't need to be engaged— I could rig in my sleep. The routine was the same every time and a decade of performing it whenever my friend, the wind, called had ingrained it in my subconscious. I unrolled the sail onto the boardwalk, sleeved the mast and pulled on the downhaul without taking my eyes from the horizon. I clamped the boom to the mast and attached the outhaul, my focus still on the waves.

A set rolled in and I watched as geometric lines of surf marched across the reef. I picked one and imagined myself riding it, my body making strange little movements like a bizarre dance to a private soundtrack. Taking my eyes from the water I met a tourist's startled gaze, bemused by my antics, intrigued that my morning had such a clear purpose. I nodded distractedly, glanced down and was surprised to find I had everything ready to go.

A gust of wind swirled up the sand towards me, tugging at my sail impatiently. I Jammed the rig into my board and sprinted to the water.

That was my first mistake: not pausing for a second to check the equipment. A windsurfing rig is attached to the board by something called a 'universal joint' ('UJ'). There's a clue in that innocuous-sounding jargon. The term: 'universal' is normally reserved for something important, crucial even. Take the Universal Declaration of Human Rights, for instance. It's more than a heap of words hastily flung together—it's a milestone document in the history of humanity, carefully constructed to safeguard lives and liberty.

The UJ is similarly worth respecting. It's more than a bendy piece of rubber connecting board and rig—it's a windsurfer's lifeline and if you care about your life you look after your lifeline. You check it before you launch and replace it before the rubber perishes. Unfortunately, that Sunday morning I *didn't* care about my life. I was desperate to leave it behind on the boardwalk and escape to that other world where I danced on water. All I wanted that morning was to be gone with the wind.

My second error was to sprint to the water without telling a soul. I was alone, of course, no windsurfing buddy to share the session with me. But if I'd just strolled over to the cafe and said *hola* to the staff, mentioned that I was the first one launching—the guinea pig testing the wind ... perhaps they'd have remembered me and called the *socorristas* when I didn't come back.

Maybe the drink had something to do with it. The alcohol was still clouding my brain, dulling the pain as usual. I was hung-over, dehydrated. I hadn't had breakfast, not even a sip of water. My most serious mistake was to take my unstable mind onto the water with me ... but even that shouldn't have threatened my life.

I could normally rely on my fitness, technique and experience. I was twenty-five and in good shape (apart from the lack of sleep, dehydration and hangover), with a decade of expert windsurfing. It wouldn't have been a problem if Sunday's session had been normal. But it wasn't. It was the day I should have drowned. Survival depended on my state of mind ... and that was a mess.

The previous evening had brought this home to me. Ironically, as a loner I was a good listener. I could sympathise with other people's problems because I had plenty myself. It made me a good barman. Customers were happy to confess their darkest secrets until the small hours of the morning. Unfortunately, there was nobody there for *me* when I dragged myself back to my lonely apartment.

El Médano was a party town, an 'Endless Summer' kind of place, a town with no winter where everybody pursued sun, sex, surf, and fun—endlessly. Médanites wanted to let the good times roll, not waste them with a sad loner.

Most nights I drank a fair bit to drown my sorrows. I guess that's why I took the job in the bar. I could handle drink well enough, it was the mornings that were the problem—except when the wind was blowing—then I could forget the loneliness, the depression, and the hangovers for a few hours.

Saturday night was always a busy shift. As usual, there was a fiesta in party-town and the Endless Summer people were in full-on Saturday Night Fever mode. They invaded the bar with their *sangría*-fuelled games, their egos and selfies, while my mood became darker as the night wore on.

Rick, the WHY Boards shaper, had promised to pop in for a drink to celebrate my new board. I was hoping he might provide some relief from the relentless posturing, perhaps even a chance to make a friend in the town. He was the one person in El Médano I'd managed to connect with—as a customer, at least ... But that night only demonstrated how shallow the connection was.

It didn't help that both of us had drunk a few too many, or that a Flamenco session in the bar made conversation impossible without yelling at each other, but my inability to communicate went deeper. You could describe it as existential (if you were being pretentious)—a classic example of Sartre's 'hell is other people'. The problem, my hell, was that other people had the impression I thought I was superior, cooler than them, simply because I said so little. But they couldn't be more wrong ...

I was on the run from my past. I'd made some serious mistakes, betrayed the people who trusted me, fucked up my life. Now I found it hard to trust *myself*, let alone anyone else. I had such a poor opinion of myself that I rarely thought I had anything *worth* saying.

When Rick walked into the bar that Saturday night my self-esteem was at an all-time low. But he didn't know that. He didn't even know my name. He propped himself on a bar stool ordered a *cerveza*, and shouted to me:

"*Hombre*, people tell me you surf well, you know what you want from a board, you look like a hardcore dude—with the tan, dreadlocks, tattoos—the ladies must love you, no? But you're a bit of a mystery ..."

I shrugged. Compliments only made me worry about a hidden agenda.

"I mean, what are you doing here anyway? You're an Ozzie, right? A long way from home, eh?"

I muttered that I was backpacking around Europe and I'd heard that the windsurfing in El Médano was good, but it didn't satisfy his curiosity:

"So, I'm a bit of a Clint Eastwood fan and when you walked into my workshop you reminded me of his character in 'Fistful of Dollars'..."

"—"

"You know, the 'Man with No Name'?"

"?"

"You don't give much away do you, *amigo* ...?"

"—" There was nothing I could say to him.

Rick had a notoriously short fuse. He didn't suffer fools gladly and now he was irritated, as well as curious:

"I mean, just who do you think you are *muchacho*? You walk into my workshop as cool as Clint, asking for customised graphics that I'd never even thought of. I make you a board that's as good as anything I've ever made, but I don't even know your name ..."

"My name is Nick" I replied. "But you can call me: 'The Man with No Name' if you like."

He laughed and shook my hand. That simple touch was the first genuine warmth anyone had shown me in months. The ice had been broken. Now I was desperate to reach out and tell him about the hell I was going through. But there was a wall around me—a wall I'd built to protect myself.

"Look mate, I don't think I'm cool like Clint Eastwood. I'm not even 'interesting'. I'm just someone who's fucked up their life and doesn't want to screw anybody else's up. So I keep things to myself, OK?"

That came out far more aggressively than I'd intended. Rick put his hand up apologetically and looked away, embarrassed.

"Hey, no problem *hombre*! Fine with me. Sorry to bother you, Nick."

He drained his glass and got up to leave. Regret surged through me:

"No, *I'm* sorry Rick."

I was sweating now, dizzy—was it the alcohol or the onset of a panic attack?

"Look mate, I don't talk much because I don't have much to say."

Rick nodded. I ploughed on, desperate to explain myself, to connect with him, but I only dug myself a deeper hole:

"Maybe it's the same with Clint? Perhaps he's not a super cool loner dude, just a bit shy? You know, lacking confidence, low self-esteem—that kind of thing?"

Now I'd definitely gone too far. Rick scowled at me like a priest who's just been told the Pope was a secret transvestite. He muttered something inaudible and turned towards the exit. Then, remembering I was one of his customers, he wished me goodnight:

"Well, *buenas noches* Nick. Good to, um ... *talk* to you. I hope you like the new board. It's looking good for tomorrow, eh? *¡Hasta mañana!* See you on the water, maybe."

With that he walked out of the bar, leaving me alone with my demons and fifty drunk revellers.

Saturday night had already become Sunday morning when I called time, kicked out the remaining punters and staggered back to my apartment, taking my emotional baggage with me. And that's where it should have stayed. But instead, I spent a sleepless few hours chewing over my problems and then hung-over, worse-for-wear, I brought all that angst with me onto the water.

Sunday, 08:00. The session, like the day, started promisingly. The wind was kind to me as I launched. I powered through the shore-break, celebrating by throwing myself into a forward loop. The world turned arse over tit and I landed still planing. Yeeha!

It was something of a breakthrough moment. For one heady moment my life was turned on its head and suddenly it seemed more bearable from that perspective. And to land it like that! I looked around to see if anyone had witnessed it but there was only empty water, a deserted beach, and the few tourists on the boardwalk busy with their breakfast.

The planing loop didn't just inspire me though, it unhinged me. With hindsight, I see it as another of my mistakes. Subjecting my unstable brain to that bare-knuckle ride only invited the chaos back in. My blood was instantly saturated with adrenaline and the rush was like an acid trip. From then on I was as high as one of those damn kites and rational thought was missing in action.

I blasted a kilometre upwind to the waves at *El Muelle*, the harbour wall, where I spent most of my sessions. It was *my* spot, but it could be horribly crowded. Not that morning though. For the best part of an hour, I had the waves to myself—as I'd hoped when I braved a hangover to greet the dawn. It was one of the best hours of my life, in fact.

Occasionally it feels like you can do no wrong and you're in sync with everything around you—the wind, the waves, the equipment, the seabirds, flying fish, turtles ... this was one of those rare sessions. It's difficult to find the words to explain it, even to another windsurfer.

I could mention the timing of the sets—the way there was a lull every time I finished a wave-ride, opening a channel for me to blast back out to sea; providing just the right ramp to launch me skywards; the ideal swell to carve my gybe on; and then another perfect wall, peeling down the line, the lip just begging to be smacked ... time after time.

I could describe the colour of the water, the exquisite graduations from aquamarine over the reef to deep ocean violet; the way that Mt Teide, the highest peak in Spain, was etched against the azure sky with a fresh dusting of snow. This island has scenery on a grand scale and that morning everything was larger than life.

I could paint a picture with my words but that's all they are and words are woefully inadequate to describe pure visceral experience like the hour I spent alone at El Muelle. I was running on feeling, intuition, emotion ... thoughts were unnecessary. But then one of my unthinking spontaneous decisions turned out to be yet another miscalculation—and it changed everything.

For some reason, I chose that morning to try something I'd thought about but never had the nerve to do. Looking way downwind I could see waves breaking on the rocky point at the foot of *Montaña Roja*, the red mountain. They looked bigger and better than the playful ones up at the harbour. The hordes would be arriving at *El Muelle* any minute now but nobody ever sailed the point—you'd have to be mental to consider it.

Of course, I knew how dangerous it could be. The surf there was seriously powerful, breaking onto razor-sharp lava, and the balance of danger versus reward was stacked against the surfer. If anything went wrong I'd be swept behind the mountain, at the mercy of the current that ripped out into the Atlantic. Once hidden behind *Montaña Roja* no-one would see me again—next stop was South America. That's exactly how people had been lost before.

I knew all this but the warnings were drowned out by a stream of ridiculous clichés repeated over a pounding beat in my addled brain like a stupid rap song: "no pain, no gain"; "if you don't go, you'll never know"; "fuck it, just go for it mate!"

I looked around, startled to hear myself shout the last of these gems aloud. A couple of gnarly old *Canarios* were fishing from the harbour wall, immersed in their own world. They had their own agenda that morning, their own connection with the sea, and they ignored me like the tourists on the boardwalk. I glanced back at them and charged off downwind on an exhilarating broad reach over huge open ocean swells.

Within a couple of minutes I was blasting past the beach I launched from and out into unfamiliar water. A few moments later I was sailing past the vertical cliffs at the foot of the mountain. I'd walked around there sometimes, marvelling at the otherworldly rock formations, but never experienced *Montaña Roja* from sea level. The cliffs towered over me, gouged by *barrancos*—volcanic ravines like gashes in the blood red rock.

For a while I sailed defensively, trying to get a feel for the setup, wary of choosing the wrong wave and getting a pounding. It was as daunting as anywhere I'd windsurfed, including some famously challenging spots I'd visited on my travels. I was in my comfort zone up at the harbour but these were waves of consequence. The sane side of my brain questioned whether I was simply way out of my league.

Then adrenaline kicked in and the same macho clichés were taunting me again. I couldn't just sail back to the beach without riding one of these monsters. I gybed onto an immense outside swell and headed back in towards the maelstrom of white water on the point. The closer I got to the rocks the more I was intoxicated by the danger. Only turn round when you hear the Sirens' song—I thought to myself, cackling manically.

I selected one of the smaller waves and dropped down the face, swooping into a gut-wrenching bottom turn that took all my commitment and nerve. I looked up at the lip, way above me, and dared myself to hit it. At times like this, you have to be completely focused, living in that precise moment. There's simply no time or brain space to worry about much else. It's best not to think, just allow the body to move.

The moment stretched out in high definition slow motion. Then an edit as I arrived at the top of the wave and everything happened at warp speed. I smashed the lip and was launched several metres into the air. This was new territory for me, like the planing forward loop earlier. I'd seen hotshot professionals do aerials on video but never thought I'd need to know how to land them. For another slow-mo moment I was weightless, eerily calm, suspended above the foaming white water. Then I was plummeting back down towards the impact zone, trying to ignore the panic, trusting my body to make the right movements.

Touchdown was far from perfect but if passengers had been on board there might have been some relieved applause. We'd survived the crash landing, so things could have been worse ... but they could also have gone better. The equipment and I were still in one piece, but for how long? A beast of a wave was about to unleash its fury on us.

I had just enough time to submerge the rig, get a firm grip on it and take some deep breaths before I was being tumbled in the classic washing-machine manner. I've had plenty of practice at dealing with wipeouts but this was different. Normally I'd just relax and 'go with the flow' but this time the flow overwhelmed *me*. I was simply scared shitless. The only things that relaxed were my sphincter muscles and my grip on the boom.

After a frighteningly long spell in the rinse cycle trying not to panic I clawed my way to the surface, gasping for air, to see my board surfing its own way towards the rocks. I've never been a competitive swimmer but I'm sure I set a personal best over those fifty metres.

Thankfully, I caught up with my kit before *Montaña Roja's* jagged teeth devoured it. Everything *seemed* intact but I knew from bitter experience that windsurfing equipment is held together by the sum of its parts—and there are plenty of them: nuts, bolts, ropes, webbing, mast, boom, universal joint ... any of them might have sustained catastrophic damage after a rinsing like that. Following this close encounter with the Grim Reaper, I realised I wasn't ready to meet him just yet, so I decided to quit while I was winning and sail back to the beach.

It was the first sensible decision I'd made that morning—proof that I did still consider life worth living, despite recent misgivings. Maybe my brush with mortality beneath those blood-red cliffs would be a turning point—literally, I thought to myself, as I turned away from the point and headed back out to sea.

Unfortunately, this moment of clarity and optimism was short-lived. Seconds after my prudent decision to head home the wind started to drop. I found myself 'slogging' out to sea—sailing at a snail's pace with most of the board underwater, unable to make progress against the current.

Normally this would be inconvenient rather than life-threatening. A lull didn't usually last too long and I'd just wait it out. If it persisted I'd drift slowly downwind to the nearest beach. If the wind dropped even more I could usually swim back with the kit and take the Walk of Shame, as we aficionados call it.

But this was a more serious situation. I was already out of sight behind the mountain, alone, and the current was taking me out to sea. The longer the lull lasted the more anxious I became. Just be patient, I told myself—the wind's bound to pick up soon. You'll get back to the beach eventually, even if it means coming in to the next bay and a longer walk home.

Ten minutes later I was still slogging slowly towards the horizon, trying not to panic as I looked back at the receding coastline. I wasn't in any *immediate* danger—I had my board to float me—but my chances of swimming back against the current were disappearing by the minute.

OK, I thought, time to turn round and try to make some headway towards land. I wobbled carefully into a slow-motion gybe, feeling the knot in my stomach tighten, painfully aware that one slip would leave me in the water without enough wind to get back up again.

The manoeuvre, like the day, started well enough. I turned the board through 180 degrees towards the beach. Now all I had to do was to rotate the rig onto the new tack. This is often the point where a gybe can fail so I focused on not falling, hardly daring to breathe ...

Splash! I was in the water, still holding the boom, treading water, watching my board disappear into the distance. Shit! I was so angry with myself for blowing this crucial gybe that it took a moment for the awful truth to sink in: I wasn't responsible for screwing up the turn, it was equipment failure—*catastrophic* equipment failure. The universal joint had ripped apart. My lifeline had been severed!

2

DRIFTING

There's no time to panic. I just put everything I have into swimming after the board. Head down, I don't take a breath for a dozen strokes. I'm not a strong swimmer but this is a life-or-death situation. Even an Olympic athlete can't compete with a five knot rip, so either I catch up with the board or I'll be lost at sea. Sink or swim, in other words.

I swim, thrashing the water like a maniac, screaming the word: "rip!" with each stroke. My world contracts to the space between me and my board. It's all that matters. "Rip! Rip! Rip!" rattles around my brain as my breath comes in ever more savage gasps. I'm just about spent, but there are still a few tantalising metres of water between us.

"This is it, mate" I scream. "Sink or swim?"

Three more strokes and I'm sinking. I stretch desperately for the board, like someone hanging over a precipice reaching out for a hand … and I manage to grab a foot-strap! I slump on board, coughing and retching.

A last bitter hysterical shout of "Rip!" resonates in my skull. "R … I … P …" a voice-in-my-head whispers. "How appropriate!"

For the past six months I'd been on the run and the people I was running from had no intention of letting me Rest In Peace until they were stood over my grave. That's why I'd been living as a ghost in El Médano. My life had fallen apart ...

No, that's me in denial again—it was all my own fault. It wasn't just the drug deal that had gone wrong, all my relationships had turned sour—or, more honestly: I'd soured them with betrayals. My business partner and windsurfing buddy (same bloke), my girlfriend (his wife), friends, family, the cops, and the Mob ... they were all after my blood. I knew one of them would find me eventually and that would be that. I was existing, rather than living, on borrowed time—a debt that would be repaid soon enough. Until then all I wanted was to ride a few more waves.

———

It's a complex web and my backstory will take a while to tell. But I have plenty of time, stuck out here, drifting around the ocean with just my demons for company.

Now I have my board my chances of survival have improved considerably (from zero) but my situation is still the stuff of nightmares. Every windsurfer fears breaking their UJ a long way from land and I'm in the worst possible place—out of sight behind the mountain, caught in a rip current taking me relentlessly away from land, and nobody knows I'm here.

Depending on how you look at things it's either an example of 'Sod's Law' or the inevitable consequence of my unstable state of mind. Either way, the ocean always punishes those who don't respect her. I hadn't looked after the UJ; it was ancient and I failed to replace it in time; I forgot to check it before launching; and, crucially, I subjected it to the vicious wipeout that terminated its useful life. But that's history now—along with my rig. With no way to attach it to the board it's useless and I abandon it to the waves.

With hindsight, that's not a good decision either. The brightly coloured sail would have made me more visible from the air—but I'm not thinking straight. My mind is already muddled, full of voices giving me contradictory advice. By the time I realise my mistake I've drifted a few hundred metres further out and the rig is sinking. I try paddling back against the current but it's obvious I'm making no progress, just exhausting what little strength I have left. So I sit on my board and try to clear my mind.

My immediate concern is how thirsty I am. "Why the hell didn't you drink some water when you were rigging up?" one of my voices demands. I nod. He's right and I'm paying for it now. My tongue is already stuck to the roof of my mouth and the seawater is looking tempting. Of course, I know that drinking salt water will dehydrate me even more, but water is water when you're as dry as blotting paper. The whingeing voice-in-my-head reminds me that I haven't eaten either but that's the least of my worries. There's every chance I'll be dead before starvation gets me.

My other regret is not telling a soul that I was heading out. The coastguard should send a helicopter to search for me once the alarm is raised ... but who would miss me?

"Yep. That's a problem for a ghost" the voice lectures me. "Nobody notices if you're there or not."

"You've been a missing person for the past six months, mate" another voice adds.

They're right, of course. I didn't have a buddy to share my session, but if only I hadn't been so obsessed with being the first to rig-up there would have been a few of my fellow windsurfers around on such a promising morning. I couldn't call any of them friends, let alone 'buddies', but a few were acquaintances. We nodded polite *holas* to each other, asked what size sails we were using, compared equipment and talked shop—after all, we belonged to the same tribe. They would have watched me launch—I was the guinea pig testing the wind, and they'd have rushed to join me once they saw how well powered-up I was. Later one of them might have noticed my absence and called the *socorristas*.

My best hope is that my boss, the bar owner, will try to track me down when I don't show up for work this afternoon. He's a windsurfer too and perhaps he'll speak to the locals, figure out what's happened and raise the alarm.

Until then I'm on my own out here. Just me and my voices. My survival will depend on my strength of will—my will to survive. I have to sit it out and stay alive for however long it takes them to find me. So I sit on my board, stare at the land receding into the distance and simply allow time to pass. Alone.

For as long as I can remember I've relied on nobody but myself. People looked after each other in the community where I grew up, but to fit in you had to conform to *their* rules, buy into *their* values. Unfortunately, I didn't.

I was born in 1990, the youngest of three brothers, in a tough little cray fishing town in Western Australia. To be precise I should say: the youngest of two-and-a-half brothers. One of the buggers was a half-brother but *none* of 'em was a brother to me when it mattered.

My dad scratched a living as a deckhand—at least when he was sober enough. My mum worked herself into the ground to support us, as a teacher in the local primary school and nights in the fish processing plant. She was outnumbered, isolated in our chaotic male household and she escaped to the sanctity of the church whenever she could. Both of them were, as far as I remember, only ever miserable.

The whole community was unbalanced, biased, macho. Academic achievement was mocked as being somehow unmanly rather than valued. My dad and my brothers branded me "soft", a "nerd", a "poof" because I preferred books to their games. I would have enjoyed school if I hadn't been bullied every day, but the kids were tribal, feral, and I wasn't in their gang. They felt threatened by someone who enjoyed learning and they took out their frustration on me.

Nobody from my town saw education as a way out of poverty. Life revolved around fishing and success meant owning a boat. When I was growing up there was heaps of money to be made from cray. The Japanese loved the bloody things. Half the town were out on the boats looking for 'em and the other half spent their working lives packing them into crates and shipping 'em off to Asia. My brothers and I were grabbed out of school as soon as we were old enough to earn a few bob to pay for dad's grog, while he skived off.

For a few years the town was booming, but the only people who got rich were the skippers. They used to lord it over us with their big houses and million dollar boats. The rest of us were grubbing around for the scraps and blowing 'em in the Tavern on skimpy night. At least we had enough to eat and a few beers. When we weren't working or drinking we had the Doctor to keep us occupied—the Fremantle Doctor, that is—the twenty-five knot breeze that blows along the coast every day in the windy season.

Windsurfing was our escape. There was a thriving scene in the town. Deckhands, factory workers, skippers all sailed together. It was a great leveller—part of the fabric of the community. Tourists came from all over Australia, and even Europe, to surf our wind and waves. They brought tourist dollars and open minds to our insular little town.

I was lucky. My English teacher was a keen windsurfer and he got me started when I was just twelve. I was the only kid in the class who liked books so we bonded. He lent me his windsurfing kit and taught me the basics. I still remember planing in the foot-straps for the first time—skimming effortlessly over the water, propelled by the invisible force of moving air, at a speed few motor boats can match, let alone other sailing craft. Yeah, that was one of *those* moments—like your first kiss, your first spliff, your first orgasm.

I turned out to be a natural, a fast learner, and it didn't take long before I was better than my teacher. Once someone experiences planing they're hooked and for many that's all they ever want, but I soon became jaded with the simple joy of blasting at top speed across the flat water of the lagoon and hankered after something more. For some this could be competitive racing, or freestyle (ever more technical tricks). In my case it was a journey into the third dimension:

waves. Once I experienced waves, windsurfing without them became two dimensional.

My mentor was a cool dude—for a teacher. He made a deal with me: study hard, pass my exams, and he'd give me his old kit whenever he bought new stuff. It wasn't difficult. I already loved reading, learning, and now I had the ultimate incentive. I began studying, obsessively—school work and weather forecasts—searching for the Holy Grail: a day with strong wind and perfect waves.

By the time I was a teenager I knew who I was. I had my identity. I'd always been an outsider, but now I was a member of a tribe. I might not be old enough to drink, but I could sit outside the Tavern and share the après-session stoke with them. I didn't need alcohol, I had adrenaline, endorphins, and the Stoke. Windsurfers know what I'm talking about: the way you feel after a good session. No stress. No worries. Mate, it's a great feeling, the Stoke!

The Doctor saved me. Windsurfing was the sure fire way to escape life's vale of tears. Still is! My dad had the booze, my mum had religion, I had windsurfing.

Then the crash screwed up the economy. The Japs couldn't afford our cray. Prices plummeted and you couldn't give the bloody fish away. The flashy boats were up for sale and people started to drift off to Perth to look for work. The town was stuffed, but by then I was sick of the place and most of its population anyway.

Mum knew I was being bullied—at home and at school. She understood why I didn't trust anyone. She was the one person who didn't mock my dreams of a better life, and somehow she found time to tutor me through high school.

The bloke who owned the fish factory, the local squire, liked to flash his money around town so he built a library next to his cray plant, in between the church and the tavern (both of which were also his). I guess he thought it completed our lives and left us no reason to leave. It towered over the neighbouring buildings, a ridiculously grand edifice for such a dump; his way of saying: "fuck you plebs, you're mine, I own you!" But it had books—piles of them.

When I wasn't windsurfing I was in his library reading everything, absorbing his books like a sponge. I wasn't choosy. I just started at A and picked out anything that caught my eye until I reached Z. Literature, trashy novels, travel books, science journals, philosophy ... everything from 'Anna Karenina' to 'Zen and the Art of Motorcycle Maintenance'. It was as well rounded an education as anyone from our town had ever received.

The cray magnate, mister Big Fish, built his library to ensnare us —to fill the gap in our lives between slaving in his factory, drinking our wages away in his tavern and repenting our sins in his church. But it was my way out of there. By the time the bottom blew out of the cray market and our town imploded, I'd grafted enough grades to grab a place at uni—the only one of us who'd ever managed it.

Mind you, the way things turned out I'm not sure it was worth all the bad feelings, bad karma, bad blood. My folks couldn't afford next month's rent let alone my fees in Perth, so I had to borrow money from my brothers, my friends, Mr Big Fish, the government ... and I'm still paying for it. I had so much resentment and envy. Everyone else was stuck in that dead-end town, gutting fish for the rest of their lives, while I was living the Life of Reilly swanning around the college on the Swan River.

It's late in the afternoon before I begin to question whether I'll be rescued. I've clung to hope all day but now the sun is sinking towards the horizon and I'm surrounded by water. Occasionally I catch a glimpse of mountains way in the distance but now I'm not even sure which of the islands is closest. The current is taking me away from Tenerife, between Gran Canaria and La Gomera. It'll sweep me out past El Hierro and then there's nothing for five thousand miles until the Caribbean.

For the past few hours I've been clinging to my sanity, arguing with my demons, occupying myself with bizarre distractions. I spent an hour fashioning a hat out of my harness, congratulating myself for having the sense not to abandon it with my rig. It must look ridiculous strapped on under my chin but its design amused me and it protects me from the sun's remorseless rays.

"Yeah mate, you've *fashioned* this harness-hat" a voice-in-my-head mocks. "It could be the next big thing on the catwalk—if you ever make it back to civilisation."

After a full day without a drink I'm beyond thirst, drifting in and out of rationality. There's an army of snakes in my head all trying to tunnel their way out through my skull. I'm delirious, dizzy, finding it increasingly difficult to balance on my board. I keep falling in the water and cackling with horrible laughter, dreaming of my days as a beginner windsurfer. I know I'm losing the plot. The voices are winning and I wonder how much longer I can stay alive, whether I'll last the night without food or water. I haven't given up yet but doubt is fighting hope in my addled brain.

All day I've assumed someone would find me. Surely *someone* has noticed my absence and raised the alarm by now? The *Salvamento Marítimo* must be out looking for me. I keep looking up, expecting to catch a glimpse of the helicopter but all I see are clouds and a few seabirds. I was hoping a fishing boat might spot me but I've seen nothing since I broke the UJ. Soon it'll be too dark anyway.

I try my best to catch a fish to eat raw. For a while, it's a game that keeps me busy. Every ten minutes a shoal of flying fish passes, flashes of silver as they leap. I flail around, clutching at thin air, inevitably ending up in the water cackling hysterically.

A turtle swims beneath me, near enough to touch. He surfaces right next to me and for a moment we stare at each other. He reminds me of ET with his bulging eyes popping out of an alien head perched on top of that absurdly long neck. I've no idea what he thinks of me but it's comforting to have company and I reach out to him. He gives me a last amused glance and dives deep, taking what remains of my hope with him.

I gaze into the emptiness beneath me and try to hold back the black thoughts. A voice pops into my head to remind me of something I'd read in mister Big Fish's library—a quote from the nineteenth-century philosopher, Friedrich Nietzsche: *'if you gaze long enough into an abyss, the abyss will gaze back into you.'*

I studied Nietzsche at Uni. His ideas fascinated me but I struggled to understand them. Now I have plenty of time to ponder what he meant, sitting on my board, drifting into the darkness. Alone.

I was an outsider again in Perth. It's a boom town for multimillionaires and it's also one of the most remote cities in the world—furthest from any other city that might make it think differently about itself. Everyone was smart, well dressed, successful ... and I was this small-town surf-punk with dishevelled dreadlocks and ethnic tattoos. I'd escaped the cray factory but I was a fish out of water there, surrounded by middle-class white kids ...

Ah, right, I didn't mention that did I? I'm what they call mixed race—that's if 'they' are being polite. Some less politically correct bastards just called me an Abo, but in fact my ethnic roots are well and truly mixed up. The black genes come from my dad. He's not a hundred per cent Aboriginal either—that might have given him more status these days, but he's black enough to suffer the consequences. Mixed race blokes were stuck with the worst jobs on the boats. When not cleaning shit off the fan they were usually to be found drinking their lives away in the tavern.

The white women in the factory poured scorn on my mum for marrying a blackfella. Her family were originally from Ireland and that gave the kids at my school yet more excuses to bully me. The white kids called me an "Abo bastard", the black kids called me a "feckin Paddy eejit" and they all hated me because I was a "poncy nerd".

I could handle the name-calling—it just gave me a thicker skin. To my mind, the mix of ethnicities made me more interesting than the rest of 'em. Irish Australians and Aboriginal people have a lot in common. They've both endured historical oppression by the British and this unites them as champions of the underdog. Irish Catholics treated the Aborigines as equals and have always been happy to intermarry, which is why Irish surnames are so prominent among Aboriginal activists.

I was equally proud of my Aboriginal and Irish roots but I hated my father and loved my mum, so when I left home I adopted her family name: Kelly. I had another reason for choosing her surname— she shared it with arguably the most famous, or perhaps the most infamous Irish Australian ever: Ned Kelly. Son of John 'Red' Kelly originally from Tipperary, the notorious outlaw lived a short, action-packed life during the late 1800s. Although he was a ruthless bandit and murderer he became something of a folk hero, a Robin Hood figure, and an anti-establishment role model for an outsider like me.

At Uni I styled myself as an indigenous outlaw—a cross between Ned Kelly and the 'angry young black man'—a working-class hero urging revolution to my fellow students. I was a loner, walled-in with my existential isolation, immersed in Nietzsche, Sartre, and all the bleakest philosophers I could find in the library. Not surprisingly, I had no friends ... until I met Robo.

The sun is low in the West now, a fiery ball sinking into the indigo sea. Ironically, the sunset is one of the most spectacular I've witnessed in the Canary Islands. Should I be bitter that nature has saved its best light show for my last evening, or shall I just let go and be grateful?

I lie on my back and drift, gazing up at the sky as it goes through its repertoire of purples, pinks, reds, and golds. There's a black dot in the distance, silhouetted against the setting sun. For one glorious moment I think it's a helicopter and wave my arms manically, like an inebriated cheerleader. But when I rub my salt-encrusted eyes and look again I realise it's just a seagull.

The bird has me in its sights. It dives towards me out of the sun, like a kamikaze pilot on his last mission. I'm expecting to be bombed with guano but it has more malevolent intentions. A moment later

I'm fighting it for my eyes. I beat it away, using precious reserves of energy, but the bloody thing keeps attacking, stabbing at my face. The struggle goes on for several minutes before my tormentor gives a frustrated shriek and flies off to find easier prey, leaving me to clean my wounds with salt water.

"That's your life, right there" a bitter voice-in-my-head announces. "You never have a problem attracting them, but whenever you let them get too close they peck your eyes out!"

———————

I've never been lucky in love—or maybe it had more to do with *me* than luck. Perhaps I was just no good at relationships. I had no problem starting them but they never lasted long and they always ended messily. Women liked my surfy looks—the sun-bleached dreadlocks, the tanned muscles, the hardcore tattoos. They loved the cute smile, the soulful brown eyes, the way I made them feel in bed. I flitted from one relationship to the next but they were only ever phys-ical, shallow. I'd built this wall around myself and they never got to know the *real* Nick—the complex individual behind the macho surf-punk. I always had a girlfriend, but never a lover. Whenever the 'L word' was mentioned I'd make my excuses and beat a hasty retreat, leaving only bitterness and regrets.

My most recent failed fling was particularly messy. I'd stolen my best mate's wife—never a good idea. My infatuation with her was brief. I never loved her, but it's no exaggeration to say that I loved Robo—like a brother, you understand. Sure I already had a brother —two-and-a-half of 'em to be precise, but the least said about them the better. My family and I had abandoned each other long ago. Robo, on the other hand ... I could write a book about him.

He was my windsurfing buddy, my business partner, and my last real friend. I met him in my first week at Uni, at the ludicrously named 'freshers' ball'. My attendance was purely ironic, obviously. I was an observer, a hardcore surf-punk Cinderella. But this wasn't some glitzy fairytale ball. No, forget the image of dinner jackets and evening gowns, this was just a bog-standard disco with an extremely loud sound system and a few hundred drunk students looking for someone to grope.

I was sitting behind a pillar in a dark corner, observing this spectacle as if it was a bizarre wildlife documentary, when I noticed a bloke similarly concealed behind the next pillar. He was older than me, bearded, wearing a Rip Curl teeshirt and smoking a joint. He met my eyes, shrugged towards the cavorting throng and offered me a smoke.

"Yeah, thanks mate" I yelled over the techno beats, taking the joint and pulling on it. "So, you a surfer or what?" I pointed to the logo on his teeshirt.

He grinned. "Na mate, windsurfer."

"Right. Me too." I passed the joint back to him. "My name's Nick. I just got here."

"G'day Nick. Welcome to this gathering of WA's best young minds. I'm Rob" he shouted, shaking my hand. "It's always good to meet another windsurfer. Where ya from? I don't see many of you blackfellas on the water."

I told him where I grew up and he nodded, adding that my hometown was one of his favourite spots to sail.

"That break in front of the pub—what's it called ..."

"You mean 'South Passage'?"

"Yeah mate, that's the one. It's a nice wave ... and handy for a glass of the amber nectar."

I grinned and nodded my agreement. I would have added that the Tavern was my home-from-home, but it was impossible to talk over the sound system now. For a while, we watched the preening, posing, mating rituals that passed for 'dancing' at a freshers' ball.

"What a bunch of wankers eh?" I yelled when the track ended. He laughed and suggested we find somewhere to sink a tinny in peace and talk windsurfing.

Robo was a third-year student, which gave him considerably more credibility than my fellow freshers. He introduced me to his mates and I was soon a member of a select gang of outlaws and misfits. They lived in a communal squat and spent their time taking drugs, listening to obscure music and not saying much. My dread-locked, tattooed Ned Kelly antihero fitted in perfectly. Robo was the only one who windsurfed so I guess he appreciated having someone he could talk to without their eyes glazing over.

We started sailing together up and down the coast, driving thousands of k's searching for perfect conditions. Whenever there was a good forecast we'd drop everything, jump in his ute and drive for twenty hours straight up the coast past my hometown, not stopping till we got to the end of the road: Gnaraloo. We'd wild camp up there for a few days and windsurf ourselves stupid on some of WA's sickest waves. Then we'd fire up the ute and blast back past Perth, past the university, ignoring the urgent demands for academic work. We'd stop over at Margaret River, before cruising for another eighteen hours down to Esperance.

We had some amazing adventures, Robo and I. My God, they were good times! We were a similar level on the water and we complemented each other well. He had a cool, controlled, smooth style, while I was more gung-ho, radical, crash-and-burn.

Robo taught me to loop properly, threatening to stick a mast extension where the sun didn't shine unless I landed one. My previous attempts had been little more than extravagant wipeouts, whereas his were controlled rotations. He showed me that there was more to it than big cojones. He taught me the value of technique, breaking a move down, visualisation ... I taught him about spontaneity, living in the moment, trusting instinct.

Robo made everything look easy, but really it was the result of a lot of thought. Sometimes I thought he was guilty of over-analysing things. "Don't think" I'd yell at him. "Just do it!" We had our differences and sometimes there could be tension between us, but we were always there for each other when it mattered and we survived some sketchy situations together—rescued each other's kit from the rocks, saved each other from drowning ... We became brothers-in-arms, trusting each other as only those who've gone into combat together do.

We clocked up a lifetime of experiences in his rusty old ute—and the stuff we used to talk about to keep awake on the road ... I was majoring in philosophy and I thought I was into some pretty heavy ideas but Robo, jeez! He got me into Carlos Castaneda and his 'separate reality'. Robo was experimenting with psychoactive substances: mescaline, Magic Mushrooms, LSD and he took me through the origins of the psychedelic counterculture—starting with Aldous Huxley's 'Doors of Perception' in the late 1950s and culminating in the 60s with the contrasting groups lead by Timothy Leary and Ken Kesey's 'Merry Pranksters'.[1]

We tripped together a few times—more amazing, crazy adventures! We were like windsurfing Pranksters rather than followers of Leary's somewhat po-faced, humourless cult. The Pranksters were a 60's evolution of Jack Kerouac and the Beats. Like them, we were on the road, constantly on the move from one adventure to the next.

Robo persuaded me to reveal more of myself than I ever had before. He could see through the dreadlocked surf-punk with the tribal tattoos and distinguish the real Nick from the fashion statement. My indigenous identity was etched on my skin—the tattoos were inspired by traditional Aboriginal art, but my tribal allegiance was skin deep. He encouraged me to delve deeper into my roots and explore what lay behind the symbols: The Dreamtime, Creation, the Ancestor Beings, the Laws of Existence.

Windsurfing on that coast can be world-class but it's not without its problems. The Doctor only does his thing for half the year, so what to do with the other half? And that's only the half of it. The Doctor can be fickle. In a good season he hits twenty-five knots most days from November to April, but then there were the bad seasons ... that's when we got well and truly skunked, driving to the end of the road on a promise of wind and finding nada: a mirror-flat ocean, nobody there, nothingness.

They were the pits, those windless days in Gnaraloo. When the Doctor didn't blow we'd be tormented by stifling (>40c) temperatures and a plague of flies. The best way to spend days like that was in an air-conditioned room, not cooped up in Robo's rust-bucket ute. A skunking meant enduring days of each other's foibles: my drinking, his smoking; my farting, his snoring; my silence, his talking. Those days tested our relationship and fault lines sometimes appeared.

When the season ended most windsurfers mothballed their equipment for six months and did other stuff (mainly surfing) until the Doctor returned in the spring. Not us though. We were addicts and we needed a regular fix. We started looking further afield, travelling to exotic locations, sailing some of the planet's most notorious wave spots: Ho'okipa in Maui, Punta Preta in the Cape Verde Islands, 'One Eye' in Mauritius ...

Windsurfing those spots on their day, when they're going off, is an extreme sport. The locals are radical, hardcore. We had to prove ourselves, earn the right to sail them. The sketchy situations became more serious, the injuries more severe. Our bond was subjected to more stress and cracks started showing. But we shared this obsession with adventure, danger. It was intoxicating. We were addicts, living on the edge. We lived for those trips, but we needed to make real money to afford them. So we began dealing drugs.

It's dark now, a cloudy night, no moon or stars to distract me. I'm lying across the board face down without the strength to sit, trailing my limbs in the water, fascinated by the phosphorescent bubbles. My mind is empty, drifting with the current as I gaze into the abyss below.

Something brushes my leg. At first I think the turtle has returned and brought hope with him. But then there's a second, heavier touch and one of my voices chuckles menacingly.

A fin breaks the surface and primal terror grips me. I'm shaking so violently that it's hard to stay on the board. I don't care who you are, however expert a survivalist, the fear of having your limbs torn off and being eaten alive can't be underestimated.

"No worries, mate. It'll be over quicker this way."

The voice-in-my-head has a point. I'm going to die a slow painful death anyway. Perhaps I even deserve it. However, I'd prefer it to be in my own good time and slightly less violently.

"R.I.P. Nick" the voice in my skull yells, as the dark shape circles me. "Ripped In Pieces!" He starts singing the infamous riff from 'Jaws'.

I lie on my board waiting for the attack, defenceless, heart racing, riff rumbling ... but it never comes. The creature seems more curious than predatory—and suddenly I know why. It's not the 'Man in the Grey Suit', *el tiburón*, it's a dolphin! Hardly surprising he's curious, considering the odds against him coming across a human floating around in his territory.

Again hope courses through my veins. There are plenty of stories of dolphins saving humans—chasing away sharks for instance. We have a lot in common, apparently. If I can just grab his fin perhaps he'll understand my predicament and tow me back to land?

I remember watching a wildlife documentary where dolphins were trained to perform tasks by scientists who learned to speak their language. So I try communicating this idea to him by emitting a bizarre series of whistles and clicks while pointing at myself and his fin.

If I managed to convey anything in dolphin-speak it can only be to confirm that I'm not to be trusted, because when I reach out to him he abandons me and swims languidly into the distance.

Of course, I knew the idea of being rescued by a large aquatic mammal was somewhat far-fetched but while he was with me there was hope. Now all I have are my voices and my memories. They replay in my head like a movie-length version of my life flashing past.

I can taste the despair, but I don't blame the dolphin. I wouldn't trust me either—after what I did to Robo ...

———

It started innocuously enough—the drugs—cultivating a few plants to supply our fellow students, but it quickly escalated. Robo knew some big players and the deals soon became significant. We began smuggling coke and weed hidden in our windsurfing bags. It was a double bluff: nobody suspected these two long-haired students, such obvious targets, would be crazy enough to conceal drugs in their enormous coffin-like bags. We made ourselves comically obvious, dragging the board-bags around like two clowns and we were always waved through customs with smiles while the suits were strip-searched.

Robo enjoyed the wheeler-dealer shenanigans but I was ambivalent about the drug deals. I had other revenue streams and some were even legal: windsurfing instructor, travel journalism, teaching English ... My real passion was writing and I dreamt of becoming rich and famous by chronicling our adventures in the windsurfing equivalent of Kerouac's 'On the Road'. That was still just a dream and none of the other activities was as lucrative as drugs, but nor did they cause insomnia.

As the deals got bigger I became increasingly worried that Robo was dragging me into a disaster. I told him we were playing with fire and we were going to get burnt. He told me to get out of the kitchen if I couldn't handle the heat. We began to argue, chucking clichés at each other like grenades. For while there was a bubble around us. Nobody could touch us. But inside the bubble things were falling apart.

Eventually we got too big for our boots and took on some sharks who were higher up the food chain than us—the Great Whites of the drug world (isn't it funny how there aren't any Great Blacks preying on smaller white fish?). These guys were ruthless predators. We knew they'd screw us unless we screwed them first so we hatched a plan to take their consignment and skedaddle (as my Irish gran might have put it)—get the hell out of Oz and never come back.

Unfortunately, the screwing also included me and his wife, Alison. It started when Robo was out of town setting up the deal. The Great Whites weren't bothered about political correctness and they refused to do business with a "cocky Abo punk" so me and Alison were left alone in their one bedroom apartment. I volunteered to sleep on the sofa but I ended up in their bed.

There'd always been an undercurrent of attraction between us. Robo knew that. Alison and I flirted and it made for a tense triangle, but he trusted us, counted on our loyalty.

"Loyalty. Remember that?" A voice in my head was telling me to stop, but another part of my anatomy was in control and I had to have her. "It's just a word, mate" another voice whispered, as we tore off our clothes. "This is real."

Passion feeds self-deception and fuels betrayal. It's like a game of 'stone-scissors-paper'—sex cuts through trust and crushes loyalty.

It didn't stop there. We couldn't keep our hands off each other and we drifted into an affair behind Robo's back. Things hadn't been going well between them and my relationship with him had also deteriorated. I was blinded by desire, drowning in guilt, and it unhinged me. But there's no excuse for what we did next ...

Alison and I split with the drugs, leaving Robo to deal with the Great Whites. It was a catastrophic decision. Stealing your best mate's woman is one thing, taking his livelihood another, but dumping him in the dunny with the Mob is unforgivable. I didn't just betray him, I put all our lives at risk. Now there was a bunch of people after my blood. So we went on the run, fleeing to the world's most remote surf spots, never staying long enough to be traced, living by selling the dope bit by bit until both it, and we, were finished.

I windsurfed all the time—to escape from myself and eventually from Alison. She didn't surf, wasn't interested. Whenever the wind blew, or the surf was up, she accused me of abandoning her. She couldn't bear to be on her own, but all I wanted was to be left alone with the wind, waves, and my guilt.

The stench of betrayal and self-loathing was overwhelming. Depression and paranoia stalked me like a pack of black dogs. I was gripped by panic attacks, living in fear of a knock on the door, a tap on the shoulder, a knife in my gut.

Finally the drugs were all gone and we couldn't stand each other any more, so I skedaddled again. I left Alison enough money to get back home to Oz and vanished—ran like the wind—to live like a ghost in El Médano ...

And that's how I ended up drifting around the ocean with just my demons for company. Now it looked like I'd be taking them with me to a watery grave.

Of course, it wasn't meant to end like this. I was only *borrowing* Alison for a fling. Robo got her back soon enough and I'd repay all my debts eventually ...

"Who ya trying to fool?" a voice-in-my head demands.

"Certainly not us" the rest of them chorus.

"You *stole* her and you didn't care a shit about him."

"Yeah, you fucked up big time." They're gloating now.

"It's payback time, mate ..."

"R.I.P. Nick Kelly!" they yell in unison.

I see lights in the distance. Perhaps it's the inter-island ferry or a tanker. It looks enormous and strangely unreal. Of course I go berserk trying everything to attract their attention. The ship passes cruelly close and the throb of its engines drowns my feeble croaks for help. The wake lifts my board from the flat sea and for a moment I'm surfing, flailing madly. Then it surges away and the lights are swallowed by the darkness.

I lie across my board on my back and drift. The sea and sky become one. Nothing to choose between them. My life is no longer worth fighting for. I'm finished. I close my eyes and allow myself to drift into the blackness.

I dream about death and it's one hell of a dream—a vision of hell! They're all in it, the principal players in my life and they're all after a piece of me ...

A beautiful bird with Alison's face dives out of the sky and pecks out my eyes, laughing as she drops them into the sea. I scream. Robo appears as a shark, tearing great chunks of my flesh and tossing them to a pack of monster crayfish to mince in their giant claws. To my horror I realise the cray also all have features I recognise: my brothers, my dad, mister Big Fish. Finally, the Great White mob in their grey suits circle me, shouting profanities while casually gnawing at the remains of my corpse.

The strange thing is: when they've finished torturing me and leave me to die, I'm not afraid any more. I simply accept it as the end of everything that's me.

3

HEAVEN OR HELL?

The Atlantic. Monday, October 26, 07:50. I'm surprised to find myself alive as the first streaks of light distinguish sky from sea. At least I hope I am, but it's far from certain. Perceptions and thoughts are floating around, but there's not much left of my sanity. Voices still crowd my head, competing for ownership. There's also a whole heap of pain but who's feeling it? Where the hell am I and how did I get here?

Then I notice something that persuades me I'm either still dreaming, hallucinating, or dead. As the sun climbs out of the sea a shape emerges with it. At first it's just a dot, then a mysterious blob travelling towards me on a collision course.

I rub my salt-encrusted eyes, trying to focus on the mirage, expecting it to disappear. Instead, it gets bigger, coming straight out of the sun, backlit like some epic Hollywood vision of an alien spaceship. From somewhere there's a hideous cackle of ironic laughter, possibly mine.

"Mate, this is ridiculous!" one of my voices sneers. "You really think your story deserves such a blockbuster ending?"

The apparition is a hundred metres away and still heading straight at me. Pure white, glistening in the dawn, perfectly reflected in the mirror-flat sea. I've never believed in a supernatural being but now I'm not so sure that God is dead. If this is the kind of show he puts on to welcome a soul into the After Life then he can count me in. "Hallelujah, I'm a believer!" my voices sing, like a demented gospel choir.

Then I hear shouts. They seem to come from the White Shape and they don't sound like celestial choirs. A smaller, darker shape emerges from the Mothership and races towards me.

"In the nick of time, eh Nick?" a voice sniggers.

The shouts get louder, more agitated, even less angelic. Now I'm not so sure it's the Good Guys coming to guide me to the White Light and I'm afraid.

The dark shape arrives beside me. Inside are two men—at least, they seem convincingly human. They're dressed in white and I'm relieved to see they don't have horns or forked tails. I lie there looking up at them and wait for the next development in this impressive dream, hallucination, or whatever. It certainly has high production values, anyway.

They throw me a lifebelt. It has a symbol or logo on it that seems somehow familiar. I stare at it, wondering if I should trust a lifebelt in a dream. But I grab it and they lift me into the dark shape.

"They're aliens, mate" a voice-in-my-head tells me. "You're being abducted by beings from another galaxy."

That's all very well, I think to myself, but they can't just leave my wave-board adrift in the Atlantic. She's a thing of great beauty and she saved my life (if indeed I *was* still alive). I desperately want these aliens to abduct her as well, but to my horror I find I can't speak. My mouth, tongue, throat and vocal cords are welded together into one solid block of salt.

"No worries mate, they can read your thoughts!" my voice reassures me.

Of course they can—they're an advanced race from a distant civilisation. My board is lifted out of the water and joins me in the floating shape.

We speed across the water to the Mothership. From close up it's even more impressive. There's a name painted on the gleaming white hull in blood-red capitals that are larger than me: THE ABYSS. Next to it is the same, strangely familiar symbol that was on the lifebelt: six black lines, two broken, four unbroken.

I gaze in awe at the ship, whispering the name reverently, and for the first time one of the men in white speaks to me: "*Sí señor, eso es correcto—el Abismo!*" Whether these beings are from heaven, hell or another galaxy it's comforting that they communicate in Spanish.

I have to climb a ladder to get onboard but I'm too weak to stand, let alone climb. A rope is thrown down and I'm hoisted up onto an immaculately polished deck. I lie there convulsing, barely breathing, but perhaps I'm alive?

Water is poured into my mouth but my throat is so constricted that at first I can't drink. Then I'm vomiting bile and salt water onto the deck. I remember feeling ashamed to behave so rudely to these kindly super-beings but a moment later I'm unconscious.

More shouts and then one of them is pumping my chest and breathing into my mouth. I observe this from above, looking down at my lifeless body.

After a few seconds my heart is beating and I'm breathing unaided again. I regain consciousness, open my eyes and try to thank them, but now the pain is unbearable.

More water trickles down my throat and this time it tastes wonderful. They pick me up, carry me inside and gently place me on the softest surface I've ever experienced.

It's as if I've observed all of this from outside my body. Now I close my eyes and feel myself return, before plunging into deep, dreamless sleep.

4

THE ABYSS

Tuesday, October 27, 08:00. I opened my eyes, after twenty-four hours of uninterrupted sleep, and wasn't surprised to see water. I tried to focus, but my eyes were sluggish. Was I dreaming? Hallucinating? It was hard to tell.

Six inches from my face, filling my entire field of vision, was a glass of water. This wasn't what I was expecting but it *was* what I needed. I drank to the bottom of the glass without pausing for breath and looked around for more. Right then I could have soaked up a bath-full!

"*¿Le gustaría bañarse, señor?*"

Excuse me? So the voices in my head spoke Spanish now? A fragment of memory from another dream popped into in my brain: superior beings from an advanced civilisation who could read my thoughts and communicate telepathically, in Spanish.

There was a knocking sound. I looked around for the source but my eyes were still adjusting and I was finding it difficult to make sense of the visual data they were sending.

"You like a bath, sir?" A deep voice with a Spanish accent.

Aha, so that's how it works—I think about drinking a bath-full and *they* answer the thought.

Suddenly it occurred to me that I was lying in a bed rather than on my windsurfing board. This made no sense but it was certainly welcome. I sat up and tried to focus on my surroundings. I'd been half blinded by the sun the previous day but my sight was gradually returning.

Now I could see that I was in a perfectly white bedroom. Light flooded in through a round window and there was a door, half open. A man, or humanlike being, dressed in a white uniform stood in the doorway. He repeated his question, again speaking in heavily accented English.

"Yes, that would be great, mate" a voice replied. It sounded like mine but I couldn't be sure.

"*Muy bien señor*, the water is ready for you. After bathing the Master will speak with you."

I stared at him, unsure of how to respond.

"Please to come with me *señor*."

With his assistance, I managed to get out of bed and follow him towards another door. He opened it to reveal an enormous white bath. He helped me climb in, pushed a button and jets of water massaged my aching limbs.

I lay in the warm foamy water thinking how strange it all was—to be surrounded by water again, floating but not drifting ... and no longer alone. I didn't know what was going on, but right then I didn't care. Heaven? Alien abduction? Dreaming? No worries if it meant luxuriating in a kingsize hot tub.

The man-in-white turned towards the door, but my eyes managed to focus on him before he left. He was my age, powerfully built, dark complexion, wearing white Bermuda shorts and a smart white polo shirt. Everyone I knew wore board-shorts, bright surfy teeshirts, torn jeans, hoodies ... surf-punk was the uniform of my tribe. But this dude had a kind of timeless, classic elegance about him.

There was a logo on his shirt—a graphic symbol with six black lines: two broken, four unbroken. Beneath it, in elegant red lettering: 'The Abyss'.

He nodded to me and closed the door, leaving me alone with my thoughts. A voice-in-my-head reminded me I'd seen those red letters and that symbol before—in another dream. But you know how it is with dreams—the more you struggle to remember things the more elusive they become, like trying to grab soap in bath-water.

I decided to relax and go with the flow. Things could be worse—I could be drifting around the Atlantic, a dismembered corpse with my eyes pecked out, or in the stomach of one of the Men in Grey Suits.

After my bath, I returned to the supremely comfy bed and my helper brought me breakfast. I'd eaten nothing since Saturday night in El Médano and I was literally starving, but I still had time to appreciate the quality of the food.

"I hope *el señor* is liking *la comida*?" he asked.

I nodded enthusiastically, my mouth full of smoked salmon and scrambled eggs.

"The Master would like to speak with you now, *señor*. Are you ready to meet him?"

I shrugged.

My helper stepped back and another figure entered the room. He was much older, perhaps in his late fifties—my dad's age, but unlike my dad this bloke didn't move like an old man. He was an imposing individual: tall, thin, grey hair, lined face, dressed in black—in stark contrast to both the room and my helper in his immaculate white uniform. I couldn't see his eyes behind the mirrored sunglasses. Somehow he commanded respect without needing to open his mouth or look into his eyes.

We studied each other in silence, until it became uncomfortable. I swallowed the last piece of toast, took a swig of the sublime coffee, and opened my mouth to speak ... but he got there first:

"So, *señor*, how are you feeling after your ordeal?" A thoughtful, urbane voice, with an accent I couldn't quite place.

"—" I couldn't answer his question. My brain, like my eyesight, was still working sluggishly.

"I hope Carlos has been looking after you?" He gestured towards the man-in-white.

I nodded and then I caught a glimpse of myself reflected in his mirror shades. It wasn't a pretty sight: sunburnt, haggard, but alive— thanks to him. I figured it was about time I showed some gratitude:

"Yes, yes, it's been ... I can't ... I feel ..." I croaked, through cracked lips. For the first time the enormity of what I'd been through struck me. The emotions poured out and I wept.

"Look mate, I can't thank you enough" I sobbed. "You saved my life. But where am I? Please tell me I *am* alive! Is this a dream? Who are you guys? Where are you from?"

He raised his hand. The gesture was kindly but it halted my hysterical raving instantly.

"All in good time. You need to rest now. We'll talk again later. In the meantime, what is your name?"

"—" Again I couldn't answer him. Who *was* I indeed? He waited while I wrestled with the question. Eventually the voice-in-my-head replied: "my name is Nick."

I must have said this aloud, or perhaps he read my thoughts, because he leant in towards me, shook my hand and greeted me:

"Pleased to meet you, Nick. Welcome aboard. My name is Alejandro Langer, but my crew call me the 'Master'. I would appreciate it if you did the same."

I nodded and he continued:

"To answer some of your questions: yes, you are definitely alive and this is not Heaven or Hell. It is the Abyss ..."

He paused, amused by my obvious confusion. I said nothing and waited to see where this was going.

"As to whether you are experiencing a dream we call 'reality' then I would ask you in return: who is dreaming it? But that is something we can, perhaps, discuss later over a glass of red wine?"

I shrugged and tried to meet his gaze, but I was once again confronted by myself reflected in those impenetrable glasses.

He smiled—the faintest of smiles—a mix of irony and world-weary amusement.

"Very well, Nick. Get some rest. Later you can tell me how you came to be drifting around in the Atlantic."

He spoke to the man-in-white: "*Deberíamos dejarle dormir ahora. Por favor, Carlos, traédmelo a la una y comeremos juntos.*"

Before leaving he explained what he'd said:

"Carlos will wake you in a few hours and we will have lunch together. I see you've enjoyed your breakfast but I expect you will be hungry for his cuisine again."

He closed the door and I was alone again. I closed my eyes and fell back into deep, dreamless sleep.

———

Time jumps. There's a knock on the door. I open my eyes, try to focus and make sense of my surroundings, but I'm disoriented again. Things are blurred and confused—like an acid trip. It feels as if time has jumped ahead and barely a few seconds have passed but I can see from the clock on the bedside table that it's now one o'clock, so several hours have elapsed.

———

The man in the white uniform entered the room and passed me a bathrobe. It was as luxurious as everything else in this dream. A voice-in-my-head reminded me that I knew his name and that I could speak a little Spanish: "*Gracias Carlos*" I croaked in my salt-encrusted Ozzie accent.

He seemed pleased by this improvement in my state of mind and its capabilities: "*Ah, veo que habla mi idioma señor* ... you are speaking some Spanish, no?"

I nodded. "*Sí, un poco, pero necesito practicar más* ... I've been living in Tenerife for three months but I only ever speak a few words."

Carlos helped me climb a spiral staircase up to a wooden deck. The first thing I noticed there was my board, propped up against the polished steel railings and secured with some white rope. Relief and gratitude surged through me—she was here with me in this dream!

Draped over the board were my wetsuit and harness. These familiar objects jolted me out of my reverie. This was no dream, nor was I hallucinating. This was for real—I really had survived! My board had kept me alive and now she was even more precious. I stroked her like a much-loved dog.

A clichéd phrase popped into my head: 'welcome to the first day of the rest of your life' and I looked around with fresh eyes. I was standing on the main deck of a large catamaran. It was a beautiful afternoon and we were surrounded by crystal-clear water glistening in the sunlight. In the distance I could see islands, mountains. I recognised Mt Teide, Tenerife's iconic volcano. We appeared to be heading back towards the coast I'd left two days ago.

There was a moderate breeze, perhaps fifteen knots and we were under sail as well as cruising with an engine—'motor-sailing' I think it's called in yachting parlance. We were making good headway on a beam reach heading for the port of Santa Cruz and it looked like we'd be there in a few hours.

Looking around I began to realise just how sophisticated this boat was. In the centre of the main deck there was a circular bar made of exquisite inlaid mahogany, complete with more bottles of exotic alcohol than should be allowed near a thirsty Ozzie windsurfer. It put to shame the humble local bar in El Médano where I'd been working for the past few months. Next to the bar was a long dining table, again constructed of fine wood, laid with places for three. Carlos gestured to me to sit and asked if I would like a beer:

"¿Le apetece una cerveza fría, señor, antes de comer?"

"Sí, gracias Carlos, eso estaría estupendo" I replied, dredging my brain for the little Spanish I'd acquired.

He handed me a chilled Dorada from the bar and I sat there sipping it in the sunshine, marvelling at the transformation in my fortune. "It's amazing the difference a day can make ..." the voice-in-my-head sang.

Two men walked across the deck towards me. One was dressed in the same white uniform as Carlos but he was, perhaps, twenty years older. The other was the man I'd met earlier—the bloke who'd introduced himself as the 'Master' (I tried to recall his real name but already it escaped me). He was dressed as before, in black, and spoke to me in the same cultured, rather formal tone:

"Good afternoon, Nick. I hope you are feeling better and ready for some lunch?"

I managed to overwrite my default shrug with a polite nod. He introduced his colleague:

"This is Pablo Vasquez, my captain. He is in charge of the boat—I just tell him where we go."

Pablo gave me a wry smile, with a hint of a wink. He seemed like an agreeable sort of chap and I warmed to him immediately. I was still wary of this Master bloke though. I just couldn't figure him out. He seemed to operate on more than one level simultaneously. Everything he said *seemed* normal enough but then resonated with layers of hidden meaning.

"So Nick, as you see we rescued your *tabla de windsurf* when we plucked you out of the sea yesterday ..." he pointed to my beloved wave-board, "but Pablo and I were under the misapprehension that this sailboard of yours required a sail to move?"

I wasn't sure if this was a genuine question or his version of sarcasm, so I said nothing. He continued in his dry, amused tone:

"I was hoping that perhaps you had invented a new form of propulsion?"

Now it was clear he was joking, so I smiled politely.

"Seriously though, Nick, I have been fascinated by your sport of board-sailing ever since I first saw it in the Canary Islands. It seems to be the *purest* form of sailing and the participants have the most direct connection with the wind and waves, no?"

I nodded my agreement.

"So, for me, it was a rather fortuitous moment when one of these board-sailors turned up and I could welcome him aboard my own sailing craft."

Again I couldn't be sure if he was sincere but he seemed to be doing his best to reassure me.

"Clearly we are members of different sailing *tribes* ..." He scrutinised my dishevelled dreadlocks and Aboriginal tattoos "... but we share this connection with the wind and I'm fascinated to find out more about *your* tribe."

I nodded, cautiously.

"Of course, for you the circumstances of our meeting had a different significance ..."

"—" I could find nothing to say to this and he sensed my unease:

"But let's eat now. Perhaps you will be happier to talk about your voyage after lunch."

He clicked his fingers and Carlos arrived at the table with plates of food. The meal was extraordinary, simply out of this world. Again I wondered if I'd been abducted by aliens—beings with highly advanced culinary skills and perhaps even an extraterrestrial equivalent of Michelin stars. The *solomillo a la parrilla* was so superior to any steak I'd previously experienced that with the first mouthful still in my mouth I announced I was giving it ten out of ten " ... and that's praise indeed, coming from an Ozzie!"

The Master nodded and acknowledged my praise on Carlos' behalf.

"So Nick, you are from 'down under' as I believe it is popularly called. I thought I recognised the accent. And if I'm not mistaken, you have indigenous roots?"

I took a gulp of red wine (again worthy of an advanced civilisation) and answered with my usual shrug. He took this as an affirmative:

"Yes, I thought these markings on your skin were familiar ..." He gestured towards my tattoos. "But this is quite unusual, no? An antipodean native who is a fellow sailor, a *board* sailor ..."

Turning to his colleague he added: "By the way, I hope you are not a 'bored sailor', Pablo?"

The captain gave a self-conscious laugh—as if it was a required response. His employer continued to interrogate me:

"So Nick, please enlighten us: were you perhaps attempting a long-distance crossing with your little sail-less craft? Something like that Thor Heyerdahl fellow did with his Kon-Tiki raft?"

Now it was my turn to laugh politely. Then bit by bit, helped along by the beer, wine, and liqueurs, the Master extracted my backstory. I tried to keep some of it to myself, but the more alcohol I consumed the more I felt compelled to open up to this strange man. He had an uncanny knack of probing with just the right question and then, once he'd uncovered one detail, he'd use it to lever out the next.

"If he isn't an alien super-being he could be a detective" a voice-in-my-head warned. "Just be careful, mate. Remember, you're the one on the run."

I was more intrigued than worried though. He had far too much empathy for a policeman. He was more like the father I never had—a father-figure who wanted to *listen* rather than kick the shit of me.

So, all was gradually revealed ... my roots in that deprived little fishing community; my obsession with surfing the wind and waves; my escape to uni; the drug deals and betrayals; my life as a ghost in El Médano; the severed lifeline; the twenty-four hours I'd spent drifting in the ocean, hope receding with the coastline; the bleak realisation that my life wasn't worth preserving; and finally, the miraculous arrival of the Abyss at my exact space-time coordinates.

Eventually, after Carlos had cleared away the dessert, coffee, and liqueurs and Pablo had returned to the bridge, the last of my confession had been extracted. I was overcome with self-loathing and gratitude—to have someone listen to my story—someone who saved my life and, perhaps, my sanity. I broke down and wept like a child.

The Master put his arm around my shoulder. Again I thought of my father—how I'd longed for a simple gesture like that from him. A brick had been removed from the wall I'd build around myself and now I could see out. I lifted my head from my arms, sat up, and looked around ...

It was already mid-afternoon. Mt Teide was much closer now and I could make out Tenerife's capital city, Santa Cruz. It looked like we'd make land before dark. Two days ago I'd watched this coastline recede into the distance, terrified I'd never see it again. Now the familiar landmarks were a poignant reminder of just how lucky I was.

"How can I ever repay you?" I asked him, tearfully.

"Don't worry about that now, Nick. Or as they say in your great nation: no worries!"

I wiped away a tear and smiled.

"I'm so sorry for exhausting you. What kind of host am I? You are my guest and I reduce you to tears. You've been kind enough to tell us your story and now I understand exactly what you've been through. You should rest now."

He helped me to my feet and beckoned for Carlos.

"We'll be back in the harbour in a few hours. I suggest you stay onboard for one more night to recover from your ordeal. You can decide what you want to do in the morning, after a good night's sleep."

I agreed that this was sensible. There was no rush to return to my life as a ghost just yet.

"In the meantime, I invite you to dine with me this evening so I might enjoy the pleasure of your company for a little longer. It's been quite a while since I was able to converse with someone in English."

I took this as a compliment. My tribe back in Oz didn't 'converse'—more yell at each other. I'd barely spoken more than a few words in the last six months and most of those had been in my broken Spanish, so I hoped I'd be able to hold up my end of the conversation.

Carlos arrived and I decided to show the Master that an Ozzie surf-punk could have a few more strings to his bow:

"*Gracias por la maravillosa comida* Carlos" I said, thanking him for the wonderful meal. "*Ha sido la comida más deliciosa que he probado en mi vida!* ... My compliments to the chef."

He bowed to us and the Master looked suitably impressed.

When Carlos woke me again it was early evening and we were already berthed in Santa Cruz marina. The sun was setting behind the mountains, leaving the usual incandescent sky, and the lights of the city were framed in the window. I gazed at the familiar skyline, determined to change my life. I'd been gifted a second chance and now it was up to me to make the most of it.

Carlos presented me with a fresh bathrobe. Then, before escorting me upstairs, he gave me a tour of the yacht and introduced me to the rest of the crew. I'd caught glimpses of them but only spoken to Carlos and Pablo. The others were like shadows. They were all young men and spoke Spanish, when they spoke at all. They seemed embarrassed when I shook their hands and thanked them for rescuing me.

The all-male crew, and their reluctance to speak, were like a religious sect—a closed community of monks who'd taken a vow of silence. Then there was their leader—what to make of him? Ostensibly, the Master was the wealthy owner of the Abyss, but he seemed more like their high priest, or guru. The name of his boat was something else that perplexed me ...

"It's a bit strange, *el nombre: 'El Abismo'*, no?" I asked Carlos.

"—" He shrugged and I recognised the gesture. It meant: "don't ask me ..." but not as in: "I don't know ..." no, it meant *literally* don't ask me.

I arrived on the main deck and the Master greeted me with a glass of his fabulous red wine.

"So Nick, now Carlos has shown you around my floating home, what do you think of her?"

"She's beautiful" I replied, "but I'm intrigued by the name ..."

"Ah yes, the 'Abyss'. Have you, by any chance, heard of Friedrich Nietzsche?"

I smiled. "The bloke who discovered that God is dead?"

He looked at me quizzically.

"Yes, that's correct Nick. Well, I named my catamaran after something else he said ..."

"... if you gaze long enough into an abyss, the abyss will gaze back into you."

He seemed surprised that I'd interrupted him and by my enthusiasm for the philosopher's work, so I explained:

"I did plenty of reading to get into Uni and I studied philosophy there for a while. I was just getting into Nietzsche until I got distracted by the windsurfing trips and drugs."

We shared a smile and he allowed me to continue:

"Funnily enough, that quote was rattling around my head while I was drifting on my board, gazing into the abyss below me and wondering what was down there. When I saw the word written on the side of your boat it was like a sign—a divine vision of a lifeboat come to rescue me. Not that I believe in a supernatural being. I agree with Friedrich: we killed him off a long time ago."

He nodded.

"As I said, Nick, I was delighted to have an English speaker to converse with, but it's a real bonus to be gifted such a knowledgeable and erudite one."

I blushed. It was the first time anyone had used either of those adjectives to describe me. Of course, I was flattered but I was also wary that perhaps I was somehow being 'groomed'.

Over dinner the Master resumed our discussion, quoting the rest of the *'gazing into the abyss'* text: *'Whoever fights monsters should see to it that in the process he does not become a monster.'*

"You see Nick, popular opinion of Nietzsche, in our age of individual freedom and liberal democracy, is that he was some kind of philosophical monster."

I nodded and said that from the little I knew about him that opinion might have something to do with the Nazis championing his ideas.

He stared at me. For a moment I thought he was about to expose himself as a proud follower of Adolf Hitler, or worse, an actual Nazi war criminal.

No, he can't be—surely he's not old enough? I thought to myself. Get a grip, mate!

"You are correct, Nick. The Nazis misappropriated many of his ideas. For example, his theories of 'Master-Slave Morality', the *'Übermensch'*, and his conviction that mankind must evolve, through natural selection, to the ultimate goal: the 'Superman' who is beyond Good and Evil."

With ideas like those it's hardly surprising the Nazis hero-worshipped him, I thought to myself. He could see I was sceptical and he was determined to put me straight:

"Friedrich Nietzsche was no monster. He was fighting his *own* monsters. After his decline into madness, his sister twisted his words and he became the most misunderstood thinker of his century."

This didn't allay my anxiety but now he was in full flow and I didn't dare interrupt him.

"The Nazis distorted everything to fit their evil agenda. I named my boat the 'Abyss' to remind the world of the consequences. I'm sure you've noticed: she has two hulls ..." He gestured expansively around the catamaran. "I considered naming them separately: 'Good' and 'Evil', but I think that would have been confusing for the harbour master."

I laughed at this attempt at humour—it seemed to be expected of me, but I was finding the conversation hard work.

"I can give you some books that will shed more light on this. We have an extensive library onboard the Abyss and you're welcome to make use of it in your remaining time with us."

"Thank you, that would be helpful"—a polite reply to buy time while I tried to work out the rules of this strange game of philosophical chess. My nose for a deal (or was it a threat?) was twitching like a dog's. I'd understood that I'd be leaving the next morning so how much reading did he expect me to get through in my "remaining time"? Besides, I objected to being groomed—as most dogs do. I decided to make my *own* move:

"Perhaps it would also help if you could tell me a little about *your* background?"

"—" No reply, just a tense pause while he probed me from behind those damn glasses.

I swallowed and tried a different strategy:

"After all, you know all about *me* now but you've told me nothing about yourself: where you're from, where you were heading with the yacht ..."

He leaned back in his chair, took a sip of wine and averted those probing lenses, gazing instead into the distance.

"Very well Nick, let me put the record straight ..."

I looked past his shoulder at the lights of the city, while he spoke softly to me, like a father telling his son a story ...

"I was born in Buenos Aires, in nineteen fifty-three. My father was a German doctor, Dr Ludwig Langer, a psychotherapist who studied with Carl Jung in the thirties. He was the leader of a group of radical thinkers who were experimenting with alternative systems of morality. They were interested in synthesising nonwestern ideas, Chinese Taoism and Indian Tantric thinking for instance, with those of the great European philosophers. You could say they were trying to give evolution a helping hand, to progress the human race towards Nietzsche's *Übermensch*."

For me, this "experiment" in human evolution had chilling resonances with Fascism and again I wondered about his politics and his past.

"They were searching for a new way of living together, an alternative to conventional society, an 'alternative lifestyle' if you like. Perhaps you could describe them as the original hippies—thirty years ahead of their time."

I smiled. Now he had my attention.

"Their ideas resurfaced and became popular in the nineteen sixties—in Timothy Leary's work, for instance. Perhaps you've heard of him?"

"Vaguely" I replied. "Didn't he have something to do with the campaign to legalise LSD?"

"That's correct. Like my father, he saw psychoactive substances as a catalyst for spiritual enlightenment, a way of changing society for the better."

"But surely drugs like LSD didn't exist in the nineteen-thirties?"

"Correct again, Nick. My father travelled extensively and he came across *natural* examples of these substances—mushrooms and cactus plants for instance. They've been used for hundreds of years by indigenous people as a gateway to a separate reality."

I was familiar with that phrase. It was the title of one of the books Robo had introduced me to. The author, Carlos Castaneda, was an anthropologist who travelled into the Mexican desert to study an indigenous tribe who used peyote as he'd just described.

"My father brought back samples of these substances from his travels and his group were experimenting with them in their commune in Bavaria during the thirties."

This was all very interesting, but I still had my doubts ...

"You mentioned that Nietzsche was a guiding light for both your father's group and the Nazis. Did Ludwig have any sympathy with their ideas or their methods?"

His lip curled, a flicker of a cynical smile.

"The Nazis plagiarised the group's ideas, distorting them and eventually putting them to horrific use in their concentration camps. They forced my father to oversee some of their appalling experiments. At the end of the war, he managed to escape from the nightmare his country had become. The rest of the group either perished or were imprisoned by the allies' war-crimes tribunal."

I nodded. So his father had collaborated with the Nazis under duress. That didn't necessarily make him a war criminal but he'd escaped the consequences nonetheless.

"My father made a new life in Argentina. He started a business which became very successful and met my mother, who was much younger than him. I am their only child and I had a privileged education at a private British school. In the seventies, a brutal dictatorship was in power. Anyone who opposed the *Junta* simply 'disappeared'. I left the country to study and eventually teach, in Dublin."

So that explains his accent, I thought to myself—a mix of the

Queen's English with some Spanish inflexions, soft Irish vowels and hard German consonants.

"Ireland is a special place for me, Nick ..."

"And for me as well!" I interrupted. "Although I've never been there."

He looked at me, surprised. I explained that my mother's family were from Ireland and I'd adopted her surname, partly because of the connection with Ned Kelly.

"You must go there one day, Nick. It's a magical place but like your outlaw namesake, it's seen its fair share of troubles."

He paused and stared into the distance.

"While I was living in Dublin my parents divorced and then my father died. The circumstances were somewhat tragic but that needn't concern us now ..."

He gazed out to sea and I sensed that grief had overtaken nostalgia.

"When we examined his will we found he'd left everything to me: his wealth, some valuable art treasures and his journal. But there was one condition: to claim my inheritance I had to promise to continue his work. In exchange for this undertaking, I would never need to earn my living again. I didn't know what to do ..."

He paused again, perhaps reliving this dilemma. It was a beautiful evening. A full moon suffused the marina with ghostly light and a warm breeze tugged at the rigging, teasing playful rhythms from the ropes. Neither of us disturbed the gentle symphony of marine sounds and the Master's story remained paused for several minutes. Eventually, he pressed the 'play' button and resumed his narrative:

"I'd never been close to my father. He was always a distant figure who rarely spoke about his work, or his past. Of course, I respected him and I was grateful for my privileged education, but we didn't have much contact after I left Argentina. I was quite happy living a modest life as an academic in Dublin and I wasn't tempted by his wealth, to be honest. But then I read his journal and it changed everything ..."

He'd built the tension to this cliffhanger moment. Now he had me on the edge of my seat:

"Everything? Really? So what was in it?"

He stared at me, weighing up whether I should be trusted with his father's secrets. Then he nodded to himself, as if he'd just made an important decision, and began to reveal the contents of Ludwig Langer's journal. It was quite a story ... his studies with Jung, his travel adventures, his spiritual journey, his experiments with psychoactive substances, 'alternative living' with his Group, his struggle for survival as the waves of hatred gathered and darkness descended over Europe ...

His father had set it all down in this journal, describing every-thing with meticulous care and it had remained hidden until his death. When the Master read it he knew what he had to do ...

"I realised I could do nothing better with my life than to continue my father's work and try to achieve his goal—the goal that had been stolen by the Nazis—the evolution of humanity to the next level."

I frowned. It was all as disturbing as it was confusing and my expression betrayed my doubts.

"I can see you're not convinced, Nick. Some of my father's ideas are unconventional, I admit. Possibly even dangerous if they fall into the wrong hands. Perhaps one day you may get the chance to read his journal and judge for yourself."

I shrugged. Perhaps ... but the next morning I expected to be back on terra firma, dealing with the next chapter of my *own* life. Right then I needed sleep. I was exhausted and a little drunk.

I mumbled my apologies, stumbled downstairs to my cabin and fell into bed. I was unconscious within seconds—no dreams, no voices in my head.

5

TERRA FIRMA

S anta Cruz marina, Tenerife. Wednesday, October 28, 08:15. Carlos woke me with a discreet knock, a cup of his superb coffee and yet another bathrobe. As I opened my eyes I was disoriented for a moment—the hangover was familiar but why wasn't I in my apartment in El Médano?

Carlos opened the shutters and light flooded in. I sat up in bed and took in the view through the porthole. The marina was bustling with activity, a reminder that it was time to revisit terra firma and confront the problems that were waiting for me there.

How long had I been cocooned in the closed world of the Abyss? I was losing track of time like a prisoner in solitary confinement. Perhaps I could work it out by the bathrobes—they were like scratches on the wall of my cell. A wry smile—of course I wasn't a prisoner, I was the Master's *guest* and I could leave whenever I wanted. But I had no clothes and no money. My only possessions were my trusty wave-board, wetsuit and harness.

Carlos announced that breakfast was served. I arrived on deck to find another lavish banquet waiting for me. How on earth could he prepare meals that would be the envy of a top restaurant in a tiny galley at sea? "No worries" I thought to myself, "just make sure you do it justice, Nick Kelly."

I sat down and greeted the Master. He wasted no time in pleasantries:

"So Nick, I've been thinking about your situation and I have a proposal to put to you ..."

He left a pause while he let this sink in.

"But first I should explain why I've chosen *you* for this opportunity. I believe it is more than good fortune that our paths coincided out there in the Atlantic ocean."

He stared out to sea and spoke quietly, as if to himself:

"There are greater forces at work here. Some people call them: 'God' but as you stated: he has been dead for some time. Others use the word: 'destiny' but I prefer to think of a gravitational field—a force that attracts certain people to each other."

I understood what he meant—Robo and I were an example of 'gravitational attraction' and perhaps he and I were another. After all, he was the only other person, apart from Robo, who'd persuaded me to reveal something of the individual behind my wall.

There was a long silence, broken only by the seagulls' plaintiff cries. I waited, eager to hear his "proposal", but he seemed lost in his own world. I wondered whether his mind was quite as sharp as I'd thought, or whether there might be a few kangaroos loose in his upper paddock. Eventually, I had to cough to remind him of my existence. He turned back to me, apologised, and resumed where he'd left off:

"You have great inner strength and enormous potential, Nick."

I blushed—this was news to me.

"Our friend Nietzsche might have been describing you when he wrote: 'to live is to suffer, to *survive* is to find some meaning in the suffering.'"

I nodded. This was just a fancy way of saying: 'whatever doesn't kill you makes you stronger'.

"I recognise this strength in you—it's something we share, but you have only just discovered it. I can help you realise your potential."

He looked straight at me. I frowned and waited to see where this was going.

"So Nick, let's cut to the chase. Yesterday you asked me how you could repay me for saving your life. I've considered this and as it happens there *is* a way you can help me. If you're interested in my proposal then I can help *you* to move on."

Of course I was interested, but I was still wary of his motives.

"There is a task, a mission, and I need someone I can trust to carry it out."

I leaned forward and tried to look him in the eye. Again I found only my own reflection in those impenetrable sunglasses.

"I had planned for Carlos to undertake this mission, but he's rather useful here, onboard the Abyss."

I smiled, thinking of the exquisite food we were enjoying.

"The task is straightforward but, as I say, it requires someone who is trustworthy, self-reliant and an experienced traveller. Does that sound like yourself, Nick?"

I gave a noncommittal half-nod.

"Very well. This is your mission, 'should you choose to accept it' as they say in the movies. I need a courier to deliver a package to someone on the other side of this ocean ..." He pointed out to sea. "... in the Caribbean Islands. Have you heard of the Dominican Republic?"

I nodded. "The country that shares an island with Haiti?"

"Yes, that's correct. The island of Hispaniola, which lies eighty kilometres to the southeast of Cuba across the Windward Passage and ..."

I interrupted: "But why do you need me to deliver this package in person?"

I was beginning to smell a rat and I smiled at the thought—surely not on *this* luxury yacht!

"Well Nick, I can't simply post this package because one: I don't know the recipient's address and two: the contents are too important to entrust to the vagaries of the international postal system. I need a courier to deliver the package in person."

Now my nostrils were twitching with the whiff of rodent.

"Can I ask what's in this package?"

"Well, I'm not at liberty to reveal the exact contents but I *can* tell you that it doesn't contain anything illegal or dangerous—no drugs or weapons."

"OK. I understand you can't tell me the *exact* contents but perhaps you can give me a clue. For instance: is it animal, vegetable or mineral? That kind of thing might persuade me ..."

He smiled.

"Very well, Nick. The package contains important documents—a letter, a contract and money—some of which is to provide for your expenses while you are there. I'm sorry, but I can't be more specific than that."

I reverted to my default gesture—a shrug. He still had to persuade the fish to bite ...

"As it happens, you may already be familiar with the town where the recipient lives, since I believe it's well known for your sport of boardsailing. Have you, by any chance, heard of Cabarete?"

I nodded. I had indeed heard of the spot—a starboard tack, right-hand reef break on the north shore of the Dominican Republic.

"Yes, I've heard good things about the place and I don't have much to keep me here in Tenerife ..."

I'd never been to the Caribbean—it was a long haul from Oz, but it had always been on my wish list. I scratched my chin, now sporting several days of stubble, and tried to come up with a reason not to accept his 'mission'.

"So, after I've delivered this package, what then? Perhaps you could explain what's in it for me."

His lips curled into an ironic smile. The fish had taken the bait, now all he had to do was reel me in.

"Well, forgetting for one moment that you owe me your life ..." I swallowed, but it seemed this was his attempt at humour "... that is indeed a fair question, Nick. You will, of course, receive a fee. Let's say: five thousand US dollars? Plus all expenses. How does that sound?"

It sounded fine to me.

"Furthermore, as I've mentioned, this is your chance to sail some new waters, surf some new waves ..."

I tried to keep a poker face but he was reeling me in fast.

"And it would be a new start for you, with a new identity. Your chance to reinvent yourself, somewhere nobody knows about your past; somewhere it will be hard to trace you."

Damn, he was persuasive, and he was right—it was just a matter of time before one of my pursuers caught up with me here. I had to keep moving. The further the better, and the Caribbean was about as far as I could get from home.

"You mentioned a contract ... do I have to deliver it back to you when it's been signed?"

A pause while he left me dangling. Then, suddenly, he removed the mirrored shades. I instinctively recoiled. He leaned towards me, looked me in the eyes and spoke softly, like a hypnotist:

"No, Nick. When you have delivered the package you have fulfilled your debt to me—the debt for saving your life. But only *you* can decide if you have fulfilled your mission and ultimately your potential or ... (another hypnotic pause) ... whether we still have unfinished business."

I waited for him to explain what this "unfinished business" might be but he replaced his sunglasses and moved on to more practical matters:

"So, the target for my package lives in Cabarete but I don't know their address. However, it's a small community and this person will certainly be well known there. Just ask around when you arrive."

I nodded. The fish had been landed and the deal had somehow been done. I offered him my hand and he gave me a firm handshake. Then he clicked his fingers and Carlos appeared. The Master spoke to him in Spanish and then to me:

"We should celebrate our collaboration, Nick ..."

Carlos returned with two glasses of Champagne and we sipped

them in the sunshine. Eventually, he broke the silence to give me further details of my mission:

"When, and I stress: *only* when you arrive in Cabarete, you will open the package. Inside you'll find a letter with the target's name on it and a second package. It's crucial that you're not tempted to open either the letter or this other package. Do you understand me, Nick? I need a solemn undertaking on this. Your word. Otherwise, I should send Carlos."

I agreed, although I found his language somewhat unsettling. We shook hands again and he continued briefing me:

"You will give both the letter and the package to the person named and they will make you welcome for as long as you decide to stay. You will receive half of the fee now and the other half from the target. I hope this is all acceptable to you, Nick?"

I nodded. His use of "target" was rather disconcerting but I put it down to English not being his first language.

"Of course you will need your passport. I could send Carlos to El Médano to collect it, along with any other belongings you require, or if you prefer I have an alternative suggestion ..."

I shrugged. There was nothing in the apartment I couldn't happily leave there. The only possession I cared about was my trusty wave-board and I had her with me. But he was right: I would need my passport, so I waited to hear his 'alternative suggestion'.

"I have contacts here in Santa Cruz—people who can arrange a new passport. Indeed, create a new identity for you if that's of interest?"

Of course it was. A new identity, with the correct documentation, was exactly what I needed. It would allow me to travel without leaving a trace of Nick Kelly.

He smiled and announced that he would contact "his people" but I must be patient—it might take a while to arrange. In the meantime, I was his guest.

"You'll need a new wardrobe to go with your new identity" he added, giving me an amused look. "It might arouse suspicion if you turn up at the airport wearing only one of our bathrobes, or your wetsuit."

I grinned and agreed that neither would be an appropriate disguise.

"So, I'll send Carlos into town to buy some clothes and tomorrow we'll take a photograph of you in your new outfit for your new identity."

He stood up, nodded to me and with that our meeting was over.

I returned to my cabin to find yet another bathrobe waiting for me and a pile of books on the bedside table. I hoped I wouldn't have time to read them all, but I glanced at the titles, trying to decipher his motives for the selection ...

Of course, there was some Nietzsche: 'Beyond Good and Evil' and 'The Birth of Tragedy'. Then there was an English translation of 'The Magic Mountain' by Thomas Mann. Beneath it was a copy of 'Dr Faustus', the Elizabethan tragedy by Christopher Marlowe, along with Goethe's version.

I'd read Mann's great novel in mister Big Fish's library and I could understand its relevance to the Master's ideas, but I was more than a little worried by 'Dr Faustus'. All I knew of the Faust legend was that it involved the protagonist being 'groomed' and then selling his soul to the Devil. The parallels with my situation were worrying.

Two other titles were contemporary, perhaps included as lighter reading: 'Zen and the Art of Motorcycle Maintenance' by Robert Pirsig and 'The Dice Man' by Luke Rhinehart. I knew the first of these was a philosophical inquiry into values, including Nietzsche's Dionysian/Apollonian dichotomy, but I hadn't come across the second. Glancing at the cover I saw that it bore the confident claim: 'Few novels can change your life. This one will!' The blurb described how the narrator uses the roll of a dice to transcend morality and move beyond Good and Evil, developing into a sort of 'Superman' and attracting a cult around him. I could see why the Master had given it to me.

There was also a copy of the 'I Ching'. I picked it up and flicked through it. Something caught my eye—a graphic symbol—six black lines, two broken, four unbroken:

I looked up from the page and found myself staring at the same symbol. It was everywhere: on my bathrobe, towels, the crew's uniforms, the lifebelts ...

Of course! Now I understood why I'd found the Master's logo familiar. Robo had introduced me to the 'I Ching' and we'd dabbled with it occasionally—throwing coins to arrive at a hexagram and arguing over what it meant. I'd even consulted the oracle the night before I ran off with his wife, reading into it what I wanted it to say, and using it to justify my betrayal.

I wondered what its significance was in the Master's story.

He clearly appreciated visual art as well as literature. There were paintings dotted all over the boat and I examined them closely, looking for further clues.

One was a portrait of a young woman, painted with bright colours and a lightness of touch. Her beauty and strength radiated from the canvas. Next to it was a painting of a middle-aged man holding a baby. The style was similar but the mood was in complete contrast. It was painted in oil, with heavy brushstrokes—thick layers of grey and dark brown. The man was glaring at the viewer and gripping the baby protectively, as if he was about to be swallowed by the darkness that surrounded them.

The signature on these two paintings was the same: Caitlin O'Connor. The first was titled: 'Self Portrait, Zurich, 1932' and the second: 'Ludwig and Martyn, Bavaria, 1940: The Waves of Hatred Gather'.

I turned my attention to a third, very different canvas. Painted in acrylic in a modern style, it was a portrait of a man surrounded by various objects, set against a tropical backdrop: deserted beach, palm trees, turquoise water and a luxury yacht. The man was dressed in black, looking out of the picture from behind mirrored sunglasses. He looked younger but it was clearly this Master bloke. The objects seemed to be floating or flying around him and the composition had the dreamlike quality of Surrealism or perhaps Magical Realism. The title was: 'Le Maître de ma Mer' and the artist had signed it: Nicole Jean-Baptiste Beauvais.

I spent the rest of the day on deck studying the books, in preparation for our next conversation. Sitting there in the sunshine, dressed in my luxurious bathrobe, sipping a cocktail, doing my homework for our next game of philosophical chess, I reminded myself that I'd had worse days—drifting around the Atlantic dying of thirst for example. The marina was a constant distraction though—a reminder of what was waiting for me on terra firma.

Wednesday, 22:00. Dinner was over (yet another superb meal). We'd finished our coffee and liqueurs and were working our way through a second bottle of the Master's excellent *Rioja*. He was more relaxed with me now and didn't need much prompting to continue his life story ...

"After my father's funeral, I remained in Buenos Aires while I settled his affairs and read his journal. Then, once I'd made the decision to continue his work, I signed the papers giving me control of his estate. It included several properties and a collection of paintings my father had brought out of Germany. They had been languishing in a vault and some of them had become extremely valuable. I sold most of them, but I kept a few that had special significance for him."

"And those are the paintings hanging in my cabin, by an artist called Caitlin O'Connor?"

He nodded.

"Did *she* have 'special significance' for him?"

Again he nodded.

"One of her paintings has the title: 'Ludwig and Martyn, Bavaria, 1940'. Your father's name was Ludwig, so Martyn must be their child —your brother?"

"My *half*-brother" he replied, dismissively.

"So, what happened to him?"

"—" Clearly the least said about him the better, so I moved on:

"The other part of the title is: 'The Waves of Hatred Gather'. I presume that's a reference to the rise of the Nazis?"

He nodded.

"You said that your father escaped after the war but what about Caitlin?"

A dark cloud passed over his face.

"The Nazis arrested Caitlin and she died in Dachau."

He paused and the moment filled with sadness.

"My father escaped with Martyn and left him with Caitlin's family in Ireland. It's quite a story ..." he added, looking at me intently. I allowed him to continue without interruption.

"As well as being a gifted artist, Caitlin was a leading light in the Irish Republican struggle against the British and her son inherited her politics. As I said, Ireland is a special place for me, a magical place, but it's seen its fair share of troubles and Martyn has had a hand in some of them."

Again I sensed anger when he mentioned his half-brother.

"The full story is revealed in my father's journal. Perhaps one day you will read it, Nick, and then you'll understand *everything*."

I shrugged. Perhaps, and perhaps it would complete the jigsaw-puzzle. Right now there were plenty of missing pieces.

"What about the other painting by the artist with a French name: Nicole ... (I tried, but couldn't remember her other names) ... it's a painting of you, no?"

"Yes, that's correct. You are most observant, Nick."

"And does the artist have 'special significance' for *you*?"

"—" I waited for his reply. When it didn't come I changed the subject:

"Did your father's estate also include the Abyss?"

He smiled, clearly much happier to talk about his boat:

"No Nick, it was my own idea to build her. My group of fellow travellers are dispersed all over the planet. I realised I could be a citizen of the *world* rather than tied to any one location. With modern communication technology, we don't need to be physically located in the same place."

I nodded. During Carlos' tour of the Abyss I'd noticed how sophisticated the onboard technology was and Pablo had proudly pointed out the various systems installed on his bridge.

"Like you, Nick, I have always been drawn to the ocean. A life on the ocean waves, as a citizen of the world of ideas, was my dream. So once I had access to my father's estate I designed my ultimate floating home and had her built by skilled craftsmen in the UK."

Finally, something I could understand! I was still unsure about his ideas and unimpressed by someone born with a silver spoon in his mouth, but his yacht was special. I congratulated him for putting his inherited wealth to such good use and told him I envied his "life on the ocean waves".

There was something else, besides the name, that intrigued me about the Abyss:

"Tell me about your logo. When I first saw it, on the lifebelt and then on the side of your yacht, I had the strangest feeling of déjà vu. I knew I'd seen symbols like it before. Then this morning I realised it's one of the graphics from the I Ching."

A hint of a smile from him.

"Correct. It is indeed one of the hexagrams from the ancient Chinese 'Book of Changes'—number sixty-one, to be precise."

I nodded. "So, why that one?"

His lip curled in amusement.

"Good question, Nick."

I blushed, flattered, but again wary of being groomed.

"Each of the sixty-four hexagrams has two constituent trigrams, which are the Kangxi radicals to be found in Taoist cosmology. I'm sure I don't need to explain this to you?"

My cheeks reddened further. I had no idea what he was talking about. Ignoring my embarrassment, he continued his lecture:

"So, one of the trigrams that make up *our* hexagram is 'Xùn'. It means: 'wind'—something that means a lot to you, no?"

I nodded. "Yes, it does. The wind and my board have been my only real friends lately."

He gave me one of his probing stares.

"I think perhaps you have been sailing *too* close to the wind, Nick, just like Icarus was tempted to fly too close to the sun. You suffered the tragic consequences of over-reaching yourself."

I scratched my head and nodded, reluctantly.

"When you get too close to the wind it ceases to *be* your friend. If you sail straight into the eye of the wind you come to a dead stop. Isn't that true, Nick?"

I shrugged, but I knew he was right.

"You need the balance provided by the other trigram: 'Duì', meaning 'swamp'. When you put the two trigrams together you get *our* hexagram, number sixty-one. It's sometimes labelled: 'Centre Returning' but I prefer the variation: 'Inner Truth'. You'll find it all around you ..."

He pointed to the nearest lifebelt. At its centre was the graphic symbol—six black lines, two broken, four unbroken.

"It was 'Inner Truth' that kept you afloat before we plucked you out of the water" he said, smiling at me.

"Yes, I suppose it was" I replied, remembering how the aliens in their white uniforms had thrown me a lifebelt with this logo on it.

The Master and I discussed the 'Ching' for a while longer but the lingering after-effects of my ordeal, as well as several glasses of his fine wines, had taken their toll. I was physically exhausted and mentally drained. He apologised for tiring me and thanked me for my excellent company. I made my way gratefully back to my cabin, into bed, and deep dreamless sleep.

When Carlos woke me the next morning he announced that he had a new outfit for *el señor* to wear for my passport photograph. I got dressed, tied back my dreadlocks and made myself as presentable as a hardcore surfer-dude could. The clothes fitted perfectly. I guess you'd call them: 'smart casual'—well-cut jeans and plain teeshirts— ideal for travelling. At last I was dressed in something other than a white bathrobe. I felt less like a prisoner, but I still had no money, and it took a few more days for my new passport to arrive.

I spent the time studying the books, discussing ideas with the Master and enjoying Carlos' fine cuisine. I was caught in a strange limbo, wonderfully well looked after, but restless to leave and increasingly depressed by our conversations. They became ever darker and more disturbing.

We'd moved on from Nietzsche to become bogged down with themes of disease and death. The Master was obsessed with the struggle of ideas in Thomas Mann's 'The Magic Mountain' as played out between the two main characters: the radical Jesuit Naphta and the enlightened humanist Settembrini. In their dialogues they discuss life and death from a metaphysical perspective and we seemed to be acting out their roles.

He hinted that like Mann's characters in their mountaintop sanatorium, he was suffering from an incurable illness and didn't have much time left to complete his father's work. He wasn't afraid of death ("I've been gazing into that abyss for a while now") but he was worried about losing his mind and concerned about what would happen to his father's work and his wealth.

Apparently, Ludwig had suffered from severe depression,

terminal dementia, perhaps even insanity. It seemed probable that he'd taken his own life, although the Master never stated it explicitly. Alejandro's great fear was that he'd inherited his father's unstable mind along with his wealth. This was the black hole he was staring into, his abyss, his monster.

Friday, October 30. I longed to escape from this claustrophobic world and rejoin the society of mere mortals, rather than 'Supermen'. I felt trapped in a state of limbo, weighed down by the bleak seriousness of our discussions and increasingly unable to contribute. Even the cloying luxury was becoming tedious. I wanted normality and terra firma beneath me. I was paranoid that I was being groomed for some unknown, unwanted role but I'd committed to the Master's mission and given him my word that I'd fulfil my side of the deal. I'd had my fill of betrayal, for the moment anyway.

Although suspicious of his motives, I was flattered by his faith in me. I'd always been an outsider—never had a proper family, never really *belonged* anywhere. He was offering me membership of some kind of exclusive club and it was tempting. Besides, my freedom depended on the money and the new identity he was providing.

So I bided my time: eating, drinking, reading, thinking, discussing interminably, and forever gazing out at the open ocean to our starboard and the bustling city to our port—marooned in this luxury limbo between them.

Saturday, October 31, 06:30. Carlos woke me early because after five days and nights aboard the Abyss I was finally escaping its confines. I had my new identity and I was ready to fulfil the Master's mission. As I prepared to reacquaint myself with terra firma I told him that I owed him my life and thanked him for looking after me so well.

"No, Nick, you owe me nothing" he replied, warmly. "If there was a debt it has certainly been repaid with the pleasure of your company. I wish you luck and remember: you survived because of your inner strength. Now you must realise your full potential. I hope that you achieve this goal and that our paths cross again one day, in happier circumstances."

We said our goodbyes and I walked down the gangplank, onto the quayside, and away from the Abyss. I was wearing my natty new clothes and carrying a backpack with my ticket, money, new passport and the Master's package. I strolled along the pavement, wheeling my board in a fancy new board-bag, feeling the same freedom I experienced windsurfing. The world was my oyster and I was as free as my friend—the wind.

I hailed a taxi, tied my board-bag to the roof-rack and set off for the airport. After the usual heated discussion with the check-in staff about excess baggage, I boarded the plane for Puerto Plata, on the north shore of the Dominican Republic.

We took off and headed west, out over the ocean where I'd so recently been adrift. I stared out of the window, thinking about the miracle of my survival and marvelling at the magnificent view of Mt Teide—the highest peak in Spain and the second highest volcano in the world. From the air Tenerife was truly spectacular: jagged red mountains gouged by deep ravines, black lava fields, green pine forests, bleached white hilltop towns, fishing villages clinging to the rocky coastline.

As the mountains were replaced by open water I settled into my seat and wondered whether I would ever return to this spectacularly beautiful island.

PART II

THE CARIBBEAN

"I think perhaps you have been sailing too close to the wind, Nick, just like Icarus was tempted to fly too close to the sun."
(The Master)

6

SALSA ON SPEED

Puerto Plata Airport, Dominican Republic. Saturday, October 31, 2015, 17:00. This is the start of a new chapter for me, I thought, as the plane touched down. I was now officially: Malcolm Fraser, an English teacher from Sydney—a name I shared with Australia's twenty-second prime minister. *Adios* Nick Kelly! He drowned in the Atlantic. R.I.P. I'm somebody else now and my new life starts here.

I stepped out of the plane and took my first breath of warm, moist Dominican air. The twenty knot breeze welcomed me like an *amiga*. It had a softness that was feminine and it smelt quite different from the harsh, dry, macho wind I'd left behind in the Canary Islands. The runway was only a few hundred metres from the surf and I'd caught tantalising glimpses of playful waves as we'd landed. I think I'm going to like it here, I thought, as I joined the queue of perspiring tourists at the passport control.

"*Bienvenidos a la República Dominicana, señor* Fraser" the immigration official said, as he stamped my new passport. I smiled, relieved at how easy it was to become someone else and still amused by my illustrious Australian namesake.

The arrivals hall had a distinctly third-world feel. It was swelteringly hot, humid and chaotic—like a fiesta in a Turkish steam bath. A melee of sweating passengers were waiting for their baggage while being harassed by the predatory porters. The usual conveyor belt and carousel were nowhere to be seen, along with air conditioning and most of the other facilities we tend to take for granted. In their absence luggage was being unloaded from a truck outside and thrown through a hole in the wall, to land randomly amongst the scrum. I waited anxiously for my beloved wave-board, dreading its imminent free-fall and trying to anticipate where it might land.

My board-bag appeared at the hole in the wall. I elbowed my way forward and just managed to catch it before major damage was done. The porters eyed the heavy bag greedily, jostling each other for possession of this windfall, keen to demonstrate their machismo. Brushing them off with the few choice words of Spanish slang I'd acquired, I dragged the aptly named 'coffin' bag through the scrum of tourists to the usual comments: "what you got in there mate? A dead body?"

Outside was just as chaotic but the breeze made it bearable. The taxi drivers were every bit as enthusiastic as the porters to have me as their client. There was plenty of shouting, posturing, even some wrestling as they argued over who would have the honour and how much they could sting me for the board-bag. Eventually, the alpha-male fought off the competition, grabbed the board and slung it onto the roof of his early sixties American gas-guzzler. Again my limited knowledge of street-slang Spanish was invaluable as we haggled over the fare. It wasn't a particularly welcoming introduction to the country but I would soon learn that the cartel of airport porters and taxi drivers were among the few Dominicans who weren't genuinely lovely people.

We set off along the coast road towards Cabarete. The half-hour journey was a crash course in familiarisation—nearly, but not quite, literally. Somehow we managed to avoid becoming dangerously over familiar with other road users and crashing, but there were numerous near misses. Clearly you needed local knowledge to drive here.

Knowing how to avoid the locals meant knowing which bit of the road to stick to. Enormous trucks, belching smoke, hogged the middle. Cars, taxis, and buses stuffed full of people, with yet more clinging on, took the rest of the road. Tiny scooters, carrying whole families plus a few live chickens and making a disproportionate amount of racket, clung to the edges, sometimes resorting to the pavement or ditch to avoid superior traffic. Lowest of all in the hierarchy, lower even than the occasional horse and rider, were the pedestrians. They crossed themselves, took their lives in their hands, and ran like hell!

It was a land of contrasts. On the ocean side of the road were grandiose resort hotels with faux ranch-style gates and frontages designed to impress. Directly opposite them, on the landlocked side, were shanty pueblos with tiny shacks of corrugated iron, palm fronds for roofs. The tantalising glimpses of surf I'd seen from the plane were just a taster. Gazing out of the taxi window I could see palm-lined beaches with fine white sand, endless reefs and empty waves.

We rounded the last corner and suddenly I was staring at a five-kilometre horseshoe bay, full of white horses. The reef was about eight hundred metres offshore here and I could just make out brightly coloured sails and kites playing in the waves. I'd arrived at my destination, my friend the wind was with me and my new life was looking promising.

Cabarete had a texture all of its own and all you had to do was walk down the main street to experience it. As I wandered along (anything more energetic was foolish in the heat and humidity) all my senses were bombarded with stimuli. Merengue music blasted out from trucks—manic, like salsa on speed. The aroma of *pollo asado*, plantain, beans and rice wafted out from the *chiringuitos*. Tattooed dudes in designer shorts strutted their stuff like peacocks, while their bikinied surf-chicks giggled and gossiped in French, German, Italian. Wasted-looking prostitutes propositioned me: "*Señor*, you liking fooky wid me, no?" *Hombres* with matted dreadlocks offered me bottles of aloe vera, ganja, *Mama Juana* (concocted from rum, red wine, honey and, believe it or not, tree bark!).

It was a heady mix, a rich tapestry: colonial Spanish, Latin-Caribbean meets trendy Euro surf-village, with a smattering of hippies to complete the picture. Merengue was its beating pulse—and what a beat! Jamaica moved to the heavy, hypnotic bass of reggae; Cuba danced to elegant, fluid salsa; Argentina to the sinuous, desperate passion of tango ... and the DR had its salsa-on-speed. Those furious Merengue guitar licks were everywhere, enforcing a manic little dance even in the heat, until you were dripping with sweat and the *niños* on the street were pointing and grinning at the *gringo*.

I followed a sandy alley away from the craziness of the main street onto the beach, sat down at a table and ordered both a *cerveza* and a *Cuba Libre* chaser. Why not? After all, I was celebrating the first day of my new life. I was tempted to try a *Mama Juana*—the barman told me it was the perfect cure for the hangover I would, no doubt, soon have. On the other hand, perhaps the exotic cocktail of rum and tree bark was a taste that could wait to be acquired.

My board-bag was propped up next to me and the rest of my possessions were in the backpack under the table. I still hadn't opened the Master's package but I was in no rush. I'd given him my word and I'd been good to it. Now I was more interested in checking out the conditions in the bay, finding somewhere I could store my board, buying some sails, locating the best steak in town, and finding a bed for the night. I addressed these priorities in that order and the day ended with me in a comfortable room in the Windsurf Hotel with a full stomach and a quiver of new sails.

Sunday, November 1, 08:05. I opened the shutters and sauntered onto my balcony to find a perfect view of the bay and the reef. I could keep an eye on the windsurfing from the hammock that was thoughtfully installed there. Not much was happening right then. Clearly, the wind, like most of Cabarete's other inhabitants, was in no rush to make an appearance.

By the time I'd finished a leisurely breakfast and jogged the length of the beach, it was a different story. White horses were dancing across the water, the surf centres were opening, people were rigging-up and the beach was buzzing with activity. It was time to 'Check De Action' as a famous windsurfer from Barbados[1] is fond of saying. There'd be plenty of time for the Master's mission once I'd ridden a few waves.

I strolled next door to the centre where I was storing my equipment, introduced myself, asked what sail size they recommended and rigged-up. The wind here wasn't as strong as in El Médano and it blew from the opposite side. I needed a bigger sail and a bit of time to get used to the unfamiliar tack: jumping on starboard, wave-riding on port. But after half an hour I was dialled in to the conditions and loving them.

Cabarete was jumping heaven. You were well powered right from the beach, blasted out across the bay meeting ever bigger ramps and then you arrived at the proper waves on the reef. I threw loop after loop and it wasn't long before I'd landed my first ever forward on the unfamiliar tack. All around me people were smiling, especially the local blackfellas—they were pulling some incredible stunts. Even the kiters were giving me whoops when I landed a high back loop. The locals could get a bit nasty at some of the more hardcore breaks I'd surfed in the past but Cabarete was refreshingly mellow.

The waves were nothing special, but the dudes in the surf-centre assured me that if I stayed long enough I should get lucky with a big day and anyway ... here I was riding waves in the Caribbean, wearing just board-shorts, looking back at a perfect beach with topless sheilas and *Cuba Libres* at ridiculous prices—what more could a bloke want?

All the while I had the manic Merengue riffs playing in my head and it was like I was dancing to them. The tempo was perfect for windsurfing—high energy, like punk, but with the flow of salsa—punk salsa, salsa-on-speed.

· · ·

I sailed for three hours without a break and was more than ready for a late lunch and a *siesta*. When I woke in the afternoon the Master's package was still on the table and couldn't be ignored any longer. My hands shook as I opened it, feeling as if he was somehow there, watching me through those mirrored sunglasses.

There was a letter and another package inside, just as he'd said. It was identical to the one I'd just opened: wrapped in plain brown paper, nothing written on it ... but there was a name on the letter: Nicole Jean-Baptiste Beauvais. No address.

I was relieved to find everything was as he'd told me it would be —no drugs, no weapons, and I was intrigued by the name on the letter. First: I wasn't expecting to find it addressed to a woman. Perhaps it was his terminology: 'the target', or the all-male crew on his yacht, but I'd assumed it would be a man. And second: I knew I'd seen that name before, but I just couldn't drag the details from my memory. It nagged at me like a déjà vu.

I stared at the letter, wondering what to do next. For a second I considered ripping it, and the package, open. He'd told me there would be money inside and now I was on the other side of the Atlantic, thousands of miles from him. What could he do if I just did a runner—disappeared into the woodwork and lived like a ghost here in the DR, as I'd done in Tenerife?

It wasn't loyalty that stopped me and I don't think it was fear of him, but a voice-in-my-head said: "you've been running long enough, mate—running from your past and from yourself—sailing too close to the wind, like he said. Your life's been stalled long enough. Let's try something different this time."

I got dressed, put the letter in my pocket and walked out onto the madness of the main street to look for Nicole.

It didn't take long to find someone who knew her. The barman in the second bar I visited smiled when I mentioned her name.

"*Si hombre*, everybody know Nicole. *Una chica muy guapa*. She one gorgeous chick but she classy, no? *Una mujer muy elegante*."

"So where can I find this beautiful lady?" I asked him.

"—" He shrugged.

The sound system kicked into life with a wah-wah guitar—the iconic opening riff of 'Voodoo Child' by Jimi Hendrix. Sixties music was cool in Cabarete, a popular antidote to the manic monotony of Merengue. Jimi's acid rock filled the space.

I placed several dollars on the bar and ordered a *Cuba Libre*, plus whatever he was drinking.

"It's just that I'm supposed to deliver a package to her" I shouted over the music.

He picked up the money and mixed the drinks. We waited for a break in Jimi's vocals before continuing the 'conversation'.

"So, you're like *un amigo* of Nicole?" He yelled, eventually.

"Not exactly. More *un amigo de un amigo*."

It was hard to make myself understood, competing with Jimi, so I took the letter from my pocket and showed him her name on it. He nodded, cautiously.

"Look, what it is, *hombre* ... Nicole, she's escaping from Haiti, *y hay un rumor...*" He tailed off, watching me carefully. Seeing no change in my expression he completed his sentence: "... *si, el rumor* is some peoples are looking for her—*unos tipos malos!*"

Jimi had reached the chorus and was belting out the hook now: "... cos I'm a voodoo child, Lord knows I'm a Voodoo Child!"

I sighed. "*Hombre, no soy un tipo malo!* Do I look like a bad guy, mate? I'm just an Ozzie windsurfer doing a favour for a friend of this Nicole sheila."

He smiled. "*¡De acuerdo!* Why you no say you're windsurfer, man? Now I know you no *mal tipo*. I *windsurfista* like you."

We shook hands—members of the same tribe. He told me to go to the little school in the jungle on the downwind edge of town and ask for Nicole. She was the teacher there. I thanked him, gave him a couple of dollars for his time and said I'd look out for him on the water.

"See you on the reef, man" he replied, "this what *los lugareños* say *aquí*"

I walked out of the bar just as Jimi launched into the famous soaring guitar solo. I grabbed an imaginary guitar and joined him, dreadlocks swaying in the breeze. Nobody batted an eyelid. An Aboriginal half-caste playing air-guitar was nothing special on Cabarete's main street.

Sunday, 16:30. I walked out of town and took a dirt track inland. Within a few minutes I'd left the cosmopolitan craziness behind and entered a different country, a world that had existed long before the tourists invaded. The one thing they had in common was the ubiquitous sound of Merengue. Here, in the jungle, it was drifting on the breeze from transistor radios in tiny shacks, rather than pumping like a hurricane from giant speakers on pimped pickup trucks.

Being a Sunday I hadn't expected to find the school open but it turned out to be quite easy to find. I followed the sound of children until I reached a clearing in the jungle and there she was, surrounded by smiling kids, painting a mural on the wall of the little school-house. I stood there for a moment taking in the scene: the kids' infectious enthusiasm, the vibrant colours and bold images of their painting, and Nicole herself.

The barman hadn't exaggerated—she was indeed *una chica muy guapa* and *una mujer muy elegante*—a pretty girl on the cusp of becoming an elegant woman. In her mid-twenties, slim, athletic, with skin like *cafe con leche*—an unusual, exotic blend of African and European—mixed race, mulatto, like myself. Her jet black hair was cut unfashionably short, like a French film star from the early sixties. The barman was right: she had a classic elegance, as if she'd just walked off the set of 'Jules et Jim'.

"*Hola*, Nicole?"

She turned to me, startled.

"*Si. ¿Qué?*" Some fear in her voice.

"*Tengo algo para usted* ... I have something for you ..."

This only increased her alarm.

"*Merde!*" She swore in French and took a step back towards the children, putting her arm around the nearest—a little girl who shared her teacher's strikingly good looks.

"From the Master ..." I blurted out, desperate to reassure her.

There was still anxiety in her eyes, but they were clouded with confusion now as she tried to make sense of this strange *gringo*. I attempted a few more words of explanation in my stuttering Spanish before she stopped me:

"We speak English if you like. Is good for me to practice and good for the childrens to hear. I am teaching them a leetle."

Her voice was musical, the accent an intriguing mix of staccato Spanish softened with legato French intonation.

"Thanks" I said, relieved. "I'm sorry to surprise you like this. The Master sent me to deliver a *contract?*"

I said the word questioningly, unsure of the effect it might have, but she seemed to understand and to trust me a little more now:

"OK. Wait some moments and I close the school. Ah, *oui*, it is Sunday, no? So, no is open and I no need close ..."

I smiled at her impeccable logic.

"... but we finish painting and is time to go home now. You come to *la casa* with us, no?"

I nodded. She cleared away the children's paint and brushes, beckoned to the pretty little girl and introduced her daughter, Jacqueline, a shy child about eight years old and already sharing her mother's beauty and poise. I told them my new name: Malcolm, remembering just in time that I was no longer Nick.

We walked a short distance through the rainforest until we came to a group of huts. Children were playing and a few chickens, goats, pigs and dogs wandered around. The usual scratchy Merengue riffs and delicious aromas hung in the humid air.

I noticed, with a wry smile, that some of the shacks had incorporated windsurfing components in their construction. Broken masts had become supporting beams, torn sails patched up holes in the palm-thatched roofs, delaminated boards made great tables. I thought how cool it was to recycle these discarded toys, my tribe's unwanted carbon, mono-film, and fibreglass, to become essential components in the fabric of everyday life.

"*Mi pueblo*" Nicole said, a measure of pride in her voice.

She nodded to her daughter and Jacqueline ran off to play with her friends and their animals. We sat down outside one of the huts. It was painted every shade of blue: from the turquoise of the ocean, with a few leaping dolphins, to the deep purple of the night sky, complete with a graphic, laughing man-in-the-moon. Someone here was an artist and it was confirmed by a stack of canvases propped up against the wall.

I put the Master's letter and package on the table—which on closer inspection appeared to be a classic Naish thruster wave-board supported on a broken boom. Nicole went inside, returned with a beer for me and opened the letter. I sipped my drink and watched a series of emotions animate her face as she read it ... initially, recognition—she glanced from the letter to me almost as if she'd been expecting both; then surprise—she looked at the Master's package as if it might be about to explode (something that had worried me as well, given his use of the term: 'target'); and finally, resignation as she read his last instructions and nodded—sadly, it seemed to me.

She put the letter on the table and stared into space. I sipped my beer and allowed the moment to stretch out. It was wonderfully tranquil here after the bedlam of Cabarete—just the faint sounds of children, animals and domestic bliss. Even the Merengue was muted, pianissimo.

Some kind of parrot squawked rudely in the trees, jolting Nicole from her reverie. She folded the letter and put it in her pocket, picked up the package and asked me, abruptly:

"What day is today?"

"Sunday" I replied, surprised how quickly she could forget.

"No, not *day* ... how you say: *¿Cuál es la fecha de hoy?* Ah, *oui* ... what is the date today?"

I told her: "November the first."

She nodded, thoughtfully, as if memorising it, and muttered

something under her breath: "Ah, *oui, Día de Muertos!*"—at least I think that's what she said.

I waited for her to explain the significance, but instead she asked me how I knew the Master. I told her my story, or at least an edited version. She listened carefully, nodding, occasionally asking for clarification. It was dark by the time I'd finished and I'd sank a few more beers. I asked her to reciprocate and tell me her own story but she sighed and told me it was getting late, they must eat and sleep— tomorrow was Monday and school started early.

She called out: "*Jacqueline, ici maintenant!*" Her daughter came running and they spoke in some kind of French Caribbean dialect.

"*Oui, c'est créole* we are speaking" she explained, smiling at my puzzled expression. "Now, I sorry, but come back tomorrow. You eat with us and I explain you about the Master, *our* story."

I thanked her and agreed to return the next day. Apart from anything else I was still owed the second half of my fee, which I assumed was included in the package I'd just delivered.

Then I followed the path back through the jungle and danced my way along Cabarete's crazy main street to the Windsurf Hotel. Manic Merengue pumped out everywhere but I was exhausted. I drifted off to sleep with salsa-on-speed running riot in my head.

7

VOODOO CHILD

The next day I repeated my routine: a leisurely breakfast, jog on the beach while waiting for the wind to wake up, and a fantastic session playing in the waves on the reef. Then lunch in a *chiringuito* followed by a *siesta*, shower, and a few beers with my friend, the windsurfing barman. I'd shouted *"hola hombre"* to him on the water earlier and we'd shared a wave, grinning manically at each other. I finished the afternoon with a stroll down the main street, along the path, to Nicole's little hut in the jungle.

She greeted with French style, planting a kiss on each cheek. Jacqueline smiled shyly from behind her mother's skirt. A couple of dogs emerged from the little house and welcomed me warmly, slobbering over me in their own version of kisses. Nicole called to them: "Legba, Simbi ... *siéger! Bons chiens. Aller! ¡Vamos!*"

"Interesting names" I said, "I never heard them before ..."

"They are names of spirits" she muttered, "names with power, from my home. One day I explain you."

She shooed the dogs away and they scampered off to chase some chickens. Jacqueline went with them to join her friends playing around the communal well at the centre of the pueblo. The children's happy voices mingled with the dogs excited barks, chickens' clucks, pigs' snuffles, parrots squawking in the trees, scratchy Merengue guitars, delicious aromas ...

I thought how fortunate these people were. They may not have many possessions but they had a community. The children could play safely, the dogs could wander freely, no-one agonised about 'health and safety'. They were living a pared-down life, without even electricity, but they made the most of what little they had. Nicole seemed to read my mind:

"We no have much. We try to look after each other, but many problems here: much diseases and no money to pay doctor when childrens sick. The houses are not strong. When hurricanes come it is terrible here. There is no work and no money for education to get work. This is why I help with teaching ..."

She tailed off into a melancholy silence. Clearly, I'd over-romanticised the picture of an idyllic unspoilt life in the jungle. Nicole was like me though: an optimist, a survivor ... and someone who enjoyed their food. She soon snapped out of the sadness and bustled me towards her kitchen.

"I cook dinner for you now. You like chicken, plantain, rice and beans, no?"

I nodded enthusiastically. It was just what I needed after several hours ripping up waves on the reef.

"*Bueno*, 'cos that all I got!" she said, with a shrug-smile familiar from my own repertoire.

We went inside her little hut. You could call the interior 'open plan' or use my own description: 'pared down', perhaps even 'minimalist' ... but only if you were being ironic as well as pretentious. There was just room for a table—again constructed from an old windsurfing board, and a couple of rickety chairs. I sat down, carefully. She opened a bottle of Tropical beer for me and placed a plastic bag on the table next to it.

"The Master, he put money for you in the parcel."

She counted out a wadge of US dollars from the bag and handed them to me—the balance of my fee. I thanked her and put the money in my pocket. I had fulfilled my obligations to the Master now. Job done.

"He is giving money to me also, for helping you. In his letter he tell me you are starting a new life in *la República Dominicana* and I must teach you about the country, the peoples."

I shrugged.

"He say you are running from things in your past—peoples from your country. You need, how-you-say, move on?"

Again I shrugged, wary of where this was going.

"This is true for me also. I escape from my country, Haiti, from bad peoples there. This is why I am afraid when I see you yesterday. I think you maybe *un tipo malo*."

I sighed. "Yes, well I'm glad we've cleared that up now. I'm just the messenger and you know what they say … ?"

"—" She looked at me blankly.

"You know: don't shoot the messenger and maybe he won't shoot you … ?"

Still no reaction. She was busy preparing the food now, conjuring up a meal in the tiny kitchen.

"So, Nicole, tell me about your work here" I asked her.

"When I come here to the pueblo there is no school for the local childrens. I ask the mayor of Cabarete and he say it possible the government make a school here in the jungle, but no possible money for a teacher."

She frowned as she chopped the vegetables, wielding the knife as if it was *los tipos malos* she was chopping up.

"I say OK. *No problema*. I no teacher but I help my daughter learn read and write Spanish, French, a leetle English, numbers, art …"

She smiled at Jacqueline who'd joined us at the table, tempted by the delicious aromas that were now wafting from the hut.

"*El alcalde*, the mayor, he say *bueno*—is possible a school … *if* I am the teacher."

She chucked the vegetables into a pan of boiling water dismissively, as if it was the mayor she wanted to boil alive.

"I tell him: OK, I teach the childrens but I no happy! I'm not a teacher, I am an artist, a painter." She gestured to a pile of canvases in the corner. "I struggle to earn enough to live and now he want me to be like how-you-say: charity?"

I picked up one of the canvases and complimented her. It was full of local colour. At the top was the ocean, waves on the reef, sails and kites, the beach fringed with palm trees, some with kids climbing for coconuts; at the bottom: her pueblo in the jungle, with children and assorted animals. She'd even included some of the cannibalised windsurfing components in her depiction of the huts.

She smiled at my compliment but her smile was tinged with irony:

"These are my tourist paintings. I sell them on the beach so we can eat. Jacqueline is helping me make them."

Her daughter smiled shyly.

"My own work is different. Come, I show you ..."

I followed her into the hut's only other room—their bedroom. There, on the wall above her bed, was a large portrait of a powerful black man surrounded by various objects, set against a backdrop of a dark, stormy sky. The man was looking out of the picture with an intense, cruel stare and he had a vicious blood-red scar on his cheek. There was a brutality about him. The objects seemed to be floating or flying around the man, circling him—or perhaps they emanated from his imagination. Some were ethnic, primitive: an African-looking mask, a drum, a machete, and others were modern: a mobile phone, cigarette lighter, car keys.

I stared at the painting. There was something familiar about the style. I couldn't put my finger on it but I could see what she meant. This was completely different from her simple, colourful 'tourist paintings'. It had a dark, brooding power and it was radical—neither figurative nor abstract, more dreamlike, hallucinatory, magical even —as if the artist had endued each object with significance, power.

I racked my brain, searching my limited knowledge of art for the influences—possibly cubism, or perhaps surrealism? No, neither. The phrase: 'Magical Realism' came to mind. I'd seen art like this before but I couldn't place it. Was it the colours, or the composition? I voiced some of these thoughts, including my Magical Realism label and asked what had been in her mind?

She smiled and inclined her head to one side, looking at the painting as a dog might.

"Interesting, your ideas Malcolm, but my picture no have these things. They are for the European artists. My work is exploring my *own* culture. It comes from Africa originally. We call it *Vodou* and you say 'Voodoo'. But you are right about the objects in my painting—they have power. You call it 'magic' and we say 'essence' or 'spirit'."

She went on to explain how her painting worked on two levels: superficially, as 'art'—an object for someone like me to look at, think about, perhaps put on the wall of a gallery. But it had a deeper purpose ... The combination of these particular 'power-objects', placed around the human subject in exactly this composition, functioned either to protect or control the subject, almost like putting an invisible force-field around him. Only someone with the 'Knowledge' would see this other level in the painting.

This was intriguing. The dual function idea reminded me of 'The Picture of Dorian Gray'—the famous film of Oscar Wilde's story in which the protagonist, Dorian, sells his soul to ensure that the picture, rather than he, will age and fade. But regardless of the Voodoo spirit stuff, Nicole's work was undeniably powerful and contemporary. I didn't know much about art but she clearly had a unique perspective and rare talent. I asked her why she'd given up her own work.

"I am single mother with no money. Nobody here buy paintings like these. They are too strange, too dark. So I must make tourist paintings to eat. No time for *Art* ... (a bitter laugh as she spat the word) ... only time for life!"

I replied that her skill and vision were wasted making pretty pictures to sell for peanuts on the beach. She should persevere with her own paintings and perhaps one day the art world would discover them. It wasn't impossible for a gifted young artist to be discovered, escape from the ghetto and have a career ...

For example, Jean-Michel Basquiat—a young, self-taught black artist, had come from a modest Haitian background to become one of the most famous artists in the New York Graffiti movement. He was championed by Andy Warhol and now his paintings sold for millions of dollars. He was known as the 'Radiant Child' and for about a decade his star burned bright. He was only in his twenties when he died from an overdose, cut down at the peak of his powers just like Jimi Hendrix. I remembered the song that had been playing in the bar when I was looking for Nicole ...

"Maybe one day you'll be as famous as the 'Radiant Child' and people will call you the 'Voodoo Child'!"

She laughed and told me she knew all about Basquiat. He was a sort of hip-hop hero on the streets of her *barrio* and his success was an inspiration to her. She'd just begun to get a bit of recognition for her own work when she had to leave Haiti:

"I was making these paintings for many years in my hometown, Port-au-Prince. People were starting to notice them and, how-you-say, to give me money: *las comisiones y honorarios*, to paint a picture for them—some important peoples, like the Master ..."

Suddenly I remembered where I'd seen a painting like this one. Of course, it was on the wall of my cabin aboard the Abyss. Now it all made sense ... The title was '*Le Maître de ma Mer*' and she'd signed it: Nicole Jean-Baptiste Beauvais. No wonder I recognised that name when I opened the Master's package.

I told her I'd seen her painting of the Master on his yacht. She nodded and went on to explain how he'd commissioned her to paint it and later helped her escape from Haiti:

"So, I am just getting a leetle successful but then I must leave my home—escape from my life there. The Master, he help me escape. But is not possible to bring all my paintings, just this one ... (she touched it reverently) ... it is not for sale."

I asked her who the subject was—the big man with the scar and those cruel eyes?

"He is *el tipo malo* who want to kill me. I run for my life from him. He is my husband, Jacqueline's father!"

I gasped. Now I understood why the barman had been so reluctant to reveal her whereabouts and why she'd been so afraid of me. She must have thought I was a hit man sent by her husband.

"This painting is protecting us. When it is close, *en la casa*, he no have power over us. That is why it is not for sale!"

I thought of the portrait of Dorian Gray hanging in his attic, protecting him from the ravages of time. What about Nicole's painting on the Abyss—was it protecting the Master somehow? Or perhaps it protected *her* from him? I asked her how she met him ...

"Alejandro see my paintings in the market in Port-au-Prince and he ask me to explain them. When I tell him what I tell you: they are about *Vodou*, then he give me good money for them."

I nodded. I could well understand the Master being interested in her work and the culture it sprang from.

"He invited me onto his boat. First I think he wants to buy my body. I say: it not for sale. I'm no hooker. I'm married with young child. He is laughing and telling me no worry—he only interested in my paintings and my mind, not my body."

I smiled. That also tallied with what I knew of the Master. She went on to describe the effect the Abyss had on her—the food, the opulence, the crew in their immaculate white uniforms, the Master, all in black, asking her question after question, probing her with those shaded eyes. Nicole taught him everything she knew of *Vodou* and her 'Dark Art', as he called it. He understood the power in her paintings and he told her she was now one of his Group.

"I no understand him" she confessed. "Then he say: I am a 'shaman with my brush'. I no understand that neither" she said, laughing.

He kept his word and was always a perfect gentleman, only ever interested in her work and her knowledge. But his patronage still created problems for her ...

"My husband is a jealous man, *un hombre muy violento*. He no want me to be an artist and he no like me to make money with my paintings. His friend tell him he see me with a rich white man, on his boat, and he is very angry. He beat me. I am used to it, but then he threaten to hurt Jacqueline. This is too much for me."

I looked into her eyes, the eyes of a survivor, and saw myself in her.

"I tell the Master and he help me to run away. He fix me a passport and he take us on his boat over the border into *la República Dominicana*. Here we are safe, but now I am single mother with no money. He give me money for my paintings and to help us here. All he ask is I teach him my Knowledge, make art, make education for local childrens, and wait for him to send me new student—*you!*"

I recognised the Master's modus operandi: rescue someone in trouble, introduce them to his ideas aboard the sealed world of the Abyss, give them a new identity, new passport, money ... and what then? Enlist them into his cult—the Group and send them back into the world to carry out his 'missions'?

Not for the first time I thought of the Faust myth, the way he sold his soul in a contract with the devil. Had I been 'between the devil and the deep blue sea' when he'd rescued me?

"So, Nicole, you have a contract with the Master?"

She gave me a strange look.

"*Oui, mi contrato* with him is starting when you give me the letter yesterday—*Día de Muertos*, the Day of the Dead ..."

She paused.

"And this contract somehow involves me?"

"*Oui,* it is involving you ... and me ..."

She paused again and seemed to rethink her answer.

"No, *this* is my contract with him: I must *help* you, like he help me. *Teach* you, like I teach him."

I thought about this, chewing it over as I digested Nicole's delicious Dominican cuisine. The Master had hinted he had plans for me beyond my present mission—ambitions for me to "fulfil my potential", as he'd put it. Now it seemed his master plan involved Nicole. Apparently, he'd assigned us roles: she was cast as the teacher and I was her pupil. It seemed impolite not to follow his script after she'd shown me such generous hospitality, and besides: this was the start of my new life. It looked like the next chapter would be a steep learning curve.

But something still disturbed me—something in her voice when she'd told me about her contract with him ... a wrong note, something out-of-tune ... Maybe it was her reference to the Day of the Dead, along with the stuff about Voodoo ... Perhaps it was just my paranoia about the Master ... But something wasn't quite right.

It was time for me to take the path back through the darkness to the Windsurf Hotel. I finished my glass of wine and thanked her for a lovely evening. She smiled coyly and asked me what I was doing tomorrow:

"You come to my school *mañana* and help me teaching the childrens English, no?"

I shrugged and considered this request—or was it a demand? It was hard to tell, given her use of the language.

"I no speaking good, your language, *N'est-ce pas*?"

I grinned. Now it was my turn to be coy. She may be correct about her incorrect grammar but there was no doubting how sexy her accent was. She gave me a positively Parisian pout, straight out of 'Jules et Jim'. It did the trick. I knew I wanted to see her again.

"Well, far be it for me, a mere Antipodean, to correct a teacher's language ..." I put on my mock-pompous parody of an upper-class-twit British accent.

"*¿Qué?*"

"... especially one who is fluent in French, Spanish and Creole" I continued in the same tone, "but yes, your English is rather what we call 'Pidgin', if you don't mind me saying so."

"What is this Pidgin?" she demanded, pouting expressively.

"It's a small bird, found in large numbers in places like Trafalgar Square, London, where they shit a lot!" I replied, trying to keep a straight face.

She looked at me incredulously, not sure if I was being serious.

"I no shitting pigeon! *Merde!*" she exclaimed, the pouting now off-the-scale cute.

We looked at each other and collapsed in laughter. Her soulful, serious artist cover was blown and the ice was well and truly broken.

"OK. *Adios. Au revoir Madame Pigeon. Hasta mañana.*"

She kissed me on the cheek and I promised to return tomorrow.

A little way down the path, slightly unsteady from the wine and perhaps also her kiss, I stopped and glanced back. Nicole was hugging her daughter and the two dogs, Legba and Simbi were trying to muscle between them for a cuddle.

8

LEARNING CURVE

The next morning I had an early session sailing the waves on the reef. It was nowhere near as good as the previous two days but that's the nature of windsurfing. No two days are the same—no two waves are the same, for that matter. It's what keeps things fresh, spontaneous. But when the wind and waves aren't cooperating, the kiters are cutting you up and yelling abuse at *you* and you're out of sync with nature, then it's time to take a rest. So I wasn't in the best of moods when I arrived at the little school in the jungle for my first day as Nicole's visiting professor of English.

She introduced me to the children: "*Este es el señor Malcolm.* He is helping us speak like the pigeons in London ..."

Blank stares.

"*Él nos ayudará a hablar inglés como las palomas.*"

The classroom erupted in giggles. Then noticing my glum expression she added: "but today he is looking like a black dog."

I scowled at them, to illustrate the sentence.

A cheeky little boy raised his hand. "Yes, Miguel?"

"*¡Él no es un perro negro, él es un pollo negro grande! y ...*"

More laughter. Nicole interrupted: "No, Miguel, today we are talking Eenglish ..."

"He no black dog—he big black cheek'n!"

I applauded Miguel and corrected him in my mock-posh British accent: "I am *not* a black dog, *nor* am I a big black chicken—I am a kangaroo! I bet you haven't seen many of those around here?"

Puzzled expressions, including Nicole, but now I had their attention. I picked up some chalk and drew a passable likeness of my nation's favourite critter. Then I hopped around the room doing occasional kickboxing moves in a somewhat bizarre impression of a kangaroo with a baby roo in its pouch. My performance seemed to go down well and the black mood soon left me, lifted from my shoulders by the kids' energy and enthusiasm to learn.

Nicole asked me to tell the class how windsurfing worked so I grabbed a brush and illustrated my explanation by painting it into their ongoing mural, piece by piece:

"This is the board: *la tabla*. This is the sail: *la vela*. This is the mast: *el mástil*. And this is the boom, um ..."

I had no idea of the Spanish word but they knew what it was—most of them had a close familiarity with these objects, on the beach, and as essential components in the construction of their houses. I added a windsurfing kangaroo just to complete the picture.

The rest of the afternoon passed in a blur of laughter, pidgin English and flying paint. Before long it was the end of the lesson and I was reflecting on how much fun it had been. Perhaps I shouldn't have been surprised—after all, teacher *was* the profession listed on my, or rather: Malcolm Fraser's passport.

Nicole seemed happy with our afternoon's work and invited me back to the hut for a celebratory *cerveza* and some more of her food. I accepted gladly—I was starving and gagging for a cold one after all my exertions, particularly the kickboxing kangaroo. She prised Jacqueline away from the mural and closed up the classroom.

As the three of us walked cheerfully along the path I couldn't help sneaking glances at this *muy elegante mujer*. It had been quite a while since I'd enjoyed anyone else's company, let alone a beautiful young woman like Nicole (the Master was more 'challenging' than enjoyable). My last romantic relationship had ended disastrously and I was in no rush to start another, but romance is like windsurfing: unpredictability is the name of the game!

When we got back to the pueblo I was greeted as an *amigo*. Kids smiled at me, adults nodded and said *hola*, even the dogs remembered me. I'd been a recluse for so long I'd got used to being an outsider, but right then I felt part of a community again. That evening I began to demolish the wall I'd built around myself.

Nicole cooked the same simple, delicious Dominican meal and we had a few glasses of the local *vino tinto*. After dinner, she insisted on initiating me into the pleasures of *Mama Juana* and that did the trick... Any remaining doubts that we would soon also be enjoying the pleasures of the flesh vanished into a euphoric rum-and-tree-bark haze.

She sent Jacqueline to a neighbour's house and we became lovers —as simple as that! No coyness, no persuasion, no complications. We simply tore each other's clothes off and got down to it like a couple of dogs on heat. Straightforward honest lust. My God, how I needed it!

Afterwards, we lay in her bed, in the afterglow, and laughed as the sweat rolled off our bodies. I kissed her, wondering what it meant, but feeling happy in the moment. Sex is like windsurfing for me—total, spontaneous immersion in the now. My previous relationships had always been sexual but the sex was shallow, skin deep, like going through the motions in the gym. Sex without passion is like windsurfing without waves—one dimensional, frustrating. I always got bored pretty quickly and moved on.

This felt different. The passion was more than skin-deep. The sex had soul. We were soulmates making love. There was an honesty in our lovemaking, a trust in our touch. It cut through the mistrust we each felt for the rest of humanity.

"You are the first man since I leave my husband" she whispered to me. "I no trust anybody after him."

I could hear the anxiety in her voice when she spoke of him, almost as if she had to lower her voice in case he was stalking her.

"But you trust *me*?"

"*Oui*, I am seeing myself in you."

She looked into my eyes and smiled. I understood what she meant. She recognised her loneliness reflected in me, as I did mine in her. We were mirror images of each other. Two mixed-up mulattos: African-French, Irish-Aboriginal. Reflections within reflections. Soulmates.

We made love again—or rather, we had glorious, uncomplicated passionate sex again. There was no need to complicate it by using the 'L word'. No talk of "us". No tears of regret. No worries.

That was the first Ozzie expression I taught her. She loved it:

"*Oui*, you are my meester No Worries Malcolm, the Kangaroo Kid!"

I kissed her laughing mouth.

"And you are Mademoiselle Pigeon, my Voodoo Child."

I explained how the Hendrix song had been playing in the bar when I'd been looking for her. A flicker of doubt clouded her smiling eyes at the mention of Voodoo and her contract with the Master. But it was soon 'No Worries' again. That would be the last time I'd think about him for almost a year.

The next day followed a similar pattern: a frustrating session on the reef redeemed by an inspiring couple of hours with the children in the classroom and a cathartic release of frustration with Nicole. After that, we went into town for our first date—a post-coital dinner at my favourite restaurant in Cabarete: 'Las Brisas'.

She looked stunning, in a dress that was spectacularly sexy and elegant. I introduced her to a few of the local windsurfers—a cosmopolitan tribe gathered from all over the world. She beguiled them, effortlessly switching from Spanish to French to her own idiosyncratic version of English, which had already started to improve with my help. She was a fast learner and I wondered if I might be able to teach her my sport as well. She laughed at the suggestion,

didn't say no, but told me she "no have much time for learn to surf..."
I corrected her grammar and she added:

"I must spend my time making tourist paintings to sell on the
beach, teaching *los niños* and ... (she looked at me significantly) ...
learn to speak English better."

The idea was shelved but it got me thinking: if not Nicole, then
perhaps I could teach some of the kids to windsurf? The empathy I
shared with them surprised me and it reassured Nicole. I loved
messing around in the classroom and she found it easier to trust one
of the male species who was just a big kid himself. I got on well with
her daughter and even the two dogs liked having me around. I took
them for long walks, exploring the jungle paths while Nicole and
Jacqueline worked on their tourist paintings.

Over the next few weeks our passionate fling evolved into a
serious romance. I spent plenty of time in Nicole's hut, gradually
leaving more of my few possessions there, but it took a while before I
moved in with her. I didn't want to rush things. We maintained a
healthy independence until the Windsurf Hotel became an unnecessary extravagance and I became a full-time resident of the little
pueblo in the jungle.

We were each fiercely protective of own space but we'd recognised we were soulmates that first night. I guess it was another
example of the Master's 'gravitational attraction'. It took a while, but
Nicole was only the third person (after my brother-in-arms, Robo,
and Alejandro himself) to get to know the Nick concealed inside the
surf-punk disguise.

December 2015. Autumn turned to winter, although the four seasons
are not well defined in the DR. It's hot all year round but some
months are also wet and some months are windy. In the autumn the
wind is unreliable—all or nothing, hurricanes or calm, and it rains a
lot. Some years there's flooding. In the summer it's humid, windy, and
the Atlantic is flatter.

After Christmas the place lit up with day after day of strong wind and waves—often challenging, sometimes majestic, occasionally even life-threatening. I had a number of long swims back from the reef with broken equipment but nothing much fazed me after my adventure drifting around the other side of the same ocean. I felt invincible and I pushed myself to the limit. Bit by bit I gained the locals' respect until it was all high-fives on the beach and whoops on the reef. Even the kiters took me seriously and we shared waves without the usual abusive shouts.

I was happy—happier than I'd ever been in my life. Every day was much the same, but in a good way. I learned to appreciate the stability of a healthy routine shared with the right people and to live in the present moment, like a dog—a No Worries dog, rather than *un perro negro*. Malcolm Fraser, the English teacher from Sydney, was happy doing what it said on his passport; and Nick Kelly, the Kangaroo Kid from WA, was happy with Nicole, his Voodoo Child.

January 2016. The new year kicked in with an epic Merengue party on the beach. Once I'd recovered from the mother of all *Mama Juana* hangovers I resolved to give something back to the community that had welcomed me so warmly.

I began with a renovation program in the pueblo and schoolhouse, using recycled windsurfing equipment from the rental centres on the beach. My first project was to build an extension to Nicole's hut. She and Jacqueline had nowhere to paint their tourist paintings when it rained, and I was fed up with the kitchen being turned into an artist's studio. My real motive, though, was to encourage her to rediscover her own work.

It worked! Paintings started to appear in the new studio and stayed there rather than being sold for a few pesos on the beach. A new style began to emerge—just as radical as the strange portrait above the bed, but lighter and less brooding. She didn't speak much about her work, but the studio had given her the space to explore art again, rather than just make paintings to live.

When the rest of the community saw Nicole's studio they were impressed. I'd come up with some new ways of cannibalising wind-surfing components, reconfiguring them in a way that hadn't been thought of before. What's more, I'd been able to persuade the rental centres to donate their unused equipment before it was falling to pieces. Some of it was still in good enough condition to use for its intended purpose and this motivated me to revisit an idea that had been drifting around my head for weeks: why not start a windsurfing school for the local kids?

Windsurfing is like a religion for me. I'd been telling them about it from my first day as their English teacher—using it to illustrate ideas, describing the places I'd visited, even telling them my survival story. They were enthralled, but none of these kids had ever been given the chance to try the sport. Here we were, a few hundred metres from one of the best spots in the world, with a thriving windsurfing economy, and yet none of them had a clue how much fun it was, let alone how it might even provide them with a job.

The only way for a poor Dominican kid to escape from the ghetto was to be discovered by a baseball scout and taken back to the USA to join a top team. That was every local kid's dream. Each Major League team has a training academy in different parts of the island to help develop upcoming players and every season the scouts scour the country looking for talent. Dominicans are famous as some of the best pitchers in the world. It's in their blood, like West Indian fast bowlers or Jamaican sprinters. Perhaps these kids were also naturally talented windsurfers? I intended to find out.

I started by setting up an old board and rig on a patch of grass outside the school and showing them the basics. Of course they loved it and Nicole had to impose strict rules: an hour of English and if sufficient progress had been made, form a queue and you get your turn on *el simulador de windsurf*.

The day came for our first outing to the beach and you've never seen a bunch of kids so keen to get their lessons done and dusted! I'd managed to persuade the French windsurfing centre at the far end of the beach to lend us some beginner equipment and even the hard-bitten instructors were chuffed to see the children having so much fun. They were used to adult tourists obsessing about looking cool and learning everything logically, but my lot just jumped straight in with manic Merengue enthusiasm. Before long most of them were tacking and gybing and some were experimenting with freestyle, inventing new ways of falling in. *Merde*, it was a joy to watch!

Our weekly lessons became daily *après*-school sessions and soon we were a regular part of the Cabarete windsurfing scene. The local dudes thought it was cool, the tourists started to notice us and the foreign rental centres' consciences were pricked. Nicole and I went round all of them asking them to donate equipment and collect money from their clients for my little *escuela de windsurf*—the 'Kangaroo Windsurf School'.

As the conditions became more challenging it became clear that one of my pupils was something special. Miguel, the little boy who'd piped up cheekily on my first day in the classroom, was more than just an unusually quick learner—he was a potential star. Within a few weeks he'd left the other kids behind and was sailing with me on the reef. A couple of months of intensive advanced coaching and he was looping. By the spring he was already better than me—somewhat humbling (and a bit galling) to see such natural raw talent.

Nicole and I persuaded the French windsurfing centre to sponsor Miguel in a local wave sailing competition. Not only did he beat the other juniors easily, but he pushed the adults hard and came third in the pro fleet! Word spread about this talented Dominican kid and a visiting journalist wrote a piece about him for 'Planche' magazine, focussing on how we'd given him the opportunity to discover his hidden talents. It was heartening to see how proud the other children were of Miguel. They weren't jealous of his success at all. They just thought it was fantastic that one of them was now a famous windsurfer.

Winter became spring (although you'd be hard pressed to notice much of a difference) and the Kangaroo Windsurf School was thriving. 'We Hop Higher!' was our slogan and 'No Worries' our message.

Children started travelling from further afield to join the local kids and Nicole managed to persuade the mayor of Cabarete to extract some funding from the minister of sport. Along with Miguel's aspirations to be a pro windsurfer, several of the other kids had the potential to become instructors and a few were already helping out in rental centres up and down the beach. For sure there was less fame and fortune in windsurfing than baseball, but it could still be a way to make a living for these kids.

For me, windsurfing was more than a sport—it was a lifestyle and a religion I practised every day. I taught them its values: freedom, self-reliance, respect for nature, stoicism and patience when the conditions didn't cooperate, and the comradeship of a tribe of fellow enthusiasts.

April 2016. After the intense winter sessions in waves of consequence, it was time for the manic partying of *Semana Santa* (Easter week)—so crazy that all water-sports were banned because there were simply too many drunk people in the water! After that, the tourists left us alone for a couple of months and the wind and waves took a break as well.

Spring was a quiet season in Cabarete. Nicole and I were happy to have some time to ourselves. She was focussed on her own work now, with a stack of extraordinary paintings in the studio. There was talk of a 'meet the artist' day to introduce her to the public, perhaps sell a few, or score a commission. She was even thinking of trying to get an exhibition in the capital city, Santo Domingo.

I finally started working on the book I always said I'd write—a memoir of my adventures with Robo, a windsurfing equivalent of Kerouac's 'On the Road'. Once I'd written the first sentence: *The day I should have drowned started well enough...* it seemed to open the floodgates and a torrent of experiences, ideas and emotions poured out. I started with my survival story and jumped in and out of my life in a series of flashbacks.

I was surprised to find I got as much of a buzz from writing as I did from windsurfing. Both activities were completely immersive. Each word, sentence, paragraph and chapter posed a challenge as unique as a gybe, jump, or wave-ride. Nothing else mattered when I was writing or windsurfing, but the big plus was that I could write whenever I had a free moment—no need to wait for wind and waves. So it was the perfect foil for my other passion.

Writing the memoir was a cathartic, confessional experience— my way of confronting the past, admitting my mistakes and moving on. It was the story of my obsession with the ocean and adventure; the story of an outsider searching for an identity; my struggle for survival; and, in the end, a story about loyalty and betrayal.

I'd never told my family what I was going through and I couldn't ask Robo or Alison for forgiveness ... but I could write it all down and tell the truth. Perhaps one day it would be published, maybe even become a best seller, and they'd understand why I did the things I did ... I thought, somewhat naively.

At one point I quoted something the Master had said to me: "I think perhaps you have been sailing too close to the wind, Nick, just like Icarus was tempted to fly too close to the sun." As soon as I quoted him I knew I had the title: 'Too Close to the Wind'. He was right: it was a perfect description of my stalled life—a series of miscalculations and misjudged angles. Nobody can sail straight into the eye of the wind—there's a critical angle beyond which you stall and come to a dead stop.

I showed what I'd written to Nicole, hoping for her approval or at least that she might understand me better. I thought reading it might bring us closer and apart from anything else, it would be good for her English. She read it slowly, digesting it like fine French cuisine—a morsel at a time, savouring some passages, laughing at others, stopping often to ask the meaning of a word, occasionally choking on an indigestible episode. When she finished it she gave me the strangest look. The mix of sadness and joy was unlike anything I'd seen from her before—but perhaps *all* emotions are just different aspects of the same truth, different sides of the same coin.

She kissed me and told me she recognised herself in my story. We were the same—outsiders. She because she was an artist, me because I was forever hopping around like a kangaroo. We were mixed-up mulattos from the wrong side of town. We shared a tough background and we were survivors, searching for a better life—not just materially but spiritually. Perhaps we'd never find it. Perhaps we'd always be alone. We were mirror images of each other. Soulmates.

Her next painting was a portrait of us, surrounded by 'power objects' in her Magic Realism manner. She explained that by placing us together, framed by these objects, the painting would protect us. It was a portrait of two spirits who shared the same consciousness. She called it: 'The Kangaroo Kid and his Voodoo Child'.

I had no idea whether the painting would really protect us. From what? What does *anyone* know of their future? All I knew was that when she showed it to me, in that precious moment, the Kangaroo Kid and his Voodoo Child were soulmates.

9

DÍA DE MUERTOS

June 2016. Spring became summer and the tourists returned to Cabarete, bringing the wind with them. The ocean was flatter but it blew every day, and that's how they liked it. The lack of surf made my own sessions rather two dimensional (waves were the missing third dimension) but it was great for teaching the kids at the Kangaroo windsurf school.

We were well established now, funded by the government and promoted by the tourism authority. Miguel was a local hero, winning contests, signing sponsorship deals and well on the way to becoming a professional athlete—at the age of fourteen! His parents were great. They kept him well grounded in reality and insisted he finish his education.

I was part of the community—welcomed by the pueblo in the jungle, respected by the Cabarete windsurfing tribe, even the mayor occasionally popped in to the school to say *hola*. It felt like the Kangaroo Kid had grown up and become a contender. Perhaps this was what the Master meant when he talked about "fulfilling my potential"?

Whatever. I'd done it for myself. It was my life, not his. Whenever

I thought about him, the black dog, paranoia, crept into my thoughts. I wasn't his puppet, but I couldn't escape the nagging feeling that he was still pulling the strings, somehow.

Nicole's paintings were selling well, and not just to tourists. A gallery in Santo Domingo was interested in showing her work, but when I asked how they'd discovered her she was unusually guarded. I thought we had no secrets from each other, so I was a bit upset.

Eventually, she confessed that the Master had provided her with a letter of introduction which had been included in the package I'd delivered. She hadn't wanted to mention it because she knew I was worried that she was still somehow contracted to him. I understood *why*—because he'd helped her to escape from Haiti, but she wouldn't tell me *how*. It was the one taboo subject between us: what did she have to do to release herself from this contract?

August 2016. We went hiking with the dogs into the hills between the DR and Haiti, Nicole's homeland. She said she wanted to show me how things were there and to teach me about *Vodou* without distractions, so we left Jacqueline with a neighbour in the *pueblo*.

Looking into Haiti from a hilltop above the border fence was like looking into hell. All the vegetation, anything edible or useful, had been stripped to leave a barren wilderness. The rainforest was being turned into an empty plain of mud, scarred by huge craters where gravel had been extracted. The banks of a river were crowded with shanty huts piled on top of each other and the river was an open sewer running with shit. There was frantic activity, angry shouts, bad smells ... The place had an edginess, an edge of darkness and violence. The dogs seemed to sense it too, growling to themselves all the time.

I wasn't enthusiastic when Nicole announced we'd be spending the night there. It wouldn't have been my choice of campsite, especially when she told me that a group of nuns had been ambushed, raped and brutally killed nearby. But she insisted, explaining that the hilltop had a special significance for her. It was a sacred place for her ancestors—a place where spirits were set free. She'd been there several times before, to take part in *Vodou* ceremonies in which animals were sacrificed. For a moment I feared for Legba and Simbi, but she assured me there'd be no live sacrifice that evening.

We lit a fire and talked deep into the night. Nicole began by telling me her life story. She was born into a large family, the middle daughter of three older brothers and two younger sisters. Crammed into a tiny, chaotic house there were plenty of mouths to feed, but they all did their bit. The extended family managed to scrape a living and they usually had enough to eat.

Her father was a black Haitian—a violent *cabrón* who ruled them like a dictator. He was especially cruel to the female members of the family and his macho cruelty established Nicole's distrust of men:

"That *hijo de puta*, he just like my husband, like all men ... except my Kangaroo Kid" she added, smiling shyly at me.

Her mother was French, white, but just as poor. She was from a broken home—the illegitimate child of an illicit affair. Nicole's father had rescued her and he never let her forget it. She was beautiful, kind and gentle, but she suffered from depression.

Nicole was her favourite daughter. Her mother taught her about French style, art, and her secret knowledge: *Vodou*. She was desperate for Nicole to get an education and escape from poverty. But one day, when Nicole was ten years old, she came home from school to find her mother had taken an overdose of sleeping pills.

"I never forget that day" she said, bitterly. "Now I have no one to protect me from my father. Life is more terrible for me and my sisters. But it make me stronger, better survivor."

Nicole grew up in a *barrio* of Port-au-Prince where gangs controlled everything, drugs were everywhere, murders were common. To survive you had to be smart, streetwise. One of her brothers was gunned down right outside her house and she told me about it in a shockingly matter-of-fact way:

"He was ... how-you-say? In the wrong place, at wrong time, with wrong *tipos*."

She would have been just another *chica* from the *barrio* but she had a talent for making pictures and this protected her. The gangs 'commissioned' her to paint the walls of their *barrio* with their tags—their logos, marking their territory like dogs. She integrated them into her own sophisticated images and people sensed her street art was special ...

"Without my painting I am nobody. Art is my secret weapon, the way I survive."

Her story struck a familiar chord. My background was nowhere near as harsh as her's but we shared the same aspirations. I'd managed to escape from a dead-end fishing town by educating myself in mister BigFish's library, while Nicole had hoped art would be her way out of the ghetto. Sadly it wasn't to be:

"When I was a teenager a teacher at my school say my paintings are special. She speak to my father, tell him I must study art ..."

She paused, staring into the fire, perhaps imagining a life that might have been.

"But my father get mad and he say: No! Nicole no is *especial*. She must clean, cook, earn her place like the rest of his women."

When she was just seventeen her father was offered money to arrange a marriage to one of his friends—a man twenty-five years older than her. He turned out to be another *malvado cabrón*, forcing her to be his domestic slave, a baby machine, beating her when she begged to be allowed to have a life of her own.

She kept painting though, in secret, and whenever she could she smuggled pictures down to the market, occasionally managing to sell one. This was how she met the Master. She taught him what she knew of *Vodou* and he helped her to escape.

Just before she ran away she took her daughter into these hills to ask the spirits to protect them ...

"This place is special. Here there is a way into the spirit world. I camp here with Jacqueline and I tell her everything I know—the 'Knowledge'. Now I do the same for my Kangaroo Kid."

. . .

It was around midnight when she reached into her bag and produced a leather pouch and a small wooden pipe decorated with oddly familiar symbols. She opened the pouch and emptied the contents into my hand: some irregular shaped brown pellets. They looked like beans or large seeds.

"The Master give me these" she explained, "to help teach the one he sends to me—you!"

I looked at her, wary as ever when his name was mentioned.

"The seeds are from a cactus plant which grow in your own country."

Now I remembered: he told me that he'd done some travelling "down under". I examined the pipe more closely and realised why the markings were familiar—they were traditional Aboriginal symbols.

"We also have plants like this here, mushrooms, but this cactus work better. Alejandro tell me your native people are using it for hundreds of years."

I grinned, proud of my heritage and our psychedelic plants.

"We smoke together and then I show you the spirits here. They are all around us!"

"Really?"

All I could see were fireflies, a full moon, and stars. The forest enclosed us in its soft, green grip.

She packed a few seeds in the pipe and crushed them into a powder. Then she took a stick from the fire, lit the pipe, and drew the smoke into her lungs. She closed her eyes and passed the pipe to me. We shared it in silence for a while.

Time jumps. Nicole speaks to me, but her voice comes from another world. She tells me to focus. Not just to look, but to *see*. She tells me to look at things as she does—as an artist. To see form instead of objects. To see curves, colours, angles, the shape of the space *between* objects ...

I look around, trying to see things as she does.

She explains how our conscious mind overlays a grid on the world to make sense of it. I must strip away the grid to see the reality beneath it. To see things as they are. To see the spirit world.

I'm trying, but now everything is blurred, out of focus. I catch glimpses, out of the corner of my eye—brief glimpses into her portal, her world—glimpses of things my mind tells me are not there ... but then they dissolve again.

She points to things: water, trees, mountains. Tells me the names of the spirits who are found there—spirits who guard and protect us.

I gaze into the fire, watching the sparks fly into the night sky, listening to these stories from another world, marvelling as she explains her Knowledge.

Time jumps and suddenly I'm seeing things differently ... I look into Legba and Simbi's eyes and I see they are spirits, not dogs. I see shapes made of air, surrounding us like magnetic forces. I see the wind—my friend for so long. Now I can *see* him! I see things I can't even begin to describe.

Time jumps, again. Has it been a dream? I don't think so, but now I'm exhausted. I'm lying in my sleeping bag, gazing at the dying embers of a fire. Drifting. Asleep.

The next morning. The molecules of psychoactive cactus have dissolved in my bloodstream. I've left the alternative reality and returned to 'normality'. Time was flowing in a straight line again instead of jumping around like a kangaroo.

Nicole woke me gently. I opened my eyes and took in the view from our hilltop campsite. The forest was bathed in the red glow of dawn. Haiti was waking up beneath us—just another day in Hell for them.

My friend, the wind, swirled around pulling at the trees. Legba nuzzled my face and Simbi licked my feet. The fire was still glowing and Nicole was making tea.

"*Bonjour*, Malcolm" she said, with an impish grin. "*Comment ça va toi? ¿Qué tal?* How are you feeling?"

"I'm not sure ..."

I told her I didn't know what to make of the previous night. It was confusing and a bit scary, but I was lucky to have shared it with her. I was privileged to be her student, to learn about *Vodou*, the spirit world, the Knowledge. It reminded me of my own tribe—not the windsurfers but my roots in the people of the Dreamtime. I wondered whether I would ever return to my own homeland and make my peace with the spirits there.

September 2016. The summer was nearly over when Nicole had her exhibition in Santo Domingo. Most of the tourists had left Cabarete and we were looking forward to the autumn—another quiet season on the north shore. Her show was a big success and for a while she was the talk of the town, heralded as the next big thing to come out of the Dominican art scene. She sold several paintings and we went on a shopping spree buying stuff for the hut, the pueblo, and the school.

I was pleased to see her receive the recognition she deserved, but I couldn't forget that it was the Master who made it happen. We'd been together nearly a year and he was never mentioned, but now his presence loomed over us again. He pulled her strings, just as he did mine.

Nicole's exhibition was the high point of that year. We were happy together, growing ever closer, soulmates making the most of our simple lifestyle, on an upward learning curve ... but we'd reached the apex of our loop.

October 2016. The hurricane hit the island just before our first anniversary. I'd never experienced anything like it but the locals were used to *los jodidos huracanes*. They battened down the hatches, rode it out in a shelter, and got on with their lives again. The shelters were built to withstand these massive tropical storms and their huts were soon rebuilt from the same palm trees, corrugated iron, and recycled windsurfing components. When you don't own much you haven't got much to lose.

But this one was different, a once-in-a-decade category five. It wasn't so much the wind, although gusts of around 150 mph were a bit much even for a wind-lover like myself, it was the rain that did the real damage. Scores of people drowned when rivers burst their banks and many more perished in devastating mudslides. The lucky ones, like us, merely had their houses destroyed.

At times like this, the community pulled together and I was proud to be part of it. We helped each other stash a few essential possessions in the shelter and afterwards, we rebuilt each other's houses. Nicole managed to save a few of her most important paintings, including the one above the bed protecting her from her husband, and her portrait of us. I chose the wave-board that had saved me from drowning in the Atlantic.

We emerged from the shelter to a scene of utter devastation. Everything we'd built over the previous year had been destroyed: Nicole's hut, her studio, the rest of the pueblo, the schoolhouse, our windsurfing school ... all gone! It was heartbreaking.

The most devastating thing was the loss of one of the dogs. We'd only been able to take Legba with us to the shelter. Simbi had run off into the jungle. When we returned to the *pueblo* we found his dead body next to the ruin of our hut. He must have come back to the village as the eye of the storm passed over and then been hit by a piece of flying debris. Legba lay there, next to his corpse, howling for his dead mate.

By the end of October we were just about coping. We'd survived one of the worst storms in living memory but Nicole became more stressed every day. We started to argue, the first fights in our year together. I knew that something was wrong but I couldn't work out what it was. The hurricane seemed to have exposed a fault-line in our relationship—as if it was the pay-back for discovering such happiness. Perhaps sadness and joy are just two sides of the same coin and this was an inevitable part of the learning curve.

The only positives were the waves that arrived in the aftermath of the hurricane. I had some of the most intense sessions of my life sailing in huge surf on the reef, often alone, occasionally with a few of the most gung-ho locals. This was what they lived for, dudes like my barman friend. It was dangerous, even life-threatening at times, but I needed windsurfing more than ever to cope with the stress. Nicole had no release, no time for her art, and I could see how much she was suffering.

It was after one of these intensely challenging wave-sailing sessions that I returned to the pueblo to find she and Jacqueline were missing.

It was Tuesday, November 1, 2016—*Día de Todos los Santos*, a holiday when most Spanish Catholics celebrate their saints, and some who maintain links with a more ancient, pagan past revel in dressing up as skeletons and zombies to mark *Día de Muertos*, the Day of the Dead.

The previous evening we'd gone into Cabarete for a meal to celebrate our anniversary. Las Brisas, the restaurant where we'd spent our first date, had survived the hurricane. It was a special place for us and they were grateful for our support. When we told them we were celebrating our year together they pulled out all the stops, starting with a bottle of champagne they'd stashed somewhere safe.

Our celebrations that evening were tinged with sadness for the devastation all around us—on the beach, in our community and the rest of the country ... But there was something else troubling Nicole. She seemed profoundly uneasy with me, as well as sad. I tried to drag it out of her but as the evening wore on she retreated into herself, into a shell of despair.

When we got back to the hut we made love with a desperation that scared me. Afterwards, she was crying but she wouldn't tell me why. Tears rolled down her face and she couldn't look at me. She turned her back and we slipped into our separate worlds.

The next morning she woke early and made some coffee. We drank it in silence, still unable to look at each other. It was already windy. The wind that had destroyed our community seemed to be tearing us apart now.

She sat there staring at the broken huts, the fallen trees, not speaking. I didn't want to leave her like that but she insisted I go windsurfing. She told me it would help, but she said it with a kind of bleak fatalism that confused me. She gave me the saddest smile, kissed me gently, and wished me luck (very strange, I thought to myself). Then we said goodbye to each other. I grabbed my board and set off for the beach.

That was the last time I saw Nicole. When I returned to the hut she and Jacqueline weren't there. There was no sign of Legba either. At first, I thought they might be with a neighbour. I walked around the *pueblo*, but nobody had seen them that morning.

Then I realised all their stuff was gone: clothes, the few school books we had, her paintings ... All but one ... The Voodoo painting above the bed was missing, but her portrait of us: 'The Kangaroo Kid and his Voodoo Child' was still hanging on the wall.

For one terrible moment I wondered if Nicole's husband had found her and kidnapped them. My stomach churned as I imagined assembling a group of vigilantes and going in chase. I don't do violence particularly well but when needs must I can hold my own.

Perhaps if we caught up with them before they reached the border ... but if they made it to Haiti—no way. All sorts of crazy scenarios flashed through my brain. My heart pumped and I felt dizzy with adrenaline.

Then I saw the letter on the table, with a package next to it wrapped in brown paper, and I knew this chapter of my life was over.

10

IN TRANSIT

I sat in the empty hut, staring at the envelope, willing myself to open it. My world had contracted to these four walls, the table, and what was on it. I looked at my watch—I'd been sitting there for an hour. What day was it? Tuesday ... and the date? The first of November.

Then it hit me: exactly one year had passed since I'd taken the path into the jungle to meet Nicole. "One hell of an anniversary" a voice-in-my-head muttered, bitterly.

"Where the fuck are you, Nicole?" another voice howled. "What happened to *us*?"

The carefully constructed stability of the past year began to disintegrate. The plans, projects, hopes and certainties all began to dissolve. My mind began to fracture, as it had when I was drifting alone in the Atlantic.

I picked up the letter, shaking as I stared at it. It was my lifeline—an explanation, a confession, perhaps even (I was shaking violently now) a suicide note ...

I ripped open the envelope.

It was none of these. It wasn't even from her. It was the original letter from the Master *to* her—the letter I'd delivered one year ago, handwritten in his elegant, formal italic script:

> *Hola Nicole,*
> *Espero que esta carta los encuentre a usted y a su hija en buen*
> *estado de salud?*
> *No, I will write in English, because one year from today HE will*
> *read this letter and understand.*

I gasped. My eyes darted around the room. For a moment I sensed his presence—as if his handwritten words had flown off the page and coalesced to form his hologram. Trembling, I read on:

> *I have sent this young man to deliver your contract, as we agreed.*
> *Like you, he is fleeing from his past and I have given him a new*
> *identity, just as I did for you. Like you, he is a survivor. He has*
> *great strength of will, but he is flawed by self-doubt and betrayal.*
> *You must help him to fulfil his potential.*
> *This is your contract: you must teach him Friendship, Loyalty,*
> *Love, Charity—through your work with the children, and your art.*

I was weeping now. So the year I'd shared with Nicole and Jacqueline had been ordered by *him*—to fulfil her contract? My life here, helping with the school and the pueblo, teaching the kids to windsurf —all of it was done on his orders. Everything? So it seemed ...

> *You must teach him the value of education, how to live with mate-*
> *rial poverty but spiritual wealth, and you must teach him the Dark*
> *Arts—the Knowledge, from your country. You have this Power in*
> *your art, as a shaman—you must show it to him, as you did to me.*

What did he mean: 'shaman'? Was she some kind of witch who could control me with the power of her 'Dark Arts'? Had I been part of some bizarre Voodoo experiment for the past year?

The voices in my head were back, tormenting me with their questions. I stared at the letter, my lifeline, desperate for some answers ...

In this package are some documents, money, a letter for the messenger, and a second package. The money is to be divided: half is for you, and half for the messenger—the balance of his fee.
You must hide this letter, along with the package and the note for him. One year from today you will leave these items for him to find in your house.
Then you will take the new passport, money, and tickets (included in your package) and leave La República Dominicana forever, to start a new life.
You will leave nothing else in Cabarete—no trace that you have ever lived there. No word of where you are going.

His words ripped through me like a patient receiving electric shock therapy or a prisoner in the electric chair. Now I knew, with shocking finality, I'd never see her again.

The clock had been ticking for us from the day I'd arrived at Nicole's hut with this letter. After she read it she'd asked me the date and when I told her she muttered: "*Día de Muertos*". Now I realised she was already mapping out the year ahead, from one Day of the Dead to the next. We'd survived the hurricane but we couldn't survive *Día de Muertos*—the day of the death of our love.

Now I understood Nicole's distress in our final few weeks together, the sadness of our last evening, the desperation of our love-making, why she'd wished me luck with such finality that morning.

I gazed around the empty room, tears in my eyes as I stared at the spaces where her paintings had been. He'd ordered her to take everything with her but she'd made one last gesture of defiance. Her painting of the two of us: 'The Kangaroo Kid and his Voodoo Child' was still hanging there. I would never see her again, I knew that now, but at least I had this memento of our year together—proof that I hadn't just imagined the whole thing.

I stared at that picture for a long time, reliving our year—a lifetime compressed into a square metre of canvas, before reading the final few sentences of his fucking letter:

This is your contract with me. It expires in precisely one year.
After you have fulfilled it you are free.
If you do not do exactly as I have instructed, the contract is invalid.
In that eventuality, your estranged husband will be informed of
your whereabouts, with the inevitable consequences for you and
your daughter.

It was signed with the initials: *A.A.L* and dated: *Sunday, November 1, 2015 (Día de Muertos)*—the day I delivered the package to her.

So, that was that. Now I understood everything.

There was a package next to the letter on the table, wrapped in the inevitable brown paper. On top of it was an envelope, addressed to me. Inside was a single sheet of paper. I recognised the Master's handwriting again:

Nick—by now you will have read my letter to Nicole outlining my
contract with her, and you will probably be wondering what
happens next.

"Fuck you!" the angry voice-in-my-head screamed. I'd kept alive a glimmer of hope there might be some word from Nicole in this second envelope. Now I felt helpless. I was his puppet and he was pulling my strings ...

When our paths crossed a year ago, in the Atlantic ocean, you told
me how you had betrayed the friend you loved. You were so
consumed with guilt and self-loathing that you believed you
deserved to die.

When you told me your story I suggested that you had been sailing
too close to the wind. Now perhaps you understand what I meant.

I stared at his words until they began to float around like a cheap video effect ... and then I had some kind of weird flashback to my vision of hell—the dream I had just before he rescued me—the dream with all the people I'd betrayed.

Suddenly it hit me: the emptiness I was feeling right then must be how Robo felt when I ran off with Alison. I didn't even leave him a note, no explanation—we just disappeared. Strange how I'd never really thought about it before. It took Nicole's disappearance to show me what he must have gone through.

Tears streamed down my face, spilling onto the page, blurring the words. I moved the sheet of paper before they became illegible, and read some more ...

When we met, your ego was defined by Loyalty and Betrayal. But
the year you spent with a member of our Group has shown you
other ways of thinking, other ways of living.
Now you must let go of your ego, just as you must let go of the year
you shared with her.

"Fuck knows what *that* means." The angry voice was back in my head, but now I understood what was at stake. He'd ordered Nicole to leave me because that was her contract with him. But did he do it to teach *me* a lesson—a lesson about 'Loyalty and Betrayal'?

Now I felt fear as well as anger. If he was capable of manipulating Nicole like that, what else did he have planned for me?

"How could anyone be so cruel?" the voice demanded.

But it was only what I'd inflicted on Robo ... and that was the lesson: love and loss—two sides of the same coin.

There were some final instructions. I fought wave after wave of panic as I read them ...

It is time for your next mission, the next stage of the journey to fulfil

your potential.
Tomorrow you are booked on a flight to London—the hub of my
communications network. You will go to the transit lounge in
Heathrow airport. Once there (and only then) you will unwrap the
new package.
You will then receive further instructions.

It was again signed with his initials and dated: *Tuesday, November
1, 2016*—today's date.

I sat in the empty hut staring at the Master's note, bewildered, while
the voices in my head argued about what I should do. One whispered: "Follow his instructions. Go with the flow. There's nothing left
for you here." Another shouted: "No! Enough is enough! Just
stay put."

I sat there for a long time, drowning in thoughts and emotions.
Eventually, emotion overwhelmed me. The sense of loss was too
strong for rational thought. It was overpowering me, taking me down.
I knew I wouldn't survive if I stayed there. The gaping hole left by
Nicole would swallow me. I was afraid for my sanity, perhaps even for
my life. At that moment suicide was a real possibility.

Blinded by despair, I stumbled out of the hut into the jungle and
wandered around aimlessly, calling her name. I looked for her for a
few hours, asking everyone if they'd seen her leave. It was pointless, I
knew that, but I needed to taste the futility, to hit rock bottom before I
could crawl back out of the pit.

Eventually, I stopped asking people if they'd seen her and started
saying *adios* to them instead. I'd come to a decision: I was going to
take that flight to London the next day. It wasn't what I'd call a
rational decision but it did have some practical implications. I had
some responsibilities to the community, to the people who'd
welcomed me. I couldn't just leave without tidying up the loose ends.

Somehow I found the strength to talk to the rental centre who'd
supported my windsurfing school. I told them I was leaving and

begged them to take it over. Of course, they wanted to know why I was going so suddenly—why hadn't I given them a bit more notice? I was in no mood to explain but thankfully they didn't need much persuading. They took one look at my face, desperation etched all over it, and promised to do whatever they could to keep the school running for the kids.

Saying goodbye to the windsurf *niños* was painful, especially saying *adios* to Miguel. I hugged him and told him he was The Man now, no longer a Kangaroo Kid, a special athlete who would do great things in our sport. I would never forget him and I'd be watching his career from wherever I was in the world.

Then I limped back to the hut, devastated, a black dog with his tail between his legs. I sat down and howled for an hour.

In the end what saved me was Nicole's painting of us. 'The Kangaroo Kid and his Voodoo Child' was still hanging there. She might be gone but I was taking a part of her with me, like an urn of ashes. I took the painting from the wall, carefully removed the canvas from the cheap wooden frame and packed it in my board-bag.

Then I got seriously wasted on *Mama Juana* and some grass I'd bought in town. At some point that night I slipped into unconsciousness—the same deep, dreamless sleep I'd experienced in my first twenty-four hours aboard the Abyss.

Wednesday, November 2, 2016, 08:00—the morning after my *Día de Muertos*. I was woken, as usual, by the sounds of the jungle and my neighbours going about their business. But as soon as I opened my eyes I knew it wasn't going to be a normal day for *me*. For a start, it felt like there was a machete buried in my head. I looked around for something to inspire me to get out of bed, rather than simply ending the agony there and then. The hut was bare—just my few possessions packed ready to leave, and the half-empty bottle of *Mama Juana*.

"Glass half-empty, or half-full?" a voice in my head demanded. A cackle of crazy, bitter laughter filled the room, frightening me—was that how my laugh sounded now?

Then I found my inspiration. I did something the locals had often urged me to try but until then I'd never been desperate enough to do: I took a slug of *Mama Juana* as a cure for the hangover—a so-called 'hair of the dog' cure—a black dog in my case. How on earth the evil concoction of rum, red wine, honey and tree bark was supposed to work God only knows, but that morning it did the trick. I dragged my protesting body out of bed, got dressed and took the path through the jungle into town for the last time.

When I'd arrived at Puerto Plata airport, a year and a day ago, I'd taken a taxi. Now I only had a few pesos in my pocket, so I waited in line for the *guagua*[1] with the locals and their chickens. They eyed the dishevelled gringo and his enormous bag with suspicion. My board-bag took the space of at least another passenger, but there was no way I was abandoning my trusty wave-board as Nicole had abandoned me.

The *guagua*'s arrival was the cue for a mini-riot. It was dog eat dog as passengers battled to get on, but this *perro negro* was desperate. I fought my way through the scrum and squeezed myself and my coffin-shaped bag onto the sweaty little bus, accompanied by angry shouts and complaints about dead bodies.

I was drained—physically and emotionally. Before my *Día de Muertos,* I could handle the stress of living in the Dominican Republic. I used to enjoy the craziness, thrive on the adrenaline. Now everything was torture: the heat, the stink, the noise …

Merengue music blasted from the speakers. Funny how I used to love merengue. 'Salsa on speed' I called it. It animated life in the DR. Everyone and everything moved to its manic pulse. Now I couldn't stand it. The music tortured me like nails scratching on a blackboard, tearing at my skin, ripping up my soul.

That *guagua* journey was hell, but eventually we arrived at the airport. The porters descended on us like a pack of vultures. One of them grabbed my wrist before I could extract my board-bag from the bus and join the queue at the check-in.

"*No tengo dinero, ni pesos*—I have no money!" I shouted, but it didn't deter him.

"OK. I take the watch, *señor!*" he yelled, grabbing my much loved Casio G-shock and spitting in my face. Luckily he was a scrawny little weasel—no match for me in my current mood, and I fought him off before his *compañeros* came to his rescue.

I dragged my board-bag up to the desk and produced my passport. The check-in girl's reaction was encouraging:

"Ah yes, mister Fraser, we have a ticket reserved for you on the London flight ... oh, and your surfboard" she added, staring at the computer screen.

I nodded, grateful for these small mercies.

"I see that it was booked just over a year ago" she announced, with some surprise.

I nodded again. This didn't surprise *me*, given what I knew of the Master's meticulous planning.

"And it's a *first class* reservation!" A mix of shock and respect in her voice now, as she studied this scruffy passenger with the designer dreadlocks.

I could imagine her wondering if I was some kind of celebrity—a famous musician or perhaps a top professional surfer.

"So you don't need to queue up here, sir."

I noted the elevation of my status to "sir".

"Just leave your board with us and you can proceed straight through to our VIP lounge."

I smiled—for the first time in twenty-four hours. I might hate the Master but I appreciated his efficiency and attention to detail. It made a dreadful day marginally more bearable.

I made my way to the VIP lounge and proceeded to take advantage of the hospitality there. It dulled my despair a smidgeon, but not for long.

As soon as we took off I wondered what the hell I was doing. I tried to gather my thoughts, but the voices in my head were doing their best to scatter them. They reminded me how Cabarete had felt like home. I'd been a member of Nicole's little community and my tribe of locals.

Teaching the kids to windsurf, to speak English, helping to rebuild the pueblo ... all this had given me an identity—even if there was a false ID on my passport. The past year had been a steep learning curve. I was a different person, no longer an outsider ... and now I was throwing it all away ...

"For what?" a voice demanded.

I shrugged. To be honest, I didn't have an answer. All I had were the Master's instructions—a paper trail of packages and notes, like clichéd clues in a contrived crime thriller.

"What about this 'Group'?" another voice whispered. "He said Nicole was one of them, so are *you* now a member?"

"I've got no fucking idea" I muttered to myself, shrugging again.

Now I was getting hostile stares from my fellow first-class passengers in their designer suits. It was bad enough when the dreadlocks and tattoos had invaded their space, but with all the muttering and shrugging I was in danger of being reported as a dangerous lunatic.

I sank a few beers and tried to silence the voices. But paranoia is another black dog, like depression—it chases you and alcohol won't make it go away. I hated this Master bloke with a vengeance, but I feared him. He knew all about me—everything he needed to control me, and he had no qualms about threatening Nicole.

"He told you to 'let go of your ego' ... but then who will you be?"

Good question, I replied to myself, keeping the dialogue inside my head now. This voice had a point. Perhaps, given time, I'd get over Nicole, but my ego was who I was—my identity, whether false or real—as Malcolm Fraser or Nick Kelly.

When I was onboard the Abyss we'd discussed the notion of free will—was it an illusion? Were we all just characters in somebody else's dream? At the time I thought it was just a game of philosophical chess, clever conversation to entertain him. Now these questions seemed to be the crux of the biscuit. Was I free to choose my own identity, or must I 'let go of my ego' to be in his Group?

I sat there, thirty-thousand feet above the Atlantic, wrestling with philosophical questions that had occupied some of mankind's greatest minds. It seemed unlikely that I, a screwed-up Ozzie surf-punk, would get very far with them. So I reclined the seat, sipped my beer, smiled benignly at the suits, and tried to empty my mind.

Wednesday, 21:00. The plane touched down at Heathrow airport, but I was none the wiser. "The hub of my communications network" the Master had called London, preposterously. He was probably sitting on his yacht somewhere, sticking pins into voodoo effigies—the puppetmaster, pulling the strings.

Paranoia gripped me. Perhaps he was watching me at this very moment via a feed of the airport security cameras. After all, if he was important enough to have an international 'communication network' with a 'hub' here in London, perhaps was powerful enough to have access to the world's CCTV systems, or clever enough to hack into them.

I was sweating now, shooting scared looks at the security cameras, the airport staff, my fellow passengers. Then I got a hold of myself. This was all getting a bit too 'On Her Majesty's Secret Service'. He was surely no 'Doctor No', and I was certainly no James Bond.

I followed the signs for 'Passengers in Transit' along interminable steel-grey corridors into the bowels of the terminal, lost in a strange limbo—a shadow world existing somewhere between Arrivals and Departures, a purgatory between this world and the next. Something in me had died the morning Nicole had disappeared and now I was just a shell, a dead man walking, a zombie trapped in transit, a ghost again.

Eventually, I arrived at the transit lounge—the waiting room between worlds. I sat down, put the Master's package on the table, and looked around wondering what to do next.

There were a few of my fellow transit zombies in the room, lost in limbo like me. One bloke, in particular, caught my eye. He looked familiar, but I couldn't quite place him. As I unwrapped the package I had the impression he was watching me.

Again I followed the Master's instructions to the letter—literally, because having removed the usual brown wrapping paper, in the specified location, I again found a letter, along with yet another package, wrapped in the inevitable brown paper. I put it on the table and picked up the letter. It was addressed to: '*el capitán,* Pablo Rodrigues Vasquez, London'.

I looked up and was startled to lock eyes with the man I'd noticed. He nodded politely to me, and beneath the unfamiliar beard and newly cropped hair I recognised him. It was indeed Pablo, the captain of the Master's yacht. He crossed the lounge and sat down beside me.

I gave him the letter without a word passing between us. He read it, nodded to himself, and unwrapped the package, placing the items that were inside it on the table: some money, an airline ticket, and a handwritten note.

He handed the note to me. I recognised the Master's handwriting and saw that it was a message to me, but before reading it I needed to have a conversation with the messenger. I stared at Pablo, waiting, until the silence became embarrassing. Clearly, he wasn't expecting to explain anything, but I wanted some answers.

"*Hola* Pablo, long time no see" I stuttered, not knowing where to start. "*¿Cómo estás?* How are you?"

"—" He shrugged.

Perhaps I should have apologised for resorting to such a lame cliché but it *had* been a long time—a year and a day to be precise. When I'd walked down the gangplank and away from the Abyss I hadn't expected to see him again, ever. Now here he was, materialising in the transit lounge as if he'd just beamed down from an episode of 'Star Trek'.

I tried again: "More to the point, Pablo, *¿Que pasa hombre?* What's going on mate?"

He would have shrugged again, I'm sure of it, but I put my hand on his shoulder. He stared at it, surprised and annoyed. I suppose he'd expected to pass the Master's instructions to me with a minimum of human interaction and then just beam back up to the mothership.

He raised his eyes from the hand on his shoulder to meet my own, and he could see my distress. The despair, confusion, paranoia—all the bleak emotions of the past two days were etched on my face, and it broke the ice ...

"OK. *Bueno*. Is good to see you, Nick. I hope you are having a good journey?" The same smooth, cultured Argentine accent I remembered from the Abyss.

"Please Pablo, I need some answers, *por favor*, before I go crazy."

He nodded, reluctantly, and I fired a round of questions at him:

"Look, all these notes and packages in brown paper—what's going on? Is it some kind of spy thing? You know, like a James Bond movie? Is he a spymaster?"

A wry smile and a shake of the head.

"So who is he? And what is this Group? He said Nicole was a member—what about you?"

He gave me the faintest of nods.

"OK. And am I a member now?"

Again there was a suggestion of a nod.

"So, what is the project, the goal? Some kind of world domination?"

My voice cracked. I was breathless, hysterical. He put his hand on *my* shoulder to stop me.

"I think you must read *las instrucciones* from the Master, Nick. He explain everything what happen next ..."

I sighed. Clearly, I wouldn't get any more answers from Pablo and there was no point in getting frustrated with him. I remembered what I'd said to Nicole when I delivered the Master's letter to her: "don't shoot the messenger and maybe he won't shoot you!" So I picked up the note and read it:

Nick—it is time for you to continue your journey.
Pablo will give you a one-way ticket to Perth, Western Australia,
and enough money for the next stage of your mission.
You will travel to the library in your hometown and log on to our
website: www.TheGroup.org
(Your username is 'Close2TheWind' and the password is below)
You will then receive further instructions.

He'd signed it with his initials again: *A.A.L* and added today's date: *Wednesday, November 2, 2016.* Below it was an 'I Ching' hexagram:

I stared at the arrangement of six lines trying to work out how it could be a clue to the password. Eventually, I gave up and decided I'd figure it out when I got to my destination. When I looked up from the page Pablo had gone. I wasn't surprised.

So, I'd been given my instructions—the 'next stage of my *mission*' as he put it. I remembered the first time he'd used that word. He'd tried to humour me: "This is your mission, Nick, 'should you choose to accept it' as they say in the movies." Should I accept it again now?

I gazed at the Quantas ticket and the money. Several thousand Australian dollars were sitting there on the table doing their best to tempt me, but it was the destination on the ticket that persuaded me.

Perth. I stared at the name and something shifted in me. The confusion and paranoia were still there, but I'd changed in the past year. I could embrace change now, live with the confusion, feed off the fear—just as I'd done when I confronted the life-threatening waves from the hurricane.

The despair that gripped me when my soulmate walked out wasn't just going to vanish as she did, but now I had a reason to move on. My destination was far more than a city—it was the eye of my hurricane. The waves generated by my past mistakes had been swamping me for too long. It was time to stop running and confront them head-on. The black cloud began to lift, the despair became a dull ache, and I could breathe again. Perhaps the glass was half-full *and* half-empty.

I was going home!

PART III

AUSTRALIA

"We saw ourselves as anthropologists from the twenty-first century inhabiting a time module set somewhere in the dark ages of the 1960s. On this space colony we were attempting to create a new paganism and a new dedication to life as art."
(Timothy Leary)

11

THE FREMANTLE DOCTOR

Perth Airport. Friday, November 4, 2016, 07:00. "Welcome back, Mr Fraser ..." the immigration officer said, as he scanned my fake passport. He was trying hard not to grin, but I could tell he was amused. As he compared my likeness to the photo, he couldn't resist commenting: "... back from the grave, I see?"

Aha, it was refreshing to hear some good old Ozzie sarcasm again. He was, of course, referring to the *other* Malcolm Fraser—the prime minister who'd died in 2015, but little did he know how close to the mark his attempt at a joke had been. Yes indeed, the ghost was back home!

I collected my board-bag, rented a car, and drove the two hours north to my hometown. It had been eighteen months since I was last in Australia and considerably longer since I'd been back to the town, but nothing had changed. I drove down the main street, past familiar landmarks: the school, the tavern, the crayfish plant, until I reached the library.

As I walked in it was as if I'd come full circle. The books on those shelves were old friends. Memories came wafting back like a heap of cray left to rot in the sun—the smell of the place was enough to trigger them.

I sat down at a row of computer screens. They were new, or at least they hadn't been around when I was doing my growing-up in there. They must be a welcome window on the wider world for the closed little fishing community.

I logged onto the internet and accessed a Wikipedia page of I Ching hexagrams. The one in the Master's note was number five, referred to as: 'Attending', 'Waiting', or 'Arriving'.

I typed the name of his website: www.TheGroup.org and was presented with a secure log-in window. I entered the username he'd given me: Close2TheWind and typed 'attending' in the password field.

The computer gave a bleep of disapproval and an error message shot onto the screen: INCORRECT LOGIN—ACCESS DENIED!

I tried again, this time typing: 'waiting' as the password. I got the angry bleep and the same message, but now it also included a threat: ONE FURTHER LOGIN ATTEMPT PERMITTED BEFORE ACCESS IS PERMANENTLY DISABLED!

I was sweating now. I'd forgotten how hot it could be in WA when there was no wind. It was forty in the shade and breathless—hell without the cooling afternoon sea breeze. That's why the locals call the wind the Fremantle Doctor—his twenty-five knot daily prescription makes life more bearable. Mister BigFish may have installed the internet in his library but his improvements hadn't stretched to aircon.

Adrenaline coursed through my body as I gave it my one last shot, typing 'arriving' as the password this time. After an agonising few seconds, a message appeared on the screen. I was relieved to see it was addressed to me, personally:

Welcome to The Group, Nick. Our goal is to realise my father's vision for humanity, and we communicate via this website. The password I have given you will allow you to read some extracts from his journal.

Below this message there were some links labelled: 'Title Page',

'Extract 1', '2', '3' etc. I clicked on the first and it took me to a page of handwritten German. The handwriting was not the Master's, but a similarly formal, elegant italic hand. There was a title in the middle of the page:

Das Journal von Dr Ludwig Langer, Psychotherapeut.
Ein Bericht über sein Leben, seine Experimente in der Ethik und die Erforschung der 'Conditio Humana'.

I stared at the screen, nonplussed. Surely he didn't expect me to read his father's journal in German? Then I realised there was an obvious solution. I typed the handwritten text into Google Translate and an English version appeared on the screen:

The Journal of Dr Ludwig Langer, Psychotherapist.
An Account of his Life, Experiments in Morality, and Research into the Human Condition.

Ambitious, to say the least—and that was just the title! I clicked on 'Extract 1', typed Dr Langer's words into Google, and read the translation of his introductory paragraph:

In this journal I chronicle my life, my studies, and my work as a psychotherapist; my expeditions to the remote regions of India, China, and Australia ...

Aha! So, he had visited my homeland. Now I was intrigued. I continued typing as fast as I could, and read on:

... my experiments with mind-altering substances; my research into exotic ideas, philosophy, religion, and mysticism; my thinking about metaphysics, ethics, aesthetics.

Quite a list, I thought. The Master had clearly inherited his father's all-embracing intellectual ambitions along with his wealth.

I recount how I assembled a group of like-minded radical thinkers; I describe The Group's experiments in 'alternative living', and our search for the 'Ultimate Solution' to the Human Condition.

So much to take in! I was drowning in a sea of ideas. For instance, his *'Bestmögliche Lösung'* ('Ultimate Solution') had frightening resonances with the Nazi's *'Endlösung der Judenfrage'*—their 'Final Solution' to the 'Jewish Problem', which involved the murder of six million Jews in concentration camps. I remembered my anxieties aboard the Master's yacht and I wondered if Dr Langer's journal would reveal that he had indeed been a Nazi war criminal. Thankfully, the next sentence put the record straight:

I describe how the National Socialists stole my work and destroyed my life. I chronicle the events that forced me to flee from the country I once loved and drove me to the brink of suicidal madness.
All this you will find in my journal. It must remain hidden until my death, when my sons will read it and understand what to do with it.

Sons? Was that my typo? I checked again, but no, the handwritten text definitely had: *'meine Söhne'*, plural. Then I remembered: the Master told me he had a half-brother. He hadn't wanted to talk about him and I couldn't remember his name. Perhaps it would all be explained in the journal.

Having concluded his introduction, Dr Langer began at the beginning:

I was born in 1901 in Vienna, the home of Sigmund Freud and the birthplace of the psychoanalytic method. My father was a Lutheran preacher and I had a strict Protestant upbringing. However, while attending the University of Vienna my mind was opened by the ideas of Freud, Nietzsche, and the other great philosophers. It led me to question the scriptures as the arbiter of morality. Of course, this resulted in estrangement from my father, which, sadly, continued to his death.

In 1929 I moved to Zurich to study with Freud's associate: Carl Jung. Freud emphasised the importance of sexual development as the key to our understanding of neuroses, but Jung focuses instead on the collective unconscious: the part of the unconscious that contains memories and ideas that he believes were inherited from ancestors.

I knew a little about Jung from the time I spent digesting the same books that surrounded me now, in Mr BigFish's library. It was a privilege to be given access to the private journal of someone who studied with him. I typed the German text into Google as fast as my fingers would allow and read on ...

Many of my ideas have been shaped by my studies with Jung and I readily acknowledge my debt to him. However, I humbly maintain that my own research has extended these ideas considerably further than Carl envisaged.

My experiments with The Group have taken us beyond mere theoretical hypotheses. We live our ideals—an alternative way of living together; a groundbreaking morality based on Nietzsche's framework; new forms of relationships to replace the Oedipal Mother-Father-Son triangle; relationships that escape the prison of jealous, possessive monogamy; relationships in which men and woman are equal; even (and I write this safe in the knowledge that this journal will remain secret until a more enlightened generation discovers it) relationships between Group members of the same sex!

As Google translated Ludwig's words the corners of my mouth twitched with amusement—the ironic smile of 'a more enlightened generation'. From the little I knew of Jung's work I was aware that he'd moved on from his mentor, Freud's analysis of sexuality, but I doubted that he'd embraced gay sex. I could certainly understand why his pupil had wanted to keep these 'experiments' secret.

Jung's concept of the collective unconscious had always fascinated me. It reminded me of my own roots, my own ancestors'
mythology: 'The Dreamtime'. So it felt as if Dr Langer was speaking
to me personally in his next couple of paragraphs:

> *My travels, in the real world as well as in the world of ideas, and
> our experiments with psychoactive plants, have unlocked The
> Group's own collective unconscious!*
> *During my expedition to the remote outback of Australia, I studied
> with an Aboriginal shaman who initiated me into the rich
> mythology of the indigenous people who have lived there for thou-
> sands of years. This shaman taught me about his ancestors, his
> tribe's collective unconscious, which they call: 'The Dreamtime'.*

I was so engrossed in the words on the screen that I hadn't
noticed the old man who'd sat down opposite me, until he spoke:

"Nick?"—a gravelly voice, barely a whisper, but then we were in a
library after all.

My head jerked back from the screen and I locked eyes with a
dishevelled blackfella. He could have been anywhere between sixty
and ancient. The lines on his face told a lifetime of stories. His skin
was stretched taut, like leather aged by the sun. His upper body was
all skin-and-bones, gnarly sinews poking out from a ragged black
vest. His matted dreadlocks looked like they hadn't seen shampoo in
years, but his eyes were alive, dancing with energy and humour.

He was supremely incongruous, sitting there in Mr BigFish's
library. The town's temple of learning was a bastion of white civilisation and to be honest (rather than simply 'politically correct') you
never saw Aborigines in there. I was about as black as it got in the
reading room. I might be sporting a few ethnic tattoos but my dreads
were positively polite compared to this gnarly old fella, and I dressed
in the designer surf-wear of my tribe rather than looking like a pack
of dingos had just dragged me in from the bush. Even so, I still got
plenty of stares for my mixed race roots.

Once I'd got over my shock, my initial reaction was to shrug and deny all knowledge of this 'Nick'—I was Malcolm Fraser, after all.

His wizened face cracked into a smile that lit up the room. He raised one gnarled finger, like an umpire answering a question of 'How's That?' or a teacher ordering a wayward pupil to hold their horses. Then he typed something into his computer. He waited for a second and pointed to my screen. Some words had appeared on it:

"I have been expecting you, Nick. The Master has sent you to help my people."

I looked at him in astonishment. My mouth opened to fire off a volley of questions, but he raised his finger again—this time to his lips, in a 'shush, this is a library' gesture. I looked into his laughing eyes. My God, what eyes!

He typed something else, and I stared at my screen:

"But before you can help me, I must teach you everything I know, as I did for the Master."

I scratched my head and tried to make sense of this. His text had underlined the connection between us and I needed some answers:

"Who are you?" I typed into the message box on my screen.

"My name is Mandu" He typed back, looking up and nodding to me politely as if we'd just shaken hands. Then he added some more text in explanation:

"(it means: 'Sun')"

His smile radiated warmth and energy.

Great name, I thought to myself. Who needs solar power with a smile like that? I also liked his use of brackets.

"I am one of the Master's group" He typed.

This was scarcely credible, but it did explain how he knew my name.

"So how can I help you?" I asked him.

"All in good time" he replied, and continued typing: "Now I have something to give you—from Alejandro."

He reached into a shabby leather bag and brought out a package. I recognised the plain brown wrapping paper. Checking that nobody was watching, he passed it to me and typed another message:

"Do not open it now. You will know when the time is right and you will know where to find me then."

He looked at me, or rather mesmerised me, with those extraordinary eyes. There was so much I wanted to ask him, but I was like a rabbit caught in the headlights of his gaze.

He smiled, this time to himself, and nodded, as if he'd just remembered one last thing. His fingers clicked on the keyboard again:

"Right now your mission is to revisit your past and put things right!"

Then, with shocking swiftness and agility for such an old man, he picked up the bag, stood up, and strode out of the library.

I sat there, dazed, staring at the empty chair. For a moment I wondered if he'd been for real or just a figment of my jet-lagged, Mama-Juana-and-cannabis-addled imagination. I rubbed my eyes, blinked, and looked at the screen. Most of the text had been erased, but his final instruction: "put things right!" was still there. The package was sitting on the desk, wrapped in the familiar plain brown paper. He had been for real.

It was a bizarre way to communicate, but perfectly suited to a library and completely private, given that we were both logged into a secure website. Text conversations were, of course, commonplace for anybody of my generation but perhaps not for someone like him. The contrast between his appearance and the sophistication of our method of communicating was shocking, but the *content* was even more extraordinary:

"I have been expecting you, Nick. The Master has sent you to help my people ..."

Where had I come across that kind of statement before? It had an almost biblical tone to it, like one of those Old Testament prophets (Isaiah, maybe?) who'd been waiting for the Messiah to arrive and save the Jews so the New Testament could begin.

He might look like an Old Testament prophet but no way was I the New Messiah. A line from Monty Python's 'Life of Brian' popped into my head: "He's not the Messiah. He's a very naughty boy! Now, piss off!"

I logged out of the website, erased the browsing history, and picked up the package. Mandu had told me not to open it until the "time was right" and I understood enough of the rules of this game by now to obey that instruction. It didn't stop me wondering what was in it though. I sniffed it and there was a hint of something musky, like an exotic herb. I shook it and there was a dry rattle, like playing the maracas in a Merengue band. Intriguing!

I put the package in my backpack, walked out of the library and went next door to revisit my past, in the other of the town's great institutions: the tavern.

My dad was slumped in his usual corner with a group of his mates, all equally worse for wear. Nothing new there, except on closer inspection he'd deteriorated even more than they had.

"G'day dad. How are ya?" I asked him.

A token grunt of recognition, at least I think he recognised me, it was hard to tell. I felt like a ghost.

"And mum?"

Nothing. Not even a shrug. Just a tense silence. Eventually one of them looked up from his pint:

"Your mum passed away, mate."

I swallowed hard.

"Not that *you'd* be bothered, Nick Kelly ..." another of them spat at me. With a shock, I recognised my half-brother.

"What the fuck you doin back here?" he demanded. "Come back to gut some cray have ya?"

A ripple of cackles from the rest of them.

"We heard you was on the run from the Mafia?"

"I stopped running and came back to put things right."

"So where's the five hundred dollars you owe us from when you pissed off to Perth to get educated?"

I reached into my pocket, extracted some notes from the wadge

Pablo had given me, and passed them to my half-brother.

"Quits now, right?"

"—" He shrugged, still oozing resentment, but he put the money in his pocket.

Silence, except for the sound of men drinking their lives away.

"I'll see you back home then. I'm staying a few days." I nodded to them and walked out of the pub.

I stuck around for a while, trying to 'put things right' as per Mandu's instructions, but it was a thankless task. Once again I was an unwelcome outsider and all my childhood trauma came flooding back. As then, the best escape was the library, but now instead of randomly reading everything from A to Z, I had the Master's website to occupy me.

His father's journal was fascinating, but hard work. Translating the handwritten German was tortuous and some of the more obscure passages were beyond me, but I could follow up Ludwig's references using the books on the shelves: Plato, Kant, Nietzsche, Freud, Jung ... Some of western civilisation's greatest thinkers were compared, contrasted, and linked to oriental mysticism in the journal. But what really intrigued me were the resonances with contemporary culture —his experiments with psychedelic drugs and group sex, for instance:

> The Group has been experimenting with mind-altering substances
> —psychoactive plants from various part of the world.
> First, we cultivated some herbs known as Cannabis—a genus of
> flowering plant in the family Cannabaceae. It has been well docu-
> mented since the classical Greeks and Romans (ref: Herodotus) and
> is usually smoked or inhaled in a vapour-bath. Group sessions
> result in a state of relaxation and euphoria similar to that induced
> by alcohol, but without the negative side-effects on sexual perfor-
> mance or philosophical thinking. Consequently, these sessions often
> become exciting adventures in orgiastic sexual experimentation and

deep existential analysis. I invited my mentor, Carl (Jung), to participate but he declined.

I could see why the Master described his father's group as the "original hippies, thirty years ahead of their time." They must have outraged conventional society. I could well understand Jung declining the invitation to get stoned with them and participate in sessions of 'orgiastic' sex, drugs, and 1930s rock-&-roll (well, maybe not the latter).

Spending my time researching the journal and reacquainting myself with the books in BigFish's library was like being back at uni. It reminded me of what I'd thrown away when I abandoned my studies. I resolved to go back and pay my fees at least, and then who knows? Maybe I'd finish my philosophy degree and one day complete a doctoral thesis linking Dreamtime creation myths with Jung's ideas, referencing material from Dr Langer's journal.

A few days with my family were enough. I tried to make my peace with them and the town, but at best it was just a temporary truce. It was time to put things right with the rest of my past. So I went looking for my old windsurfing buddy, Robo.

I'd returned to Australia in early November, just as the windy season was starting in WA. You could say the Fremantle Doctor provided a cure for my *Día de Muertos*. My timing was good and the time was right to chase the wind again. I knew I'd find Robo wherever the conditions were firing.

However much I hated the Master I had to admit: he wasn't tight with his money. Pablo had given me the equivalent of a generous salary plus expenses. Whether this meant I was contracted to him, as Nicole had been, or an employee like Pablo, hadn't been made clear, but I was fairly sure I was now a paid-up member of his Group. I could repay Robo the money I owed him and still have more than enough for six months of chasing the wind.

I set myself up with a quiver of secondhand sails and a rusty old

V-dub 'splitty' (as my tribe called the classic Volkswagen split screen camper-van). I tied my trusty wave-board to the roof, stuffed the sails inside, stocked up on tinnies, and set out on a tour of WA's wind-surfing spots.

The season was looking promising. The Doctor was doing his thing and the locals were buzzing. It was wonderful to be back, sailing familiar waves with my own tribe. I'd forgotten just how good the windsurfing was—world class conditions in my own backyard. After each memorable session I used the après-surf debrief to ask after Robo and put the word out that I was looking for him.

I used some more of the Master's money to equip myself with an extremely smart phone and a state-of-the-art tablet. I'd survived without these gadgets while I was living a pared-down life in the jungle, and before that as a ghost in El Médano, but they made life as a nomadic surf bum easier. I justified spending the Master's money by telling myself I could use these devices to log into his website and keep in touch with him. Of course, I could also use them to check wind and wave forecasts, look at webcams up and down the coast to see if I could spot Robo, and give myself a presence on social networking sites.

In the end it was Robo who spotted *me* on a windsurfing forum and messaged me. It wasn't what you'd call a friendly message. In fact it was decidedly hostile, but I was expecting that. Since Nicole had done to me what I did to him, I was able to empathise. Putting myself in his place, I wouldn't have been overjoyed either—to hear from an old 'mate' who'd run off with my money, my drugs, and my wife.

I replied that I wanted to repay the debt and put things right, or at least have the chance to tell him how sorry I was. To his credit (or perhaps it had more to do with his *lack* of credit) he agreed, and we arranged to meet at one of our favourite beaches close to Perth. The forecast was looking good for the next day.

I arrived early and the conditions didn't disappoint. It wasn't one of WA's classic big surf spots but the waves were fun for jumping and doing a few wiggles on. I was loving being there, going for all kinds of crazy moves and laughing manically when I crashed them.

Our paths finally crossed on the water, or rather *in* the water. I came to the surface after one of my more extravagant wipeouts just in time to see Robo several feet above me, about to land on my head. He splashed down next to me, his fin just missing slicing into my skull.

"You got some nerve, Nick, you evil bastard!" he shouted at me.

"G'day to you too mate. Still spinning out on the landings then" I yelled, as a wave washed us towards the beach in a tangle of rigs.

I offered him my hand. He ignored it. For a moment I thought he was going to clobber me, but we were too busy rolling around in the shore-break.

A few minutes later we were both spat up on the beach covered in seaweed, looking like two clowns with circus wigs. We stared at each other in stony silence for about ten seconds ... and collapsed in help-less laughter. He was the first to spit out the weed and speak:

"Mate, you look f-ing ridiculous, but at least you're looping more like a kangaroo than a koala these days."

"Robo, what can I say ...?" I spluttered, choking with emotion as well as salt water and seaweed.

"You could start by giving me my money."

"For sure. No worries. It's in the van."

We sat in the splitty, dripping seawater everywhere, and cracked open a tinny. It was just like the old days; just like I'd never ran off with his drugs and his wife; just like we were still mates—except that we weren't. Not right away at least.

Robo was a lot happier once I'd given him back the five grand, but it took a while for the rest of the wounds to heal. It was difficult talking about Alison, but at least now I understood what he'd been through. I'd been taught my own lesson in love, loyalty and betrayal and it forced me to face up to what I'd done to him.

I told him I was desperately sorry for betraying him. The blame was all mine. I'd never be free of the guilt unless he could forgive me. That was what I told him, and it was all true, but it wasn't the whole story ...

I hadn't simply stolen her from him like I had the drugs. There are three sides to every triangle. Our friendship had deteriorated, their relationship had turned sour, and she'd been more than willing. The plan to skedaddle with his stash had actually been hers and she'd worked hard to persuade me. But I didn't expect him to believe that, so I kept it to myself.

Later it turned out she'd confessed everything and he'd eventually forgiven her. Their relationship survived and now they had a daughter approaching her first birthday. Perhaps Alison's fling with me was the catalyst they needed ... but I kept that thought to myself again, and instead told him I was really happy he'd patched things up with her.

Robo wasn't one for hanging on to a grudge and letting it fester. We both knew he couldn't hate me for ever. We'd been like brothers before I screwed it all up. I'm not talking about my *actual* brothers who were wasting away in my hometown—we'd always loathed each other. No, Robo and me had the kind of bond that can only exist between brothers-in-arms, the kind of love that goes deeper than blood ties. We trusted each other as only those who've gone into combat together do. We'd faced so many sketchy situations, survived close shaves with the law and the Mob, saved each other from drowning ... I'd betrayed that bond but eventually he forgave me, and I loved him for it.

It took a while—a few road trips, beers, joints, truth and reconciliation sessions, but we got there in the end. The breakthrough came when I gave him the manuscript of 'Too Close to the Wind'—the story of our adventures together, a memoir of my mistakes, a confession of the betrayals. When Robo read my survival story, how I'd drifted around the Atlantic for a day and a night, he was moved to admit that however much of tosser I'd been, he'd miss me if I disappeared for ever. We embraced and I knew that I'd finally put things right with *him*, at least.

I still didn't know what the Master's role in all this was, what game he was playing with me, but if he *did* order Nicole to disappear to teach me a lesson, then perhaps it had worked.

Of course, there were still a few other people after me. Alison was far from happy to hear of my return. She'd never forgiven me for abandoning her when the fizz went out of our fling. Her pride had been hurt when I chose the wind and surf over her company. Now she was worried I was going to steal Rob away from *her*—ironic really. She knew how much our windsurfing trips meant to him and she wanted me out of their lives for good.

I never managed to put things right with her but we negotiated a truce, as I'd done with my family. As long as Robo did his time with her and the baby, she allowed him time off for good behaviour.

Perth University was also looking for me. I'd quit without telling anyone and left the country without paying my fees. Eventually, they told the police I was a missing person. The cops started a halfhearted search, but they were quite happy for me to stay missing.

My other pursuers were the bad guys: the Great White drug sharks. Robo had told them I'd done a runner with the drugs and that he was as keen to find me as they were. He'd cut a deal with them, paid off his share, and he was no longer on their hit list. Not so me.

To be honest I didn't lose sleep over it. Sure I'd have to watch my back but I wasn't unduly worried. Nick Kelly was a missing person and my false ID protected me. I had no intention of getting back into dealing drugs and they certainly weren't clued up enough to know where to find me: at the coast, wherever the conditions were firing. You had to be one of my tribe, chasing the wind, to know where that was. I reckoned that as Malcolm Fraser, nomadic surf bum of no fixed address, I could evade them indefinitely.

So, now I was an outlaw like my namesake, Ned Kelly. I was a missing person, but no longer a ghost. I was on the road, but no longer on the run. Robo and I were brothers again, gone with the wind.

12

BROTHERS IN ARMS

That season in WA was exceptional. The Fremantle Doctor blew consistently from November 2016 into April 2017. Those five months were some of the happiest of my life (along with the year I'd spent with Nicole). Robo and I were on the road again, like Kerouac's beats, chasing the wind and escaping from normality—from Alison and shitty nappies, academic expectations, job prospects, failed drug deals, brown paper packages, gun-toting Mafia sharks, and all the rest of life's humdrum hassles.

The Doctor laid his healing hands on us and our friendship was repaired. We were brothers-in-arms again, with a bond that was forged in the vastness of the ocean and the emptiness of the outback. A bond that could withstand the forces of nature, let alone the trivial pursuits of society. We were nature's outlaws, defying her formidable power, facing whatever she could throw at us, day after day. We existed in our own bubble, like a rock band on tour, and nothing could harm us—for a while ...

One night in March we were in a pub way up north—a hangout for blackfellas—a place where the people I shared half my genes with spent half their lives; where they went to get drunk and forget how hopeless the other half was. A sad pub that made the morose crayfish workers in my dad's tavern seem full of the joys of spring.

Robo and I were tolerated because of my genetic credentials and because our tribe were the only tourists who ever made it up there. We weren't included in the locals' conversations, but we weren't explicitly excluded either. So I was keeping a polite distance, while half listening to their conversation about a political storm that was brewing over some aboriginal land up in the Purnululu national park. When I heard Mandu's name mentioned I sidled up to the group of blackfellas and asked them who he was and how he was involved—was he well known around there?

"Yeah mate, he's like a tribal elder. Y'know, the bloke who protects the traditions and lays down the law."

I nodded. The old fella I'd met in the library fitted that role perfectly. I asked them what the problem was.

"The White Man wants their land. Word is the Plant grows there, but the land is sacred."

"The Plant?" I asked, intrigued now. My curiosity was met with stony looks and sullen mutters. We were outsiders after all.

I brought a round of beers and introduced myself and Robo. I told them where I was from, down south. A few of them had worked on the cray boats down there and one bloke even knew my old man. Then I mentioned I'd met this Mandu bloke, briefly, in my hometown and that seemed to break the ice. I asked them, again, to tell me about this plant growing out in the desert. What was it and why was it so important to Mandu's people?

"Well mate, it's a cactus. They cut it open and take the seeds. Then you see things different. Y'know, like magic mushrooms or somethin'. And it works like med'cine. It can fix yer head straight when you got roos loose in the upper paddock. The tribe up there's bin usin' it for centuries. Now the Whitefella's heard about it and he wants it."

I nodded. I was no stranger to mental states like that and had been known to use 'medicinal plants' myself to 'fix my head straight'.

I remembered the night Nicole and I camped out in the rainforest above Haiti. I still had vivid flashbacks from that night.

"The park's 'sposed to be protected, but when the White Man wants land he just takes it. Don't make no difference if it's sacred and they've bin buryin' ancestors on it fer thousands of years. The tribe aint got no way to stop 'im. No money and no leader."

"What about this Mandu bloke?" I asked. "He seemed to know a thing or two when I met him."

Robo glanced at me. I hadn't mentioned anything to him about meeting the strange old fella in the library.

"Mandu? He's like a shaman y'know, but he don't know White-fella politics."

I nodded again. Yes, that made sense. He'd seemed wise, but it was the wisdom of a tribal elder, a shaman, rather than a charismatic leader. I told them the tribe would need to involve the media, get themselves on TV and in the newspapers, start local and then go national; get themselves a lawyer who specialised in land rights; win over the liberal white politicians who supported their cause; organise protest marches, hunger strikes, whatever it took to stop the White Man from stealing their land ...

"Yeah mate. You tell Mandu when you see 'im. Maybe *you* should be their Main Man?"

I shrugged and replied that politics wasn't really my thing.

Robo told me not to be so modest—I had just the right qualifications to lead their campaign. The blackfella agreed:

"I mean you're a 'domino dingo' ain't ya?"

"That's right mate" Robo said, laughing. "But is he black with white spots, or white with black spots?"

The blackfella held his hand up, embarrassed now.

"No offence meant, mate" he added quickly.

" ... and none taken" I replied, raising my glass to him. I was used to a whole range of racial slang and slurs, this was one of the mildest.

"Na. I just meant that you got a foot in each camp, like. So you could work good for everyone. Plus you seem like you got y'self educated. And good on ya for it!" he added quickly.

I shrugged modestly.

"Ain't no way any of *us* lot are goin' nowhere 'cept this dump!"

He made an expansive gesture taking in the pub and his fellow drinkers, to general grunts of agreement.

Robo made a sarcastic comment along the lines of: "... and look where education gets you—a surf bum living rough in the outback."

We all had a laugh, but the conversation had got the cogs in my brain turning.

The windy season was nearly over when I decided the time was right to open Mandu's package. I hadn't touched it for five months, but I'd been thinking about it since the conversation in the pub up north. It was late March and the Fremantle Doctor was thinking about shutting his clinic for the winter. I was sitting in the van on my own, smoking a spliff and gazing at the Windguru website on my tablet, hoping for one last session before we mothballed the equipment. There was a pulse of long period swell heading our way from the Southern Ocean, and a hint that the pressure systems might just bring some wind if we managed to be in the right place at the right time, but it was a long shot.

I was feeling bored, lethargic—the onset of a seasonal depression that only the Doctor could fix when he reappeared in the spring. I wondered how I was going to get through the next six months without my fix of adrenaline. I was a wind junkie and without windsurfing life was drab, monochrome, meaningless.

On impulse I grabbed Mandu's package from my rucksack, put it on the table, and continued surfing the online weather sites, obsessively searching for the most optimistic forecast. I needed something, anything, to get me out of this rut and I kept glancing from the tablet to the parcel, wondering if now was the time to open it.

Eventually, the lack of wind on the internet became too depressing, so I put down the tablet and picked up the package. I shook it, listening to the dry maracas-like rattle, smelt it, noting the musky aroma, and finally ripped off the plain brown wrapping paper.

Inside was a plastic medicine bottle containing a number of brown pellets. They looked like beans, or large seeds, rather than any kind of drug you could get in a pharmacy.

I wasn't surprised by the contents of Mandu's package—the bloke in the pub up north had given me the clues, but I certainly hadn't expected it to be capable of altering the weather forecast! That came as something of a bonus. When I refreshed Windguru for one last look I couldn't believe what I was seeing. The forecast had improved —dramatically!

The small pulse of swell had become a dark red blob of waves heading straight at the south coast of WA and the gentle sea breeze had turned into a three-star hoolie! I checked the map for a beach that would be exposed to the swell and lined up with the wind direction—it looked like Esperance would be the place to be.

It would almost certainly be our last road trip of the season, but it looked like it could be epic. Hopefully, the season would end with a bang rather than a whimper. I fired off a text to Robo: *Esperance going off. Get your arse in gear. We leave tomorrow pronto.*

As I sat there, feeling the familiar knot in my stomach: anticipation, adrenaline, nervous energy, I stared at Mandu's medicine bottle. It had a label, but rather than medical information there was simply a graphic symbol: a set of six lines. I recognised it as another of the 'I Ching' hexagrams.

I opened Wikipedia on the tablet and looked it up. The knot in my stomach tightened when I discovered it was number twenty-nine: 'The Abyss'. I accessed the Master's website, logged in with my username: 'Close2TheWind', entered the name of his yacht as the password, and was again taken to a scanned page of his father's journal. I typed Dr Langer's handwritten German text into Google and was presented with this English translation:

In 1933 I travelled to a remote region of Western Australia to study with an Aboriginal shaman. Of all the mythologies I have researched, their's is the most fascinating. They call it the 'Dreamtime'.

The shaman introduced me to a potent psychoactive substance: the seeds of a cactus growing in the desert, on land that is sacred for his tribe. I do not know the scientific name for it—the shaman referred to it simply as 'The Plant', but I would hypothesise that it might be related to the peyote genus of cactus seed we obtained from Mexico. I took a photograph of this mind-altering cactus and brought back some samples to share with The Group.

The 'Plant' is an irregular brown seed pellet that can be ingested or smoked in a pipe. The effects are similar, but less intense, when smoked. If ingested it is very important that the dosage is correct. The shaman warned me that it may be dangerous to take too much —especially if the subject has underlying psychological issues.

The indigenous Aboriginal people use it as a treatment for adverse mental conditions such as depression, and even (I suspect) schizo-phrenia. So the effects are beneficial, as long the correct dosage is not exceeded.

My own experiments with this Plant have included some extremely powerful experiences in which all my senses were enhanced and it seemed as if I was 'seeing reality' for the first time. These experi-ences are undoubtably amongst the most creative and spiritual of my entire life.

I believe that mind-altering substances such as the Plant may one day be seen as powerful medicines, leading to the eradication of mental disorders, and perhaps even the evolution of mankind.

Following this extract, there were a few black and white photographs of the cactus plant and some closeups of the seeds. I looked from the image on my tablet to the medicine bottle next to it, emptied a few of Mandu's brown pellets into my hand, and compared them. They were identical. Dr Langer's 'mind-altering substance' was clearly the same plant the blackfella in the pub had been talking about.

Now I realised I'd seen these seeds before—the night I'd camped out with Nicole, on the hillside above Haiti—we'd taken some of them together! The Plant had opened the 'Doors of Perception' for me that night, and now I held some in my hand. I felt like Alice when she found the bottle labelled 'DRINK ME!' I was tempted to follow her and the White Rabbit into Wonderland there and then, but the next day we had an early start and a long drive south. So I put the cactus pellets back in the bottle and stashed it in my rucksack, until the time was right, as the ancient shaman had advised.

Saturday, April 1, 2017. It was our third morning in Esperance when I opened Mandu's medicine bottle again. We needed time to recover after the twelve-hour drive in my ageing camper-van and then to get used to the conditions down there.

Esperance is a beautiful place: wild, rugged, remote, with one of the best beach breaks on the planet. The waves that explode on Nine Mile Beach have come thousands of miles from the deep Southern Ocean and are not to be taken lightly ... but it was April Fool's Day and as the expression goes: 'Fools rush in where angels fear to tread.'

The forecast was good for one more day of wind and it might well be the last of the season, so I decided to make it special. It wasn't the first time Robo and I had windsurfed while stoned, drunk, or high on something other than adrenaline. Many times we'd smoked some weed, even done a bit of coke, and the sessions were always interesting, often exhilarating.

This was different. The Plant was more than a mood-enhancing stimulant, it was a gateway to a state of altered consciousness, an alternative reality. We were about to open the 'Doors of Perception' and follow Dr Langer's path into the unknown—pioneers, exploring the limits of mind and body. This would be 'Extreme Sport' at its most extreme!

Nicole and I had smoked the Plant and I knew roughly what to expect. This time we were planning to swallow some seeds, but I had no idea how many to take. Dr Langer warned about the importance of ingesting the 'correct dosage' but he hadn't specified what that was.

It was pure guesswork. So, in a state of blissful ignorance, we crushed several of the cactus pellets into a powder and washed them down with a tinny. Then we drove along the beach for a few miles until we found a spot where the waves were peeling nicely and we went wind-surfing.

There's plenty of space on Nine Mile Beach. We weren't just at the end of the road, we were at the edge of the continent—next stop: Antarctica. We launched into that empty space like astronauts and soon we were weightless, escaping gravity as we floated high above the waves and carved vertical turns under translucent lips.

The effects of the Plant began to kick in after about twenty minutes, but it took at least an hour before we were peaking. It's difficult to be precise about timings, or to be objective about the events of that day, to be honest. All I can do is describe what I was experiencing, what I thought I saw, and then step back and tell you what might have really happened. I'll give you my best shot at an objective account of an intensely subjective experience, as Huxley tried to do when describing his mescaline trip in 'The Doors'.

Taking a psychedelic substance is like taking a detour down a scenic route that isn't on the map. Normal life is about using the motorway to get from A to B efficiently, but sometimes as you're cruising along in fifth gear you catch a glimpse of an intriguing little lane snaking off into the hills and you find yourself wondering what is out of sight around the bend. That morning Robo and I had chosen to step off the well-trodden highway and take an excursion into the unknown.

Unlike alcohol or cannabis, the Plant neither impaired nor enhanced our windsurfing, just allowed us to come at it from a different angle. I didn't feel intoxicated, nor did it make me braver or more foolhardy, it was more like I was able to use parts of my brain that weren't normally involved.

Time jumps. The first indication that something unusual's happening is when I find myself right in the pocket of a large wave, wondering how on earth I got there. Somehow I've managed to link a forward loop straight into a wave-ride. Objectively, I know this isn't possible, but now isn't the time to worry about it.

I discover that I can use my appreciation of music to time my moves in a rhythmic dance that's also a mathematical equation. I can draw lines on a wave that are both guided by visual aesthetic (how would this look if it was a drawing?) and determined by geometric rules (the sum of these angles should be one twenty degrees for a perfect shape). I can harness the creativity we use to write poetry to order spatial awareness—if I can choose the right words to describe spinning through a loop, then I can land the jump perfectly.

Subjectively, this is how it all felt at the time. Objectively, we were probably both just going for our usual moves, but timing them differently and linking them in unusual ways.

Time jumps. I see Robo way outside, suspended upside down above massive swells at the apex of a huge back loop, framed against a cloudless sky. A shutter clicks in my mind's camera and I carry this image of him with me to this day. As he reaches the apex of his jump and I capture this memorable mental image, I gybe onto the same set of waves, turn back towards the beach, and ride a mast-high wall of water all the way to the inside.

That wave-ride is as close to perfection as I've come. Turn after turn (I lose count), each one tighter, more vertical, more radical than the last. Athletes sometimes talk about being 'in the zone' or 'feeling the flow', and board-riders of all kinds (surfers, snowboarders, skateboarders) often say that when they're performing at their best they're 'one with the board', like it's 'part of their body' ... but these are all inadequate descriptions of that wave in Esperance. I see all the possible lines I can draw, with absolute clarity, as if I'm watching myself ride the wave in a high definition slow-mo video, shot at hundreds of frames per second, with time to analyse each frame and choose my line.

I finish the ride in a state of bliss and head back out expecting to find Robo riding in on an equally perfect wave. I'm preparing to let rip with an ecstatic shout when we cross, but there's no sign of him. At first I think perhaps he's seen a better peak further down the beach and gone exploring ... but as the minutes pass with no sign of his sail in the distance I begin to suspect something's gone wrong.

It takes a while longer before panic has me in its grip, and then I'm shouting his name, screaming it, shaking violently now. No! This can't be happening! He can't have just vanished. This can't be real—it must be the drug fooling me somehow. Maybe he's playing games with me. Yes, that's it. He's back on the beach, a tinny in his hand, having a laugh.

I race back to the beach. Throw my equipment in a heap. Run up the sand to the van. Look inside, panting like a dog. He's not there.

Now I'm howling like a dingo. No! This can't be happening!

I spend the rest of the day sailing geometric search patterns and roaming the beach. Time passes, but instead of flowing past like a river it jumps in discrete steps, like bad edits, or a film with missing footage. I'm losing the plot.

Sometimes I glimpse a fleck of colour on the horizon ... the sun glints, as if from a sail ... and I think it's him. I shout his name and watch the shout splinter into pieces, echoes spreading out over the water: **Rob**-bo-o-o-o ... They bounce back at me in reverse: o-o-o-ob-**boR** ...

I'm disorientated, hallucinating, plagued by ever more horrific visions: flashbacks to the night I took the Plant with Nicole, and more disturbingly, to the dream I had while drifting around the Atlantic ...

Time jumps. I'm surrounded by sharks with human features, Great

Whites in grey suits, giant crayfish with enormous claws. A prehistoric bird with Alison's face dives out of the sky and ferociously attacks my eyes.

I fight off these monsters, knowing them to be products of my addled brain, but I can't escape the awful reality of Robo's disappearance. It gets worse as the effects of the Plant wear off and the hallucinations are replaced by overwhelming emotions: hopelessness, despair, guilt.

I search all day, but eventually, exhausted, I realise he's simply vanished, disappeared into that vast empty space, and he isn't coming back.

That night I sat on the desolate beach, my head in my hands, wondering what to do. As the traces of the Plant left my bloodstream and I came down from the trip, I was overcome with loss. Emotions overwhelmed me, as they had when Nicole vanished, and left no space for rational thought.

Robo had disappeared from my life just when I'd repaired our bond. I loved him, my brother-in-arms, as I'd loved Nicole, my only other soulmate.

R.I.P. brother. At least you died doing what you love.

Love and loss—once again—two sides of the same coin?

13

THE BUSH OF GHOSTS

As the sun rose at the edge of the continent I walked the length of Nine Mile Beach looking for Robo's equipment, or his body. I felt numb, drained. All the emotion had been sucked out of me, leaving me empty, and I'd accepted that emptiness. Now I understood the Master's message: "let go of your ego completely". Tragically, it had taken Robo's death to show me what he meant.

Perfect sets were still rolling in. Wave after wave peaked, then crashed onto the beach, unloading its energy spectacularly. People are like waves: energy on the move, in transit between birth and death. One second there's energy, and the next it's gone. The energy that was Robo had moved on, just as it does when a wave breaks, and I had accepted it.

That beach is so vast, so empty, so primal. I felt like a ghost drifting through the dawn, lost in limbo, in transit again. I saw nobody and I never found Robo's body. It was several days before it washed up down the coast and I was long gone by then.

The most likely explanation is that his life ended shortly after I captured that mental image of him midway through a back loop, about half a mile out to sea. My guess is he'd become disoriented in mid-air and fell from the sky—like Icarus when his wings melted. He must have landed the loop all wrong, smashed his head on his board, knocked himself out and drowned. The rip current would have taken his body out to sea, just as it did when I broke my mast-foot off the coast of Tenerife.

With hindsight, perhaps I could have saved him. If I'd been there next to him, instead of taking that wave back to the beach, I would have seen it happen, watched him screw up the loop, witnessed him smash his head, lifted his unconscious body onto to his board, given him mouth-to-mouth ...

With hindsight, April Fool's Day had been another catalogue of errors. It was a mistake to combine the altered consciousness induced by the Plant with the adrenaline-high windsurfing naturally produces—a recipe for disaster, in fact. With hindsight, it was also a mistake to ignore Dr Langer's warning about the dangers of taking too much of the stuff. But as the cliché goes: 'hindsight is better than foresight' and as someone else once said: 'Before, you are wise. After, you are wise. In between, you are otherwise.'

We'd been fools to rush in where angels feared to tread. The ocean always punishes those who don't respect her ... but I felt no guilt. It had all been sucked out of me, leaving just egoless acceptance of these errors, and anyway: feeling guilty wouldn't bring my brother-in-arms back.

I tied my board to the van's roof-rack and drove north. I was a ghost on the run again, but it was different this time. I was different. Robo's death had changed me.

We drove, my board and I, straight past Perth, the university, Alison, aiming for the horizon. Mile after mile of black tarmac splitting the red desert, hour after hour of bleak nothingness.

Well, not quite. We made a brief detour into my town and drove slowly down the main street. As we passed the pub I caught a glimpse of my dad sitting outside with his mates, drinking sullenly. They didn't see me. Nobody saw me—I was a ghost, after all.

Then we rejoined the highway and didn't leave it again until the

Pinnacles. I had to stop somewhere—to gather my thoughts, to sleep, and it was a good place to do it.

The Pinnacles are natural sculptures, formed millions of years ago from limestone, sitting in the desert like chess pieces in a game played by giants. The landscape is lunar, or perhaps Martian. It reminded me of the volcanic crater at the centre of Tenerife. As an outsider, I'm attracted to these desolate spaces and the solitude you can find in them.

I arrived at dusk, after the tourists had left, and I felt at peace there. Losing Nicole, and then Robo, had ripped out my ego, guilt, my dependence on society and its rules, perhaps even my fear of death. I'd looked into the abyss and now I was beginning to understand how the Master and his group were trying to live.

This ancient place reminded me of what I had to do next—find Mandu, the tribal elder. I'd done my best to put things right with my past and I'd moved on. "You will know when the time is right ..." he'd told me, " ... and you will know where to find me then."

I left at dawn, before the tourists arrived. As the sun rose behind the Pinnacles it bathed everything in red light and cast eerie shadows on the desert floor. For a few perfect moments I watched emus, galahs and kangaroos wander around the weathered rock spires. Then I rejoined the highway and drove north, towards the horizon.

When I stopped for fuel at a gas station with wi-fi I sent a message to Alison, explaining what had happened in Esperance, but omitting any reference to the Plant. It was simpler that way. All she needed to know was that Robo had died doing what he loved—a tragic accident, in powerful waves, at a notoriously remote beach-break. I told her that I loved him like a brother and I was devastated. Now I had to 'go bush' for a while and sort my head out.

Fourteen hours later I arrived at the pub where we'd heard about Mandu's tribal land. It was a quiet night and it looked like they'd be closing early. As before, I wasn't exactly welcomed, but I bought a round for the few blackfellas in there and the landlord was happy for me to overnight in the car park. Luckily, I recognised one of the locals —the bloke who'd called me a "domino dingo". He asked me what I was doing back there so late in the season:

"You too late, mate. The Wind-Doctor been finished for a long time. We ain't seen none of you surf-boys up here for weeks."

I told him I wasn't there for windsurfing. I'd been thinking about what he'd said about the tribal lands up in the Purnululu national park—what was growing there, how the tribe needed to organise to stop the White Man grabbing their land, and how maybe I could help. Did he know where I could find Mandu?

"No worries mate, I'll point ya in the right direction. Them folk need all the help they can get or else their life up there is history."

He told me that Mandu's tribe were Karjaganujaru people. Some of the time they were nomadic, but they had a base near some caves in the Bungle Bungle hills, or 'Billingjal' as the Karjaganujaru called them (meaning: 'sand falling away').

He drew me a map on a beer mat. It looked a bit sketchy—a long way further north on the Great Northern Highway, then a series of tracks heading east with the crossroads marked by a big cactus or some roo bones, followed by a hike into the desert to some red rocks with caves ... that kind of thing. He wished me luck and advised me to stock up on water, food, and fuel or else as he put it: "You'll end up a dead dingo out there!"

He drank up, turned to leave, and then paused.

"By the way, where's yer mate? The white bloke that was with ya last time?"

"I left him down South, in Esperance."

"Shame. Y'could've done with 'im in the Bungle Bungles. Ain't nobody out there if it all goes pear-shaped."

"Yep" I agreed, "I'll miss him."

The next morning I was on the road again as the sun rose. I was starting to enjoy these early starts. The highway was empty and the light was cool and soft before the ferociously harsh sun took over.

I stopped at the next town (eighty kilometres up the road!), stocked up on provisions, and logged on to Facebook to find a series of increasingly hysterical messages from Alison. They culminated in threats to find me, have me arrested, send a hit man after me ...

I sent her a brief reply saying I was about to 'go bush' and I didn't know when I'd be able to connect again. I'd contact her when I rejoined civilisation. In the meantime, she should report Robo's death to the police and tell them I was a missing person. It was up to her what she did after that.

I rejoined the highway and resumed my epic journey up the western seaboard. It was late when I reached Spring Creek Track— the start of my off-road, off-grid adventure, so I parked-up and waited for it to get light again.

At first light I turned off the highway and began to navigate the track. It was a stressful experience, even for a gung-ho explorer like myself. I was breaking all sorts of rules: the route was only supposed to be accessible by proper 4WD vehicles, and then only in the dry season —April to December. It was early April and I was attempting it in my decrepit old camper-van.

It took all day, but somehow we made it up the track to a makeshift camp at the trailhead. Any further progress would have to be on foot, so I joined the few vehicles that were parked up there for the night.

As usual, I was awake as the first rays of dawn were dancing over the desert. I locked my board in the van, wondering when I'd see her again, and packed a few things into a rucksack. For some reason I brought Nicole's painting with me, rolled up in a piece of old sailcloth and strapped to my backpack. Perhaps I thought it might somehow protect me, but if I perished out in the desert at least it would be with a memento of a happier period in my life.

I looked at my beermat map and set out on what I hoped was the correct path. Ahead of me were the Bungle Bungles—strange beehive-shaped towers made of sandstone, with orange and grey stripes caused by differences in the layers of rock. The combined effects of wind from the Tanami Desert and rainfall over millions of years have shaped the domes into a surreal, alien landscape. At its heart is the eroded remnant of an ancient meteorite crater. I was heading for some caves there.

It took me two days to locate Mandu's camp. Wandering around those primaeval hills was cathartic. I had no idea if I was following the right path, but I wasn't worried. I loved tramping through the empty landscape without seeing a soul, a ghost in the 'Bush of Ghosts'. At night the sky was a vast black dome studded with stars— the ultimate planetarium. The silence was total, and I was at peace.

In the end, I stumbled across the camp by chance. Late in the afternoon on the second day I came round a corner above a canyon and there they were below me. The tribe was living in some caves around an oasis, in a remarkably picturesque setting. It looked like a brochure shot for a tropical paradise. There was a small lake, with palm trees growing around it and shacks constructed from the fronds. Sounds and smells drifted up to me: children, dogs, a didgeridoo, bongos, the aroma of meat smoked over a wood fire ... It was all rather reminiscent of Nicole's pueblo in the Dominican jungle, and I felt at home already.

Nobody seemed bothered as I wandered into the camp. Most of them smiled and a few even waved hello. I doubted they saw many visitors out there, so it was an extraordinarily warm welcome. A familiar old man loped out of one of the huts, moving with lithe agility, and greeted me:

"G'day Nick. We've been expectin ya."

He smiled at my astonished expression—the same radiant smile that had lit up the library. It had been six months, and three thousand kilometres since our brief meeting, but here he was, in the middle of nowhere, treating me like an old mate who'd just stepped outside for a smoke.

I shook his hand and returned his greeting:

"G'day Mandu. You're not an easy man to find. I hope the time is right?"

"Nobody said it'd be easy, mate. But y'made it, like I knew y'would. Welcome to our Shangri-La."

We sat outside his cave hut and he introduced me to the tribe. There were about thirty of them, mostly middle-aged, some like him as old as the hills, plus a few children and dogs. Mandu told me that his people, the Karjaganujaru, had been living in the area for twenty-thousand years. He was trying to maintain their connection to this ancient landscape but the young people were drifting back to the towns. Those in the camp still lived the traditional way for part of the year and went 'Walkabout' for the rest of the time. The time was indeed right to find him there, he told me, smiling.

I was welcomed as an honoured guest in the camp. They shared what little they had and Mandu even gave me his own cave-hut. The tribe treated me like royalty and I was intrigued to find out why ...

When I first met Mandu in the library he was sitting there, waiting for me. How was that possible? After our typed conversation, I'd speculated that he was like an Old Testament prophet waiting for the Messiah (me) to arrive and save his tribe. Now, when I turned up out of the blue at his camp in the middle of the desert, again he seemed to be expecting me. It seemed as if he and I were another example of what the Master called: 'gravitational attraction'—individuals whose orbits were inescapably linked.

That night, as we sat around the fire, I asked him to explain what he'd meant in the library when he'd typed: "I have been expecting you, Nick. The Master has sent you to help my people ..."

For a while he said nothing. Silence enveloped us. I gazed into the fire, watching the sparks fly up into the night sky. A shooting star blazed across the blackness. Way out in the desert a wild dog's cry punctuated the stillness. Then, as we sat in that remote, infinite space, Mandu told me how he met Alejandro Langer.

Many years ago, when they were both young men, the Master hiked into this wilderness to find a shaman like the one his father had written about. Mandu taught Alejandro about his culture and their mythology: the Dreamtime, Creation, the Ancestor Beings, the Laws of Existence. The shaman introduced him to the consciousness-raising Plant, and they experienced it together several times.

The Master told Mandu about his Group—a 'virtual tribe' of free-thinkers financed by Alejandro's inherited wealth. The Group's goal was to fulfil Dr Ludwig Langer's ideals: the evolution of our species to the next level. Mandu wasn't interested in the Master's lofty objectives for humanity, but he *was* worried about his own tribe's survival. Alejandro told him that one day he'd send somebody else to study with him and that this person would be able to help his people.

Mandu kept in touch the same way I did: via the Group's website, and recently he'd received word that the new student was on his way. Alejandro told Mandu his name and where to meet him: in the library in my hometown. Now here I was.

The next day Mandu began my initiation into his tribe. He scrutinised my surfy dreadlocks and pseudo-Aboriginal tattoos, smirked, and told me that his mission was to give me back my identity. He was going to show me: "who ya *really* are, Nick, instead of who yer pretending to be."

He began by explaining the Dreamtime, drawing diagrams in the sand with a stick—pictures of their cosmology, their understanding of the world and its creation. Dreamtime is the beginning of time, when the Ancestor Beings created the universe and the lifeforms that inhabit it. It's the beginning of Knowledge and the Laws of Existence. For survival, these laws must be observed. The Dreaming connects an individual to the accumulated knowledge of the Ancestors through rituals and trance-like states produced by psychoactive catalysts, such as the Plant.

It wasn't the first time I'd heard this stuff. The blackfellas in my hometown occasionally spoke about the 'old ways' and Robo had encouraged me to delve deeper into my roots, but it had never been properly explained to me. I'd always thought of Aboriginal myths as elaborate ghost stories, fairytales, never as something real. For Mandu Dreamtime was as real as TV, movies, the internet—a 'separate reality', just as they are. White folk pressed a switch on a remote control, clicked an icon, and pictures appeared on their screen. His people smoked some Plant seeds, entered the Dreaming, and connected to the Ancestors. He promised to show me how this worked ... as soon as the time was right.

I asked Mandu about the package of seeds he'd given me in the library. He told me it was one of the Master's tests—to prepare me for my initiation into the Dreaming. I'd survived the test and I'd found him, so now I was ready for my next challenge.

It wasn't quite as simple as that for me. Yes, I'd survived the test, but Robo hadn't. He was an innocent victim, collateral damage in the Master's mission for me. I was swept up in a maelstrom of conflicting emotions: guilt over Robo's death, anger at the Master, but eagerness to learn more from this ancient shaman.

I decided the time *wasn't* right to tell him about Robo, but of course I'd already experienced the Plant once before—in the rainforest bordering Haiti. So I told him my own story: how I'd met the Master, how I'd travelled to the Dominican Republic and learnt about Voodoo from Nicole, and how we'd smoked the Plant together.

Mandu nodded and told me it was another of the Master's tests. I wasn't sure how much he knew about Nicole, so I told him about her art—how her paintings had the power to protect or control people. I showed him her portrait of the two of us: 'The Kangaroo Kid and his Voodoo Child'.

He stared at it for a long time, nodding and muttering under his breath. A smile lit up his face, gradually, like a sunrise. He looked up, and I was bathed in the warmth of that smile.

"Thank you for showin' me this, Nick. I see what it means f'ya, and I understand ya better now I've seen it. It means something for me too. I see a system of knowledge that's like our own."

"You mean you can see connections between *Vodou* and Dreamtime?"

He paused, lost in thought, weighing up options before replying.

"I can *show* ya these connections if y'like mate?"

I nodded. He leaned in closer to me.

"Tomorrow I'll take ya to a place that's sacred for our people. A place where no Whitefella has ever bin ..."

He spoke softly, almost whispering in my ear:

"There's a cave, where the Ancestors are restin' ..."

I said nothing. The silence was spellbinding.

"The cave has paintings like yer one!"

My eyes widened in surprise. He leaned in, even closer.

"That's how I know I can trust ya, Nick, and why I'll take ya there."

He looked at me. I was struck, again, by how he shared the Master's piercing gaze.

"We'll take the Plant together there, in the cave. The time is right."

He smiled—an enigmatic Mona Lisa smile. Then he winked at me.

The next morning the two of us set out on a hike deep into the Bungle Bungles. Our destination was an ancient meteorite crater at the centre of the tribe's land. I was half a century younger than Mandu and wearing hi-tech walking boots, while he was barefoot, but I struggled to keep up with him.

After a couple of hours we stopped to drink at a waterhole in another canyon. Cactus plants were growing there—strange shapes with human-like limbs. Mandu took his machete and chopped off a cactus hand. He put it on a rock, split it open and showed me what was inside.

"This is it, Nick. What the Whitefella is after. What he want to steal from us: the Plant!"

He dug the tip of his knife into the soft cactus flesh and extracted some familiar brown seed pellets. I stared at them and the knot in my stomach tightened. I coughed nervously and swallowed hard. Mandu looked at me and asked what was wrong. There was no hiding from his gaze. The time was right for a confession, so I told him what had happened to Robo on April Fool's Day. He listened carefully, without reproach or sympathy, and simply asked how many seeds we'd eaten. I told him I couldn't remember exactly, no more than half a dozen. He nodded, sadly.

"That's why the Whitefella must *never* have the Plant, Nick. They want t'make money from it, but they don't understand the danger if y'take it wrong. If y'take it *right* it'll put yer head straight. If y'don't, it's like a snake—not dangerous, but it can kill ya!"

He gathered some pellets, put them in a pouch, and we resumed our journey. As we walked he told me more about the Plant. His people had been using it for thousands of years, but not as a recreational drug. No, for them it was a 'medicine for the head'—a cure for adverse mental states, as well as a way to enter the Dreaming and connected with the Ancestors. But there were also risks attached.

The people who were trying to acquire it: businessmen, politicians, even a multinational pharmaceutical company, knew about the beneficial properties but they knew nothing of the dangers: panic attacks, neuroses, perhaps even schizophrenia. Other people were after it as well—bad people: criminals who just wanted to push it on the black market as the latest psychedelic trip. They'd all be putting people's sanity, perhaps even lives, at risk just to make a quick buck. They were disrespecting something Mandu's tribe considered sacred. In his opinion, white people shouldn't be messing with the Plant at all.

I looked at him and shrugged.

"No worries, Nick" he said, winking at me, "like I bin telling ya, yer not really white, mate. The Plant is in yer blood ..."

"Yes, it probably *will* be, in a few hours" a voice-in-my-head whispered.

"... but yer mate, Robo, now he *is* a white kid?" he asked.

I nodded.

"... and that's why he shoulda bin more careful."

I told him how experienced Robo was with all sorts of stuff. How it was him who introduced me to acid, for instance, at uni. Mandu replied that the "stuff" Robo knew about was white kids' drugs. They were different from the Plant. It was more powerful and potentially more toxic, depending on how much you took, as well as the age and state of the cactus. You needed to be aware of these things to take it safely:

"Yeah, mate. The stuff Robo knew about is chemical. The White-fella make it in his pill factories. It should be the same every time y'buy it from 'im. The Plant only grows *here*, on our lands. We're the only people who know how t'take it safe. Yer mate took too much, too quickly, and he couldn't handle it right."

I tried to explain that it was just one of those things, that Robo was going for a massive back loop and shit can happen in those situations, but he wasn't having any of it:

"So, how good is yer mate normally with these loopy things? When 'is head's straight?" he asked.

I told him that Robo had been looping for a decade and had taught me how to do them.

"Yeah, so there y'go Nick—shit don't usually 'appen to 'im, even when he's 'angin upside down, unless 'is head's working different."

He chuckled to himself, ruefully, and explained how you had to respect the plant's powers. You had to *earn* the right to enjoy its benefits by gradually increasing the amount and monitoring the effect.

Suddenly I had a flashback to my wave-ride in Esperance. I tried to describe it to Mandu—how I could see all the possible lines with absolute clarity like I was watching myself in a slow-mo video.

He nodded and told me I was lucky I could handle such a big dose. It proved the domino dingo was more black than white! His tribe only used it sparingly and for specific rituals. They collected the cactus plants personally, so they knew their origin and potency.

This was why his people had such a problem with alcohol—the white man's drug of choice. It was never a part of their own culture, so they abused it:

"The booze is Whitefella's poison for us blackfellas. It makes us weak 'n sick. It rots our minds and then we're just pissed Abo fools. That's how they want us to stay ..."

He tailed off into bitter mumbling—the first time I'd seen him angry and less than lucid. But he didn't slow his walking pace. Again I struggled to keep up as we climbed the steep trail to the crater rim.

Eventually, after walking for most of the day, we descended into the crater and stopped outside a cave. Mandu announced that we'd arrived and must prepare our camp before it got dark. He bustled around collecting firewood, lighting a fire, boiling water for tea, unrolling our sleeping bags, and getting us ready to spend the night in the mouth of the cave.

When everything was in order we sat down beside the fire. He took the cactus pellets from his pouch, crushed a couple into a powder, mixed them into his tea and drank it. I did the same. We sat there in silence for a while, listening to the gentle moaning of the wind.

Then, as dusk descended, he stood up abruptly and announced that the time was right. He entered the cave and beckoned me to follow him.

Time jumps. As darkness encloses us I'm aware that I'm entering a special place, a shrine. Mandu switches on a torch as we crawl through a narrow rock passage deeper into the cave interior.

Eventually, it opens out into a much larger space. Bats are circling above us, their strange cries echoing from the walls. Mandu shines his torch on them and for the first time speaks:

"This place is sacred f'my people" he whispers. "The spirits of the

Ancestors are restin' here."

He pans the light around and now I see that we're in a vast, cathedral-like space. Stalactites hang from the roof far above us like enormous icicles. Bizarre stalagmites rise from the floor like smaller versions of the Pinnacles' spires. We stand there in silence for a moment while I take in the scale of the place. Then he speaks again:

"No Whitefella has been here before. Not even the Master. Yer the first to see it who's not one of my tribe."

He allows his words to sink in for a moment, and then suddenly, shockingly, he switches off the torch, plunging us into darkness. I jump with fear and he puts his hand on my shoulder to reassure me.

"Now I'll show ya why I brought ya here ..."

He pauses, and then with the timing and panache of a showman, he switches the light back on and illuminates the wall in front of us.

It's covered in paintings—hundreds of them, making an astonishingly complex mural, like an Aboriginal Sistine chapel.

I gasp, and gaze in awe for a long moment.

"Now y'see why I trusted ya, Nick?"

"—" I'm not sure what to say.

"Why I chose ya t'be the first outsider t'see these paintings?"

I'm overcome with gratitude. I can imagine all the eminent anthropologists and art historians who'd give anything to be standing there, and I wonder if I'm worthy of his trust.

He moves the torchlight over the paintings, pointing out details, objects:

"Y'see the connections, mate? How our system of knowledge is like the painting y'showed me?"

———

Time jumps. I look at the cave wall more closely, and suddenly I understand. It's as if Mandu has switched on a light in my brain and illuminated whole areas that have previously been dark.

In a flash of awareness I see Mandu's 'connections'—the connections between Voodoo and Dreamtime; the connections that link *all* knowledge; the links that connect things; the things that are 'out there' in the world and the things that are inside our head, and where they meet: the interface between subject and object. It's a moment of rational awareness, not a hallucination. The full effects of the Plant have yet to kick in and work their magic on me.

You had to look beneath the surface, beyond style, to see the connections between these ancient cave paintings and Nicole's work. There were people and objects depicted in the cave, just as there were in Nicole's paintings, and they were quite different stylistically ... but the relationship between subject and object was supernaturally high-lighted in both.

The choice, and placing, of objects in space around the human subjects was crucial in Nicole's work. Her art was spiritual. She aimed to harness the power of spirits to create 'power objects' that had meaning for her subjects, or even protected them. It looked as if the same thing was going on in these cave paintings. The subjects: people and animals, were surrounded by objects that looked as if they were flying through space: a spear, a rock, cactus plants ...

Mandu points to the latter: "Y'already know what *they* are, Nick, but what d'ya make of this ... ?"

He directs the torch into a corner of the cave he's previously left dark. There, at the very edge of the painting, are some objects in the sky that look remarkably like spaceships, flying saucers, whatever terminology you want to borrow from popular science fiction.

I stare at the cave wall, speechless, dizzy. I sit down on the floor and say nothing. Neither of us speaks for a long time. Quite how long I'm not sure.

———

Time jumps. Now the paintings are animating, coming to life! Objects start to move. Mandu begins to scrape painted objects from the mural and liberate them. He does this with the elaborate care and skill of an expert mime artist. Soon the cave is filled with painted objects flying through space.

"This is the Dreaming, Nick."

His voice seems to come from everywhere at once: in my ear, six feet from me, from the edge of the universe ... I'm not sure how long I remain there, spellbound, saturated, dissolving, vanishing into dark, empty space ...

———

Time jumps. Now we're in darkness, outside the cave. I have no idea how we got here. No recollection of leaving that space. But the paintings are still with me, in my head. Has it been a dream? I don't think so, but now I'm exhausted. I'm lying in my sleeping bag, gazing at the dying embers of a fire. Drifting. Asleep.

———

Time jumps. It's the next morning. I'm still asleep. The molecules of psychoactive cactus have dissolved in my bloodstream. I've left the alternative reality, the Dreaming, and returned to normality.

Mandu woke me, gently. I opened my eyes and took in the landscape. The desert was bathed in the red glow of dawn. My friend, the wind, swirled around us kicking up the sand. The fire was still glowing and Mandu was making tea.

"G'day, Nick. How ya feelin?"

I shook myself awake, rubbed my eyes, and tried to work out what had happened.

"I'm, not sure, mate" I replied, scratching my head.

He gave me an impish grin.

"Well, tell me what y'saw last night in the cave, then."

I shrugged. "I don't know if I really saw what I *thought* I saw."

He laughed—a big-hearted roar of amusement. I tried again:

"I mean ... I'm not sure if I was asleep and just dreamt the whole thing?"

"No, Nick, y'weren't asleep. Y'were awake in the cave."

I nodded, reassured.

"And y'weren't dreamin' ..."

He paused.

"The paintings were dreamin' of *you*!"

I stared at him, unable to make sense of that, but he simply compounded my confusion, without compromise or concession to my feeble half-white brain processes:

"What y'experienced was the Dreamtime, not a dream in yer head. We all shared it: you, me, the Ancestors, the beings in the paintings. And, by the way, as y'may 'ave noticed ... (a dramatic pause) ... some of 'em are not from this planet!"

He paused, for a beat. Then he winked at me.

I shook my head, slowly. There was clearly a cultural chasm to cross before I could get anywhere near understanding what he was talking about. I thanked him for showing me this special place and told him I would remember the experience for the rest of my life. Then I asked him how I could help his people in their struggle with the white man.

Mandu was busy packing, preparing to decamp. He looked up and met my gaze.

"Well, Nick, *you* must tell *me*. That's why the Master sent ya. I'm just an old man tryin' to 'ang on t'what's important before he joins the Ancestors in that cave."

I looked at him, drowning in those eyes.

"My tribe depend on me and my knowledge. We've survived 'ere in these hills f'thousands of years, but I know nothin' about the Whitefella's politics."

Suddenly I sensed his frailty and I was filled with compassion for this ancient shaman who just wanted to be left to rest in peace.

"I hope I've taught ya somethin' Nick, out here in the bush, in the cave. Now it's time for you to teach *me* ..."

We set off back down the steep trail, and as we walked I told him what I thought needed to be done.

14

THIS LAND IS OUR LAND

W e arrived back at the camp late in the afternoon, to find that they'd had some unwelcome visitors. A gang of white men had turned up on quad bikes, belching fumes everywhere and throwing their weight around. Some had been dressed in paramilitary uniforms and armed with rifles. The two in charge had portrayed themselves as figures of authority—politicians or civil servants, but they could just as well be working for the Mob as the government. The others were probably hired heavies.

The two big-shots had employed the classic good-cop-bad-cop strategy to interrogate the tribe, while their henchmen stood around looking menacing. Mister Nasty wanted to know about the Plant, demanding to be shown where the cactus was growing and threatening painful consequences if they didn't comply. The tribe had feigned ignorance, telling him it was a secret known only to the tribal elder and unfortunately he was currently unavailable (although they hadn't put it quite like that: "we told 'im to bugger off!")

Mr Nice Guy apologised for his colleague's brusque manner and announced he was there to negotiate about the land rights issue. He explained their "delicate situation" in the face of "market forces, political pressure, and the March Of Progress." The tribe had shrugged and told him (truthfully this time) that only the elder understood stuff like that.

The unwelcome visitors soon realised that nothing could be achieved without Mandu, so they strutted around the camp for a while issuing vague threats, before announcing that they'd be back to deal directly with the 'head honcho'. Then they got on the quads and roared back down the track in a cloud of dust.

I asked the tribe to describe these two reprobates and from their descriptions, I had a hunch I was acquainted with one of them. Mister Nasty sounded less like a bad cop and more like one of the big-shot criminals Robo and I had crossed—the Great Whites of the drug world. It looked like he was now in cahoots with a crooked politician, Mr Nice Guy, and planning to muscle in on the tribe's land to get their hands on this lucrative new recreational drug.

Mandu had already told me that a multinational pharmaceutical company were also after the Plant. They were interested in it as a potential treatment for bipolar, manic-depressive conditions. The pharma guys probably wouldn't resort to tactics like these sharks, but they had almost unlimited resources to pit against the tribe's complete lack of anything with which to fight them in the courts. Their traditional way of life was threatened unless they organised a fightback. The plan I'd outlined to Mandu on the long walk back from the cave must be put into action straight away.

The next morning I woke with the dawn, full of enthusiasm for my new mission, determined to do whatever I could to help Mandu and his people. We arranged to meet in the nearest proper town, Broom[1], in a week or two. He wasn't specific about exactly when or where, but he said that he'd find me "when the time was right."

Before I left he gave me a parting gift: a pipe, carved from the branch of a eucalyptus tree, with markings that reminded me of the cave paintings, along with a leather pouch full of cactus seed pellets.

"This is f'you, Nick" he announced, handing me the pipe. "My father gave it t'me before he left this world t'join the Ancestors. I want ya to have it, t'show yer one of us now."

I was overwhelmed with gratitude, but I told him I couldn't possibly take something so full of significance for him.

He laughed. "No worries mate, I can make a new one. It's a lot easier than makin' a new friend."

Then he gave me the pouch of cactus pellets, telling me:

"Most of the time we smoke the Plant, not eat it. It's safer like that."

I nodded—I could vouch for that.

Mandu's gifts meant a lot to me. The pipe and pouch of seeds were identical to those that Nicole had used the night we smoked the Plant together. Along with her painting, they were a reminder of the connection between us—a link running all the way from the remote Australian outback to the haunted Haitian rainforest, connecting her *Vodou* and his Dreamtime ... via the Master. As always, he was at the centre of things.

I packed them in my rucksack and said goodbye, thanking Mandu with all my heart, and assuring him I'd be fighting to protect their land and their way of life. We embraced and I set off back down the trail to my camper-van.

The rusty old VW splitty was still parked at the trailhead, with my board inside. We were just at the start of the windless winter season and it would be at least six months before she saw any action again. In the good old days, Robo and I would have been off on a search for wind and waves elsewhere in the world. Now here I was, in the middle of nowhere, with just my board for company and no chance of renewing our bond with the ocean any time soon.

I sat in the van, in that desolate spot, wondering what on earth I was doing there. I'd committed myself to a hair-brained scheme to help some people with whom I shared a tenuous connection, at best. If my board could speak she'd be asking me: Why?

I stared through the dust-encrusted windscreen at the maze of trails leading east, out into the empty desert, and the track that led west, back to the Great Northern Highway.

"I'll tell you why ..." I muttered, startling myself with unexpected conviction. I was at one of those crossroad moments when you choose your next path—a coming-of-age moment. This was my chance to do something that mattered in the *real* world—the grownup world of politics, business, the media; something that might change this world for the better, in however small a way.

Perhaps, once again, this was what the Master meant when he talked about "fulfilling my potential"? Whatever. I'd made the decision myself, without him pulling the strings. It was *my* life, not his. I wasn't his puppet. I'd told Alison that I had to "go bush" for a while and "sort my head out." The time I'd spent in the desert, with Mandu, had sorted it. I didn't need the Master, I had my *own* mission now.

I put the doubts out of my mind and turned the key in the ignition. The trusty VW engine started first time and I set off west, on the tortuous journey back to civilisation.

Twelve hours later I made it to Broom. I based myself there because it had most of the things I needed: an airport, local media, politicians, lawyers. The campaign would be fought on several fronts: media, political, legal, and possibly commercial. My strategy involved all of these:

1. Make contacts in the local radio and TV stations and get some journalists onboard.
2. Launch the political campaign with their publicity— organise protest marches, lobby politicians, and try to win over those who might support our cause.
3. Argue our case in the courts.
4. Take control of the commercial opportunities offered by the Plant.

I began contacting local journalists and it was soon apparent that they were interested in the story. It had some popular ingredients: the 'noble savage' underdog struggling against marauding big business and greedy politicians, a whiff of corruption and scandal, and last (but surely not least) a charismatic spokesman.

I might say so myself, but it turned out I was something of a natural in front of the cameras. The dreadlocks and tattoos got their attention, my mixed-race background gave me politically correct kudos and credibility, and I was surprisingly articulate for a domino dingo surf-punk. Even my assumed name fitted—the media loved the irony that a half-caste kid fighting for Aboriginal rights shared his name with an Australian prime minister. Within a week I'd established my media presence, kick-started the campaign, and moved it on to phase two: the political arena.

Our first demo attracted a few hundred people—a fair sized crowd for Broom: a diverse mix of local blackfellas, white liberals, the curious, do-gooders, bandwagon-jumpers, and those who were just after a good knees-up. We marched down Main Street like warriors, with our banners and warpaint, and camped outside the mayor's office chanting, singing, wailing with didgeridoos, and banging the drum for Aboriginal rights. The banners had slogans like:

AUSTRALIA—A STOLEN CONTINENT!

HANDS OFF OUR HERITAGE!

THIS LAND IS OUR LAND!

The last of these was a rewording of the famous Woody Guthrie protest song: 'This Land Is Your Land' and it became our rallying cry. As the TV truck arrived to film us we launched into a rousing version, which made the local news that evening. It was picked up for prime-time nationwide coverage and the video went viral. The local airwaves, national networks, and international social media reverberated with a bunch of bizarrely painted Abos laying down a groove on didgeridoos and blasting out the lyrics to a white folk singer's dust-bowl anthem:

This land is my land, this land is our land.
This land was made for you and me.

.   .   .

One afternoon, a couple of weeks after I arrived in Broom, I was sitting in the library researching stuff for the campaign. Since spending half my youth in BigFish's temple of learning, libraries had always been favourite places to escape to, after the ocean of course. I was staring out of the window, planning our next move and thinking that it was time to involve Mandu, when I spotted something that made me drop the book I was reading ...

The Man himself was riding majestically down Main Street on a motorcycle that looked as ancient as he was, dreadlocks flying from beneath his classic leather helmet and goggles. He looked like a cross between Mad Max and Wallace & Gromit. It was a moving picture straight out of the movies, but there were no cameras rolling and this was no film set—just the gnarly old shaman rolling into town like Wyatt Earp arriving for the Gunfight at the O.K. Corral.

"Expect the unexpected when this bloke makes an appearance" a voice-in-my-head reminded me. When we first met, his presence in a library had seemed supremely incongruous. Since then Mandu had shown me how he was the master of his *own* world, expertly eking out an existence from the desert's meagre resources. Now here he was, happily hanging out downtown, looking completely at home in his trendily weathered biker's jacket and cutoff jeans.

He pulled up outside the library and sat there grinning at me through the window. I got up from the desk and strode outside to greet him. He removed the Mad Max helmet and the Wallace & Gromit goggles and said G'day. We embraced and I gazed at the motorcycle, admiring its classic lines.

"Yeah mate, it's a Royal Enfield Bullet" he announced proudly. "They started makin' 'em in 1948 when the Poms still made the best bikes in the world. I've 'ad 'er goin' on for what ... (he did a quick calculation on his fingers) ... fifty-five years now!"

He added that he'd trained as an apprentice mechanic when he was a young man and he still did all his own maintenance and repairs.

"But it's gettin' harder keepin' the old girl on the road these days. Can't buy parts no more. Me mates tell me about anythin' I can scavenge and some of 'em even make bits for 'er. I give 'em some cactus seeds in return. We 'ave a smoke and everybody's 'appy. She's still runnin' sweet but sooner or later she'll get crook—like me" he chuckled.

I was impressed and mentioned that a classic bike like his Enfield might be worth a lot of money to a wealthy collector. He could sell it and buy a spanking new modern motorcycle. He chuckled, ran his hand lovingly over the Enfield's bodywork, and asked me why the hell he'd want a fancy new bike when he already had one he trusted with his life?

"Y'can't work on these poncy new Jap cycles like y'can on my Bullet. Somethin' goes crook with 'em and y'just chuck 'em away, like everythin' else these days. No-one knows how to fix things no more."

I knew what he meant. It was in line with his whole philosophy: preserve rather than throw away; make the most of what you've got; don't screw up the planet by wasting its resources; live in harmony with nature. Having said that, I knew, from our initial communication via computers, that he wasn't averse to modern technology when it suited him, so I presented him with a brand-new smart-phone and told him that we'd need to be in regular contact as the media campaign got into gear.

"OK mate, whatever y'say, but I doubt this thing'll work out in the bush." He looked at the phone sceptically. "Maybe we should get some homin' pigeons and camels?"

He winked and flashed one of his radiant smiles.

Smalltalk over, we got down to business. I outlined my four-phase strategy and updated him on how things were progressing. He complimented me on my high profile media presence and added, sarcastically, that he hoped I'd still have time for him now I was a local hero and a TV celebrity.

I blushed and replied sharply that I wasn't interested in fame. The last thing I wanted was to take all the credit for helping to protect *his* tribal land, but the campaign needed a spokesperson and *he* hadn't been available.

I happened to have an interview with a local TV station arranged for that afternoon, followed by a meeting with the mayor, so I invited Mandu along. With hindsight, it was a mistake. The problem was: Mandu was a bit too 'ethnic' for both mainstream media and politics. It didn't help that he'd smoked some Plant and then we'd had a few beers together before the live interview ...

The presenter introduced me with the usual joke about my name and then turned to him:

"So, Mr Mandu, tell us how long you've had the job of tribal elder?"

"Job? Na mate, it doesn't work like that ..."

Mandu stared into the camera, his smile posing questions only he and the Mona Lisa could answer. There was an uncomfortably long pause. Eventually, he continued:

"The Ancestors were here first. Thousands of years before you lot. And let me tell you somethin' else ... (he gazed into the camera) ... not many people know this ... (another long pause) ... some of 'em weren't from this planet!"

He paused, for a beat. Then he winked, straight at the camera, straight into thousands of living rooms.

The presenter coughed nervously.

"Ahem. I see. Thank you for explaining your role, Mr Mandu."

He turned back to me: "Now, Malcolm Fraser ... (the usual snigger at my name) how does it feel to be the focus of so much attention?"

I shrugged.

"Some people are comparing you to other great freedom fighters: Nelson Mandela, Martin Luther King, Malcolm X ..."

I blushed, swallowed hard, and avoiding Mandu's amused gaze, attempted a reply:

"Well, it's a great honour to represent the indigenous people of the Karjaganujaru tribe and if I could just explain why we're so angry ..."

Mandu butted in: "*We're* angry? *Malcolm*?"

For a moment I thought he was going to blow my cover, then he remembered who I was supposed to be.

"Oh yeah, that's right mate (he giggled, and then pointing at me, addressed the presenter) ... he's like a dingo with a roo bone. A domino dingo!"

He guffawed, so loudly that the sound man had to remove his headphones. And so it continued, with me trying to keep the interview on track while Mandu sidetracked it with increasingly bizarre interjections and his stream of consciousness weirdness.

Our meeting with the mayor didn't go much better. In deference to the bloke's status I scrubbed up and put on some smart clothes, but Mandu's dishevelled appearance didn't help. We were ushered into the Head Honcho's office and he greeted me politely, but he could barely hide his distaste for the scruffy old blackfella with the matted dreadlocks and torn-up biker gear.

Once we were seated in the plush leather office chairs the mayor addressed us from behind his imposing desk. He began positively, by stating that the local council were "broadly sympathetic" to our cause, and of course he "respected the human rights and cultural heritage of our indigenous cousins." (Mandu guffawed loudly at this.) He added that they were "fully committed to protecting Aboriginal traditions at a local and state level."

I nodded my gratitude for these platitudes, but before I could ask him for more concrete support the dishevelled elder butted in:

"Yeah, OK, let's cut the crap. What about our land, mate?" he demanded.

"Well, Mr Mandu, as you know it's a delicate situation" the mayor replied. Then, choosing his words carefully, he explained:

"There are market forces at work, political pressures, and the March Of Progress to be taken into account ..."

Mandu angrily interrupted him again:

"Yeah, that sounds just like the bullshit that other smooth bastard told my people. I guess he's one of yer mates then?"

The mayor shuffled some papers, avoided looking us in the eye and replied, warily:

"Ahem. Yes, I *am* aware that a colleague recently visited you on-site ... but I have to say that he's a member of the *opposition* rather than being in a position of *authority*, as, ahem, *I* am."

He looked at us directly now, as if to reinforce the power *he* had over our future.

I nodded, cautiously. Mandu shook his head in frustration. The mayor went on, in an increasingly oily tone:

"In fact, I would like to put on record, given your high profile in the media Mr Fraser ... (he gave me that smarmy smile politicians do so well) ... that I distance myself from my opposition colleague's opinions, methods, and *especially* his, ahem, business *associates*."

More cautious nods from me and exasperated shrugs from Mandu. The mayor gave us his 'serious, thoughtful, and concerned' look as he continued:

"There is, however, the difficult issue of this psychoactive cactus plant that's apparently growing in the region. Some of my colleagues have concerns that it might be used as a recreational drug ... (he stared accusingly at Mandu) instead of for its medicinal properties."

Mandu guffawed so violently he almost fell out of the fancy leather office chair. The mayor tried to ignore him, and ploughed on:

"I have it on good authority that a Swiss pharmaceutical company are interested in trialling this, ahem, 'herb', with a view to licensing it as a treatment for various mental conditions. Of course, we would do everything we could to *facilitate* this project, given the *exciting* business opportunities it might offer to a relatively deprived region of the state."

The mayor looked straight at me as he said this and gave me a little wink, as if he was offering me a piece of these *"exciting* business opportunities". I gave him the faintest of nods in return, and as they say: 'a nod's as good as a wink'. It seemed like we'd tacitly agreed some kind of deal. But Mandu wasn't so easily fobbed off:

"Look mate, it might be 'a relatively deprived region of the state' t'you lot, but those hills have been our home for centuries. In fact, the

Ancestors have lived up in the Bungle Bungles for *thousands* of years! Ever since the Dreamtime."

He paused to allow the gravity of this to sink in. Then he leant forward in the fancy leather chair, put his elbows on the mayor's desk, looked him straight in the eye and whispered:

"And I'll tell ya somethin' else ... (his eyes drilled holes into the politician) ... not many people know this ... (pause, enigmatic smile) ... some of 'em weren't from this planet!"

He paused, for a beat. Then he winked at the mayor.

For a moment Broom's Head Honcho was lost for words. He looked at us, shrugged, and stuttered nervously:

"Well thank you, ahem, g-g-gentlemen. I can assure you I'll do everything in my, umm, my power ... to f-f-facilitate things ... at a local, state, and possible even n-n-national level."

I nodded. Mandu shrugged. And, with that, our meeting was over.

The next morning we got together again in my camper-van to discuss tactics. Following the previous day's media and political engagements, Mandu wanted to know about the other two aspects of the campaign: legal and commercial.

I explained how, in my opinion, saving their land and protecting the Plant from the bad guys were linked. I'd already had a meeting with a lawyer who specialised in land rights and he'd suggested that we also try to get the Plant recognised as a religious sacrament in the tribe's traditional rituals.

Mandu wasn't convinced. His people had never considered themselves 'religious' in the sense of believing in a supernatural being, heaven, hell, and all the other paraphernalia of a 'faith'.

"Look mate, Dreamtime ain't some kind of religious mumbo-jumbo. It's real, Nick—like I showed ya in the cave."

To experience this reality all you had to do was to smoke some Plant—and that wasn't a religious ritual, like munching some bread and pretending it was the body of your guru ...

"Na mate, it's what y'do to get stoned and chat to the Ancestors."

I told him I understood all that, but it didn't matter—this was a legal tactic, not an accurate description of the 'truth'. He shrugged and said he didn't understand the distinction. So I tried, again, to explain what the lawyer was advocating: that making the Plant legally integral to the tribe's ceremonies would hopefully pre-empt any attempt by the government to make it an illegal drug. It would, however, require expert anthropological evidence and possibly Mandu himself to testify at the hearing.

He was sceptical and thinking it through, so was I. Not only would he need convincing, but also some coaching. It was hard to imagine him in the witness box without a mix of trepidation and hilarity, so I told him I'd give evidence myself in his place if it was at all possible. Unfortunately, this didn't go down well either. He took my suggestion completely the wrong way, accusing me of disrespecting him, his people, and of seeking fame on the back of *their* struggle:

"Y'like playin' at being one of us blackfellas, Nick, but really yer just like the rest of 'em white bastards—out t'make a quick buck."

I blushed. There was an uncomfortable silence, the start of a rift between us. The two sides of my mixed race genes were pulling me in opposite directions. A voice in my head was shouting: "Fuck that for gratitude! If that's all the thanks I get for trying to save his patch of dirt from some seriously heavy dudes, then he can fuck off back to the Bungle Bungles and wait for the shit to hit the fan!"

Our standoff lasted several tense seconds, then he mimicked my trademarked shrug and smiled his marvellous Mandu smile. I tell you: that smile would melt the heart of the most frigid ice queen.

"OK, we'll do it yer way mate" he agreed. "But y'know, them lawyer buggers don't come cheap."

I nodded and suggested that he contact the Master to request his financial support for the campaign. I thought this was more likely to succeed coming from him since his relationship with the wealthy philanthropist went back a lot further than mine. I added that I'd be organising some fundraising events.

Mandu was happy enough with these suggestions, but my next

idea was more problematic. I told him we had to take control of the commercial opportunities offered by the Plant and bring it to a wider market responsibly, before the Mob got their hands on it:

"We have to control the marketing and distribution ourselves, Mandu; educate consumers about the cultural context—where it fits in your people's traditions; tell people how to take it safely. At the same time, we should be talking to the pharmaceutical companies about licensing the Plant as a medicine."

Mandu nodded, reluctantly. He understood all this and agreed with me, up to a point. Of course it was better to be proactive, rather than wait for the bad guys to grab their land and crush them, but for him marketing the Plant was the lesser of two evils, rather than a *positive* choice. He'd never agreed with the Whitefella's ways of doing business:

"It's all just greed, Nick. Like the song says: 'this land is *our* land' but *he* can't share it peacefully, he's gotta grab it and own it."

Mandu had no desire to bring the Plant to a 'wider world' let alone make money from it. All he'd ever wanted for his people was to be left alone to live their lives as they'd been doing for centuries, in harmony with what was around them. Now I was telling him we must follow White Man's rules, argue our case in his courts, go into business together ...

I tried to reassure him, told him he wouldn't need to compromise his beliefs, his traditions, his culture—I could handle all the White Man stuff myself ... but deep down there was an issue of trust, and it was splitting us just as his people used fire and water to split rocks.

Mandu got back on his classic motorcycle and roared off back to the bush. He took the smartphone with him and I promised to keep him in the loop with regular text messages. He said he'd check it whenever he could get a signal, but reiterated that in his opinion homing pigeons or camels would be more reliable.

15

DREAMTIME PLANT PRODUCTS

My time in Broom passed quickly. Days were filled with frenetic activity as the campaign progressed on all four fronts. Before I knew it, three months had shot by—half the windless season, and it was July already. I still grieved for my windsurfing buddy, Robo, and I was unsure how things stood with Mandu, but at least I could look forward to the reappearance of my old friend, the Fremantle Doctor.

The campaign was going well. We had the support of the local media, the story was trending on social networks, whipped up by our 'This land is our land' video, and our cause had been endorsed by some important pressure groups. I was on first name terms with the mayor and I was well known in the town, something of a local hero. People listened to me, and for the first time in my life what I said, and did, mattered.

With funding from the Master, we were able to proceed with the legal case and start a business selling the Plant via the internet. Every week Mandu made the arduous journey on his Enfield Bullet with a consignment of freshly harvested cactus pellets. He wasn't too happy about the disruption to his idyllic life in the bush, and he was uncomfortable with all this Whitefella stuff, but he loved riding his motorcycle, so he didn't grumble too much.

I rented a warehouse and assembled a team of workers to handle packaging and despatch, while I took care of the website, marketing, and finances. We called ourselves: Dreamtime Plant Products and thanks to the power of the internet the little local business soon became a surprisingly successful international enterprise.

Orders rolled in as word spread about the Plant's psychoactive properties. Our customers bought into the indigenous cultural thing and they loved that their money was helping to support the tribe's struggle against greedy businessmen and crooked politicians. Demand began to outstrip supply and Mandu was no longer able to provide us with enough product, so we hired a team of delivery drivers. The business grew exponentially and I became a workaholic, focussed on marketing, profits, legal issues and politics, while Mandu became increasingly distrustful of my motives. There was nothing I could say, or do, to ease his doubts, but I was simply too busy to worry about him anyway.

To my surprise, I relished my new role as an entrepreneur. When I was welcomed into Nicole's community it felt like the Kangaroo Kid was no longer an outsider. Now it felt like I'd finally come of age and joined the grown-up world of commerce and politics. It wasn't Mandu's world, for sure, but it was somewhere I had some influence, responsibilities, status. I'd been avoiding stuff like that ever since my childhood in a dead-end town, with a family who convinced me I'd never achieve anything. Now I was a contender. Who could blame me for embracing this brave new world?

With Dreamtime Plant Products going from strength to strength, I began discussions with the pharmaceutical company who were interested in licensing the cactus as a medicine. With the help of our lawyer and some 'facilitation' by the mayor, I negotiated a contract to supply them with samples for their trials. In exchange for the sole rights they stumped up an advance of a hundred thousand dollars—a sum that was, of course, peanuts for a multinational company, but for a penniless windsurfer living in a rundown camper-van, and a bunch of Abos camped out in the bush, it was a fortune.

I never found out whether the mayor received any financial incentive for 'facilitating' the deal, but the council were praised for bringing an 'exciting new business opportunity' to this 'relatively deprived region of the state' (quotations from the mayor's press release). The praise was certainly well-timed, coming just as the mayor was starting his bid to be re-elected.

I ploughed most of the money back into the campaign and the business, but I felt entitled to spend a bit on myself. After all, my newly acquired status demanded I look the part, as well as walk the walk and talk the talk. So I rented a suitable apartment and bought myself some smart clothes and a fancy Japanese motorcycle.

Mandu was predictably scornful of the bike, calling it: "a pile of Jap dingo dung", but his misgivings went much deeper—to the heart of our joint enterprise. He was worried that fame and fortune would corrupt me, the tribe, and their traditional way of life (I noted he didn't include himself in the list of potentially corruptible subjects). I should have listened to him, but I dismissed his anxieties as an inability to embrace change, to 'think out of the box', and the rift between us grew ever wider.

As Dreamtime Plant Products prospered and news of the pharmaceutical deal broke, I was portrayed in the media as a kind of mixed race Ozzic version of Richard Branson, the British billionaire entrepreneur. Like Branson, I'd started a small, local business at a relatively young age (in his case as a student, selling records and promoting rock events), but I was really more interested in spreading the word than making money. Rather than a Branson-style business magnate, I preferred to think of myself as a latter-day Timothy Leary.

Leary was a writer, academic, psychotherapist, and one of the first people to experiment with psychedelic substances, such as psilocybin ('Magic Mushrooms') and LSD, in the 1960s. His research for the Harvard Psilocybin Project focused on treating alcoholism and reforming criminals (the 'Concord Prison Experiment'). Many of his research subjects told of profound mystical and spiritual experiences which they said positively altered their lives.

Leary believed that the drug itself didn't produce the transcendent experience, it merely acted as a chemical key to open the mind and free the nervous system from its routine patterns. He argued that psychedelic substances, taken in proper doses and in a stable setting, could benefit society, urging people to: 'Turn on, Tune in, Drop Out'.

Like him, I advocated the legal use of such powerful catalysts to raise consciousness, enhance creativity, and open the 'Doors of Perception'. I was trying to educate people about the Plant and how to use it safely, just as he'd done with LSD back in the sixties. Leary later wrote:

> We saw ourselves as anthropologists from the twenty-first century inhabiting a time module set somewhere in the dark ages of the 1960s. On this space colony, we were attempting to create a new paganism and a new dedication to life as art.

I'd come across something like that before. Leary's time-travelling anthropologists were just like Dr Ludwig Langer's group of fellow travellers—a 'space colony' in a 'time module' stuck in the 'dark ages' of 1930s Germany, but far ahead of their time—looking forward to the 1960s—experimenting with psychoactive substances, alternatives to conventional morality, 'attempting to create a new paganism and a new dedication to life as art'.

Now here I was, in 2017, like one of Leary's 'anthropologists from the twenty-first century', perhaps not attempting anything as grandiose as Dr Langer, or Timothy Leary, but it was still early days for Dreamtime Plant Products and I was excited to see where it would take me.

Another couple of months raced past in frantic activity. I did my best to live up to my Branson-esque image and fulfil my role as a Leary-like advocate for the Plant. As spring replaced winter, three of my original four goals had been achieved: I'd established a significant media presence; politicians supported our cause and were cueing up to be photographed with me; our commercial projects were going well ... Only the legal battle remained to be fought and won.

It was the most difficult nut to crack because, unlike the other goals, I had no control of the labyrinthine process. We were in the hands of lawyers who were paid (excessively, in my opinion) to argue the merits of our case, rather than believe in it passionately. The outcome would be decided by supposedly knowledgeable, impartial judges who actually knew nothing about Mandu's people, and were riddled with prejudices and bias.

Worse still, I'd become a victim of my own success. The media were so besotted with me, and Dreamtime Plant Products had expanded so quickly, that the government got wind of this new psychedelic drug and intervened in the legal process.

Stories of harmful side effects were starting to circulate. Despite my best attempts to educate our customers there were always people who ignored my warnings, played Russian roulette with their sanity, and suffered the consequences: neuroses, schizophrenic episodes, bad trips. The rumours were blown up into full-on horror stories in the tabloid press, and the bad publicity persuaded the authorities to call for the Plant to be banned.

Mandu had always maintained that white folk shouldn't mess with the Plant because they couldn't handle it. Robo's death was a tragic example of how things could go horribly wrong. Now I was becoming aware of the downsides of being a user myself.

By then I was smoking it regularly—most days, and I had to keep increasing the amount to get the same effects. I was ignoring my own warnings, exceeding the safe dosage, and finding myself becoming increasingly dependent on those little cactus pellets. I started suffering memory loss, inability to concentrate, dizziness. The only way I could function was by smoking more Plant.

Along with the physical symptoms, there was a worrying loss of perspective in my life. My notoriety meant I'd be a key witness at the forthcoming hearings, but instead of taking this responsibility seriously I arrogantly assumed the judges would simply roll over and be swayed by my celebrity status.

As our day in court approached, my relationship with Mandu deteriorated. He accused me of becoming more like a drug dealer than a campaigner—a pimp, obsessed with making money instead of raising consciousness. He said that I was hanging out with the wrong people, cosying up to wheeler-dealer types instead of the liberal politicians who could support our case in court. What we needed to win the Whitefella's legal game was credibility, not status.

Deep down I knew he was right, but I was too far gone to admit it. My judgement had become clouded by ego, ambition, and mind-altering cactus seeds. I was a high-flyer now, over-reaching again, sailing too close to the wind, flying too close to the sun ... a fall from grace was inevitable.

Committee Room 1, Parliament House, Perth. Monday, September 4, 2017, 10:00. I arrived at the inquiry, looking the part in a new suit and tie, to do my civic duty as an expert witness. I'd made the 4,500 kilometre round trip to argue against the criminalisation of a humble cactus plant—a criminal waste of time in my opinion. No doubt WA's great and good would be persuaded by my evidence and agree with me.

As soon as I'd been sworn in I faced a barrage of questions from the state's lawyers:

"Is it not true that ingesting these cactus seeds is not without danger, Mr Fraser?"

"Yes, that's correct" I replied, wondering why the hell lawyers have to overcomplicate everything with double negatives. I qualified my answer:

"The Aboriginal people who've been using the Plant for hundreds of years advocate *smoking* it, rather than ingesting it, and that's the advice Dreamtime Plant Products gives to our customers. We also publish guidelines about safe doses on our website."

"So there *are* harmful side effects?"

"Possibly, but there's currently no proof. The research has yet to be carried out."

"So, what about these reports of people suffering anxiety attacks, paranoia, and generally 'freaking out' with so-called 'bad trips'?"

The lawyer formed ironic 'air quotes' with his fingers and apologised to the committee for resorting to "contemporary ergot" (or slang, as the rest of us call it).

I replied by quoting Timothy Leary's testimony at the 1966 Senate hearing. When Senator Ted Kennedy asked him if LSD was surely "extremely dangerous?" Leary replied: "Sir, the motor car is dangerous if used improperly ... Human stupidity and ignorance is the only danger human beings face in this world."

I went on to include a list of other familiar products and activities that were "dangerous if used improperly": alcohol, tobacco, electricity, cooking, sport, and so on ... In other words, we were both arguing that what's needed was education, not criminalisation.

I told the inquiry that like Dr Leary I was focussed on informing people of the dangers, as well as raising consciousness about the benefits of this powerful psychoactive plant. It had been used for centuries by the indigenous people of the Kimberley region who knew it to be a 'medicine for the head'. This was why we had a contract to supply samples to a multinational pharmaceutical company for their research.

I suggested that instead of banning the Plant, the government should license it—make it available only as a prescribed pharmaceutical drug, or from reputable suppliers (such as ourselves), to be used solely by responsible adults.

I concluded my testimony by suggesting that if the state of Western Australia in its wisdom, and with the benefit of half a century of hindsight, licensed the Plant, they could then tax it, and who knew how much revenue that might generate for the state?

There was a thoughtful silence as the assembled politicians and lawyers considered this argument. Nobody could think of a reason why the tax man shouldn't be allowed to get his hands on this extra revenue and there were no more questions for me, so I left the stand feeling reasonably satisfied with my performance and muttering "I rest my case" under my breath.

The inquiry adjourned for lunch at this point, which was a blessed relief. Expert witnessing was hard work. My testimony had taken most of the morning (the account I've given here is just a bullet point summary) and I was starving.

I walked out of the committee room to find someone waiting for me in the crowded lobby. Dressed in a dark suit and tie, he looked familiar. At first I thought he was one of my journalist friends expecting to interview me, but I couldn't quite place him. Our eyes met across the lobby, he smiled at me, and with surprise verging on shock, I recognised him. There was only one human being who could smile like that.

"G'day Nick. Quite a show y'put on in there for those fat galahs."

"Mandu! What are you doing here?" I gasped. "You look ... umm, you look ..."

I tailed off, lost for words for once. Having told me he wouldn't be testifying I never expected to see him in Perth, but it was his appearance that threw me. I shook his hand and looked him up and down, taking in the complete outfit. From the newly shined formal shoes and sober black socks to the neatly sweptback dreadlocks ponytail, he was immaculate. There wasn't a hair out of place, but the most shocking detail was definitely those shoes and socks. I'd never seen him wear anything other than ratty old sandals before, and that was only when he was riding his motorcycle.

He laughed at my confusion. "Yeah mate, I scrub up OK when I need to. I wanted t'hear what y'ad to say to those buggers, but I don't think they'd 'ave let me in if I showed up in the Abo biking gear."

Over lunch he told me he'd always fancied "a bit of a trip" on his motorcycle before they both "bit the bullet." So, on a whim, he'd borrowed the smart togs, jumped on the Royal Enfield Bullet, and ridden the 2,250 kilometres down to Perth—just to watch me testify!

We spent a pleasant hour together and it was just like the early days of our friendship, before all the White Man stuff got in the way. He complimented me on my performance—the way I'd delivered my evidence, the mix of research and passion, and he told me that now he understood why I'd made such an impression on the Master. I blushed and smiled my thanks, lost for words again.

Then his tone darkened. He predicted that the inquiry's verdict would be negative and that it would give the bastards the green light to trample all over us. I told him not to be so pessimistic, to have some faith in the legal process. Hadn't he just told me I'd made a convincing case for legalising the Plant?

He laughed, bitterly, and said he'd had enough experience of the Whitefella's ways to know how these things would turn out. Yes, I'd made a good fist of it, but I shouldn't delude myself into thinking I had any real power in this world (he gestured around the smart city eatery full of similar besuited professionals). It was *their* world. *They* made the rules and we'd always be the little guys fighting the system.

I pointed out that David beat Goliath fair and square. He countered that it was just a story. This was real life—a reality he knew only too well. I mentioned that we had plenty of support: I'd fraternised with the right politicians; I knew the right people in the media; I was doing deals with the right business people … He looked me in the eyes and smiled, sadly this time.

"Remember what Alejandro told ya, Nick?"

His laser-like gaze probed me, just like the Master, and suddenly I felt as foolish as I had aboard the Abyss. I shrugged, resorting to my default defensive gesture.

"Y'know: be careful not t'sail too close t'the wind, not t'fly too close t'the sun in case yer wings melted … Remember that, mate?"

I frowned, wondering what else he'd said about me. For the past six months I'd been in control of my own destiny, no longer a puppet. But suddenly he was a presence, the elephant in the room again.

Mandu smiled his smile and imitated my trademark shrug, ludicrously exaggerating the gesture. It was comical—the gesture of a

clown dressed as a city slicker. It lightened the atmosphere, cleared
the air, and we both laughed a little.

He told me he was just giving me a friendly warning to be careful,
not to over-reach myself, watch my back—the shit was about to hit
the fan and the dung was about to hit the Domino Dingo.

Mandu's pessimism proved justified. My appearance as an expert
witness was a complete waste of time. My testimony was ignored and
the state's lawyers persuaded the committee to make the Plant illegal
in WA. A total ban across the whole country was soon enshrined in
law by the federal parliament in Canberra.

I should have seen this coming. If I hadn't been so distracted by
delusions of grandeur and those addictive little cactus seeds perhaps
I'd have heeded Mandu's warnings. I was well aware of the historical
parallels and this was definitely a case of history repeating itself ...

Timothy Leary's testimony had also proved ineffective. On
October 6, 1966, just months after the subcommittee hearings, LSD
was banned in California, and by October 1968 it was illegal in all
states. In an attempt to maintain some kind of legal usage he founded
the 'League for Spiritual Discovery,' a religion with LSD as its holy
sacrament. This was unsuccessful and Leary found himself and his
followers forced underground, criminalised, his work discredited.

Here in Australia, fifty years later, there were a few glimmers of
hope. First, the inquiry allowed the pharmaceutical company to
continue their research into the medicinal benefits of the cactus.
Second, unlike Leary's attempt, here the 'freedom of religion' argument proved successful—a court in Broom decriminalised the Plant
for Mandu's tribe and exempted them from prosecution. Third, the
same court upheld the tribe's rights to their land.

The mayor was influential in all three of these positive developments. As promised, he testified in Perth to support the deal he'd
'personally facilitated' with the pharma company, and in Broom to
support our 'indigenous cousins'. He received plenty of favourable

publicity in the local media and shortly after his appearance at the land rights hearing he was re-elected with an increased majority.

Mandu enjoyed the 4,500 kilometre round trip on his Enfield (although it proved terminal for the motorcycle—the Bullet finally 'bit the bullet' and was retired). I think he secretly relished taking on the White Man at his own game and in the end he got pretty much everything he wanted. The tribe's land was now legally protected, as was their right to use the Plant in their 'religious ceremonies'. The fact that it was now banned for everyone else didn't concern him. In any case, he wanted nothing more to do with the business of selling it. The money we'd made together had done nothing for his people except distract them with useless consumerism and the White Man's poison: alcohol.

As for me? Well, the inquiry verdict and the ban were a massive disappointment—a sad anticlimax to my career as an activist and entrepreneur. It was the end for Dreamtime Plant Products and my newly acquired status in the community. It looked like the end of my relationship with Mandu, as well.

For the past few months we'd been travelling in opposite directions. My ambition was to be a contender, whereas Mandu just wanted his people to be allowed to live their lives as they had for centuries. His objectives had been achieved, but mine had been thwarted by the government. He'd been proved right and I was wrong: you can't beat the system playing by the White Man's rules.

Now I was drifting in limbo again, but there was one more glimmer of hope: at least the windless season was nearly over. For the past six months I'd been a workaholic and a Plantaholic, now there was something else to distract me. My old friend, the Fremantle Doctor, had just made his first tentative attempts at a reunion. I was dusting down my windsurfing equipment, looking forward to feeling some wind in my sail again, eagerly anticipating my first session, when events intervened ...

16

THE CONSORTIUM

I n October, several weeks after my appearance at the inquiry, the mayor invited me to a "little soirée" he was having to celebrate his re-election. He'd benefitted from his association with the pharmaceutical deal and our land rights campaign, and he wanted to thank me personally, perhaps even to reward me "more substantially".

I was in two minds whether to go. I was intrigued to find out just how substantial a carrot he was dangling, but I was in no shape to soirée. Since the inquiry, I'd gone from drifting around in limbo into something of a downward spiral. My life had fallen apart—again.

The Plant was now a banned substance and Dreamtime Products were defunct, but I was still dependent on those little cactus pellets—those *illegal* little cactus pellets. I was suffering from panic attacks and paranoia. I lived in fear of a knock on my door. If I was arrested it wouldn't be long before the police found out I wasn't who I said I was, and once they discovered my true identity it would open a can of worms. Apart from Malcolm Fraser's false passport, there were my previous drug deals, I was still on the run from the Great White Mafia sharks, Robo's death, Alison ...

I agonised over it but in the end the carrot beat the worms. I decided I had too much to lose by not going. I had to get my life back together before it was too late, so I accepted the mayor's invitation. Perhaps his 'little soirée' would be my lifeline out of this downward spiral.

Saturday, October 21, 21:00. The party was held at a luxury beach villa some way out of town, the home of one of the mayor's colleagues. I arrived on my swanky Japanese motorcycle, looking the part, to find a gathering of Broom's great and not-so-good: lawyers, politicos, businessmen, the chief of police, and some rather more nefarious individuals.

From the moment I walked in, I felt something wasn't quite right. For one thing, all the guests were men, nobody had brought a female partner. The only women were employees, paid to serve us food and drinks, or to provide additional services—'hostesses', to use a polite term—elegantly dressed, sophisticated, but clearly 'ladies of the night'. It was all very civilised, but the kind of polite, superficial bonhomie you get at the *start* of a party. The calm before the storm.

People were getting on with each other rather too well for my liking. Sworn enemies from opposing sides of the political divide were fraternising with rival 'fat cat' developers, and the chief of police was deep in conversation with a burly wheeler-dealer with a shaved head and tattoos. There was something disconcertingly familiar about him, but before I could work out who he was the mayor sidled up and greeted me with exaggerated warmth:

"G'day Malcolm. I'm so glad you could make it."

He pumped my hand as if I was his most loyal supporter. I congratulated him on his election victory.

"Thanks, mate. I have to say that it helped a lot to have the backing of our indigenous cousins and your media presence."

I nodded graciously, but to my mind it was more a matter of political expediency—he aligned himself with *our* campaign, rather than the other way around. Anyway, he was grateful and he wanted to keep me "in the loop" (as he put it):

"I invited you here this evening to tell you about some interesting developments ... (he left a significant pause as if waiting for a drum roll). I've been asked to lead a new consortium of like-minded players ... (he gestured around the room) ... and we'd like you to join us."

I nodded, cautiously. Perhaps it had been the right decision to turn up after all.

"There are going to be some exciting new investment opportunities for you, Malcolm."

I shrugged and replied that now Dreamtime Plant Products had ceased trading, I doubted whether I could be considered a "player".

He looked disappointed but he was determined to have me on board: "OK, well perhaps there might still be a position in the consortium for you—in a consultant or PR role ..."

I responded with a polite, noncommittal reply, and that seemed to satisfy him:

"Great. I'll flesh it out over the course of the evening."

His eyes roamed around the room, located his next contact, and he moved on to do more meeting, greeting, back-slapping, and hand-pumping.

We sat down to eat a sumptuous five-course meal. It was all very formal—multiple cutlery options, fine wines, place settings reserved with name tags. I found myself sitting between the mayor and his opposition colleague, our host. Opposite us were an executive from the pharmaceutical company, the chief of police, and the burly businessman.

The seating arrangement had, no doubt, been chosen by the mayor's colleague—it was his house after all, and it soon became clear that these were the main players in the mayor's consortium. Looking at us seated at the long banqueting table I was reminded of paintings of the Last Supper. I wondered who was playing the Jesus role and who was Judas Iscariot.

As I was mulling this over, the mayor put his hand on my shoulder and introduced his colleagues. Adrenaline and paranoia hit me as I realised they included the two reprobates who'd threatened

Mandu's tribe: Mr Nice Guy politician and his sidekick, Mr Nasty 'businessman'. With a shudder, I finally recognised the burly, tattooed wheeler-dealer. Mister Nasty was indeed one of the Great White drug sharks who'd pursued me and Robo. Did he remember me? That was the crucial question. If he did, then Malcolm Fraser's days were numbered.

Smalltalk over, we got down to business. The banquet became less like the Last Supper and more like a game of poker, with stakes that were worryingly high. The mayor was the dealer and he opened the bidding:

"So, gentlemen, thank you for coming to my 'little soirée' ... (he gave us his smarmy politician's smile). Welcome to the inaugural meeting of the Consortium."

We raised our glasses in a toast.

"You're here because you all share an interest in developing the resources of the region, which as you know includes a rather unique cactus plant growing out in the Bungle Bungles."

I gulped down some wine. So, that's what this was all about.

"Now, following the government's decision to make this plant illegal, we need to think out of the box and look for less, ahem, *conventional* ways of exploiting it."

Nods of approval from his guests.

"That's why I was asked to convene this brainstorming session with the key players."

He looked around the table, sat back, and invited our input.

The pharmaceutical executive made the first move. He was holding a strong hand and he heaped his chips high. He told us that initial trials of the cactus had been positive and he was looking to take the project to the next level:

"Since the inquiry in Perth banned the recreational use of this psychoactive plant, our negotiations with the government have been going well. We have every hope it may become an important drug in the treatment of mental disorders, but there still remains the problem of the indigenous people."

A couple of the other guests muttered to themselves, expressing their opinions about this obstacle and how they would deal with it. The pharma executive was looking for a negotiated settlement with Mandu's people:

"We need someone to represent us and mediate with the tribal elder to *persuade* them to accept a deal."

He looked at me and added that now Dreamtime Plant Products had bitten the dust our contract was no longer valid, but his board had authorised him to offer me a job as a 'consultant'.

I gave him a noncommittal response. Of course I was tempted, but I was worried by his use of the word: "persuade". What he said next did nothing to allay my concerns:

"The thing is, Malcolm, this window of opportunity is limited. It'll no longer be possible for you to use kid gloves with these people. The gloves are off and you'll need to be a lot more *persuasive*."

He left a pause to allow this to sink in as I swallowed another gulp of wine.

"If this isn't acceptable to you, Malcolm, then unfortunately we will have to look for stronger partners."

He glanced around the table at our host and his burly sidekick.

Mr Nice Guy politician chipped in, eagerly accepting the pharma executive's gambit and declaring his suitability for the role of "troubleshooter", citing his ability to deal with trouble, his expertise with shooters and his lack of scruples when it came to "booting that bunch of Abos out of the bush!"

Mr Nasty covered his friend's bet and raised the stakes:

"Look guys, we're into a totally different ball game now. This bloody cactus has been criminalised, so with respect, Mr *Fraser* and his operation are no longer relevant."

He gave me a menacing stare as he said my false surname. So far he'd given no indication he knew my true identity, but now I was paranoid he was keeping that particular ace up his sleeve.

"Fair dinkum to him and his Dreamtime Products for creating a demand, but the rules of the game have changed. Me and my associates are the experts now."

He sat back, grinning malevolently, knocked back a whole glass of wine and belched smugly. It looked like the Great White drug sharks were intending to feed on the corpse of my business and muscle their way to controlling the lucrative recreational market for the Plant.

The mayor gave Mr Nasty one of his unctuous smiles and agreed that this was exactly what was needed: "out-of-the-box thinking and non-standardised solutions ... and I'm convinced that the synergy in this room can provide them."

We raised our glasses and toasted the consortium again.

The chief of police had maintained a stony poker face so far, keeping his cards close to his chest. Now he revealed his hand. He could see the logic of Mr Nasty's argument that a newly criminalised drug needed genuine criminals to bring it to market, but it put him in a difficult place professionally:

"Obviously my hands are tied when it comes to supporting such a venture *publicly*, but I might well be open to exploratory overtures if privacy was guaranteed."

He gave Mr Nasty a meaningful glance and the drug shark nodded in return. I was again reminded of the expression: 'a nod's as good as a wink'. The Chief continued to play his cards adroitly:

"Meanwhile, if our colleague (he gestured to the pharma executive) could speak to his board about making a contribution towards the cost of policing their operation, then I can guarantee my wholehearted support."

The executive replied that perhaps if the Chief could outline what kind of support he could provide, then he would see what he could do.

"Well, if things turn nasty out in the bush then you'll need our backup."

"I see" the executive replied, "and when you say: 'turn nasty' what exactly did you have in mind?"

"I mean the kind of protests that are organised by leftie do-gooders who want to obstruct progress and dump us back in the dark ages."

He glanced in my direction as he said this.

"So where do you stand on the political spectrum, Chief?" Mr Nice Guy politician asked him. "Vis a vis the land rights issue, I mean?"

"Well mate, I can tell you I've got no time for the Abos' crazy idea that they have prior rights to *our* land, and I'll do everything in my power to stop anyone from getting in your way."

His steely expression, as he looked straight at me, made it quite clear who he had in mind.

At this point I decided the stakes were far too high for me. I would have been happy to cash in my chips and leave the game, but the others had laid their cards on the table and now they demanded to see what I had in my hand. They expected me to join their consortium (although Mr Nasty insisted on calling it the "Syndicate"). I had to choose: either I was *with* them, or I was *against* them, and they made it clear: there'd be serious consequences if it was the latter. So, was I *in*, or *out*?

The more I thought about it, the more trapped I felt. I may have done a few things in the past that weren't strictly legal, but I wasn't ready to become a full-time criminal. I had over-reached in the White Man's world, been seduced by fame, fortune, and my inflated ego, fallen out with Mandu, but there was no way I could betray him.

On the other hand, if I declared myself *out* the consequences would be serious, probably painful, possibly even fatal.

I was caught between the proverbial rock and a hard place. Wedged in so tight I might have to cut my own arm off to get out. I needed to buy some time, so I thanked them for including me in such an 'exciting opportunity' and told them I'd give some careful thought to how I could contribute.

Unfortunately, this didn't satisfy them. They called my bluff and demanded an answer that evening, or else they'd assume I was *out*. In which case, it would not be possible for me simply to get back on my motorcycle and leave.

OK, I said, I'd give them my answer a.s.a.p … but please, let's at least finish this superb meal. I picked up my crystal glass of vintage Hunter Valley red and re-toasted the success of the consortium … "and The Syndicate, of course" I added, winking at Mr Nasty.

Dusk set in as we progressed through the five-course meal, but it was difficult to enjoy the excellent food as the darkness at the edge of the party closed in on me.

Once dinner was over, the serious drinking started. The waitresses cleared everything away and then disappeared, leaving the hostesses to service the guests. The mayor's 'little soirée' abandoned all semblance of sophistication and began to resemble a scene from Hogarth's 'A Rake's Progress' or a Roman orgy.

The noise level cranked up until there was an edge of violence to it. The banter became aggressive shouting. The mayor and his opposition colleague were arguing over one of the girls, yelling political slogans at each other like drunken dictators. The chief of police was locked in verbal combat with my predatory stalker, the Great White drug shark, arguing the merits of various weapons and comparing their guns, knives, tasers.

Underwear littered the strobe-lit dance floor, the swimming pool was full of naked revellers, and the dark recesses of the party were occupied with cavorting couples.

I retreated from the mayhem and found myself in a corner of the room discussing the Plant with the team from the pharmaceutical company, extolling the consciousness-raising benefits and bemoaning the government's shortsightedness in banning it. The pharma executive asked me if I had any cactus seeds with me—he was interested in trying it … "for research purposes, you understand."

I wasn't sure. There was just so much going on that night—so much scheming, manoeuvring, posturing. It all felt like an elaborate game, a setup, a trap ... or was I overcomplicating things?

I looked around the room nervously. The main players all seemed occupied, shouting at each other or boozing and carousing with the hostesses. It didn't *seem* like I was being observed, but that didn't stop me from *feeling* like I was being spied on.

Truth was, I needed a toke to relax and take the edge off the paranoia. It was a vicious circle—smoking the Plant produced paranoid delusions (along with delusions of grandeur), and then I needed to smoke some more to cope with the delusions. I understood this, but it didn't stop my dependence on those illegal little cactus seeds.

I reached into my jacket and produced the pipe Mandu had given me. It was a constant companion these days, along with the leather pouch of pellets. I packed some seeds in the bowl, lit up, and drew the smoke deep into my lungs, feeling the familiar calming rush. I passed the pipe to the pharma executive. He drew on it, passed it to his colleague, and for a while we shared it in silence.

The effects of the Plant kick in and now we're in the zone, inhabiting the present moment like dogs or babies. Time jumps in discrete steps, instead of flowing past like a river. The doors of perception open and I'm flooded with stimuli. Sounds become shapes. Colours become smells. The music becomes blurred, out of focus. I gaze at the faces around me, trying to read them, but they're closed books.

Time jumps. My thoughts become darker. I'm no longer enjoying this. I can't work out who is friend, who is foe ... The chief of police is staring at me and whispering with the mayor. Chinese whispers or paranoia? He picks up his mobile and makes a call.

It feels like they're *all* looking at me now, shuffling closer, surrounding me. The party implodes, becomes a claustrophobic world like a prison cell. The darkness at the edge of this world presses in on me.

Paranoia is a strange sensation. It creeps up on you slyly, hiding in the shadows. You turn round, catch a glimpse of something ... It inches closer and you feel it tighten its grip ... Confront it and it dissolves in the darkness, like an echo, but the feeling doesn't go away.

———

Time jumps, again. It's now later, or rather it's now *and* later. Perhaps it's now or never.

Suddenly people are coming out of the shadows towards me—men, carrying nightsticks, searching for something or somebody.

They stop and take in the scene of depravity, nodding to some of the guests. For a moment I think that they're just friends of friends, that they're not out to get me, that the darkness is all in my mind. But fingers are pointing ...

"Malcolm Fraser?"

The question is directed at me. It's a good question and it requires some thought. But I'm looking at them through a telescope the wrong way and my answer is vanishing in a cloud of possibilities ... Who am I, indeed?

I smile and shrug.

Somehow this is the wrong response. They aren't amused. They surround me. Grab me roughly. Bind my wrists. Drag me outside. Throw me in the back of a windowless wagon. Hit me repeatedly with their nightsticks. A blow smashes into my skull.

Am I being kidnapped by these heavies? Is this the end?

These are my last thoughts as I sink into the blackness.

It's a funny thing, paranoia. You start to wonder if you're delusional, and events prove you wrong.

17

FALL FROM GRACE

Sunday, October 22, 2017, 07:45—the morning after the night before. I woke up in a police cell, covered in cuts, bruises, my own vomit and urine. My head felt like it had been used as a punchbag by a gang of kickboxing kangaroos. I tried to focus on the events of the previous evening, but they were a blur.

The party had spiralled out of control, that much I knew. The noise level was insane. Sex, drugs, and rock-'n-roll (well, hip-hop and gangster rap) had breached acceptable limits. Violence threatened. Perhaps the neighbours had complained? No, that couldn't be it. The villa was so secluded, with acres of space and a private beach.

I vaguely remembered the chief of police whispering with the mayor, staring at me, making a phone call ... Then the party had been raided, by thugs who weren't in uniform. The last thing I remembered was a blow to my skull and then I must have passed out. At least I wasn't being held hostage by the Mob, but why had I been arrested?

I tried to clear my head, to think straight, but there was just a dull aching void. There must be some memories left in there, a clue somewhere, surely? No, nothing but panic. I gazed around the grim, lonely cell, buried my aching head in my hands, and wept.

. . .

Later that day I was charged with possession of a banned substance with intent to supply, and resisting arrest "... and that's just for starters" the detective told me, producing the confiscated pipe and pouch full of seeds. It would do, for now, to hold me for a few days while they investigated allegations of further misdemeanours. He cautioned me ("it may harm your defence if you do not mention something which you later rely on in court ...") and asked if I had anything to say?

There wasn't much I *could* say about the first charge. The evidence was there on the table and I didn't bother to deny it, but resisting arrest...?

"That's bullshit, mate!" I told him. "It was you lot who used violence against *me* and I've got the bruises to prove it."

I pointed to the egg-sized lump on my forehead.

"I'll be going public with my complaints of police brutality as soon as I speak to the press and my lawyer ... and by the way, I demand that right immediately."

"No problem, all in good time Mr *Fraser*" the detective replied, "*if* that is indeed your real name ...*"

He gave me a searching stare.

"In the meantime, I suggest you take a look at the arresting officer's report."

He handed me a typed document.

"You'll notice it's been corroborated and countersigned by the other three officers who were present."

I read the report with a mix of dismay and anger. It claimed that following a tip-off from 'undisclosed sources' they'd been engaged in a surveillance operation at the luxury beach villa (which explained why they weren't in uniform). An unnamed informant (presumably one of the guests) had witnessed illegal drugs on the premises, so they decided to 'infiltrate' the party. They 'mingled with the revellers' for a while, and then observed the use of a banned substance. When challenged, the suspect (me) had been inebriated, incoherent, abusive, and aggressive. They'd used the minimum force necessary to restrain and arrest the suspect.

A doctor had apparently examined me at the police station and declared that I was under the influence of a psychedelic drug, suffering from paranoid delusions and hallucinations, but nothing much was wrong with me physically. The suspect had sustained a few minor cuts and bruises as a result of his 'lack of motor control', but he wasn't at risk of harming himself, and so had been detained in a cell to 'sleep it off.'

I told my interrogator their report didn't tally with the truth. They should speak to the other guests at the party—the mayor and the detective's own chief, for instance. They would, I'm sure, support me. Then I gave him my version of the facts:

"The mayor invited me to the villa to participate in discussions with a multinational pharmaceutical company about licensing the cactus. Discussions which could bring wealth and employment to the region."

The detective looked at me blankly.

"An executive from the company approached me, wanting to get first-hand experience of the Plant for research purposes."

I ignored his grin and continued my statement:

"We were peacefully enjoying the experience when four men grabbed me, dragged me outside, beat me, and threw me into an unmarked van."

He looked down at his notes and nodded—at least we agreed about the number of men that had beaten me up.

"They weren't in uniform and they didn't show me any ID. I assumed they were criminal thugs and that I was being taken hostage."

Another snigger. My statement seemed to be the most amusing thing he'd heard that year.

"I was heavily outnumbered so I offered no resistance. Their so-called 'minimum necessary force' involved punching me and hitting me with their batons."

He was trying to hold back actual laughter now.

"And I have absolutely no recollection of any doctor examining me!"

The detective was seized by ugly, rasping, guffaws, like a coughing fit.

"Well, yes, there you go mate" he spat back at me, when he'd regained his composure. "No recollection, you say? Obviously too out-of-it! Your version of the facts? As the doctor says: hallucinations and delusions."

I shook my head, sadly.

"And by the way, Mr *Fraser* ... (he smirked as he said my false name) ... we *have* interviewed other witnesses, including, as you correctly mentioned, my boss, and they broadly corroborate the arresting officer's account."

He sat back and stared at me smugly.

I tried to gather my thoughts and plan my defence. It seemed unlikely I could challenge their twisted version of events if it was corroborated by witnesses like the mayor and the chief of police. It was clear they were all in cahoots and out to get me. I decided to confront my fears there and then, rather than suffer endless anxious hours in my cell, so I demanded to be told about these allegations of "further misdemeanours".

My interrogator smiled—not a pretty sight. Whereas Mandu's smile lit up a room, this bastard's smirk turned out the light and extinguished all hope.

"Well now, where do we start?" he crowed. "Fraud, corruption, criminal negligence—all relating to your dodgy cactus enterprise ... (a glance at his notes) ... 'Dreamtime Plant Products.' Ha, that's a joke! Just the ticket for a domino dingo trying to sell Abo shit to druggies."

He dissolved in another fit of rasping laughter.

I ignored the racist abuse and stayed silent until he stopped cackling. Then I asked him for the details of these allegations. He replied with a formidable list, starting with the financial irregularities: tax fraud, improper accounting, bribery and corruption—all linked to the pharmaceutical deal. He continued with possible charges of criminal negligence arising from bad trips experienced by our customers (who'd done stuff like jump out of windows while believing they could fly). Then there were allegations (no doubt from Mr Nasty, the Great White drug shark) of misdemeanours in my past—crimes I may have committed using a different identity. Finally, a possible link to the suspicious death of a windsurfer down in Esperance six months ago that might well result in a manslaughter charge.

"These are all ongoing investigations, Mr *Fraser* ... (again the sinister emphasis on my assumed name) ... and plenty to be getting on with for the moment!" He sat back and smirked.

I was escorted back to the cell with much to think about.

The massive steel door slammed shut and I was alone again in the stark tiled room. I tried not to panic, but paranoia and self-loathing had me by the throat. I remembered how Mandu had warned me to be careful, to watch my back, but my ego had got in the way. I'd convinced myself that I'd fraternised with the right politicians, knew the right journalists, done deals with the right men-in-suits ... but *he* was the one who was right—I was sailing too close to the wind, flying too close to the sun. A fall from grace was inevitable.

The can had been prised open and the worms were wriggling around my brain, along with a lot more dodgy metaphors. I was clearly in some deep and smelly water, wading through all the shit that had previously just missed the fan. My chickens had come home to roost and now my goose was cooked—they would go well with the worms! Manic laughter filled the cell.

"Enough!" I shouted. My voice echoed down the corridor, jolting me back to my senses. I was losing the plot. I needed to think clearly and speak to my lawyer. But could I trust him? How could I be sure he wasn't one of *them*, a member of their syndicate?

Part of me, the rational bit that hadn't been addled by the Plant, was aware this was just another paranoid delusion, but I decided to keep my dealings with him on a need-to-know basis anyway. What I needed to know was: if I pleaded guilty to possession of a banned substance, could he get me out on bail?

Yes, he replied, when I was eventually allowed to speak to him, that might be possible. It would take some time and I would need to come up with the bond. I told him to speak to Mandu and take the money from Dreamtime Products' bank account. He gave me a blank look, so I reminded him that he'd met the tribal elder when the three of us had discussed strategy. He shuddered at the memory but assured me he'd do his best.

Moving on, he thought that with the appropriate plea bargaining it might be possible to persuade the police to drop the resisting arrest charge. They would, however, no doubt continue their ongoing investigations into my affairs and I should be prepared for a lengthy (and expensive) legal battle.

After a five-minute court appearance I was remanded in custody in the local prison to await a bail hearing. In theory that wasn't a complete disaster. A person on remand is not usually treated as a convicted prisoner. For instance, they should be able to wear their own clothes, have more visits, more rights ... that's the theory, anyway. In practice, it didn't work out like that. Not in *that* prison.

The long-termers were at the top of the hierarchy there and us remanders at the bottom of the heap. Our stay was limited—either we were judged innocent and walked out the front gate, or if convicted of something serious we moved on to the state prison. So whatever malevolence we had coming to us was administered as swiftly and harshly as possible.

What's more, qualities that had previously elevated me shoved me even lower down the ladder in there. I was young, good-looking, something of a local hero ... a prime target for 'tall poppy syndrome'—an Ozzie expression describing the tendency to distrust anyone too ambitious, the need to cut them down to size. The knives were definitely out for this particular poppy. My assumed name and mixed race identity didn't help either. As an activist and entrepreneur I'd used both to my advantage, but in prison they were further reasons to single me out for a beating.

So, I was the lowest of the low in there—a cockroach to be stamped on. I was beaten by the white guards because I'd sided with "them Abo bastards out in the bush", and by the black prisoners because they thought I'd sold out; picked on by everyone who thought I was a jumped-up poppy punk, and by anyone who hated Australia's former prime minister; and battered by those who simply loved violence and didn't need an excuse.

At first I tried fighting back, but I've never been good at that and it only made the beatings worse. At times I feared for my life, but I clung to survival as I had when I was drifting around the Atlantic.

The mental torture was just as bad. The windy season had started. I could hear the Fremantle Doctor blowing outside and watch the clouds scudding across the patch of sky visible through the bars. As a wind-surfer I'd taken my freedom for granted—I was as free as the wind. Now I was a prisoner, time and space were no longer my own, and it was agony.

I thought back to my time teaching the Cabarete kids to windsurf, the emotions I tried to communicate to them—the joy of harnessing the wind, living in the moment, feeling truly alive as you left your problems behind and blasted out towards the horizon. Locked up in a six-by-eight-foot cell I felt these things viscerally. They gnawed away at my soul. As the walls closed in around me I vowed never again to take my freedom and the ocean for granted.

It was a lonely, terrible time. Hours of bleak, fearful introspection waiting for them to grab me again, then minutes of violence, terror and pain. Several days of this nearly broke my spirit, as well as my body. I might have looked for a way to end my life, but thankfully there were lifelines I could cling to.

One of these was my memoir: 'Too Close to the Wind'. I'd started writing it in the Dominican Republic, chronicling my adventures with Robo and my survival story. There could hardly be a better time or place to update it. Following my fall from grace, I had plenty of new material and shitloads of time for scribbling.

Writing was an immersive activity. I got as much of a buzz from it as I did from windsurfing. Now it became a cathartic escape from the agonising confinement. I even found that composing passages in my head as I was being battered allowed me to escape from my body and the pain.

The other thing that saved me was going 'cold turkey'. Now that I could no longer take the Plant, the paranoia was finally under control. The delusions stopped, my head cleared, and I vowed never to touch psychedelic drugs again.

Best of all, it turned out that I needn't have worried about my lawyer. He was motivated more by money than malice, and he did as good a job as any of those greedy bastards ever do. After another brief appearance in court, I was released on bail.

As I walked out into the sunlight, free again for the moment, I was met by a posse of reporters yelling questions at me. My lawyer read a brief, non-committal statement on my behalf and then I was bundled into a chauffeur-driven limo with blacked-out windows.

There were two men in the back. One was the mayor. He nodded coldly to me and ordered the driver to get us out of there. For a moment I thought I was being abducted by the syndicate, then I realised the other bloke was Mandu. He was wearing his fancy court gear: dark suit and tie, and those shiny black shoes and socks. He giggled at my confused expression.

"G'day mate. Like I told ya—I scrub up OK when I need to. This time it was t'get ya out of jail. But the bastards still wouldn't let me stump up bail for ya, even if I weren't wearin' the bikin' gear. So I needed yer Head Honcho here ..."

The mayor shrugged, and explained the situation:

"Mr Mandu came to my office yesterday and asked me to help him get you released on bail. Apparently, the bond was not the problem. Luckily for you, a wealthy supporter offered to provide the funds for your guarantee (must be the Master, I thought to myself) ... because your company account has been frozen (a hint of a sly snigger). Anyway, the issue was one of credibility. Your lawyer advised that the bail bond should be lodged by a person of, ahem, *standing* in the community ..."

Mandu interrupted: "Rather than a bloody Abo! Even if he is the tribal elder and kitted out like a fuckin' tailor's dummy!"

"Whatever ..." the mayor continued, tetchily. "So I agreed to do what I could, because of your support for my election campaign, and because your case is generating a great deal of, ahem, *interest* ..."

He paused, and I could see why. The journalists outside the courtroom had shouted questions about shady goings-on at the luxury villa of one of the mayor's friends, rumours of dodgy deals, political shenanigans. The mayor was rattled. He wanted me out of the way, but the media attention made it difficult to gag me or keep me in prison for long.

"Anyway, because of the interest in your case, Malcolm, I wanted to demonstrate my commitment to the shared issues we brought to the wider public. Indigenous land rights for example ..."

Mandu chortled, and the mayor rattled on before he was interrupted again:

"So, I agreed to lend my credibility as a person of, ahem, *standing* in the community ... (an ostrich-like preening of feathers) ... to facilitate your *temporary* release from prison."

There was a slight emphasis on "temporary", as if articulating a subtle threat.

"But I have to say, albeit reluctantly you understand ... (he gave me his best 'reluctant-but-sincere' frown) ... that this is the last time I can be publicly associated with you, Malcolm. I shall, of course, expect you to reciprocate by keeping our conversations out of the public domain."

He preened and looked at me smugly, clearly expecting to be showered with gratitude. I shrugged. Was that a bribe or a threat? I asked myself. Probably a bit of each, so to be on the safe side I nodded deferentially, gave him the slightest of winks, and thanked him for giving us a lift. He tapped the chauffeur on the shoulder and asked him to stop the car. Mandu and I got out. The mayor drove off, and out of my life.

. . .

We were somewhere on the edge of town—somewhere empty, desolate, windy. The kind of street you expect to find tumbleweed blowing down. I gazed around, lost, wondering what to do next.

Then I spotted my camper-van. The rusty old VW splitty was parked there with my trusty wave-board sitting inside!

Mandu smiled, his dazzling smile the perfect response to my bewildered gawp.

"D'ya remember what I told ya when we met in the library?" he asked me.

Now it was my turn to smile as I recalled our extraordinary first conversation, tapping away on computer terminals.

"You said the Master sent me to help your people ..."

"Yeah, that's right, Nick. Well, it's mission accomplished and now it's time for ya t'move on."

He looked at me, that smile still tweaking the corners of his weathered face, the lines etched there like canyons in the desert.

Then it hit me—I was never going to see him again. This was our final conversation, the last time I'd see that smile. We'd come full circle and that's why he was talking about our first meeting.

I was overcome with regret. He was doing his best to end things on a high, but I'd let him down—I failed, miserably, to accomplish my mission and help his people. Suddenly I needed to turn back the clock and reboot our relationship:

"I wish I'd made a better fist of it, mate" I told him, surprised at the depth of sadness in my voice. "If I could start again I'd do things differently ..."

"Yeah, well I know we've 'ad our differences ..."

He paused, reflected, and moved on:

"We *are* different, Nick, but we're also the same. You're the domino dingo kid from the other side of town, and you're a bit mixed up because of it, but us Abos out in the bush could never 'ave sorted things with the Whitefella without someone like you t'help us."

I shrugged—a gesture of regret rather than modesty.

"When y'look back at what ya *did* do for us, y'might feel different."

"Like what?" I asked him, bitterly.

"We got our land back and we got the Plant protected by the Whitefella's law, just for us, as part of our *religion*."

He giggled as he spat out the last word and formed ironic air-quotes with his fingers, like a lawyer explaining slang to a judge. Seeing him do it dressed in his fancy court getup made it all the more amusing.

"For sure I never wanted nothin' t'do with the business of sellin' the Plant" he added, "but no worries. That's all over now, and I don't 'ave t'make that fuckin' journey into town every few days. The Bullet's knackered anyway, so I've been using that poncy Jap bike y'bought with *our* money. Hope that's alright with you?"

"No worries, mate!" I replied, creasing up. You had to hand it to him, the old fella had some cheek.

He looked at me and reverted to 'serious shaman' mode again. The smile might be temporally absent but the twinkle in his eyes was ever present.

"Like I say Nick, we've 'ad our differences, but yer still the only outsider I've ever taken to the cave. I want ya to remember what 'appened there, what y'saw, what y'learned."

I stared at him, drowning in those eyes.

"The Dreamtime, mate. It's not a story, it's reality. And it's in yer blood, Nick. Remember that when yer poncin' around like a pimp, playing *their* game."

I tore my eyes from his and gazed around, bewildered, like an abandoned child, wondering what was going to happen to me now, what to do, where to go next. Silence. Tumbleweed blew down the desolate, empty street ...

Then it hit me (the tumbleweed and the thought, simultaneously) —the wind was blowing! My friend, the Fremantle Doctor was there to heal me. The ocean was waiting. I was free again. There *was* hope!

He watched me smile, saw the look in my eyes as I gazed west, out to sea.

"D'ya remember me tellin' ya what my name, Mandu, means?"

"You told me it means: Sun."

His face lit up like his namesake.

"Remember me, Nick. When the darkness comes for ya, just remember me ..."

He embraced me and it was, indeed, like embracing the sun. I could feel his warmth, his energy. Light streamed from him, almost too bright to look at.

"So, this is it mate. G'bye Nick."

He handed me a package, along with my phone and the keys to the van. I took them from him and stared into those eyes, for the last time. Did I detect a smidgeon of sadness there? No way! The gnarly old shaman was laughing!

"I'm goin' t'join the Ancestors in the cave soon ... (I understood that he was talking about his death, and yet he was giggling) ... and y'know what, mate? ... (the laughter stopped and his eyes drilled holes into me) ... not many people know this ... (pause, enigmatic smile) ... some of 'em weren't from this planet!"

He paused, for a beat. Then he winked at me.

As I drove away it felt like I was waving goodbye to the heart and soul of the continent, the essence of the land, to Australia itself. Seeing him disappear in my rearview mirror was like watching an eclipse of the sun.

18

ON THE RUN

I drove for several hours in a trance, hardly aware of where I was heading. Anywhere south would do for now—anywhere, as long as it was away from that bloody town. Eventually, I pulled off the highway and opened the package Mandu had given me. Inside there was a passport, an airline ticket, and some cash—a mix of Australian dollars and euros, several thousand at a quick glance.

I examined the passport. It had my photo and the name: Brian Cowen. I smiled as I checked his occupation. This time, rather than English teacher, it was listed as 'public relations consultant'. So, the past eight months hadn't been wasted. I'd moved up in the world, and the Master had recognised my progress—because, of course, this was his doing. When I switched on my phone it was confirmed by a text. I read it with the familiar feeling that he was somehow there in the van with me, pulling my strings again.

Nick, by now you will be aware that I provided the funds for your bail, but I do not expect you to return to Broom. You must leave Australia forever, so I will never get my money back from the court. You now owe me AU$100,000.
This debt will be written off once you have accomplished your next

mission. It will be your final mission for me and the details will be revealed in due course.

As usual, the message ended with his initials: *A.A.L* and the date: *Wednesday, November 1, 2017.* I'd always wondered about the extra 'A' in those initials. I knew his name was Alejandro Langer—that strange combination of a Spanish first name and German surname, but I couldn't recall his middle name however hard I tried. Again I was left with the nagging feeling it was somehow significant—why else would he bother to include it?

I stared at the date. There was something significant about that as well. What was it? Of course, the first of November: *Día de Muertos*, the Day of the Dead. The year I'd spent with Nicole spanned from one of these macabre fiestas to the next. Now I realised my year in Australia had the same span—a bridge between two more of these decisive days. Today was terminal for my friendship with Mandu and any connections with my homeland; the end of the road for Malcolm Fraser, Australian entrepreneur, and a fresh start for Nick Kelly, as Brian Cowen, exile.

I looked at the ticket. Brian was booked on a one-way flight from Perth to Dublin on Friday morning at 08:00. Broom to Perth is 2,240 kilometres, about twenty-four hours driving, nonstop. I'd done four hours already and it was 4 pm on Wednesday afternoon, so it should be possible, with a couple of stopovers if I kept the pedal to the metal.

A few minutes Googling my new name revealed that it was again carefully chosen. I shared it with Ireland's fifteenth prime minister (2008 – 2011), or the 'Taoiseach' as they called him there. Unlike my previous Australian namesake, their bloke Brian was still alive, so there shouldn't be any "back from the grave" comments when I arrived in Dublin. But why on earth was I going *there* rather than London, as before? After all, the Master told me it was the "hub of his communications network".

Thinking about his mixed Spanish-German name toggled something else buried in my memory. Didn't he have some kind of Irish connection as well? I tried to unearth it, but I just couldn't remember what it was. Perhaps it would pop back into my mind once I stopped trying to drag it from the depths of my consciousness. Nothing is ever really forgotten, just the links in our neural network are temporally broken, like a badly constructed web site. Once we focus on something else they often repair themselves.

A closer inspection of the ticket revealed that Alejandro had again included my windsurfing board. He'd realised, some time ago, that I didn't go anywhere without her. I stared at the ticket and wondered about the windsurfing in Ireland. The waves were supposed to be world class and there were often storm-force winds. It was the most westerly edge of Europe, the Atlantic at its most extreme, and the conditions could be insane, 'sick' as we aficionados say. The more I thought about the destination on my ticket, the more excited I was to be going there, and there was another reason …

I had my own connection with the Emerald Isle. My mother's family had emigrated from there and my grandmother used to tell me stories about the "old country" when I was little. This journey would be another return to my roots—just as the past year had been a crash course in my Aboriginal cultural heritage.

Now I knew where I was heading and it was time to hit the road again. I rejoined the endless ribbon of tarmac that would take me to Perth and, ultimately, to the other side of the planet.

Several hours later I managed to piece together what I knew of the Master's Irish connection. The light was fading fast, but we were making good progress south, the VW maxed out at a steady 100 kph. I rounded one of the few curves on that supremely straight highway to find a six-truck road-train juggernaut bearing down on my defenceless little camper-van. As I swerved, cursing the bastard, I had one of those whole-life-flashing-before-you moments, and one of the details that flashed past was the missing link.

When I was aboard his yacht he'd told me how he left Argentina during the dictatorship of the 1970s to study and work as an academic in Europe. Now I remembered where—in Dublin, of course! He said that he'd been perfectly happy in Ireland—until he read his father's journal. It had "changed everything", as he put it, and he left his life in Dublin to continue his father's work. Now he was sending me back there. Why?

I had the uncomfortable feeling there were other links I was missing. Pieces of the jigsaw that linked Alejandro Langer, and his shadowy cult, with Ireland's dark history. Apart from the world class waves, the only other thing I knew about Ireland was that it was a divided country with a troubled past. Could this final mission have something to do with 'The Troubles'?

I pondered all this as I drove south. Mile after mile of black tarmac splitting the red desert. Hour after hour of emptiness. I'd been here before, moving in the opposite direction—travelling north, away from the catastrophe of Robo's death towards my meeting with Mandu. Now I was on the run again, escaping from my past, that familiar country, my homeland.

Wednesday, November 1, 24:00—midnight on the Day of the Dead—day one of my escape. I'd been driving for ten hours, with just a few breaks for fuel, food, and a little rest. I was too exhausted to go any further, so I pulled off the highway onto a dirt track and stopped for a few hours sleep.

It was there, in that remote, desolate place, that I had the idea. Closure. Time to end it all. After all, I wouldn't be coming back. This was goodbye Australia, for ever. Let's do the job properly this time— do what I should have done when I skedaddled the first time with Alison: cut the ties cleanly, instead of leaving a sticky mess behind. There were so many people after me, or a piece of me, and simply running away again was not the solution. I needed them to believe I was dead. I needed closure, or else I'd spend the rest of my life on the run.

My first thought was to leave the van parked up on a cliff with a suicide note inside. I started working on a rough draft in my head:

I've had enough. There's no future. I'm going to jump off this cliff (no that wouldn't work—no smashed-up body at the foot of the cliff) ... *I'm going for one last sail, into the darkness* (yes, that's more like it) ... *I want to disappear into the ocean.*

Not bad. It might just work if the note was convincing enough. But then I had a better idea. I thought about the time I disappeared from El Médano—the day I should have drowned. My pursuers had no intention of leaving me to Rest In Peace until they stood over my grave, but I hadn't given them that satisfaction. Instead, the ocean and a severed universal joint had intervened and cut the ties for me. They never found my body or my board. There was no note, but I gave them a broken rig to think about. I left Nick Kelly's passport in the apartment, became Malcolm Fraser, and simply vanished.

Of course, none of that had been planned, but it had worked. When no body turned up most people assumed I was at the bottom of the Atlantic or in some lucky shark's stomach. The story died and I was soon just a ghost again. That was the way to do it. Closure.

Thursday, November 2, 06:00—day two of my Great Escape. I woke at dawn. As the sun rose out of the desert I said goodbye to the emus, galahs and kangaroos; to that ancient red land, my homeland. Then I rejoined the highway and drove south, towards the horizon, towards the next chapter of my life.

Again I maxed out the VW for ten straight hours, hardly stopping for more than a few minutes until we reached Geraldton. I was shattered, but elated at having broken the back of my final epic Ozzie road trip.

It was around 16:00 when I arrived at Point Moore, the location of one of WA's classic windsurfing spots—the aptly named 'Hell's Gates', a left-hander that breaks fast and can hold a huge swell. Not for the faint-hearted. A locals' spot. A connoisseur's wave.

The Doctor was blowing twenty-five knots and a good crowd had skived off work that afternoon. Some knew me vaguely and nodded g'day as I rigged up, but nobody seemed keen to get closer. Perhaps they were discouraged by my intense expression. Anyway, it was fine by me—I'd always been known as a bit of a loner.

Once we hit the water the vibe was more friendly, super relaxed, party time. The conditions were excellent and everyone was firing on all cylinders, whooping and waving, sharing waves, cheering each other's moves. My last session in home water was as memorable as it needed to be. We would all remember that day.

As the fiery sun sank into the ocean everyone else packed up. I sat there, next to my still rigged kit, gazing out to sea, receiving curious looks. The wind was dying, dusk was descending, and the looks became concerned. One of the last stragglers asked me what I was doing? Why wasn't I de-rigging and coming to the pub with them?

"No worries, mate" I told him, "I'm going to have a sunset session, without the crowds, just me and the sharks ..."

I allowed my voice to tail off into an uneasy silence and gave him a particularly intense stare—an expression I was sure he'd remember. He shook his head, shrugged, and half-heartedly warned me to be careful, clearly deciding I was beyond help. They left me sitting there alone, in near darkness.

A few hours passed until I was sure they weren't coming back and nobody was arriving for a spot of late-night fishing. There was no moon that night and everything looked good for my plan. I removed the rig from my board and attacked the UJ with a knife and some gusto.

After an hour's work the UJ had been significantly distressed and no longer deserved the accolade: 'universal'. As Monty Python might have put it: it was an ex-UJ. It had gone to meet its maker, suffered catastrophic failure and was in two pieces. I left one piece attached to the mast extension, buried the other piece in the sand, and chucked the rig into the shore-break.

I was in luck—a combination of the offshore night-breeze and a strong rip current took it out to sea. I watched as it disappeared into the blackness, feeling liberated. The sail was old and battered, well past its sell-by date. Now it was ancient history, along with Malcolm

Fraser. I left his passport in the camper-van and became Brian Cowen.

Leaving the VW splitty was harder. We'd covered a lot of ground together, seen the good times roll, and been to hell and back. Now it was time to say goodbye. One of the locals would find the empty van parked there and call the coastguard. My rig would be washed in down the coast, or be spotted by a fishing boat, or from the air. When they discovered the broken UJ Malcolm Fraser would be classified as missing, presumed drowned. Closure.

Thursday, 22:00. I packed a few essential possessions in my backpack, leaving everything else behind. Mandu had stashed Nicole's painting of us: 'The Kangaroo Kid and his Voodoo Child' in the van. He'd told me it would somehow protect me and I was beginning to think he was right. Regardless of any magical powers, it meant the world to me. I strapped it to the rucksack, still rolled up in a piece of old sail-cloth. Then I packed my wave-board in its fancy board-bag with wheels and set off on foot.

I'd initiated the first part of the vanishing act, but it wouldn't be complete until I'd boarded the plane as Brian Cowen. Somehow I had to get to Perth airport leaving no trace of Nick Kelly along the way. That would be tricky. If I took a bus somebody would be sure to remember the scruffy mixed-race bloke with his coffin bag. Same if I hitchhiked. There was a solution, but it involved breaking the law again. So what? I thought, as I trudged along the deserted highway. I'm already a criminal on the run, an outlaw, like my namesake: Ned Kelly. What did I have to lose?

A couple of hours later, around midnight, I found what I was looking for: a farm, in darkness, with several vehicles parked in the yard. I got lucky when the second one I tried, a rusty old pickup truck, proved to be unlocked. I chucked my board in the back and hot-wired the ute, calling on skills from my misspent youth. A dog was barking as I drove out of the yard, but no lights came on in the house.

. . .

Friday, 00:05—day three of the Great Escape. My flight was due to leave at 8 am, so I had about six hours to do the last 440 k's to Perth, dispose of the ute, and get myself to the airport in time. I drove nonstop, thrashing that ancient truck to the limit, light-headed from sleep deprivation, dangerously free.

I reached the suburbs of Fremantle at around five-thirty in the morning. It was still dark and I had no trouble finding a suitably deprived location (or "daggy shithole" as my mates would say) to torch the ute—an auto graveyard where it would be just one more burnt-out truck. Then I hopped on the bus to the airport.

It was 06:00 now and there were only a few passengers—tourists speaking a variety of languages, about to disappear, like me, to far-flung corners of the planet. They paid no attention to another back-packer with his surfboard.

I arrived at the airport with my well-travelled board-bag, a ruck-sack, and a whole lot of anxiety. I hadn't slept for thirty hours and it was catching up with me. I was exhausted, disoriented, almost as if I'd been smoking the Plant again. So far my escape had gone to plan, but it could all go wrong at the last hurdle. Checking in could well prove to be the stumbling-block and paranoia was gnawing at me again. The Master may have taken care of everything, but I was carrying plenty of excess baggage in my head.

As it turned out, there were no issues with the ticket, passport, or my new identity, but it left me wondering who the hell I was now. I'd returned to Australia as Malcolm Fraser and I was leaving it as Brian Cowen. Somewhere along the way Nick Kelly, the Domino Dingo, the Kangaroo Kid, had grown up, become a contender, and suffered a spectacular fall from grace. I'd hit rock bottom and now I was a convict escaping from this land of convicts, my homeland. This land might be your land, but it was no longer *my* land. It was time to turn the page and start a new chapter.

19

FLIGHT

Perth Airport. Friday, November 3, 2017, 08:15. The plane took off and a new chapter began. I was moving on. I knew *where* I was going—the destination on my ticket said: Dublin, but it wasn't clear who, or what, was waiting for me there. I settled into my seat as we began the journey out over the Indian ocean. The flight to the other side of the world took a whole day and night—plenty of time to ponder these questions. Right then I needed to catch up on some sleep.

I reclined the seat and was just drifting into blissful unconsciousness when I was jolted awake by a tap on my shoulder. Irritated, I opened my eyes expecting it to be one of the staff. Instead, I found another passenger had occupied the seat beside me. As I looked up I was astonished to lock eyes with the captain of the Master's yacht, Pablo Rodrigues Vasquez. Without a word, he handed me a package.

I stared at him, trying to make sense of his presence. It was as if he'd just been teleported onto the plane, 'beamed aboard' like a character from 'Star Trek' and materialised in the seat next to me. Questions jostled for space in my brain, vying to be the first out of my mouth. The winner dribbled out:

"What the hell are you ..."

He silenced me with a finger to his lips, shaking his head like a deaf-mute advising that conversation was futile, and pointed to the package, motioning me to open it. Then he reclined his seat and closed his eyes.

I sat there for a while, staring out of the window, sneaking occasional glances at Pablo. There wasn't much to see in either direction —clouds, glimpses of water far below, and Pablo's serenely composed features, enigmatic, like a bearded Buda. He was already asleep and I was desperate to join him, but curiosity overcame exhaustion. I opened the package and found seventy pages of typed A4. The title page was familiar, and I was relieved to see that it had already been translated into English:

The Journal of Dr Ludwig Langer, Psychotherapist.
An Account of his Life, Experiments in Morality, and Research into the
Human Condition.
Translated by his son: Alejandro Aidan Langer

The cogs turned slowly in my tired brain and eventually meshed in a moment of cognition. Now I knew what the other 'A' in the Master's initials stood for, but it made him an even stranger mix: German father, Argentine mother, and perhaps some kind of Irish connection to explain Aidan?

I began reading Dr Langer's journal, silently thanking A.A.L for saving me from spending the rest of the flight struggling through seventy pages of German text. The first few pages were familiar—I'd already read extracts on the Master's website. A few hours later I'd reached page thirty-five and was fast asleep. In between, the journal filled in the historical background, explained Dr Langer's theories, and took me to the halfway point in his incredible life-story.

He begins with an account of his studies with Carl Jung, in Zurich. It's an exciting time for him. Ludwig is in his late twenties, and Jung opens up a brave new world of ideas. His fellow students are a gifted bunch—some of the brightest young minds of their day. Together they explore the frontiers of their mentor's intellectual universe and are soon taking his ideas far further than he'd envisaged. Their discussions form the theoretical framework for the Group (it's always written with a capital 'G' in Alejandro's English translation).

Langer is one of the founding members, and their archivist. He documents their history and their ambitions—nothing less than the evolution of our species to the 'next level': Nietzsche's '*Übermensch*'. He describes how they develop their own system of morality, a new way of living and working together, an alternative to conventional society—what we might now call an 'alternative lifestyle'. By 1932 (and page ten) the Group is well established, with Langer as their leader—although he accepts the role reluctantly:

Of course, we all wanted Carl (Jung) to lead the Group, but he declined. This was disappointing, but he has his position in society and his reputation to protect, while we are unencumbered by such responsibilities. Eventually, it became clear he considers our views and behaviour to be too "experimental".

The Group gradually distances themselves from Jung's circle, both theoretically and, in 1933, physically—moving their base from Switzerland to Germany. When the National Socialist party begin to dominate German politics they find themselves increasingly marginalised.

By the mid-1930s intellectuals must confront a crucial dilemma: whether to collaborate with the Nazis and function within their system or oppose their repugnant ideology. Some choose the path of least resistance—a charge that has been levelled at Jung himself, others leave the country, a few stay to fight the propaganda and perish. Langer's Group abandon mainstream society altogether, establishing what might now be called a 'commune' in the Bavarian countryside. He writes at length about this moral dilemma, and throughout the period (1933 – 1939) the journal is full of prescient anxiety:

I fear for my country when so many of my fellow writers, thinkers, and artists turn a blind eye to what is happening. I wonder how these sympathisers can sleep at night as they observe our homeland being overrun by fascists. Perhaps they have no contact with anyone outside their own 'racially pure' Aryan tribe, but the Group actively embraces other cultures. We welcome members who are Jewish, as well as other diverse ethnicities.

Sometimes Langer adopts a more relaxed, anecdotal style—especially when he's writing about one of these ethnically diverse Group members. It becomes clear, within the first page of meeting her in the journal, that she's someone special for him:

In the spring of 1931 a young Irish woman, Caitlin O'Connor, arrived in Zurich to study with Jung. Caitlin was only twenty-one when we met, ten years younger than me, but she was already a talented artist, writer, and one of Carl's brightest students.
She is also one of the most strikingly beautiful women I have ever been fortunate to meet: tall, slender, jet black hair contrasting wonderfully with translucent, pale skin. She has a certain Celtic wildness about her, and she carries herself with a confidence that belies her years.
She commandeered one of the communal rooms, set up her studio, and began running painting workshops with an enthusiasm that is, frankly, a breath of fresh air here in stuffy old Zurich! She is a free spirit, questioning everything, and she soon became a valued member of our Group.

Ludwig is obviously besotted with this beguiling young Irish woman, and it seems to be a case of 'opposites attract' …

In some ways, she is a more radical thinker than myself and we disagree about many things, but the mutual respect between us has become a closer bond. We have had many heated discussions, often stemming from her revolutionary political convictions. She has

studied Marx and Lenin's socialist theories and believes passion-
ately that the world's wrongs can be righted by the correct ideology,
whereas I look for salvation within the individual's psyche, as
argued by Nietzsche.

Even though each of us rejects religion, agreeing with Nietzsche
that God is dead, we are both products of our cultural heritage. She
was raised in a staunchly Catholic family, the middle child of six.
The whole family attended mass religiously and Caitlin was
educated by nuns in a convent school. I was born into a strict
Protestant family, the only son of a Lutheran preacher who laid
down the law.

Our arguments, and personalities, often seem to reflect these
archetypal extremes: Caitlin's flamboyant Catholic excess versus
my puritanical Protestant restraint.

So much for the opposites, now he succumbs to her attractions:

From the moment I met Caitlin, I was struck by her fierce intelli-
gence, physical beauty, and inner strength. My respect for her only
increased when she told me about her humble origins.

She was born in 1910 in a tiny, remote village on the Dingle
peninsular—a rocky headland jutting out into the Atlantic on the
wild west coast of Ireland. Her family struggled to eke out an
existence with subsistence farming, fishing, and foraging.

Growing up she barely had enough to eat, but she managed to
escape from the prison of poverty by the sheer force of her intel-
ligence.

To their credit, the nuns who schooled her realised that she might be
capable of great things and encouraged her to continue her educa-
tion. They helped her to win a scholarship and attend the Univer-
sity of Dublin—the first student from the convent who had ever
managed this.

My roots might not be quite as deprived as Caitlin's, but her story
resonated with me. We both managed to escape from poverty and a

miserable future by becoming the first of our tribe to go to university. Education is a great leveller for people like us.

Ludwig's next entry reveals that Caitlin and I shared something else—a love of the ocean and a need to be close to her:

> *Caitlin often speaks of what she misses most in her new life: the*
> *wild sea, the surf, the beach where she used to take long walks:*
> *Brandon Bay. It was her solace when life became intolerable; her*
> *special place, where she could be alone to think.*

So, she was clearly a kindred spirit—someone who understood the true meaning of that modern cliché: 'life's a beach'.

Her birthplace also struck a chord with me—the Dingle peninsular. Where had I come across that evocative name? Of course, in a windsurfing magazine! Her 'special place', Brandon Bay, was the location for one of the notorious Red Bull 'Storm Chase' events, in which a select group of the world's best, most hardcore wave-sailors seek out and compete in the most extreme conditions the planet can produce. I closed my eyes and pictured the majestic, empty beaches (reminding me of those in Esperance), wild weather, epic waves ...

An hour had passed since we'd taken off. We were thirty thousand feet above the Indian Ocean and I'd read twenty pages of the journal. Pablo and most of the other passengers were asleep. I was exhausted, but the story of Ludwig Langer and Caitlin O'Connor had me hooked. I returned to the manuscript and read on ...

As I'd guessed, their story is about the attraction of opposites. Ludwig is captivated by Caitlin's wild nature, but he doesn't share her love of the ocean or her obsession with politics:

> *Caitlin is passionately committed to the struggle against British rule*
> *in her homeland. She believes that the island of Ireland should be*
> *an independent republic and that political violence is necessary to*
> *achieve that goal. Politics and violence are alien to me, but her*

*ancestors have suffered hundreds of years of British conquest. Resis-
tance and rebellion are in her blood.*
*In April 1916, when Caitlin was six years old, the Easter Rising took
place. Members of the Irish Volunteers and Irish Citizen Army
seized the centre of Dublin, proclaimed a republic, and held off
British forces for almost a week. Although only a child, she remembers how the execution of the Rising's leaders was the talk of her
village. It led to a surge of support for republicanism and the forma-
tion of a local brigade of the Irish Republican Army.*

Langer goes on to explain that Caitlin was never openly a
member of the IRA—she's too astute, but he suspects she's working
for them covertly. As a staunchly apolitical pacifist this worries him,
but by the time his suspicions are confirmed, it's too late—they're
in love ...

*In 1935 Caitlin invited me to travel to Ireland with her to witness
the struggle at first hand. We spent several weeks in Dublin—
meeting prominent activists, writers, and artists, attending political
rallies, doing a great deal of talking and, I have to confess, drinking
a lot of the local stout. The Irish are a vibrant people, excellent
company, and quite fond of these latter two pursuits.*
*Later, we travelled to the rural west coast to visit her family. The Dingle
peninsula is just as beautiful as Caitlin described it, and as beautiful as
she herself is. We spent many happy hours walking the length of
Brandon Bay, her 'special place', and it was there that we fell in love.*
*As I listen to her stories of poverty, famine and ruthless exploitation
by the colonial oppressors, I began to understand her people and
their struggle to survive on this extreme frontier, where Europe
vanishes into the Atlantic rollers. I am sympathetic, a Republican
sympathiser, but I find it impossible to condone violence.*

Over the following pages, Ludwig describes how Caitlin makes
regular trips back to her homeland. As her involvement in the armed

struggle deepens and the political situation in Germany worsens, he becomes increasingly anxious about their future ...

We both abhor the National Socialist thugs who have taken over my country, but Caitlin tells me: "whoever is the enemy of your enemy is your friend, or at least, your ally". She means that Irish Republicans share a common enemy with the Nazis—the British. I fear the IRA may already be collaborating with Hitler, negotiating an invasion of Northern Island, and that Caitlin may be involved in these negotiations. Of course, she denies this, and my feelings for her prevent me from being objective.
My love for her is like a noose around my neck, choking the breath of reason. I fear for us, for her country, and I fear for my own, as the waves of hatred gather.

As the decade progresses towards the inevitable conflict, Ludwig's journal entries become ever more desperate. At least he manages to find some solace in their love and as darkness is about to descend over Europe there's a chink of light ...

Christmas 1938—Caitlin has just discovered she is pregnant! She told me as we sat down to celebrate Christmas Day with the Group. It was a joyful way to mark a day neither of us feels a connection with. However, just as Catholics and Protestants unite to celebrate the birth of their prophet, so we joined with our fellow travellers to toast this new life. If only the rest of the Christian world could unite against the evil that seems intent on overrunning Europe and smashing the continent to pieces.

As he fears, it's not long before war is declared, but as the armies prepare to fight each other to the death, a new life, and fresh hope is born:

On September 1, 1939 the Nazis invaded Poland. Subsequently,

*France and the United Kingdom issued declarations of war on
Germany.*

*The very next day, Saturday, September 2, our relationship was
blessed with a son. Our son! He is a light in the darkness that
threatens to destroy our lives.*

*Caitlin insisted on travelling home to Ireland for the birth and I
accompanied her. Neither of us required our love to be encumbered
with a conventional marriage ceremony, so he was born out of
wedlock. Of course, her tightly knit Catholic community did not
approve of this, but she won back some goodwill by giving our son
her father's first name: Martyn. For his middle name, we chose her
grandfather's, which is also the name of her special place. And we
decided that given his place of birth, and the uncertainty
surrounding our situation in my homeland, he would take her
surname and be Irish, rather than German.*

So, we named our son: Martyn Brandon O'Connor.

I put Dr Langer's manuscript down at this point and gazed out of
the window. There was still nothing to be seen, but several thousand
kilometres of that nothingness had passed beneath us while I'd been
engrossed in the journal. I'd reached page thirty-five, the halfway
point, and there was a lot to digest.

Pablo was still sleeping soundly in the next seat. There was much
I wanted to ask him, but it would have to wait. I closed my eyes and
allowed myself to drift into blissful unconsciousness.

Several hours later I was again woken by a tap on my shoulder. This
time it *was* a member of the crew. Pablo and I opened our eyes and
the flight attendant served us lunch (or perhaps it was breakfast, or
maybe supper—I didn't have a clue). Eventually, he broke the
silence:

"*¿Quieres una cerveza, señor* Nick?"

I smiled, relieved the deaf-mute act was over. Perhaps I might get
some answers now, and yes, a beer would be most welcome.

"*Sí, por favor, gracias Pablo, pero* ... Do you mind if we speak English?"

"OK, Nick. I hope you are resting a little now, but please to tell to me: what are you thinking about the journal?"

"Well, I've only read half of it. I just reached the point where Caitlin has a baby son, Martyn—he must be the Master's half-brother, no?"

Pablo nodded.

"So, what happened to him?"

"Ah, that is a good question, Nick ..."

A pause.

"And ...?" A voice-in-my-head demanded.

"You must finish the story, and then this is becoming clear."

I looked at him sceptically.

"No, I promise. It is becoming clear when you finish the journal."

Another pregnant pause. I ate my plastic airline meal, sipped my beer, and wondered if he'd say more. Eventually, he did:

"Also ... this is explaining why we are going to Dublin."

I let that sink in for a moment. It seemed unlikely there'd be any further 'explaining' until I'd finished Dr Langer's journal, so I tried a different tack:

"Tell me about yourself, Pablo. How did you come to work for Alejandro, and what's your role in his Group?"

He shrugged, but I continued probing:

"I was under the impression that you're the captain of his yacht, but one year ago you pop up in the transit lounge at Heathrow airport, and the next—here you are escorting me from Australia to Ireland ... You seem to spend a lot of time in the air, for a seafaring man?"

He grinned, not a gesture I'd seen from him often.

"Is true, Nick. I am master of the Abyss when the Master is not aboard. Other times he is sending me on missions everywhere he cannot go to. I'm like a ... how-you-say ... a mister ..."

He looked at me for help as he struggled to find the appropriate English expression.

"?" A shrug from me. Then he found the description he was looking for:

"... a Mister Fix-it!"

Now it was my turn to smile. I liked Pablo. He was an amiable bloke and I felt at ease with him in a way I never did with his boss.

"When you return to Australia last year, Alejandro send me there to keep the eyes on you—is that correct, my English?"

"Not really" I muttered. Now I wasn't quite as relaxed about Mr Fix-it. So, he'd been spying on me for the past year and keeping Big Brother updated. He sensed my unease and did his best to reassure me:

"No worries Nick ... (he said this with such a ridiculous imitation of an Ozzie accent that, against my will, my face creased into another smile) ... the Master is pleased with you. I am in Perth when you give evidence to the politicians ..."

I interrupted him, astonished: "You mean you were at the legalisation hearing? I didn't see you there."

"I am wearing ... how-you-say ... a dress? No, *no es correcto ... un disfraz ...*" He looked at me for a translation.

"A disguise?"

"*¡Sí!* I am wearing disguise, but this no matter. I tell Alejandro what you say to the important peoples, how you say it to them ... and he very happy, you know? He say you are learning how to change the world."

He had me smiling again now, but I had to put him straight:

"Well, Pablo, I tried my best, but it wasn't good enough to change *anything*, and in the end it all went pear-shaped."

"*¿Qué?* I no understand. Why this fruit?"

He gave me a look of such comical confusion that I struggled to keep a straight face. But he'd understood the gist of what I'd said:

"OK, yes, I know what happen. You go to prison, no?"

I nodded, ruefully.

"The Master, he send me with money for your friend, Mr Mandu. Money to get you out of jail. And I buy tickets—for us, travel to Dublin."

"Ah, I see. Well, I suppose I should thank you. *Muchas gracias señor* Fix-it."

He looked at me with genuine warmth, clinked my glass with his own, and replied, in his indomitably comic version of my own accent: "Cheers. No worries, mate!"

I just couldn't hold back the laughter this time, and he joined me. The two of us collapsed in giggles, and the besuited business men around us pretended not to be appalled.

20

MISSING PIECES

W e were in mid-air—halfway through the twenty-four hour flight to Dublin. I was halfway through Dr Ludwig Langer's journal, but no nearer to understanding why I was going there. It was like trying to solve a jigsaw puzzle with half the pieces missing. Pablo insisted they could all be found in the journal. It was certainly fascinating reading, and it explained the historical context, but what did it have to do with me? I needed more information to complete the picture.

Over the next couple of hours, as we sank a few more beers, I probed him about the Master's modern version of his father's Group: how it functioned, his role in it, and how I fitted in. Pablo told me it included influential writers, scientists, philosophers, artists, and wealthy entrepreneurs—likeminded individuals sharing knowledge across disciplines. Their aim was to fulfil Dr Langer's ideals—the evolution of human society to the next level. They were distributed all over the planet, communicating and collaborating online. Apart from Alejandro and himself, I'd already met two other members: Nicole and Mandu—the Master called them his 'shamans'.

My throat was dry now. I gulped down the rest of my beer and ordered another. Pablo had reawakened my paranoia by mentioning

Nicole. I told him the Group sounded like a religious cult, an elite secret society like the Freemasons, a clandestine political party ... I even mentioned the Knights Templar. I'd been groomed and then lured into the cult by forming a close relationship with a 'teacher', who'd then been snatched away, to leave this poor sucker waiting for the next carrot to be dangled.

Pablo laughed off my comparisons, scoffed at my paranoia, and tried his best to reassure me:

"Not true, Nick. This in your mind only. You must not worry about Alejandro. He not a *bad* man. That *no es correcto, ¿entiendes?*"

I tried not to shrug, but he could see that I wasn't convinced.

"The Master, he is *above* good and evil. Ah, my English is so bad. I cannot explain this ..."

He tailed off in frustration, but I understood him. If anybody could persuade me of the Master's integrity it was Pablo. It was hard to imagine anyone grooming *him*. He didn't seem to have the kind of brain that could be easily washed. He wasn't interested in grand ideas, just focussed on practical matters—the Group's Mr Fix-it, indeed. But he still hadn't allayed my doubts about my current mission:

"I'm sorry Pablo, but I *am* worried about this trip to Ireland. Why are we going there?"

He pointed to the journal, but I needed answers:

"Alejandro said this would be my 'final mission' and it would clear my debts to him. I'm scared that I'll have to do something extreme—like maybe even kill someone, assassinate someone important ... ?"

There, I'd said it! It had been nagging at me ever since he sent me that text.

"—" A long pause, pregnant with possibilities. He picked up the journal, handed it to me, reclined his seat, and closed his eyes again.

I sighed. So many pieces of the jigsaw were still missing. I could only hope that Pablo was being straight with me and that Dr Langer would complete the picture before we got to Dublin. I turned to page thirty-six, and continued reading from where I'd left off ...

.   .   .

Ludwig and Caitlin return to Germany with their newborn son, Martyn, to find a country at war—with the rest of Europe and with the 'enemies within': Jews, Socialists, Nonconformists, anyone not prepared to bow, scrape, and salute der Führer and his Swastika.

The Group have always been outsiders, shunned by conventional society, but now, in the Third Reich, they're considered dangerous deviants. What's more, their baby son, born illegitimately outside the Fatherland, has no rights to citizenship. Langer wants them to go into hiding, perhaps even to leave Germany for ever. He begs Caitlin to consider moving back to Ireland, but she has work to do in Berlin:

> *May 1940. Caitlin is in Berlin again, acting as translator for Seán Russell, chief of staff of the IRA. They are meeting Hitler's aids to seek help from them and, I fear, planning a Nazi-sponsored revolution in her homeland.*
>
> *But then events intervene. On his way back to Ireland in a U-boat, Russell becomes ill and dies. Caitlin suspects foul play. She no longer trusts the Nazis and, belatedly, she is finally realising there can be no collaborating with these monsters. The terrible reality of what they are doing to the Jews is becoming clearer day by day. Now Caitlin has decided they are even more despicable than the British and she must devote all her energies to fighting them. I am trying to restrain her, to counsel caution for the sake of our son. I implored her to escape while we still could, but she has the heart and soul of a revolutionary. There is nothing I can say to change her mind. She will not run away, but perhaps I can persuade her to hide Martyn, at least. I am very afraid for us.*

Ludwig and Caitlin take refuge in the commune, hoping they'll be left alone. For a while they are. Three years pass and it seems they may survive the conflict that's raging all around them. But the Nazis are well aware of Langer's Group. The only way they'll tolerate these dangerous deviants is by appropriating his research for their own evil ends. They've always been fans of Nietzsche's ideas, or more accurately: his sister's distorted revisions of the great philosopher's work, so they are naturally attracted to Langer's search for the *Übermensch*, the 'Superman' who is beyond Good and Evil. Now they order him to perform experiments on the prisoners in their concentration camps. If he refuses he'll become an inmate himself. Langer agonises over this moral dilemma ...

*Monday, July 5, 1943. I received an official letter from the RMVP—
the letter I have been dreading.*
(Here Alejandro adds a footnote with the full German title: 'Reichsministerium für Volksaufklärung und Propaganda' and the chilling English translation: the Reich Ministry of Public Enlightenment and Propaganda).
It informed me that they are taking control of my research. From now on, all my experiments with psychoactive substances etcetera will be conducted under 'laboratory conditions' in the 'controlled environment' of the 'correctional facilities' at Dachau and Auschwitz. I will be provided with a plentiful supply of 'suitable subjects' (chosen from the Jews and dissident political prisoners interned there) and the results of these experiments will be published as official government documents.
If I do not agree to this, there will be serious consequences for myself and the Group. Instead of conducting these experiments voluntarily, as a member of staff, I (and presumably other Group members) will become a 'permanent resident' at one of the camps and forced to conduct my research 'under strict supervision'. The implications of this are quite clear.
What should I do? They have me trapped in the straight-jacket of a dilemma. If I agree, they will steal my life's work. I will be forever labelled a collaborator and a coward. If I refuse, they will imprison me, and then what will happen to Caitlin and our son?
I realised today that, unlike Caitlin, I am not a hero. I want to survive more than I want to make a grand moral stand. Perhaps this is a betrayal of my ideals, but all I want is to be left alone to continue my work. If that makes me a coward then so be it.

Reading this, I had a great deal of sympathy for Ludwig. I asked myself the same questions: what is more important, survival or morality? How far would *you* go to survive? Like him, I would probably choose to be a survivor rather than a hero—so did that make us cowards?

For me, he's not a worse person than Caitlin. He's caught up in a situation he can't control. He just wants to be left in peace to explore his personal space (no wonder Alejandro called his father a prototype hippie), but he finds himself in the wrong place at the wrong time—a familiar location for me! Others might judge him as morally weak, or a coward, but I was in no position to make those kinds of judgements.

From page fifty the journal becomes increasingly harrowing. Ludwig and Caitlin disagree fundamentally over the solution to Langer's 'straight-jacket of a dilemma' and it destroys their relationship ...

> *I can see no way out of this. No chance to escape now. In my*
> *despair I contemplated ending it all. For a while, suicide seemed the*
> *only solution. But when I suggested it, Caitlin was disgusted with*
> *me. For her the only honourable course of action is resistance. I*
> *asked her if this justified abandoning our son? She looked me in the*
> *eye and told me that yes, for her it does!*
> *I cannot accept this. However courageous her stance, it cannot*
> *justify a mother abandoning her child. Surely survival overrules*
> *political correctness?*

I grimaced at Langer's use of the expression 'political correctness', which has become so diluted in modern times. My sympathies were with Ludwig rather than Caitlin. The path he chooses now seemed to me to be the only way out of this moral maze:

> *I told her that the least disastrous option (the lesser of two evils)*
> *was to agree to the Nazis demands, for the sake of our son, but to do*
> *everything in my power to help the inmates in the camps, to ease*
> *their pain as best I can. I will undertake these experiments, give*

psychoactive substances to the prisoners, and monitor the results.
But I will offer it to them as an escape from the horror of their lives
in Dachau and Auschwitz.
Perhaps this research might even advance my ultimate goal: that
these mind-altering substances may one day be used as powerful
medicines, possibly contributing to the eradication of mental disor-
ders, and perhaps even leading to enormous advances in society.

Unfortunately, Caitlin doesn't share Ludwig's optimism. For her, his choice of survival over resistance and his pragmatic strategy are quite simply cowardice:

Caitlin accused of me of being a coward and we argued violently.
Our relationship is being torn apart day by day. She no longer loves
or respects me. If it wasn't for our son I think she would take a gun
and shoot me as a Nazi collaborator!
For the past six months, she has been working with an underground
resistance movement, hiding Jews in the commune and helping
them reach safety via a network of safe houses. She has been
responsible for saving dozens of escapees and she is a hero, but it has
put her life, and our son's safety, at grave risk.
Eventually, we came to an agreement. I gave her my word that I
would try to escape with Martyn to Ireland if she is no longer able
to look after him. I must take him to her family, where he will grow
up in a safe, loving community, as she did. I made this solemn
promise with dread in my heart.

I'd reached page fifty-six now and Ludwig's manuscript had me gripped. Tension has been building steadily over the previous few pages and now I'd reached the climax. Tragedy seeks out Ludwig and Caitlin with awful inevitability. The date of his next entry is significant:

Monday, November 1, 1943. A day I will never forget …

That decisive, terminal day again: the Day of the Dead—the end of the road for Ludwig and Caitlin ...

The Gestapo arrived at our commune to arrest Caitlin. The officer in charge handed me a warrant with her name on it. There was no mention of Martyn, but I feared for him when I heard them talking about her "illegal bastard child". Caitlin distracted them with her courage and defiance—questioning their authority and insisting that the warrant is for her, and her alone.

Luckily there were several children playing together, and our little Marty blended in with his blue eyes and blond hair. It is ironic how inheriting my Aryan genes, rather than his mother's Celtic looks, saved him.

There was nothing I could do to save her, though. As they dragged her away she shouted at me, accusing me of betraying my ideals, collaborating with these monsters to save my own skin. I was filled with despair and guilt. She is the hero. I am a coward.

The soldiers escorted her to their vehicle and threw her inside, brutally. I dare not think about what they will do to her. I must be strong—for Marty.

Caitlin looked into my eyes—a look I will carry with me to my grave. There were tears in my eyes, but not in hers—just defiance, courage, and ultimately, resignation.

"Don't forget what you promised, Ludwig" she said, calmly but firmly, reminding me of my responsibility for our son's survival. Then, as she was taken away: "Remember me ..."

The events Ludwig describes were not unexpected, but I was still shocked and moved as I read his words. There might not have been tears in Caitlin's eyes, but I confess to a little moisture in my own.

I looked up from the manuscript and gazed around the plane, blinking in the dimly lit cabin, wrenching my focus back from the horror of Nazi Germany. Pablo was still asleep and there was still nothing to see below us—hardly surprising, as it was now dark.

When did that happen? I wondered. No matter. I wiped my eyes, took a deep breath, and read on ...

Caitlin is taken to Dachau and Ludwig begins his experiments for her captors, there and in Auschwitz. Over the next year he's able to help her a little, smuggling food and medicines, but despite numerous requests, he's never allowed to see her. As you can imagine, and as her jailers intend, this is torture for him. He's wracked with guilt and remorse, but he's the one who survives and he knows what he must do:

Wednesday, November 1, 1944. The day has come. The day when any remaining hope dies ...

So, another Day of the Dead, I thought to myself.

Caitlin has been interned for one year now. Her final words: "Remember me ..." are the last I will ever hear from her. I gave her my word that I would escape with Martyn and today we leave my homeland forever. There is nothing here for us any more. I know I will never see her alive again. In any case, she despises me.
The war is going badly for Germany. The allies are advancing on all fronts and soon the Reich will be history. Some of the Group are interned with Caitlin but a few have already escaped. Today Martyn and I will join them. It has cost us everything—all my money, my reputation, my self-esteem, and the love of my life.

He signs his name and adds this note:

Note to my reader: if my journal ends here, then so be it. You will know we failed. I hope you have found some of my ideas of interest, and that my work may, one day, be revisited.

I turned the page, not daring to breath ... and the journal continued. I exhaled, and read on ...

Page fifty-eight. Langer has managed to escape from Germany, and there are still a dozen pages of his life left. He takes Martyn to Ireland, where he receives a bitter-sweet reception from Caitlin's family. Her parents are overjoyed to see their grandson safe, but inevitably they blame Ludwig for their daughter's predicament.

While he's there the Russians enter Berlin, Hitler commits suicide in his bunker, and British and American soldiers liberate the camps. Ludwig and Caitlin's family are initially hopeful that perhaps she's survived. But then they receive the cruellest of news:

Tuesday, May 8, 1945—Victory in Europe Day. The war is over, and everybody else is celebrating. But I have just received news of Caitlin's death. Nine days ago Dachau was liberated. Since then we have kept alive a glimmer of hope. Her family have been praying for her and lighting a candle every day in their church. But today the light of our hope was extinguished.

It seems that she was one of the last people to be murdered by the Nazis. I can hardly believe the cruelty of her fate. She resisted for so long and came so close to surviving that terrible place.

Now I must leave this beautiful country. As Martyn's father I have been tolerated here, but now I am an unwelcome intruder. Caitlin refused to give in and was murdered. I faced the same moral dilemma, took the coward's way out, and survived.

Now I am no longer tolerated in her community. It cannot be my home, but from now on it will be little Marty's. It breaks my heart to leave him, but he will be safe here. His father is labelled a collaborator, perhaps may even be accused of being a war criminal. I am a lead weight dragging him down, a noose around his neck.

For his sake, Martyn's grandparents have agreed to keep my existence a secret from him. They will tell him that after our escape I returned to Germany to rescue Caitlin and died in the attempt. He will grow up here, believing that both his parents perished fighting the Nazis. I hope he will inherit his mother's courage and the struggle to reunite Ireland will become his cause, as it was hers. That would be a fitting legacy for a remarkable woman.

At this point, the plane's loudspeakers crackled into life and there was an announcement. The captain informed us that we'd soon be landing in Dubai to refuel. The lights were turned off and I could no longer read. I put Langer's journal down and nudged Pablo. He woke with a start and a comical where-the-hell-are-we? expression on his face.

Fifteen minutes later we were sitting in the transit lounge—an air-conditioned, hermetically sealed, futuristic netherworld of a shopping mall. There were no windows and no clues to our time zone or location. We may as well have been in a space station rather than in Dubai.

I watched, amused, as the smokers amongst us were compelled to indulge their habit in a smoked-filled perspex bubble. Every time the door opened a great cloud of smoke belched out, as if from the bowels of a volcano.

Pablo asked me how far I'd got with the journal …

"I've nearly finished it. Caitlin has been killed by the Nazis in Dachau, but Ludwig has escaped to Ireland. He's leaving Martyn there and he's running off somewhere else, to avoid being arrested as a collaborator. I assume he travels to your own country, Pablo?"

Mr Fix-it nodded.

"When Alejandro first told me about his father, aboard the Abyss, I was worried he might have been a war criminal. I mean: Argentina was their favourite bolt-hole, I believe?"

Pablo nodded. "I not know about this 'hole', but is true, Nick—we have some bad peoples in my country. People who do terrible things in the war and escape from justice. But Ludwig no is a *bad* man, similar to his son. *¿Entiendes?*"

"Yes, Pablo, I understand. And I sympathise with him—as someone who has been forced to flee from my own homeland."

He nodded again. "Dr Langer start a new life, make a new family in Buenos Aires. He is respected there. But he never is happy again."

"What did he do there? Continue his work? Start a new group?"

"You must finish reading his journal, Nick, and then you will understand everything. I promise."

I nodded reluctantly, again frustrated by his insistence that all the answers were in this damn journal.

"And what about Martyn?" I demanded. "What happened to him?"

"—" Pablo pointed to the manuscript. I sighed.

Our flight was called. We left transit lounge limbo, boarded in silence, and took our seats for the final leg of our journey: Dubai to Dublin.

Once we were in the air again, dinner, or breakfast (or whatever else they were calling it—I was past caring by now) was served. After we finished the meal and sank a couple more beers Pablo reclined his seat and closed his eyes, but I wasn't going to let him escape this time:

"Look mate, we've got eight hours left—plenty of time to sleep. How about staying awake while I read the last few pages of the journal, eh *compañero*? I'll keep my part of the deal and finish it, then perhaps you can explain why we're going to Dublin. Fair Dinkum eh?"

I smiled as he stroked his beard. Confusion emerged from beneath it and slowly spread across his features. His expression was complete when it reached his forehead and his brow wrinkled into a frown. He'd never understand the Ozzie vernacular, but it was amusing watching him try.

"OK Nick. No worries (again the comically exaggerated version of my own accent). I stay awake with you (I nodded my thanks) but I need *un café fuerte*."

I grinned and we ordered double expressos. I picked up the manuscript and resumed reading from page sixty ...

Ludwig arrives in Buenos Aires with hardly any money, but over the past two decades he's been collecting art and he manages to smuggle some paintings out of Germany. Some are by Group members, including Caitlin, and a few by artists who've since become famous: Otto Dix, George Grosz, and Paul Klee. The Nazis condemned them as 'degenerate', but after the war they're recognised as central to the development of twentieth-century art. Their work is sought-after and highly prized. Langer only needs to sell a few paintings and he has enough capital to start a publishing business ...

July 1950. I have been in Argentina for five years now—long enough to call Buenos Aires my home. I can never go back to my real homeland so I must make the best of my situation, but I fear I will never be happy here.

Since selling the paintings my finances are more secure now than they ever were in Germany. I have become wealthy, but wealth can never compensate for what I have lost.

I miss Caitlin desperately, but at least I managed to salvage a few mementoes of our time together: her sketchbook, a few photographs, some of her essays, and two of her paintings. They are some comfort.

The sketchbook contains drawings from Ireland: sketches of her family, their village, the beach, waves, even a few of me that she did during our walks along Brandon Bay strand, her special place.

The earlier of her two paintings is a self-portrait, painted in Zurich while we were studying with Carl (Jung). Her beauty and strength radiate from this canvas. There is a lightness of touch and the colours are bright. We were materially poor then, but rich in happiness.

The other is a portrait of myself and Martyn, painted in September 1940 to mark our son's first birthday. However, it does not celebrate the occasion. Painted in oil, with heavy brushstrokes—thick layers of grey and dark brown, it is a reflection of the tension between us, the angst we were both feeling by then. I am glaring out of the picture and gripping Martyn protectively, as if he is about to be swallowed by the darkness that surrounds us. Caitlin gave it the title: 'The Waves of Hatred Gather'.

Of course, I'd seen these two paintings hanging in the Master's yacht, along with some of Nicole's work. I checked with Pablo and he confirmed this:

"*Si*, Alejandro have Caitlin's paintings on the boat. He take them from the house in Buenos Aires when his father die."

I told him how beautiful I thought she was in the self-portrait, and that the other canvas seemed to be filled with gloom and doom.

He nodded. "Is true, Nick. The Master tell me about Caitlin, and he tell me about his own life in Ireland—how it is a special place for both of them."

"Have *you* been there?" I asked him, hoping that perhaps he might reveal another piece of the jigsaw.

No, he replied, this would be his first visit.

I waited for more information, but none was forthcoming. The expression: 'like getting blood out of a stone' came to mind. Instead, he returned to the paintings aboard the Abyss:

"I know nothing about art, but is *muy importante* for Alejandro— is how he meet Nicole, *por ejemplo*."

I nodded. "Yes, I know. Nicole told me all about how she met him."

I still had her painting of the two of us: 'The Kangaroo Kid and his Voodoo Child' strapped to my rucksack in the overhead locker. It seemed like a good time to show it to Pablo.

He stared at it, and I was reminded of the time I showed it to Mandu. Mr Fix-It's reaction was similar:

"Thank you for showing me this, *señor* Nick. I see what she is meaning for you. You must show it to Alejandro."

"Yes, I will" I replied. "So, will I be seeing him soon?"

"—" The usual enigmatic silence. He pointed to the journal. I sighed, turned back to the manuscript and continued reading. There were only six pages left ... and then I wanted some answers.

Langer is in his fifties now. His business prospers and he's resigned to making the best of his situation. In 1952 he marries his secretary, a woman fifteen years younger than him, and a year later their son is born. They name him: Alejandro Aidan Langer-Alvares. Ludwig explains why on Page sixty-five:

> *My wife is a modern woman. She insisted on equality when it came to naming our son. Her grandfather's name is Alejandro, and that would be his first name—no alternatives were discussed, but it's fine with me. Her family name is Alvares and that was added to mine, giving her a 50% stake. I was permitted to suggest his middle name, and I decided that it should honour Caitlin's homeland. After researching Irish boys' names I decided on Aidan, which is an Anglicisation of Aodh, meaning 'bringer of fire', and is the name of a Celtic sun god.*
> *My wife is a devout Catholic and there was no need to explain this ancient pagan reference. Alejandro will be christened in the cathedral here.*

So, the A.A.L. puzzle had been solved and now I finally understood the Master's exotic mix: German father, Argentine mother, and the missing link: an ancient Irish sun god. No wonder he was drawn to that other fiery star: Mandu.

Ludwig never finds happiness in Argentina, despite his material prosperity. His research is incomplete, but he lacks the energy and enthusiasm to continue it. His marriage is one of convenience, rather than love, and he's consumed with guilt over Caitlin's fate. At least Alejandro never needs to worry about money. He receives the best possible education at a private British school, but not the love of his parents. They remain distant figures and he's brought up by a succession of nannies, housekeepers and tutors.

In the seventies, a brutal dictatorship seizes power. For Ludwig, it's horribly resonant of the Nazi's inexorable rise in the 1930s. He becomes a recluse, ever more depressed, and in 1979 his marriage ends. By then Alejandro has left Argentina to escape the *Junta*. He rarely has contact with his father, but Ludwig helps him find a safe haven in Ireland. He tells his son that he has connections there (something of an understatement, I thought to myself). Alejandro ends up studying, and then teaching, in Dublin.

Langer is now alone in Buenos Aires. Both of his sons are in Ireland, unaware of each other, but somehow this pleases him. He has never forgotten Caitlin, nor their child:

> *In February 1950 I set up an anonymous trust to fund Martyn's education and provide him with a modest allowance. It is administered by a solicitor in Dublin who is sworn to secrecy. My son knows nothing of me, only what Caitlin's family have told him— that both his parents died in the war, and whatever explanation they have seen fit to give him for the money.*
> *It was the least I could do for him. Martyn can never inherit my wealth—I intend to leave everything to Alejandro, on condition he continues my work. I hope, with all my heart and soul, that when he reads this journal he will agree to this.*
> *My other great hope is that after my death my sons may one day meet each other and that Martyn may also read this journal and learn the truth. He may not forgive me for his mother's death, but at least he will understand the appalling dilemma I faced.*

I looked up from the manuscript and stared out of the window. The endless ocean had been replaced by empty desert. There were only two pages left now and four hours of the flight to read them, but I needed another beer, and conversation.

I turned to Pablo and nudged him. He opened his eyes, guiltily— he had a dog's ability to fall asleep, instantly. I ordered two beers and he smiled at me gratefully.

"Have you finished the journal, *señor* Nick?"

"Very nearly" I replied. "Perhaps now you can tell me why we're going to Dublin?"

He considered my question, took a sip of his beer, and told me, for the umpteenth time, that I was close to an explanation but I must finish the manuscript first.

"OK" I sighed. "At least you can tell me what happened to Martyn? Is he still alive? He would be, what, seventy-eight years old by now?"

"Yes, Nick, he is alive—as far as I am knowing."

I waited for him to elaborate, but he said nothing.

"So where is he then?"

Silence. We finished our beers. I stared at the emptiness beneath us. Then, just as I'd decided that no more blood could be squeezed from the stone, he answered:

"He is in Dublin."

I nodded. Now we were getting somewhere. I put down my empty glass and picked up the journal again. Page sixty-nine, the penultimate page ...

November 1980, Buenos Aires. This will be the last entry in my journal. Thank you, dear reader, for taking the time to read it. I apologise if you are expecting a satisfying conclusion. There is no happy ending I'm afraid, just a weariness with life and a desire to end it.

For the past two decades, I watched as others appeared to rediscover the values our Group explored, only to abandon them in the morass of modern society. In the late 1950s and early 60s, I was hopeful that we might have reached a turning point, through the work of writers such as Aldous Huxley, and researchers such as Timothy Leary. For a while, it seemed that psychedelic substances would open the doors of perception, reveal the truth within, and that society would evolve. I hoped that cheap travel and mass media might open people's minds to explore the world of ideas, other cultures, ancient wisdom. For a few years, in the 1960s, it seemed that we were witnessing the birth of a new age ... But it was not to be. Now all I see around me are Nietzsche's 'Last Men'. They surround me, with their suffocating culture of convenience, comfort, triviality, mediocrity. Friedrich is turning in his

*grave. He saw this coming, and for some years now I have also seen
my own end coming.*

*The doctors first diagnosed severe depression and prescribed drugs.
They didn't work. A psychoanalyst made the laughable suggestion
that I, a student of Carl Jung, should voluntarily commit myself to
a psychiatric institution.*

*Eventually, I found a doctor who told me the truth: I was suffering
from an incurable form of dementia, which would only become
more acute and would soon rob me of my mind. He suggested that
my condition could be hereditary and that I might have inherited it
from my father. When I think about his mental state in his last
years, this seems plausible.*

*Now my greatest fear is that one, or even both of my sons will
inherit it from me. This is too much to bear. I do not want to be
alive to witness that, let alone my own slide into the abyss.*

*So, all that remains is a bitter death and the slim hope that
Alejandro might escape this terrible disease and continue where I
leave off.*

*Again I thank you, my dear reader, for your time and patience. I
hope you have found something of interest in this journal.*

Auf Wiedersehen.

(These final, poignant two words were left untranslated)

My eyes were wet again, as I put Langer's manuscript down. Such
a bleak ending. The final few paragraphs were effectively a suicide
note. Now I remembered that Alejandro had hinted this was how his
father had met his end—with open arms, a "bitter death" indeed.

Then I realised it wasn't *quite* the end. There was a note attached
to the final page with a black paper clip. It was handwritten in the
Master's familiar elegant script and addressed to me personally:

*Nick, now you have read my father's account of his life and his
work, and you understand what I have inherited from him.*

*When I read his journal, after attending his funeral, it changed my
life. I learnt that he suffered from severe depression, terminal*

dementia, perhaps even insanity, and that he had taken his own life. I understood that his condition could be genetic and that I might inherit his unstable mind, his incurable illness, along with his wealth. However, I couldn't simply ignore his plea to continue his life's work. So, in 1981 I started a modern version of his Group, with the goal of creating an alternative to Nietzsche's 'Last Men' in contemporary society.

As the years passed and the New Group pursued this goal, I knew time was limited. If I succumbed to the same problems that finished him then what would happen to his ideals, his research, his wealth? I was grappling with this dilemma when you showed up, in October 2015, drifting around the Atlantic, and I am still grappling with it. Now time is running out for me and there are pressing matters to be resolved. This is why I have sent you to Ireland. The first part of your mission there is to locate my half-brother, Martyn, and meet him. I would like you to give him our father's journal so that he learns the truth.

As you know, for a while I lived and worked in Dublin. Ironically, I was unaware of his existence in the same city. It was only when I read this journal that I discovered I had a brother. However, after all this time I am not sure how he will react. We are as different as his mother and our father were—polar opposites. I need you to be my envoy.

When I was living in the Republic, in the 1970s, Northern Ireland was embroiled in 'The Troubles'. My brother fought for his mother's cause and played a significant role in the armed struggle against the British. Some terrible things were done in the name of political expediency. Innocent people died. I would like you to hear his side of the story and then make up your own mind.

Pablo will help you find him and then tell you what to do next.

As usual, he'd signed the note with his initials: *A.A.L* and dated it with today's date: *November 4, 2017.*

"At least it's not the *first* of November this time" a voice-in-my-head whispered.

Too true, I thought. No more *Días de Muertos*, please!

I sat back in my seat, exhaled (I'd literally been holding my breath), and handed the manuscript to Pablo. He handed it back to me.

"No Nick, you give this copy to the Master's brother, *señor* Martyn. Like I promise you: now you know why we go to Ireland, no?"

PART IV

IRELAND

"Like as the waves make towards the pebbled shore,
so do our minutes hasten to their end."
(William Shakespeare)

21

THE TROUBLES

Dublin Airport. Saturday, November 4, 2017, 09:30. As the plane touched down I had the strangest feeling of déjà vu. I'd never been here before, but there was something familiar about the open, welcoming faces and the buttery Irish accent. I felt at home and, of course, I did have a connection with the Emerald Isle—my mother's family had emigrated to Australia from there. But that wasn't it. It was more a feeling of finality and a familiarity with *that* feeling, rather than with Dublin airport. So, was this the final chapter, or would there be an epilogue? I wondered.

Pedro interrupted my cogitations before the cogs could get up to speed, with his own urgent burst of questions:

"You remember who you are, no?" he whispered.

Ignoring my habitual tendency to agonise over a question like that, I hissed back:

"*Si señor Fix-it.* I'm Brian Cowen."

"*¡Muy bien!* And what is your job?"

"I'm a public relations consultant."

"*¡Correcto!*"

We were waved through customs and passport control with the predictable ironic banter:

"Good morning to you Mr Cowen, *Sir* ... (he looked from my passport to my wave-board in its coffin bag) ... I'm so glad you've taken up something other than golf, now that you've retired from the Taoiseach job."

I smiled nervously, and that was that—passports stamped, formalities concluded, my Irish mission was up and running. I followed Pablo as he strode through Arrivals towards the throng meeting and greeting passengers. A man was holding up a sign: 'Mr. Rodrigues Vasquez'. Pablo nodded and our driver handed him a package. Inevitably, it was wrapped in brown paper. We made our way out of the airport and into the 'Fair City' of Dublin.

As our taxi turned into O'Connell Street the feeling of familiarity returned, stronger now. This was where Irish Republicanism erupted. We passed the infamous General Post Office, epicentre of the 1916 Easter Rising—events that had such an influence on Caitlin's life. Only a few hours earlier I'd finished Dr Langer's life-story and now here I was, on my way to meet their son, Martyn O'Connor.

It was a typical morning in the Fair City. Grey, misty drizzle blurred everything—'soft rain' the locals called it—so different from Perth's sharp, clean light. Tourists sheltered under umbrellas, children splashed through the puddles, working men wondered if it was too early to skive off for a pint of the 'Black Stuff'. We crawled along streets clogged with traffic, steeped in history and enveloped in that ghostly half-light, as if driving through a set for a film-noir thriller. Nobody spoke, but the silence was filled with tension.

Pablo closed the window between us and the driver, pulled down the blind, and handed me the package. As usual, there was no explanation. If this *had* been a movie there might have been a flashback sequence now, a montage of previous packages and dramatic twists in my life—the parcel I delivered to Nicole; the letter telling me I would never see her again; the one Mandu had given me, telling me to open it 'when the time was right'; the fresh identities, false passports, money, missions ... The scene would have tense music—a dramatic, discordant crescendo building into the cut back to real-time action ...

I looked at the package, then at Pablo. He nodded. The music built to a climax. I opened it ... and immediately I was shaking, sweating, breathing in frantic gasps of damp, foggy air.

Inside there was a gun.

I stared at it, praying that it was just a prop in my imaginary movie. Pablo confirmed that it was real, it worked, and it was loaded.

"What the fuck is this for, mate?" I whispered to him, my voice like fingernails on a blackboard. "I don't even know how to use it."

He told me not to panic: "*No hay problema*. It is just for safety and security. Better you safe than be sorry, *no amigo*? And no worries, mate ... (his attempt at my own vernacular was no longer amusing) ... is easy to use. You point, pull trigger, shoot it. Bang! Easy."

I shook my head and tried to control the violent shakes that had seized the rest of me. I wanted an explanation, but it was too late. The taxi pulled up outside a pub. Pablo paid the driver and told me he'd be waiting for me. I put the gun in my leather jacket, grabbed my rucksack, and entered the Oval Bar.

It took a while for my eyes to adjust to the gloom. The dark wood, dim lighting, musty smell, and overbearing atmosphere of tradition all reminded me of a church, although the sign above the bottles hinted at a less pious ideology: 'Est. 1820. Rebuilt after 1916 Rising, in time for Civil War and Resistance.'

A few old men in sombre black suits were drinking at the bar. I approached them and ordered a pint of Guinness—my first taste of the holy water. One of them turned to look at me, perhaps alerted by my Ozzie accent. His lined face, grey stubble, and shabby black suit reminded me of an Irish version of Mandu.

"You're a long way from home, son." His voice was as dark as my pint of the Black Stuff. "What brings you to our neck of the woods?"

He stared at me with the same piercing gaze as the Master and the Aboriginal shaman. There was a lifetime of experience behind those eyes, just as there was with those other two old blokes.

"G'day mate" I replied. "I'm a windsurfer and I'm here to chase storms." It was a ridiculous statement, here in a bar on Dublin's main street, but it was the best I could come up with at short notice. "I'm told you normally get a few coming in off the Atlantic in the autumn?"

His face creased into a grin. Mandu's smile was radiant, like the sun, this bloke's was a black hole—sardonic, cruel, sucking everything in and giving nothing back.

"That we do, son. You'll be wanting to get yourself over to the west coast then. To the Maharees, where my family's from."

"Yeah. Right. I'm heading over there soon. I'm just doing the tourist thing first. You know, checking out the history and stuff."

"So, you're interested in our history ... What about our politics?"

"Yeah, well mate, I don't know much about politics, but I know that just like there're a lot of storms here, there's always been plenty to talk about—the Troubles and all that ..."

I tailed off into embarrassed mumbling. There you go Nick, sailing too close to the wind again. Oh well, might as well bite the bullet (a sly grin, given what was in my jacket pocket) ...

"Actually, mate, there *is* another reason I'm in Dublin. I'm looking for a bloke called Martyn O'Connor. I gather he's a regular in here?"

There was an awkward silence, a tumbleweed moment. Heads turned to eyeball me. I was acutely aware of the gun in my pocket. He left a bar's rest for the tension to build ... then defused it, masterfully:

"Ah yes, well you're in the right place, t'be sure." He offered me his hand. "Good morning Nick—or would you prefer I called you Brian? Nice choice of alias by the way, Mr Cowen."

My mouth opened to respond, but I struggled to connect brain and vocal cords. I stared at him, like a goldfish. After several uncomfortable seconds I realised his hand was still extended towards me. I shut my mouth and tried to look him in the eye as I grasped it. His handshake was firmer than necessary, his eyes stabbed me, and he still had that mocking grin.

I gulped down the rest of my Guinness. It helped. He ordered another for me. There was silence as the barman went through the required ritual: fill glass to within an inch of the top, wait a minute until the head settles, fill the remaining 5%, chop off the overhanging creamy bit. We watched patiently—it seemed inappropriate to speak while this was going on. The barman put my pint down in front of me and the old bloke in black broke the silence:

"So, we'll call you Nick then. I never could stand that Cowen fella. Anyway, I believe my charlatan brother sent you?"

"Umm, yes, that's right—but how did you ..."

"Ah well, there's not much in this town I don't know about. For instance, I know ... (a pause worthy of Mandu) ... that you're carrying a weapon."

The piercing gaze and cruel smile tortured me. I cringed into my barstool, completely out of my depth, a boy amongst men. He ignored my discomfort and ploughed on:

"No worries, as I believe you fellas say, I'd 'ave done the same. In fact, we're all armed ourselves, aren't we boys?"

He gestured around the bar, to general poker-faced assent. I felt like a stooge in a game they were playing with me.

"To be honest with ya, I got a message from a fella called Pablo that Alex was sending you to settle things between us. Now that's typical of my eejit brother—he sends some punk to do his dirty work because he's not sure how I'm going to react if he turns up here again."

"Again?" I picked up on his implication: "You mean you've met Alejandro in here before?"

That sardonic smile again.

"You're sharper than you look, Nick. Yep, that's right. I met this feckin brother fella just the once, in 1981, and it was indeed in this very bar. I haven't seen him since. Then you turn up, thirty-six years later!"

His accent made this sound like: "dirty-six years" and I couldn't suppress a grin. I looked him in the eyes and caught just a hint of a twinkle there. He was seventy-eight years old—ancient, like Mandu, but I was beginning to feel a similar connection, bridging the generations.

"So, Mr O'Connor ..." I began, but he interrupted:

"Please, Nick, call me Martyn."

He put his hand on my shoulder—a gesture familiar from block-buster Mafia movies.

"OK, *Martyn*, Alejandro didn't tell me you two had met before ..."

I was wondered what else he'd left out, and how much of what he *had* told me was true.

"Didn't he? It didn't go well, so I'm not surprised. It was a few months after he'd been back to Buenos Aires for the funeral. Alex was just twenty-eight, not much older than you. We all think we can solve the world's problems at that age, don't we?"

I shrugged. If the past two years had taught me anything it was that there was no chance of me solving *any* of the world's problems.

"I was a revolutionary in my twenties," he added, "but I was forty-two when my brother showed up here. Old enough to be a cynic. He had a hard time getting me to listen to his story, that's f'sure."

A flicker of a smile, as he replayed their meeting.

"For a start, it was news to me that I *had* a brother. This was the first I'd heard of him."

I nodded.

"Then he told me that our mutual father, Ludwig Langer, had been living in Argentina and only just passed away ... and that was news to me as well."

I nodded, again. Of course, none of this was news to *me*.

"Y'see, I was raised by my mother's family, over in Dingle, and they'd told me that both my parents had died fighting the Nazis. I was only five when my Father escaped from Germany with me and I hardly remember anything about him or our life there. It was all so long ago ..."

He scratched his head, searching for something from his early childhood.

"There is *one* memory in here ... (he tapped his forehead). I remember the day my mother disappeared, the day she was arrested ..."

He paused and closed his eyes, reliving that terrible day seventy-four years ago. He shook his head sadly, and continued:

"My grandparents didn't know much about Ludwig either—just that he had a funny German name but he wasn't a Nazi; he didn't share my grandparents' religion or their politics; he had some strange ideas; and he was in love with my mother but he never married her. Granny O'Connor had an old photo of them, taken on Gowlane strand before I was born. They look happy together ..."

He smiled, wistfully.

"So, my father was never mentioned, but they were always talking about Caitlin. She was a real hero in our village—getting herself educated, then fightin' the Nazis and the Brits. I grew up worshipping her, tryin' to follow in her footsteps, live up to her legacy. Then this brother fella showed up, to tell me all about Ludwig Langer ..."

He frowned, and now I understood his cynicism: a stranger turns up out of the blue, claiming he's a blood relative with a closet-full of family secrets ...

"Anyway, he managed to get me t'listen to his story—how my parents met, how my mother died, how Ludwig had never forgiven himself. I told him I could see why—it sounded as if the bastard had sold her short, given in, and collaborated with the Nazis."

I shrugged and said that in my opinion it was more complicated than that.

"Is that right, Nick?" His lips twisted in amusement, his black hole of a smile. "Perhaps you know more about this Langer fella than I do?"

I shrugged, again. There was no need to reveal my hand just yet.

"So, when Alex told me about the will, how he'd inherited the lot, I suggested that he'd inherited his father's guilt along with the money."

I nodded and wondered if he knew about all the other stuff Alejandro feared he'd inherited—depression, mental instability, terminal dementia. None of it seemed to have affected Martyn though.

"Now, here's a thing ... Alex told me he only found out about *me* when he read our old man's journal, and then it turned out we'd been living in the same town!"

He shook his head and grinned at the memory.

"You couldn't fekin make it up, eh? Anyways, after he read this journal he even went over to Dingle to dig into my mother's family. Of course, anyone who'd met Ludwig was dead and buried long before he got there."

He took a swig of Guinness.

"We talked for a long time, my half-brother and me, sat right here at this bar. The more we talked the more it was clear that we might share the same father, but we didn't share much else."

Yes, that made sense. I could see now that they were polar opposites.

"Alex told me that to satisfy Ludwig's will, and inherit everything, he had to promise to continue his work. Apparently, that meant starting some sort of hippy group, like the one Langer had in Germany in the thirties, when he met my mother. They were playing around with drugs and eastern mysticism. You know, the kind of thing that was big in the sixties?"

I smiled, thinking of Timothy Leary's work with LSD, not to mention my own experiences with the Plant. But Martyn was not amused by that sort of stuff:

"Well, let me tell you, Nick, we weren't messin' around with feckin drugs and the like in the sixties. Not here we weren't. I was brought up to fight for something—something that matters—to get our country back, centuries after it was stolen from us. Like I said, in the sixties I was a revolutionary, a soldier. In those days we were fighting the British army on the streets of Belfast, not getting high on dope."

He gave me a look of such intensity that I felt like a naughty schoolboy being reprimanded by his stern headmaster. Then he relaxed a little, and the twinkle returned:

"OK, so we drank a fair bit of the Black Stuff and we might have smoked the odd spliff or two ..."

I smiled, nervously.

"... but the point is: we were fighting for something we believed in —something we were prepared to die for—something we still believe in! Don't we boys?"

The men-in-black at the bar nodded in agreement, still poker-faced.

"Do the words: 'Bloody Sunday' mean anything t'you, Nick?"

I nodded and told him I'd heard of it. For me, it was a historical event—something that happened on the other side of the world, twenty years before I was born—a few minutes of grainy news footage. But not for Martyn:

"I remember that Sunday like it was yesterday. I was there, in Derry, working with Martin McGuinness in the Bogside, mobilising against internment. British soldiers shot twenty-eight unarmed civilians that day. Some of them were my friends. It's not something you forget ..."

Silence. I wasn't sure if he expected me to react, but I couldn't think of anything to add. Bitterness surrounded me in the bar. Then he snapped back to the present:

"When I met this brother of mine, I was still locked into violence as the only way out. But let me tell you this, Nick: Thank God, those days are behind us now! OK, we didn't win, but in all honesty we were never going to win the armed struggle. It was always just a stale-mate, and it went on for too long. The so-called 'Troubles'—what a feckin euphemism that is! So many people died ..."

Now he was looking his age, sadness etched into his face along with the anger and defiance.

"Now we've got to win the peace. That's where we're at now: playing politics instead of waging war. Martin McGuinness made the same journey as me—from soldier to politician, and the Good Friday Agreement is his legacy. When he shook hands with Ian Paisley some of his friends down here said he was selling us out, but not me. Like I said: too many people have died already."

I nodded in agreement but I was way out of my depth, drowning in all the history and politics. It was time to reveal my hand and bring the conversation back to my current mission:

"Alejandro gave me a copy of your father's journal. I read it on the plane coming over here."

"Did you now?" That menacing grin again.

I gulped down some more Guinness.

"It explains things—the truth about Ludwig and your mother."

He stared at me—a make-my-day-punk stare.

"Alejandro wants you to have it, Martyn. I think he's hoping that when you read it you'll see Ludwig's side of the story, maybe even be able to forgive him."

He looked at me. The intense stare softened, he stroked his stubble and gave me a slight nod.

I reached into my rucksack, aware of the tension surrounding me. I had the feeling that one false move and I'd be confronting the 'armed struggle' personally, but I managed to extract the manuscript and hand it to Martyn without adding to the Troubles.

He started to skim through it, speed-reading sections that caught his eye. I told him to keep it. Then I drank up, thanked him for his time, said I'd convey his feelings to his brother, and turned to leave the pub—mission accomplished ...

A couple of his comrades-in-arms shuffled into my path and blocked my exit. Their leader wasn't finished with me just yet:

"Let me get you another pint, Nick (he gestured to the barman). Thirty-six years since I last heard from him and then you show up here ... (he stroked his chin thoughtfully). He tried to get me to join his feckin group, you know—started rabbeting on about Langer's philosophy, his travels, his 'knowledge' ... I told him where to stuff his hippy nonsense!"

A ripple of laughter from his mates. I sat back down at the bar and drained some more Guinness. I didn't seem to have much choice but to accept his 'hospitality'.

"When I got a message from yer man, Pablo, I thought there might be more to it. That maybe this feckin eejit half-brother might be sending someone to do me some harm. Then *you* walked in here, with your hand on the gun in yer pocket ..."

He showed me that ironic grin again, evidently amused by the idea that anyone would send *me* to do *him* some harm.

"By the way, Nick, after sixty odd years in this game I can usually tell when someone's packin' a pistol—it's why I'm still around and not proppin' up the daisies."

I nodded, completely out of my comfort zone now.

"So when you walked in, tooled up, I was thinking that this might be some sort of assassination attempt ... (another stroke of his stubble) ... until you opened yer mouth."

I felt the start of a blush. Too embarrassed to shrug, I smiled. He matched my awkward smile with his black hole of a grin.

"Let me give you some advice before you walk out of here. Watch yer back, Nick. There's a reason why he gave you that gun. There's plenty of bad fellas down here in the South y'know, from both sides, on the run, still killing people. It's in their blood. They'd be lost without the kick they get from shootin' people. So you watch yer back, OK?"

I nodded and thanked him for the warning. The cynical, mocking grin softened into genuine warmth.

"You're a good lad, Nick. I can see that." He patted me on the back, and I felt like a kid again. "I know what the blackfellas in yer country went through when those convicts arrived from England, and what you've had to put up with ever since. We're comrades, y'know. Both of us have been colonised by those feckin Brits!"

Murmurs of agreement from our fellow drinkers. I was halfway through my third pint and the Black Stuff was working its magic. We grinned at each other and now the smiles were genuine.

I told him about my own connections with the Emerald Isle—how I shared my surname with the famous half-Irish Ozzie outlaw, Ned Kelly, although of course I couldn't match his high standards in the role. I told Martyn that I might not be much cop as an assassin, but I certainly shared his views about the Poms.

The laughter in the Oval Bar was unambiguous. I was one of

them. A fellow outlaw, a brother-in-arms. Martyn asked to look at the pistol I was "packing". I showed it to him and he appraised it expertly:

"Yeah, not bad Nick. It'll get you out of a sticky situation ... (he aimed it playfully at my head) ... but only if it has bullets in it!" he added, squeezing the trigger.

It was still raining when I stepped outside—grey, misty drizzle that made everything ghostly. Did it ever stop here? Martyn's advice to "watch yer back" was still rattling around my brain as I peered into the murky half-light, scanning the street. Could I trust anyone in this city of shadows?

Pablo was waiting for me, in a smart black van with blacked-out windows. He opened the passenger door and I climbed in. As usual *señor* Fix-it said nothing—no greeting, no questions about my meeting in the Oval Bar, no hint of where we were going. Instead, he gestured behind him. There, in the back of the van, was my trusty WHY? wave-board and a quiver of new sails. It looked like he'd been busy while I'd been talking to Martyn, and it explained why he'd been so keen to discuss windsurfing equipment after I'd finished reading the journal. A quick glance confirmed that he'd made the correct choices.

We set off in silence, travelling west. The grey city streets became suburban sprawl, and then we were on a highway through lush green countryside. It had been quite a while since I'd seen fields, farms, cows, sheep ... I'd got so used to WA's stark monochrome deserts. Ireland was a relief, a breath of fresh air. Now we were out of the city the soft rain made sense—the softness was beguiling, mysterious. Instead of the harsh Australian glare there was this pale, misty, soft-focus light. I sat back, stared out of the window, and enjoyed the scenery.

Pablo eventually broke the silence, announcing that our destination was the Dingle peninsular. He pointed to the map on the GPS display and said that it would take us most of the day to get there. I nodded and told him that was fine with me. It was exactly where I wanted to go—the idyllic location described in windsurfing magazines and, of course, Caitlin's 'Special Place'. The second of these was presumably the reason we were going there?

No reply, just the hypnotic rhythm of the windscreen wipers and occasional directions from the robotic voice on the dashboard. I closed my eyes and allowed myself to drift.

When I opened them again several hours had passed. Soft rain was still falling. We were travelling between rounded, grassy hills towards mountains that were just emerging from the mist. Every now and then we passed through small towns, with gaily painted houses and equal numbers of churches and pubs.

Eventually, the disembodied voice of the GPS prompted us to turn off the highway onto a country road, which then became a lane. We found ourselves stuck behind tractors, moving at the locals' pace. I was just starting to get a little bored with the overdose of misty softness when we rounded a corner and there she was: the Atlantic Ocean!

Instantly everything changed. I forgot about Martyn, his brother, the gun in my pocket, the Troubles ... and gazed at one of the finest beaches I'd ever seen—and I've seen some good ones. So, this was the famous Brandon Bay—Caitlin's 'special place'. Neither Langer nor the magazine articles had exaggerated its pristine beauty. It reminded me of the beaches in Esperance, or the Caribbean, but on an even grander scale.

The green fields ran straight down to dunes, then just an empty expanse of sand which stretched out forever, disappearing into the mist as it became a rocky headland way in the distance: the Dingle peninsula. At the other end of the bay was a narrow spit of land sticking out like a single raised finger, a peninsula off a peninsula—the Maharees.

Lines of swell were marching in and peeling cleanly, breaking right across the bay. From this distance it was difficult to judge the size of the waves, but I knew they'd come thousands of miles to detonate on this exposed spot. This was where they arrived first—the most westerly bit of Europe. Looking out to sea, the next land was America.

We drove along the coast road, past abandoned houses looming out of the mist like ruined castles, monuments to a battle with nature. There was a primal feel to the place, a majestic rawness which went far beyond the usual tourist description: 'unspoilt'.

The GPS voice directed us to turn off the road, down a farm track, and onto the beach itself! As we drove onto the sand the robotic voice announced that we'd arrived at our destination: Gowlane strand.

I had no idea what I was doing there, but somehow I knew my journey was over. There'd been so many twists and turns, and no doubt there'd be more, but I'd definitely arrived at *my* destination. It was a spiritual thing for me—the ocean was in my soul. I was back in my spiritual home again.

22

———

THE CRAIC

Pablo turned off the engine and we sat there in silence for a few minutes, gazing at the waves. Viewed from sea level, close up, they were much bigger. These were waves of consequence—powerful, unforgiving. This was a beach break to challenge anyone. Pablo looked at me and gestured towards the ocean:

"So, Nick, now you can show me how you are sailing this board, no?"

I opened the window and stuck my head out. Driving, salty rain stung my eyes. This was no tropical paradise—there were no palm trees and the water wasn't turquoise. The sea was steely grey, streaked with white in the gusts. It looked wild out there—the wind was blowing at least thirty knots and the waves looked like mountains. It was cold, raining, and late—there was perhaps an hour of light left, and there was nobody else out. The beach was empty, desolate, immense. It reminded me of Esperance, the day Robo died ...

"Yeah, OK mate. No worries. Looks perfect for a swift session before the pub" I said, trying to ignore my demons.

Windsurfing is often like that—you watch the weather forecasts obsessively, desperate for wind, then when shedloads arrive you know you want to be out there and it'll be fine once you are, but all sorts of excuses are available to dampen the enthusiasm.

"OK. Let's do it!" I said, to myself as much as to my nautical amigo.

I rigged up in the lee of the van—a four metre sail—the smallest he'd bought. Oh well, it would have to do. I flattened it off with as much tension as I could apply, to handle the gusts. Most places I'd sailed this would be called a storm, but I was aware that here it was just an average November day. The weather on Europe's most exposed, westerly coast could be far more extreme—all four seasons in one morning was quite common.

Pablo watched me rig, fascinated by every detail, comparing it to his yacht. "You know Nick, this is something we are sharing: sailing, the wind, the love for *la mar*. It is, how-you-say, in our blood, no?"

I nodded and told him we had salt water in our blood. It was his job and my obsession. I remembered a fascinating quirk of nautical Spanish grammar: true sailors, fishermen, watermen always refer to the sea as feminine—rather than the more usual: *el mar*.

"Many times I am in the middle of the ocean in a storm like this, but never I *choose* to go sailing in this wind. You are crazy, Nick!"

"Well, Pablo, perhaps you're right. But I'm a windsurfer—it's what we do."

I'd finished rigging now and was struggling with the thick winter wetsuit he'd provided. I'd never worn so much rubber before. It felt like a straight-jacket and I was beginning to share Pablo's doubts about the sanity of this session. I muttered to myself, trying to stem the panic before it had me in its grip, reminding myself that the Gulf Stream kept the water relatively warm. Pablo interrupted my mutterings:

"The Master, Alejandro, he is also sharing this with us, Nick. Alejandro has the same love for *la mar*." Again the implication was that love for the ocean was like love for a woman.

"He tell me what his father write in his journal: how Caitlin love the wild ocean in this place. He say: when he meet you, drifting in the Atlantic, he already know you must come here one day—to Brandon Bay."

That was prescient of him, I thought, or did he have all this mapped out two years ago? No worries—it was indeed a 'special place' and I had him to thank for bringing me here.

"When Alejandro see windsurfing in the Canary Islands, before you show up, he is also fascinating with it. He make me drive the Abyss to where you do windsurf—how is it called, the surfing *pueblo* in Tenerife?"

"You mean El Médano?"

"*Si, vale.* We park the boat there and he watch the *windsurfistas* for many hours. He is telling me how special he think it is, what they do, how they are connecting to the wind and waves."

I'd managed to squeeze into the wetsuit and was more-or-less ready to go, but his talk of the Master had me intrigued now …

"So, tell me Pablo: is Alejandro here in Ireland at the moment? Will I be seeing him soon?"

"—" He reverted to the deaf-mute gestures again.

"OK. Well, at least let me give you back the gun. I won't need it now, will I?"

"—"

"And in any case, it didn't actually have bullets in it, did it?"

A significant pause. It would have been another tumbleweed moment, except the wind was so strong the weed would've been shredded in milliseconds. Finally, he replied:

"Correct, Nick. The Master, he tell me give you the gun for protection, but not to kill Martyn. So you no need bullets."

Somehow this made sense to him, but his logic was lost on me.

"Now I give you bullets."

"What, you think I'll need a gun while I'm windsurfing?"

He laughed—a refreshingly unambiguous sound, in his case.

"No, Nick. Not on the water. But when you finish windsurf, you have a mission for Alejandro, no?"

I nodded, wearily. I'd hoped that it had been fulfilled in Dublin, but apparently not …

"For this mission you need a gun, and … (a Mandu style pause) … you need bullets."

I sighed. No wonder the Troubles went on for so long. Could I trust anyone here? I'd had enough of this conversation—enough talk, enough paranoia, it was time for some action ...

"See you later, *señor Fix-it*" I yelled, picking up the board and rig and struggling to carry them into the wind, through the rain (which was certainly no longer 'soft'), down to the water's edge.

When it's this windy, carrying the equipment is often more stressful than sailing it, but as soon as I step on the board I leave the stress, doubt and anxiety behind. Once on the water, they all evaporate. I'm free again, living each present moment—no worries about the future, no regrets from the past—just packets of now, instantaneous decisions, intuitive movements, flow.

The wind is strong, for sure, but it's quite constant and not unfriendly. The waves are big, yes, but they're super clean, predictable, not too threatening once I suss out their behaviour. The rain is a bit of an issue—making visibility difficult, but the biggest problem is the water temperature. The first time I wipe out it feels as if all the breath has been knocked out of me. I've never experienced water this cold before, but I don't panic and sensation gradually returns to my numb hands.

You can do this, I tell myself, and anyway, Pablo's keeping an eye on me—if anything goes wrong he'll call the coastguard. I relax and start to enjoy myself. After a while I forget about the cold water, the rain, Alejandro, the Troubles ... and I'm going for loops and swooping wave rides. For the next forty-five minutes I'm in the zone.

Eventually, the light starts to fade and it's hard to see anything in the gloom. I can just make out the van, but I can't see Pablo. Doubts creep back into my mind. I think about Robo and decide it's probably time to come in.

I sail out to sea for one last run, hard upwind to gain ground for a final ride down the line. A set approaches from the deep ocean, perhaps all the way from America. I fly over a few swells and gybe onto the final one—the biggest. I stalk this pulse of energy as it prepares to end its life on the edge of Europe.

The swell becomes a wave, a clean wall of water stretching downwind for perhaps two hundred metres. I choose my moment carefully —timing is crucial in wave sailing. Go too early and there won't be a lip to hit, too late and you get eaten by the wave. Time it right and you find yourself in just the right place—the critical part of the wave— the 'pocket'.

This is it, the right moment. I take the drop and swoop into my first bottom turn, defying gravity for an instant, weightless. I sheet the rig in, lean forward, bank the board onto the toe-side rail, feel it bite, feel the fins grip.

I'm going seriously fast now, heading back towards the lip at warp speed, fully committed. So many ways it can go wrong at this point: catch a rail, bury the nose, hit some chop, spin out … a mistake could have serious consequences, but I trust this board completely—like an old friend, like my much-missed brother-in-arms, Robo.

She doesn't let me down. I hit the lip, feel the fins lift out of the water, then reconnect, and we're flying down the line again with acres of wave still left to carve up.

My God these waves are special, world class. No wonder they hold international competitions here. I want more of them, but it's nearly dark now. As I sail in through the shore-break I think about making this place my home for a while. Never mind the cold water, the rain, the Troubles … Waves this good made life worthwhile.

As I stepped off the board and felt terra firma beneath my feet, time reverted from 'in the moment' to 'normality'. Past, present, and future were separate worlds again and I rejoined the highway of everyday life. I struggled back up the beach to the van, shivering as I came down from my adrenaline fix, and dumped the equipment on the sand.

There was no sign of Pablo, but an old man was sitting in the dunes watching me. He was dressed in the traditional black suit, head covered in a black felt hat, eyes hidden behind dark glasses—a shadow in the twilight. As I watched him watching me I had another of those déjà vu moments—they'd dogged me ever since landing in Dublin—an overwhelming feeling of finality and a familiarity with that feeling.

My old enemy, paranoia, gripped me and Martyn O'Connor's advice to "watch yer back" played in my head like a clichéd movie-trailer. Tense, dramatic music underscored his words in my mental movie, accelerating in time with my pulse. It occurred to me that Martyn, or one of his henchmen, had followed me across the country, watched me windsurf, and was now going to kill me!

I wrenched open the door of the van, reached inside and grabbed my jacket. The gun was still in the pocket. I had it in my hand and my finger on the trigger. The music built to a climax ...

Then, as quickly as they'd overwhelmed me, the paranoia, panic, and déjà vu left. I put the gun back in my jacket, packed my equipment away and changed out of the wetsuit.

When I stepped out of the van the old bloke was still sitting there, in the gloom. I strolled over to him wearing my leather jacket, the gun in my pocket, 'tooled up' just in case ... but he seemed harmless enough—probably just a local who liked to watch windsurfers.

As I approached he removed his hat to greet me, but it was only when I was a few feet away that I recognised him. He'd aged, terribly, in the past two years. What was left of his hair was white, his eyes sunk in a skeletal skull, the body twisted and shaking like an ancient tree in a gale, a walking stick propped up beside him.

"Good evening, Nick."

The voice was frail, but it still had some of the same authority.

"G'day, Alejandro."

I knew he was fourteen years younger than Martyn, but he seemed so much older than his brother now. The black suit didn't help. Goodness knows why old people here dressed like they were going to their own funeral. No wonder the pubs felt like churches.

He removed his glasses (still those impenetrable mirrored lenses) and looked at me. His eyes were dimmer, but he could still hold me with that hypnotic gaze.

"I've been watching you sailing your board and now I understand who you are."

"I'm a survivor, mate—that's who I am!" I replied, pleased that he'd witnessed me sailing as well as I could. "The bloke you dragged out of the Atlantic has been around the block a few times and grown up. Now he's wondering what he's doing here?"

"It's *good* to see you here, Nick. There have been times when I wondered if I *would* ever see you again, but as you say: you are a survivor."

He looked at me warmly and for a moment I thought he was going to embrace me, but that wasn't the Master's style. As we shook hands I could feel tremors running up and down his arm like an electric current. Parkinson's, I thought to myself, wondering if he'd inherited the rest of his father's problems.

"So, Nick, you asked me why you are here, in Ireland. I intend to answer your question—in due course, but first, you must be hungry and thirsty after today's adventures? We should go to my favourite pub in this part of the world: Spillane's bar. They do the best pint of Guinness on the west coast and their steak is almost as good as in my own country, or yours for that matter."

I presumed he meant Argentina and Australia—we were both a long way from home.

"By the way, where's Pablo?" I asked him. "Is he meeting us in the pub?"

"No Nick, his job here is done. He delivered you to me and now he will return to the Abyss, in the Canary Islands."

"I see. That's a shame. I was just beginning to bond with your *señor* Fix-it."

A hint of a smile appeared, fleetingly, like a crocus bud poking through snow in early spring. It was replaced by an expression of deep sadness I hadn't seen from him before.

"Yes, *el capitán* Vasquez is a good man and a loyal friend. I shall miss him." He picked up the walking stick and levered himself painfully to his feet. "Now, let's drown these sorrows and fill our stomachs."

We drove for a few miles along muddy country lanes that wound their way tortuously between stone walls and high hedges, spinning us in circles, so that when we arrived at the pub I had no idea which direction we'd travelled. I did the driving, thankfully, and he did the navigating.

Spillane's lived up to its billing. It was a very different experience from the earnest, church-like ambience of the Oval bar in Dublin. Spillane's shared the same traditional, sombre, dark wood interior, but little else. First, there was the location—a stone's throw from some of the finest reef breaks in Europe: Mossies, Garry William, and the ironically named: 'Shitties'. Then there was the 'craic', the local term for letting the good times roll. Spillane's had plenty ...

The customers were a mixed bag of ages and types, ranging from the by-now-familiar old-men-in-black to families with kids, and they were all sharing the craic. Several dogs roamed around, scavenging for food, joined by a pack of hungry windsurfing dudes in designer surf-wear. As we walked in the music started up—a fiddle, guitar, and penny whistle, making the kind of infectious groove that had even the black suits' feet tapping. I'd be happy to call Spillane's my local if this was a typical night in there.

Alejandro had more serious plans for the evening, however. We sat down at a table in the corner, away from the more raucous punters. He ordered seafood, steaks, pints of the Black Stuff, and then got straight down to business:

"So, Nick, we have much to discuss ... Do you remember: when you were onboard the Abyss I expressed the hope that one day you'd read my father's journal, and I told you that it would reveal the full story?"

I nodded.

"So, what did you think of it?"

"Well, it feels like there's still a lot I *don't* know" I replied, "but yes,

I read the journal and I must admit: I found it fascinating."

He nodded, approvingly.

"Your father, Dr Langer, was an extraordinary man. I sympathised with him over the dilemma he faced. He chose survival, as I would, but it came with a high price—to abandon the love of his life, Caitlin, and his son, Martyn, and then find himself accused of betraying them."

He nodded again, appraising my critique.

"I gave the journal to your brother, by the way, as instructed."

"Thank you, Nick. And what did you make of Martyn?" He probed me with those laser eyes.

"Well, he's another fascinating man ..." I swallowed a swig of Guinness. "I can see that he's nothing like you. His life has been politics, the 'armed struggle' as he put it, the Troubles ..."

"And *my* life ... ?" he asked quietly.

I looked at him, again shocked by how much he'd aged.

"You're more like your father. You value ideas over politics or violent action."

"Yes, that's true Nick. I am glad you see this. It makes me hopeful that you'll understand what we must do tonight."

He left a pause, heavy with significance, but our food arrived before I could ask him what he meant. I hadn't realised how hungry I was. For a while we ate in silence, both of us lost in thought and Spillane's excellent cuisine.

Eventually he looked up, but a light had been switched off in his brain. He appeared to struggle to remember who I was, why he'd brought me there, even my name:

"I'm sorry, Mister umm ... I'm afraid I've lost track of this conversation." His voice was frail now. "It has been happening more frequently lately. But don't worry, it will come back to me in a moment ..." He stared into the distance.

I sat there embarrassed, unsure what to say, what to feel. So, it seemed that Alejandro *had* inherited his father's dementia. I wondered if he'd also been saddled with Ludwig's guilt and depression. But then the light was switched back on:

"Ah yes, Nick, of course. Please forgive me. Remember how I told you that after I left Buenos Aires I lived in Dublin?"

I nodded.

"Well, ever since then this country and the people have always been special for me. I fell in love with their traditions, their myths, the deep mystery that surrounds things here. The Irish have always welcomed strangers, but there are fault lines that run deep and have divided them for centuries."

I gulped down the rest of my Guinness and hoped he'd notice the empty glass, but he was in full flow now:

"These fault lines can also be seen between myself and my brother—even though I'm not Irish and I have no political allegiance. There is a chasm dividing us. Ironically, as I told you in my note, I didn't even know he *existed* when I lived here in the 1970s. It was only when I read the journal that I found out I had a brother. I contacted him and we met once ..."

He faltered, lost for words as he searched his failing memory. I helped him find them:

"Yes, Martyn told me it was in 1981 and it didn't go well. He said you disagreed about everything. He accused Ludwig of selling out his mother's ideals and you of inheriting your father's guilt along with his money. He said you asked him to join the Group?"

"Yes, well that was a mistake. He hated our principles, our goals, as I despised his. He has blood on his hands, Nick. He carries a weapon and he has to watch his back for the rest of his life."

He spat out the last sentence with such bitterness, such venom, that I wondered, again, whether this final mission might be to assassinate Martyn, or one of his associates. But before I could press him on this, a young man in a Rip Curl fleece wandered past, glanced in my direction, gave me a second look, and asked me in a friendly Irish drawl:

"Excuse me for interrupting fellas, but were you the sunset sailor with the Severne sail and a custom board, sailing Gowlane on your pat late this afternoon?"

I sighed and glanced at Alejandro. He'd already retreated into his shell again. We seemed to be stuck in a loop—a bit of story revealed and then an interruption. But perhaps that was part of the charm of the place.

"Yep, that's right. G'day mate, my name's Nick" I replied, forgetting that it *wasn't* my name. I should have said Brian, of course, but it was too late now.

He shook my hand and told me his name was Niall. "You're Ozzie right, Nick? I spent a whole season in WA driving up and down that coast. You fellas have some feckin marvellous spots there!"

I'd already guessed that he'd spent time in Australia when he used the expression: 'on your pat'—short for 'on one's Pat Malone', as in: 'on your own'—Ozzie rhyming slang.

"Pleased to meet you Niall" I said, raising my glass. "Your back yard's not too shabby either, mate. I can see why Red Bull come here for the Storm Chase. Bloody good waves you've got here, and not exactly crowded either."

He grinned at my understatement. As usual, I felt an instant connection with a fellow windsurfer which cut across race and nationality. He didn't give a damn about my 'exotic', half black ethnicity. He just wanted to welcome me to his home spot and share the craic:

"Welcome to Brandon Bay, Nick. I watched you for a bit, until it got too dark. I was going to rig up and join ya, but I didn't fancy it —too late, raining, bloody windy and the shore-break looked heavy."

I smiled and agreed that my session had been a bit sketchy, but having spent most of the day driving over from Dublin I was desperate to get on the water.

"Respect dude! You were pullin' some cool moves out there! But listen: you should be careful, Nick. Don't be an eejit, OK? Those waves are heavy, and with zero visibility like that …"

I shrugged, but I knew what he was saying—I had Robo's death to remind me not be an "eejit".

"The locals here are a friendly bunch y'know." He gestured expansively around the pub. "Not like some places I've been to. You don't need to sail on your pat. We share waves and then we share the craic in here."

I smiled and told him I was looking forward to sailing with him and his mates. I'd have loved to have spent the rest of the evening with them but I was getting a little worried about Alejandro. He'd slumped down in his seat, head drooping towards the table, ageing by the minute. Niall picked up on my anxiety:

"Ah, look at me jabbering on like this. It's the gift of the gab we Irish have, t'be sure. I'll see you around, Nick. How long are you staying in the Maharees—you and your dad here?" He gestured towards Alejandro.

I laughed, self-consciously. "No, Niall, Alejandro isn't my dad. He's a ... friend."

"Ah, right. Pleased to meet you."

Niall offered his hand to Alejandro but there was no response. I grabbed it instead and said I'd see him on the water. Niall went back to his friends, who were now contributing enthusiastically to the music-making and general revelry in the other corner.

I went to the bar and returned to our table with fresh pints of Guinness, hoping this might revive Alejandro. After a couple of sips of the Black Stuff he looked up, but he seemed confused again:

"Nick, you're here?"

"Yes, Alejandro, Pablo drove me from Dublin this afternoon, as you instructed ..."

"Yes, of course, now I remember. Pablo ... he's a good man ... I shall miss him."

The voice was barely audible, dragged up from a deep well of pain and despair. He was coming apart at the seams. Slumped there, in his black suit, he looked like he'd just attended his own funeral and his ghost was getting morosely drunk at the wake. He picked up his pint, spilling most of it as his hand shook, and drained the rest of it in one gulp. Then he sat up, stared at me, and tried again:

"Let me tell you why we are here, Nick ..."

I leant forward to hear his fragile voice over the din.

"I returned to Ireland to complete my father's work and to show that he made the correct moral decisions. I've always maintained that his guilt was unfounded, that his depression and mental instability could have been avoided, that his suicide was a tragic mistake ..."

The old look was back in his eyes again.

"I hoped my return would be a healing process, but I was wrong. It seems I have inherited the same troubles that ended my father's life."

Again that word: troubles. It seemed to be *the* theme here.

"I came back to Dingle to put things right with Caitlin's family. I needed to do this before I die. This was *my* final mission—to die correctly."

His voice had the familiar, steely conviction now.

"But then I had to confront the terrible things my brother did during the Troubles."

I shook my head. It was all such a long time ago—twenty years before I was even born. There was a peace process now. The country had come to terms with the past and moved on—why couldn't Alejandro? Why couldn't he make peace with his brother? But no, he had to prove that his father was right and Martyn wrong:

"My brother needed to understand that Ludwig chose the right path in 1943—there was no betrayal. Martyn had to read Ludwig's journal, just as I did. I had to give it to him so he would understand the importance of our father's work, but I knew he'd never agree to meet me, so I sent you, Nick."

"Why didn't you send Pablo?" I asked, frowning.

"Yes, that would have been a possibility, but I needed to give you one more test—to prove that you were ready for your final mission."

A pause, while I thought about this.

"What do you mean: 'test'?" I asked him.

"Your last two years have been a series of challenges" he replied, "tests that have taken you on a learning curve."

I swallowed hard—a large slug of Guinness, and waited for him to continue.

"The year you spent with Nicole in the Dominican Republic was one such test ..."

I looked up sharply and locked eyes with him, trying to hold his gaze. He could feel my bitterness, my anger, but he put his hand up to prevent my intervention.

"When I sent you back to your homeland, to put things right there and to help Mandu's people, it was another test ..."

Again I tried to butt in, to register an opinion, and again he raised his hand to stop me. It was shaking, and tremors were racking his body. I could sense the effort it was taking to control them and somehow I knew he didn't have much time left. We were in the end game now and he was telling me, with that gesture, that there couldn't be any more interruptions.

"You survived these challenges and you grew stronger, Nick. Then when you met my brother in his stronghold, his *bunker* ..."

I could hear the anger, the disgust in his voice as he spat out the word: 'bunker' with its connotations of Hitler's final days in Berlin.

"... it was your last test before your final mission—the solution to these *troubles*—the final solution ... here ... in the next few hours."

I shook my head. This 'final mission', his 'solution', had chilling overtones of the Nazi's own 'Final Solution'. I shuddered at the thought and opened my mouth to protest. For a third time, he held up his trembling hand.

Now everything was shaking, falling apart—Alejandro, me, even the room itself. The music had erupted like a volcano, going from a gentle foot-tapping jig to a full-on stomping rave, and literally *every-thing* was shaking. It was impossible to continue our conversation and I needed to escape, so I got up and merged with the merry throng enjoying the craic.

Time jumps. For a while I lose myself in the music, surrendering to the rhythm as I do when I'm windsurfing—in the moment, in the zone. The original three musicians have been joined by several others: on accordion, banjo, and bodhrán—a traditional drum struck with energy, dexterity, and a stick. The audience are contributing enthusiastically: singing, clapping, stamping, whooping and dancing wildly.

Music, passion, and audience participation all remind me of the flamenco sessions that used to spontaneously erupt in the bar where I worked in El Médano, or the manic Merengue salsa-on-speed fiestas in Cabarete.

The crowd is like a wild animal—twisting, contorting, roaring, sweating. Spillane's is a heaving, bacchanalian orgy, minus the sex. The craic is like the Plant, minus the paranoia. It strips away my layers. I let go of my self and merge with the crowd. We are one now, no longer individual egos.

I don't know how long it went on, but it was late when the musicians finally packed away their instruments. The audience looked around, dazed, as if they were just waking from a trance.

I'd forgotten all about Alejandro, but he was still there, slumped in our corner of the room. His eyes were closed and for one shocking moment I thought he'd kicked the bucket, right there, while I'd been dancing the night away. A closer inspection revealed that he was still breathing, just sleeping.

Looking around the bar I realised he wasn't the only one. All around us punters were either fast asleep or preparing to bed down. A few were still talking quietly in another corner. The bar staff seemed to have melted away and the proprietor had simply locked the front door and gone up to bed himself, leaving us to our own devices. So, this was the notorious 'lock-in'—an eminently civilised approach to licensing bureaucracy, I thought to myself, as I made myself comfortable, closed my eyes, and drifted into blissful unconsciousness.

23

THE CLIFFS OF MOHER

Spillane's bar, the Maharees, County Kerry. Sunday, November 5, 2017, 04:00. I'm lost in the same dream that's haunted me for the past two years—a nightmare that's followed me, like my paranoia, subtly mutating to include my latest fears ...

I'm drowning. A beautiful bird, with Alison's face, dives out of the sky and pecks out my eyes, laughing as she drops them into the sea. Robo appears, as a shark, tearing great chunks of my flesh and tossing them to a pack of monster crayfish to mince in their giant claws. The cray all have features I recognise—my brothers, my dad, mister Big Fish. An old man, in funereal black, points a gun at me and shoots me in the back. The consortium of Great White Mafia sharks, led by the mayor of Broom, circle me, shouting profanities while casually gnawing at the remains of my corpse ...

I'm thrashing around in my sleep, making hideous noises, trapped in the dream's ever-present moment ... then, mercifully, I'm wrenched from the horror by a hand on my shoulder.

I opened my eyes to find Alejandro staring at me. For a moment I was confused. I looked around the pub, unsure of where I was, what I was doing there.

"I was dreaming" I mumbled, rubbing my eyes.

He nodded.

"It's time, Nick."

I looked at my watch—it was 4 am for fuck's sake!

"Time for what?" I demanded, tetchily.

"Time for your final mission—your ultimate test."

He raised his hand to block any further discussion.

"We have a long way to drive, Nick, and we must get to our destination early, before any unwanted spectators arrive."

I had no idea what he was talking about, but the puppetmaster was pulling my strings again. He struggled to his feet. I handed him his walking stick and followed as he hobbled toward the back door of the pub.

We stepped outside, into the darkness. It was still raining, same as it ever was, and bitterly cold. We sat in the van, shivering. I started the engine and turned on the heater full blast. Alejandro punched some coordinates into the GPS and the disembodied voice announced that our destination was 203 kilometres and a three hour drive away. It ordered me to proceed, along the only road that led away from the Maharees peninsula.

We drove most of the way in silence, just the ghostly voice giving directions and announcing the names of towns: Castlegregory, Tralee, Limerick, Shannon, Ennis, Lahinch ... names that were steeped in Celtic mystery. I caught glimpses of majestic scenery through the darkness and mist, but mostly I just focussed on the rain-swept tarmac in the headlights and the hypnotic rhythm of the windscreen wipers.

Eventually, the voice announced that we'd arrived at our destination —an empty car-park at the very edge of the continent. I parked the van and turned off the engine, exhausted. We sat there in silence. It was still dark, but the first flickers of dawn were just starting to show themselves in the East.

I closed my eyes and was just drifting off when Alejandro abruptly reached down and produced a small black briefcase. He took out a package wrapped in the inevitable brown paper, handed it to me and told me to open it. Inside was a book and a brown A4 envelope addressed to me.

The book was beautifully bound in red leather—the kind of old-fashioned notebook that no longer has a place in our world of digital communication. I opened it and recognised Dr Langer's spidery German script, familiar from the scanned extracts on the Master's website. I was holding his father's original handwritten journal.

"I want you to have this. It is yours now, Nick."

I opened my mouth to protest, but he stopped me:

"We don't have time for questions. No time for doubts. Time has run out for me, but for you, it starts here. You are the guardian of my father's work now."

The look he gave me was as penetrating as ever, but there was such sadness in those eyes. I couldn't meet his gaze so I stared out of the window. The landscape was just emerging from the gloom. A path led off to the West, up a grassy hill, and then disappeared into space. Beyond that was just sky. I turned back to him and listened as he explained why we were there, in that desolate spot.

"Last night I explained how your previous missions have prepared you for this, Nick. If you are able to complete this last test you will be free of me, and you will be the leader of our Group."

I couldn't hold back my snort of derision.

"I'm sorry Alejandro, but that's a ridiculous idea. Why on earth would I want ..."

Again he held up his hand to interrupt me.

"Hear me out, please. I think you will change your mind when you appreciate what this could mean for you."

I shrugged—what else could I do?

"Shortly, I will ask you to show me you are ready for this role by confronting the ultimate test—an action that is 'Beyond Good and Evil', to use Nietzsche's terminology."

I grimaced. For me, an amoral act was an immoral act.

"If you are capable of this action then you are an '*Übermensch*' and you will inherit everything: my father's wealth, the Group, my yacht ... You will be free to go where you like, do what you like, for the rest of your life!"

Now he had my attention. He pointed to the envelope:

"Here is my will and all the other documents necessary for you to take control of my estate and the Group. I have already signed everything."

He replaced the envelope and the leather-bound journal back in the briefcase.

"When you have completed this final mission you will return here and sign the documents. Then everything will be yours."

I was tempted. Of course I was—who wouldn't be? I decided to play a waiting game, find out exactly what he wanted me to do, before committing to anything.

He reached into the briefcase and produced something else. I swallowed hard as I recognised a pipe, identical to the one Mandu had given me, and some familiar brown seed pellets. He crushed the seeds into a powder, filled the pipe, lit it, drew the smoke into his lungs, closed his eyes, and passed it to me. We shared it in silence for a while.

Sunday, 07:43—dawn at the edge of the world. The effects of the Plant kick in as the sun rises, and I'm living in the present tense again. Time jumps in discrete steps, instead of flowing past like a river. The doors of perception open and I'm flooded with stimuli. I can smell the pink of the sky and hear the green of the grass.

"Do you still have the gun Pablo gave you?" Alejandro asks.

I look at him, bewildered. I'd forgotten about it, but I reach for my jacket and reply that yes, it's still there in my pocket.

"Good. If you check you will find he has put bullets in it this time, no?"

My mouth drops open and I'm breathing hard, but I do as he says. There are, indeed, bullets in the gun. I'm trembling now.

"Alejandro, please ..." I mutter, but he interrupts me:

"So, put on your jacket and come with me."

He picks up his walking stick and gets out of the van. I follow—reluctantly, dragged along by some kind of magnetic force.

We walk past a sign: 'The Cliffs of Moher Visitor Centre'. The feeling of déjà vu returns, stronger now. Have I been here before? No, that's not possible, but something clicks in my memory—a video of someone windsurfing at the base of these cliffs.

The visitor centre is deserted and it triggers another fragment of memory—arriving at the Pinnacles in WA at dusk, after the tourists had left, and waking up there at dawn, alone. This is another of those empty, desolate spaces—like the volcanic crater at the centre of Tenerife, Nine Mile Beach in Esperance, the Pinnacles ... There's no time to contemplate the solitude though. Alejandro tells me to hurry, in an hour the centre opens and we'll no longer be alone.

We walk up the hill towards the cliffs. I'm terrified someone will be waiting for us there, waiting for the assassin: me! I don't know who I'm expecting—Martyn, perhaps? I desperately want to turn round and walk away, but again a magnet is pulling me irresistibly towards the edge.

Thankfully there's nobody there. We're alone—tiny specks in this vast landscape. I venture to within a metre of the drop and look into the abyss. My mind's eye plummets down two hundred metres. Far, far below, huge waves are exploding onto massive slabs of rock. Now the magnet is pulling me vertically down. The rocks are beckoning me to join them and I'm fighting the hypnotic pull of vertigo.

As I gaze down at the waves I remember more about this place. It's Ireland's Beachy Head. People come here to end it all, to take that last leap into oblivion. The surf break at the foot of these cliffs is a graveyard for many lost souls. It's known as: 'Aileens'. Kamikaze surfers are towed into the waves there by jet-ski, but it's only been windsurfed once, to my knowledge, by an Irish windsurfing champion. When I read about it and watched the video I remember thinking he was pushing the limits of what's possible in our sport.

I feel dizzy standing there, high above those waves, fighting the urge to surrender to gravity ... but thinking about windsurfing reminds me of everything I live for, and returns me to the moment.

Time jumps. I tear my eyes from the drop, look up, and see that Alejandro is beside me. I stare into those hypnotic eyes, but they're blank, empty. There's nobody inside now.

"It's time, Nick"

The voice of a ghost.

He stumbles to the edge, throws his stick into space, and stands there swaying gently.

"I am gazing into the abyss and it is gazing back into me!" he mutters.

He's going to jump ...

The moment stretches out and splinters into parallel possibilities, confronting me with a dilemma: I must choose which future becomes the present. What should I do? Should I try to stop him?

"It ends for me here. Now. I reject the slow decline into insanity my father suffered and I refuse his choice: to die like a coward."

What does he mean? That he's *not* going to jump?

"Take the gun from your pocket, Nick."

Suddenly I understand who I must assassinate.

"If you can do this, everything is yours."

He stands there, on the very edge of the world, waiting ...

Time jumps, again ...

I hand him the gun, turn, and walk away.

There's a gunshot.

I turn round, but he's no longer there.

I panic, stumble away from the cliff, run back down the path past the visitor centre to the van, open the door, grab the briefcase and run back up the hill.

I stand on the edge again, barely able to breathe. My eyes plummet vertically down to the rocks below and I feel the magnet pulling me into the abyss.

There's no sign of him. No smashed body down there. He's vanished into the ocean, like Robo, like Icarus. For a second I think I'm going to join him. The urge to jump is so strong. The magnet has me in its grip.

I gaze down. Wave after wave peaks, then explodes onto the rocks, dissipating its energy spectacularly. People are like waves: energy on the move, in transit between birth and death. One second there's energy, and the next it's gone. The energy that was Alejandro has moved on, just as it does when a wave breaks.

I feel nothing. All the emotion has been sucked out of me, leaving nothing—no ego, no guilt. The sun rises at the edge of the world and I'm a ghost again, drifting through the dawn, lost in limbo.

I take the envelope from the briefcase, remove the documents, tear them into small pieces and throw them over the edge, into the void. The wind carries them out to sea.

"Offshore wind" I think to myself, and a crazy idea occurs to me.

I run back to the van, get in and drive back down the road, towards the foot of the cliffs, towards the rest of my life.

24

TO THE EDGE OF THE EARTH

As I drive I remember more about the windsurfer who sailed Aileens. His name is Finn Mullen, a legendary Irish waterman. The story was documented in a magazine, with stunning images and the title: 'To the Edge of the Earth'[1]. I read it a few years ago but it made a lasting impression, inspiring and terrifying me, and the details are imprinted on my memory.

Now I'm going to attempt the same feat. If I drown trying then so be it. I'd just rejected the path the Master chose for me and thrown away his version of my future—literally, chucking the pieces over the cliff. I'm free of him now, free to choose my *own* mission.

Of course, molecules of psychoactive cactus are still coursing through my bloodstream, time is jumping in discrete steps and I'm living in the present tense, so that might have something to do with my 'crazy idea' ... but I prefer to think that this is a turning point in my life, a defining moment—the moment when I decide to 'live my dream' (as reality TV might put it).

A few minutes later I arrive at the spot where Finn launched. The wind is a stiff ENE breeze, as it was when he sailed here, but thankfully the waves are smaller—perhaps fifteen foot—half the size they were for him.

I struggle into my wetsuit, rig a 4.7 metre sail and plug it into my wave-board, the friend I trust with my life. Her logo confronts me with that familiar question: "WHY?" This time my answer is immediate: "because I'm here, now, alive, free!"

I throw the equipment in the water and jump on the board. The run downwind to the cliffs is truly memorable. I'm flying over huge rolling swells with the most dramatic backdrop imaginable, a particle in the ocean, a grain of sand against those giant cliffs. The Plant magnifies all my senses and even if I don't catch a single wave at Aileens I'll remember this moment for the rest of my life.

But I *do* catch a wave. A single wave, yes, but what a wave!

For a while I'm cautious, watching from the shoulder, trying to get a feel for how the break works. But the more I watch, the harder it is to get in sync with nature here. The waves don't peel predictably. They break in multiple, complex sections, sometimes dumping all their energy on the slab at the foot of the cliff. The wind is fluky as it bounces around these towering walls of rock. It's not exactly chaos—there is order, but it's an order beyond my comprehension.

I decide to trust intuition, not over-think it, just wait for a set and choose the one that feels right, the one with my name on it. As I make that decision the horizon shifts upwards.

The set arrives. I make my choice and pick my swell. It steepens below me as I watch from the top of this mountain of water. It's the high point of my windsurfing career and I feel like I'm in a video.

I choose my moment and drop down the slope into the valley. The board and I plummet downwards at an insanely steep angle. We accelerate until I'm planing faster than I thought possible. For an instant I'm terrified the board can't handle it. She'll bury the nose and we'll crash and burn ... Then I remind myself: I trust her with my life!

Now I'm walking on water. Weightless. Silence, except for the hiss of water flowing over the fins. I trim the board with subtle shifts and lean into a flowing bottom-turn. We accelerate up the wave till I'm vertical, hanging under the lip, poised between a sweet top-turn and disaster. As we fly out of the turn I thank Rick, the man who shaped my board and gave me this experience.

My wave charges towards the cliff like an express train and I feed off its energy, making turn after turn on this monster. In smaller, crowded surf, you have to slash the waves to pieces to stand out. Style is measured by technical tricks. But this ride is not about style. It's about Flow and Respect. The wave is the star, not me. Inspired by its power, I make a dozen turns (I lose count), taking me hundreds of metres down the line, perilously close to the rocks ...

Then I make a mistake—a minor miscalculation, but here, beneath these cliffs, any mistakes have serious consequences. 'Pride comes before a fall', as they say. I leave it a fraction too long before I pull out of the wave and in that fraction of a second the scales of my life are held in balance ...

On one side of the tipping point: I gybe out of the wave and sail back upwind to the van, elated as never before.

On the other side: I go for one more turn and the wave closes out onto the slab.

The moment lasts for a few tenths of a second but there's a whole lifetime, compressed, right there.

Time jumps. The balance tips. The wave closes out and dumps its energy onto me. Now instead of pin-sharp high-definition slow-motion, everything happens in an out-of-focus speed-blur of white-water. I'm tumbled in the washing machine, dizzy and disoriented.

"Don't fight it" a voice-in-my head warns. "You'll only run out of air more quickly."

So I begin counting—a mantra to control the panic ...

One, two, three ... I grip the boom, hanging on for dear life as I spin, head over heels.

Crack! What was that? For a second I think it's my neck or my back breaking. The contents of my stomach arrive in my throat. But it's just the mast snapping.

"Ha! *Just* the mast snapping?" my voice mocks. "How ya going to sail back now?"

"Yeah, you're stuffed, mate" the rest of them gloat.

I try to ignore the demons, keep counting and focus on clichés: '*que será, será*', 'go with the flow,' 'feel the craic' ...

Eight, nine ten ... The boom is torn from my grasp. Now I have nothing to cling to. I surrender to the forces of nature and count ...

I reach fifteen and come to the surface, breathless but still relaxed ... until I see the next wave. It's another monster with my name on it. I'm right in its path. It's going to smash me like a meteorite smashing into the planet.

I just have time for a gulp of air then I dive as deep as I can and start counting again—this time backwards from fifteen ...

Fourteen, thirteen, twelve, eleven ... I hit rock bottom, helpless as tons of water pin me to the slab, crushing the air from my lungs.

Ten, nine, eight, seven ...

"This is it—the countdown to your end!" a malevolent voice whispers in my head.

I'm hypoxic. My vision begins to blur. I'm seeing things—things I shouldn't see ... ghostly sea creatures ... a broken surfboard (my own?) wedged between the boulders like a tombstone—marking my grave? Is that a skeleton?

Six, five, four ... I'm seconds from passing out, giving up, joining the lost souls down here ...

Three, two, one ...

"Zero!" the voices hiss, gleefully. My final moment of consciousness?

But the ocean releases me. I claw my way to the surface. I'm right under the cliff now, next to the rocks, resigned to be smashed to bits on them.

"Yeah, you can't cheat *us*. There's no escape" the demons crow.

I turn over onto my back, stare up at the cliff and glimpse a tiny figure way up there, where the land meets the sky.

Then the whitewater picks me up and I body surf the surge, bracing for the impact ... but it places me gently onto a smooth ledge. I wait for the next wave to crush me ... but it never comes!

There's a lull in the sets. For several minutes Aileens is as flat as a lagoon. The ocean has spared me. My breathing gradually becomes normal. Feeling returns to my numb limbs. The voices have gone. Emotion floods back in to fill the void. I check myself for damage. My wetsuit is shredded. Cut and bruised skin shows through the rips, but nothing is broken.

What about my friend? I look around, expecting to find her in pieces but miraculously she's been spared as well. The rig is destroyed but the board is sitting on the ledge beside me, intact, having used up another of her nine lives. I run my hand over her, checking there's no damage, thanking the gods of the ocean.

Then I unplug the wrecked rig and throw it into the sea as a peace offering—a sacrifice to appease them. I remember doing the same thing in Geraldton the night I faked my disappearance. That was the end of Malcolm Fraser and the start of my journey here—to the ledge at the edge of the earth. Now this is the end of another chapter and the start of ... what?

I'm not sure how long I sat there, trying to answer that question— long enough for the effects of the Plant to dissipate and time to return to normality. It was like waking up onboard the Abyss. I'd survived, again, and now I had a future to contemplate.

The tide was ebbing, leaving my ledge high and dry. The magazine article had mentioned a last resort exit strategy for Finn—a goat track leading back up the cliff. I looked around and there it was, steep and slippery, but definitely climbable.

I grabbed my board, but those bold, black 3D letters confronted me with the same old question: 'WHY?' I couldn't move on without an answer. I sat down again, gazed at the logo and thought about it.

I'd been drifting through life when the Master had rescued me. The past two years had been a search for a goal worth pursuing. I'd rejected the path he'd chosen for me and I was in control of my own destiny again ... So, what now?

Well, I quite liked the idea of staying there for a while—not *right there* on my ledge, but in Ireland. I felt at home in the Emerald Isle. After all, I had family connections—it was in my blood. Spectacular beaches, wind, world-class waves, friendly locals, Guinness, wildly exuberant music, the craic ... What more could you possibly want, Nick?

Travel maybe? (and perhaps a bit less of the soft rain and troubled politics). I could imagine making Ireland my base for a while, but I'd always be a drifter, permanently in transit. The grass may be greener here but I still had the urge to see the rest of the world and I had unfinished business in El Médano and Cabarete. So, stick around for a while, chase a few storms, ride a few waves, enjoy the craic ... and then hit the road again?

It was a good plan, but I had to find something more in my life—something, or some*body*, to love. I'd been a loner, a ghost, for too long. I'd put things right with Robo but then the bloody eejit had gone and died on me! There was Nicole, of course, and Mandu ... They'd all left an aching hole in me. It was time to find another soulmate, no question about that.

But it wasn't the only answer. I needed a dream to follow. My brief experience as an entrepreneur and activist had proved that to me. For a while, back in Australia, I'd been a contender—somebody who mattered, somebody whose energy might not just vanish when their wave broke. Perhaps I could find something similar here in Ireland?

Perhaps ... but I had a feeling that commerce and politics weren't for me. There *was* one thing I'd started and had yet to finish—my memoir: 'Too Close to the Wind'. Writing it was a cathartic, confessional experience—my way of confronting the past, admitting my mistakes, moving on ...

Writing was certainly an immersive activity. I got as much of a buzz from it as I did from windsurfing. Each word, sentence, paragraph and chapter posed a challenge as unique as a gybe, jump, or wave-ride. Nothing else mattered when I was writing or windsurfing, but the big plus was that I could write whenever I had a free moment —no need to wait for wind and waves. So it was the perfect foil for my other passion ...

But perhaps it could be more than that? More than a mere obsession. Perhaps it was the answer, the goal, the dream.

Was that who I was: a writer?

I could give it go.

Why not?

So, that was that. I was a survivor and I was free now. Free to leave my ledge and climb the cliff. Free to go anywhere, do anything I wanted. As free as my friend—the wind.

25

EPILOGUE: WHY?

E l Médano, Tenerife. One year later. Rick's Sunday starts, as usual, with a hangover. The previous night he'd worked late in his workshop finishing a new board and then gone into town to celebrate. The *sangria* and *cerveza* had been flowing, and Saturday night had already become Sunday morning before he staggered back to the little apartment above his surf shop.

He's hardly slept. The wind woke him as always, even before the sun hit the window. Looking out, the mountains are caught in that unnaturally pink light. The sky is immense here, and every dawn is a performance. The beach is still in shadow, deserted, but white horses are dancing towards the bay, driven on by *Los Alisios*, the northeast trade-winds.

Now he's awake and the day has a purpose. He grabs a 'WHY Boards' teeshirt, surf shorts, a strong black coffee, and heads downstairs to his basement workshop. It's like descending into the Underworld. The walls are painted black and there are no windows, no distractions. It's claustrophobic, chaotic, cluttered with half-finished boards ... his sanctuary—a temple to his dark art.

· · ·

Rick is the owner of 'WHY Custom Wave-Boards'. He was one of the first windsurfers to make El Médano his home and he's kept the business alive for three decades, through thick and thin. But it's taken its toll on him—all that fibreglass dust, epoxy resin, alcohol, partying ... He lives for a day like today, with exceptional conditions and a new board to test.

He switches on the harsh fluorescent lights and cranks up the volume on the sound system. Heavy metal blasts from the speakers. He sits down next to the new board and waits for the caffeine and guitar riffs to defeat his hangover. Rick has been half deaf for the past decade and his customers know to bring earplugs with them to the basement. In exchange, they get his craftsmanship, banter, and to smoke a spliff or two.

The shaper sits there for a moment assessing the new board, running his hands over her, feeling the subtleties of the rails and rocker. It's a prototype—a radical new shape, and Rick can't wait to try her.

He fires up his laptop and checks the online wind meter ... twenty-five knots NE'ly, with gusts in the low thirties—*¡Perfecto!* He paces around the workshop, using the music to fuel his adrenaline, feeling the expectations build. Then he grabs the board and heads outside to the boardwalk.

The morning has real promise. The wind is the perfect strength for a 4.7 metre sail—every wave-sailor's favourite size, and the swell has been building all night. The waves on the reef look excellent—decent size in the sets, peeling cleanly ... and hopefully, he'll have them to himself for at least the next hour if he gets his act together.

It's still early and the other surf shops aren't open yet. A few tourists are having breakfast in the cafe on the boardwalk but there's nobody on the beach, and Rick is the only windsurfer rigging up. Today is Sunday—the busiest day on the water, and he's eager to get going before the crowds arrive. He has a new toy to test and he's in a hurry to escape gravity for a few hours, into that other world where he dances on water.

He throws the equipment together in something of a frenzy, working on autopilot. His brain doesn't need to be engaged—he can rig in his sleep, the movements familiar from decades of doing just this whenever the wind calls. He unrolls the sail onto the boardwalk, sleeves the mast, pulls on the downhaul, clamps the boom to the mast and attaches the outhaul—all without taking his eyes from the horizon, his focus still on the waves.

A set rolls in. Rick watches as geometric lines of surf march across the reef, mentally picking one and imagining himself riding it, his body making strange little movements, like a bizarre dance to a private soundtrack.

Taking his eyes from the water he meets a tourist's startled gaze, bemused by his antics and intrigued that his morning has such a clear purpose. Rick looks away, and glancing down he sees he has everything ready to go. A gust of wind swirls up the sand, impatiently tugging at his sail. Jamming the rig into the new board, he picks them both up and sprints to the water.

But then, just as he's about to launch, something catches his eye—another board, sitting alone on the beach. One of his own designs, in fact. Rick gazes at it and a wave of nausea breaks over him. No! It can't be! It's not possible! He's shaking now.

He remembers this board only too well. It was always one of his favourites—a classic, elegant shape with flowing lines and brutally effective graphics. The customer had wanted a pure white board with just Rick's company name in bold, black 3D letters. But he'd wanted something unique, a one-off, so he'd asked Rick to add a question mark after the WHY logo and specified that his should be the only board ever produced with it.

Rick stares at the board, with its unique logo, and tries to picture the individual who'd commissioned it. He was a young Australian dude with surfy dreadlocks and tattoos, that much he's sure of, but Rick is struggling to remember his name. He was a loner and no-one in the town knew much about him.

What Rick *does* know is that three years ago this Ozzie *hombre* disappeared, in tragic circumstances. Now, as Rick gazes at the board on the beach next to his own new design, he begins to piece together what happened ...

It was a windy Sunday with good waves, just like today, and ironically this dude's board, like Rick's, was brand new when he vanished with it. He'd only just collected it from the workshop the previous afternoon. Rick remembers being relieved that at least he'd paid in full, and then feeling guilty for such an uncharitable thought.

It's all coming back to him now. Of course, the night before he disappeared they'd toasted the new board in the bar where the Ozzie dude worked. Rick still can't remember his name, but fragments of their conversation are playing in his head now ... Rick had joked that he reminded him of a Clint Eastwood character—a strong-and-silent loner like the 'Man with No Name' ... but this *hombre* did have a name ... what the fuck was it?

Rick looks around the beach with wild eyes, searching for the missing piece of the jigsaw. Then, suddenly, he remembers ... Nick! Of course, that's it!

Their conversation had been brief, and awkward. They'd both had a few drinks and they had to yell over the racket in the bar, but that wasn't it. This Nick bloke clearly had a few problems. Rick had become impatient with his reticence, his secretive, reserved manner. Nick explained that he wasn't being arrogant, just that he had nothing worth saying about himself. He tried to justify this by suggesting that perhaps even Clint suffered from a lack of confidence, low self esteem, shyness   and that was why he didn't say much in the movies ... but Rick didn't want to know about that. It was a ludicrous idea. In fact, as a huge fan of the 'Man with No Name', he'd been offended by Nick's suggestion and walked out of the bar in disgust.

Later he wondered if he'd made a mistake. Perhaps Nick had been joking about Clint's personality and *he* was too stupid to get the joke. The more Rick thought about it the more worried he became. Why would anyone make a joke like that? Probably because he, Nick, was lonely, depressed, fucked-up himself. Maybe he'd needed someone to listen to him, to help him. But Rick had ignored him, perhaps even let him down that night.

When Nick went missing the next day, presumed drowned, Rick felt guilty. If he'd been a better listener maybe he could have helped —perhaps even been a friend, a windsurfing buddy. Then Nick might have called him that Sunday morning, told him he was taking the new board out early, arranged to meet at the beach ... They might have sailed together ... Maybe then Nick would still be alive. Shit! It was three years ago and now he's haunted by guilt again.

At the time Rick presumed, like everyone else, that this Nick dude had broken something and been swept out to sea, behind the vertical cliffs at the foot of the red mountain. Once hidden behind *Montaña Roja* no-one would see him again—the next stop was South America. That's how people had been lost before.

His rig had washed in down the coast a few days later, with a broken UJ, but they never found his board or his body. The *Guardia Civil* still had him listed as a missing person and no death certificate was issued, but most people assumed he was at the bottom of the Atlantic, or in some lucky shark's stomach.

His disappearance was briefly the talk of El Médano. There was a mention in the local newspaper, *La Opinión*, but he was forgotten soon enough. After all, he'd been living incognito, like a ghost. He had no friends and no-one to miss him.

Now it seems his board has returned, to haunt the town.

· · ·

Rick scans the beach, the boardwalk, the rocks ... but there's no sign of the board's owner. How could there be? He stares at the logo and it confronts him with a simple rhetorical question: "WHY?"[1]

AFTERWORD

Thank you for reading 'Too Close to the Wind'. I hope you enjoyed it, but even if you didn't I hope you'll post a review on Amazon (and tell me where I went wrong :-)

Indie writers depend on reviews, shares, and word-of-mouth recommendations. If you post a review and share my books on your social networks you'll motivate this author to Keep Scribbling (my motto).

Go to this link: smarturl.it/TooCloseToTheWind and it should take you to the book's Amazon page to post your review.

If you'd like to receive my newsletter, advance copies of my books, special offers, and get a FREE PREQUEL STORY with exclusive scenes from Nick's eventful backstory ... subscribe by going to this link: BookHip.com/KCQKJX

My motivation for writing 'Too Close to the Wind' was to 'share the stoke' (as Nick might say) with both my fellow surfaholics and a wider audience. It would be fantastic if you could take a photo with the book on your home beach (if you're a windsurfer), or in an exotic holiday location, and share it.

You can connect with me on my FaceBook page: <u>Richard Attree - Author</u> and at: <u>www.RichardAttree.com</u> ... I'd love to hear from you, and it would be great if you could help spread the word about the book.

A NOTE TO MY READERS

Reading a novel differs from watching a film, listening to music, or looking at a painting in one important respect: the reader lives with the story, characters, and themes for a lot longer—anything up to several weeks (if, like me, you're a slow reader and/or like to savour a book). That's one reason I love novels. The best can live with you long after you reach the last page ... but there's always a poignant moment when you put the book down and say goodbye.

'Parting is such sweet sorrow' and this is my parting gift to you. Thank you, again, for reading 'Too Close to the Wind'. You finished the main course, so here are a few extra pages for dessert—a 'look behind the scenes' for anyone who's curious about how, and why, I wrote it; and a way to connect with you for a little longer—a bit like the 'Extras' clips that you find on a DVD.

Write about what you know ...

As I say in my 'About the Author' copy: I always wanted to be a writer but was diverted into a career as a media music composer. Plenty of water had flowed under the bridge before I sat down to write my first novel[1]—a lifetime of material, in fact. So what should it be about?

Well, the usual advice is: write about what you know and are passionate about. I asked myself what that might be, and I came up with these three ideas:

1. My life story.
2. A novel about a musician.
3. A novel about a windsurfer.

Obviously, I knew a bit about the first of these, and it seemed the most straightforward to write, so I started working on an autobiography, with the title: 'The Wind of Change—memoir of a Windsurfing Baby Boomer'. However, my wife, Nikki, persuaded me to shelve it. She pointed out that nobody would be interested in the true (but arguably mundane) story of an unknown composer and average windsurfer. She suggested that I should write a novel.

When it comes to these sorts of decisions I trust Nikki 100% (even though I thought she was a bit harsh re 'nobody', 'mundane', 'unknown', and 'average' :-) so I put the autobiography in the 'Future Projects' folder and started thinking about the other two ideas.

Music and windsurfing have been major distractions in my life—simultaneous, but very different obsessions. I've spent half my life exploring these parallel worlds, getting to know the people in them, amassing a treasure trove of experiences, adventures, anecdotes ... so the raw material was already in place. A story based on either of these themes could be a fictionalised version of my autobiography. That was Nikki's point: fiction is sexier than real life—especially when it's the real life of a nobody! 'The Wind of Change' would have to wait until I was a *somebody* (and the jury's still out on when that might be).

The other two ideas competed to make it out of my brain into my word processor and become my debut novel. Windsurfing won, but an outline for my next book: 'The Rhythm of Time', with music as the central theme, has joined 'The Wind of Change' in the Future Projects folder.

What windsurfing means to me (and Nick) ...

I've been a windsurfer for most of my life. Since discovering it, with Nikki, in the mid 1980s, windsurfing has influenced many of our decisions: where to go on holiday (somewhere windy), what vehicle to buy (a van), what to spend the rest of our money on (windsurfing kit) ... and more crucially: what job to do, where to live, and even whether to have children![2]

Windsurfing is an obsession that has taken us around the world searching for wind, waves, and adventure. Like Nick (my narrator) I sometimes joke that it's my 'religion'. A primary motivation for writing 'Too Close to the Wind' was to 'share the stoke' (as Nick might say) with both my fellow surfaholics and a wider audience.

Marketing ...

A further reason to write about what you know and are passionate about, is that after writing a book you have to market it to the right people. This is less daunting if you're trying to connect with readers who already share your passion—the tribe of English speaking windsurfers, in my case.

It isn't exactly a mass market, more of a niche, but equally, there's not much competition. I jokingly describe my book as the world's first windsurfing novel. There are a few, non fiction windsurfing books (technique manuals, memoirs, location guides, for example), and no doubt windsurfing makes an appearance in other fiction, but I've yet to come across a book that you might call a proper windsurfing novel (if you know of any please let me know).

There are far more books that feature surfing, and even a few authors writing surf fiction[3]. So, although windsurfing is a smaller niche than surfing, there *is* a gap in that market. There may be fewer windsurfers than surfers (especially if we include the wannabes, hangers-on, followers of surf fashion etc who like to call themselves 'surfers' without necessarily going near a proper wave), but there's no reason why the search for wind should not be as authentically chron-icled as the search for the perfect wave.

With all this talk of a niche tribe of core readers, you may be wondering: what about non-surfers, wind or otherwise? Does he have anything to say to them?

Well, yes, I certainly hope so. I'd like to think 'Too Close to the Wind' has cross-over, mainstream appeal and that my windsurfing readers will share it with their non-'windie' friends. If they do, then perhaps their friends might understand our obsession with surfing the wind and waves. Word-of-mouth and personal recommendations are the best way for an author to build a readership, so of course I'm also hoping that another reason to recommend my novel to a non-windsurfing reader is that it's simply a good read.

I'm not a climber, but I love reading about mountains, travel, adventure ... and being a novel (as Nikki suggested) my book also has plot, characters, and a few other themes besides windsurfing ...

Philosophical Chess ...

My main character, Nick, talks about playing 'philosophical chess' with the Master. I studied philosophy for my undergraduate degree and I've always been fascinated with the interplay of ideas. I wanted to weave philosophical threads into the story without it becoming as introspective as, say, Thomas Mann's 'The Magic Mountain' or Robert Pirsig's 'Zen and the Art of Motorcycle Maintenance'.

Two thinkers have always intrigued me: Friedrich Nietzsche, the nineteenth-century German philosopher, and Carl Jung, an associate of Sigmund Freud, who become influential in the twentieth century with concepts such as the 'Collective Unconscious'. I had fun playing with their ideas—moving them around like chess pieces to see how they might impact on each other.

Mind-altering Substances ...

Another theme that interested me was psychoactive / mind-altering substances. As a baby boomer coming of age in the 1960s, a student in the early 1970s, and then playing in rock bands, I did my fair share of experimenting with psychedelic drugs. They were part of my (arguably misspent) youth, along with long hair, electric guitars, and open-air rock festivals.

I was too young (and living in the wrong country) to be a genuine hippie, but I was a trainee 'freak' (as we Brits preferred to call the counterculture kids). I read Carlos Castaneda's 'A Separate Reality', Aldous Huxley's 'Doors of Perception', Tom Wolfe's 'The Electric Kool-Aid Acid Test', Timothy Leary's writing about LSD ... and I got my hands on some hands-on experiences.

On balance, weighing up the dangers and benefits, I'm glad that I had these experiences, and relieved that I survived them. There's an element of 'whatever doesn't kill you makes you stronger' in this, but I *am* glad to have experienced these unusual mental states. It gives you a different perspective on 'normality' as just one of the many threads in life's rich tapestry.

Nick takes the psychoactive cactus Plant four times: with Nicole in the haunted Haitian rainforest; with Robo, windsurfing in Esperance; with Mandu, in the Ancestor's cave; and at the Mayor's 'soirée'. Two of these are positive, mind-expanding experiences (the first and the third), and two are negative, bad trips (the second and the fourth). The fifty-fifty good-to-bad ratio pretty much mirrors my own experiences.

Survival at Sea ...

When I started plotting the story arc for 'Too Close to the Wind' I knew I wanted to begin the book with Nick's survival story. It was based on various real incidents of windsurfers and surfers rescued after drifting for many hours on their boards. A further inspiration was Hemmingway's 'The Old Man and the Sea'.

In the ten years I've lived here, in El Médano, there have been several cases of windsurfers going missing. Some were rescued, some drowned. A few just disappeared and their bodies were never found. I imagined myself in Nick's situation and asked myself how I'd cope. Would I have the strength of will to survive? How long would hope remain?

I first read Hemmingway's heroic story of survival at sea when I was fifteen, for my English Literature O level. As I said, the best books live with you long after you first experience them. I reread it, fifty years later, while writing chapter two and I readily acknowledge his influence.

Nick's Missions and Travel Writing ...

The main story begins when the Master offers Nick a way out of his stalled life: a series of missions that lead him around the world on a journey of self-discovery—first to the Dominican Republic, then back home to confront his past in Australia, and finally to Ireland. The novel is the story of Nick's travel adventures and his spiritual journey.

These locations are all places Nikki and I have visited in our own search for wind and waves. The descriptions, texture, and some of the local incidents are often fictionalised extrapolations from my autobiography.

The Caribbean, Nicole ...

Nikki and I first visited Cabarete, the location of Nick's first mission, in the early 1990s. We've been back many times since. We have a painting in our living room that we brought back rolled up in one of our sails. It depicts the waves on the reef, the beach, and the little huts in the jungle incorporating bits of old windsurfing equipment in their construction, as described in the book. It could be one of Nicole and Jacqueline's 'tourist paintings'.

My wife's name is Nicole Jacqueline. She's also an artist, and she's *my* soulmate. She helped me a lot with these chapters.

The Outback, Mandu ...

I've been to Australia a few times, spent time in Sydney, Perth, and some of the well-known windsurfing spots. Nick's hometown is loosely based on the windsurfing / cray fishing town of Lancelin. It was there that I heard about the Bungle Bungles—ancient, strangely shaped hills hidden away in the remote Kimberly region of WA. I was fascinated by the evocative name. Twenty years later when I was searching for Mandu's whereabouts, I looked up the Bungle Bungles on the internet. Through the magic of Google Earth, I was able to make a virtual visit and explore the extraordinary landscape.

Mandu, the Aboriginal shaman, is my favourite character in the novel. If you know Carlos Castaneda's books you'll find similarities between Mandu and Don Juan, the Yaqui Indian *brujo*, or sorcerer, who teaches Castaneda about his way of knowledge. They each use naturally growing psychoactive substances (peyote for Don Juan and the cactus Plant for Mandu) to access altered states of reality. They both live self-sufficient lives off-grid in the remote desert/outback, but they're also completely at ease in a modern city. When Nick meets Mandu in Perth, dressed as a city slicker, he's as shocked as Castaneda when he finds Don Juan in downtown Mexico City.

Mandu's knowledge, the Dreamtime, the Creation Myths, have been passed down from the Ancestors and live on in his people's collective unconscious. When Nick shows him Nicole's painting: 'The Kangaroo Kid and his Voodoo Child', Mandu sees the links between his Dreamtime and Nicole's *Vodou*. He takes Nick to the tribe's most sacred place, a cave in a meteorite crater at the centre of the Bungle Bungles. They take the Plant together and Mandu shows him the Ancestors' paintings on the cave's walls. The idea of 'scraping' the figures, animals etc from the paintings and watching them come to life was based on a similar, hallucinatory experience that I had during an LSD trip.

Living the Dream ...

At its heart, my novel is the story of Nick's journey to discover who he is, to 'fulfil his potential' (to quote the Master), and 'live the dream' (to use the jargon of reality TV). It's a 'coming of age' story in which the hero eventually realises he needs to find a goal worth pursuing.

In some ways, Nick is me at twenty-five. When he dreams of being a writer he is, of course, expressing my own aspirations. I'm incredibly fortunate to be able to 'live my dream', here in El Médano, writing about what I love. I've left it quite late to write my first novel, but 'better late than never', no?

What's Next? ...

Earlier, I mentioned my 'Future Projects' folder. Let me share some of the contents with you ...

'The Rhythm of Time' is about three musicians who live in the same city, London, in three different centuries (17th, 21st, and 24th). They are so interlinked by the 'reincarnation of ideas' that it seems as if they share one life. The novel explores the magical, mysterious phenomenon of music, and the soul of that labyrinthine city—how they can change through the centuries, and yet stay the same. It will combine historical fiction, contemporary fiction, and science fiction.

As mentioned, I'm also working on an autobiography: 'The Wind of Change—memoir of a Windsurfing Baby Boomer', which will unite windsurfing and music with the story of my generation. We've lived through some of the most exciting, eventful decades in human history ... and we've also witnessed climate change, extremism, Thatcher, Trump, and selfies. So you should expect a few rants. As mentioned, this project has been put on hold until it becomes the real life of a somebody, rather than a nobody :-)

I'm also considering a sequel to 'Too Close to the Wind'. **Here's where you, my readers, can influence me.** I'm not going to promise anything ... but perhaps, just maybe, if enough people convince me that it's worth doing, I might be persuaded to revisit Nick and write a sequel. After all, I didn't kill him off along with the Master, and in some ways, his life is just beginning.

Signing off ...

So, that's it from me. I hope you enjoyed this peek into an author's mind and that you'll be with me for the rest of my writing journey.

If you'd like to receive my newsletter, advance copies of my books, special offers, and get a FREE PREQUEL STORY with exclusive scenes from Nick's eventful backstory ... subscribe by going to this link: BookHip.com/KCQKJX

My motivation for writing 'Too Close to the Wind' was to 'share the stoke' (as Nick might say) with both my fellow surfaholics and a wider audience. It would be fantastic if you could take a photo with the book on your home beach (if you're a windsurfer), or in an exotic holiday location, and share it.

You can connect with me on my FaceBook page: Richard Attree - Author and at: www.RichardAttree.com ... I'd love to hear from you, and it would be great if you could help spread the word about the book.

Indie writers depend on reviews, shares, and word-of-mouth recommendations. If you post a review of 'Too Close to the Wind' on Amazon, and share my books on your social networks, you'll motivate this author to Keep Scribbling (my motto).

Go to this link: smarturl.it/TooCloseToTheWind and it should take you to the book's Amazon page to post your review.

I'll sign off now, with Ludwig Langer's final words:

Again I thank you, my dear reader, for your time and patience. I hope you have found something of interest in this journal.
Auf Wiedersehen.

Richard Attree, December 2018, El Médano, Tenerife.

FOOTNOTES

2. Drifting

1. Chronicled in Tom Wolfe's book: 'The Electric Kool-Aid Acid Test'.

6. Salsa On Speed

1. The legendary waterman Brian Talma, the 'Irie Man'.

10. In Transit

1. A local bus, literally 'stuffed' with people.

14. This Land Is Our Land

1. Author's note: I changed the name of the main town in the Kimberley region of Western Australia from Broome to Broom to make it quite clear that *my* town, and its citizens, are fictional.

24. To The Edge Of The Earth

1. 'To the Edge of the Earth' by Brian McDowell, Windsurfer International magazine, issue #14, December 2010. Title used with Brian's permission.

25. Epilogue: Why?

1. As a postscript ... Timothy Leary died on May 31, 1996, aged 75. His death was videotaped for posterity at his request, capturing his final words. According to his son Zachary, during his final moments, he clenched his fist and said: "Why?" Then unclenching his fist, he said, "Why not?". He continued to repeat these rhetorical questions, in different intonations, and died soon after.

A Note to my Readers

1. 'Too Close to the Wind' is my first *solo* book. I've co-written two others with my wife: Nobody's Poodle (2013), a short novel written from the perspective of our rescue dog, and Somebody's Doodle (2016), a fast moving, heady mix of crime, humour, romance, and a few dogs.
2. The solution? Live as close as possible to the beach, only take on work that allows one to skive off whenever it's windy, and as for children ... do dogs count?
3. Notably Kem Nunn, credited with inventing the surf-noir genre.

ACKNOWLEDGMENTS

I'd like to thank all the people who encouraged me to make writing more than a distraction, and helped me to make the novel that was rattling around my head, real.

Thanks to all my beta readers for their generosity and constructive, critical feedback. Especially: members of the Tenerife Authors' Group: Linda Wainwright, for insisting that I flesh out my narrator; Erica Greaves for spotting a plot inconsistency; Bradley Chermside for his attention to detail and style; Leonie Brook, for her eagle-eyed proofreading; novelist Randy Landenberger https://randco.me for paring down my worst excesses—especially my addiction to adverbs; writer and expert windsurfer, Brian McDowel, for his excellent feedback, local knowledge, brilliant suggestions re the Cliffs of Moher, windsurfing Aileens, and for permission to use his evocative title: 'To the Edge of the Earth'.

Spillane's Bar (www.spillanesbar.com) is a real pub and makes an appearance with their permission. If you are ever in the Maharees pay them a visit (and mention my name :-)

A huge thank-you to John Carter (Facebook: JohnCarterPhotography), one of the world's leading windsurfing photographers, for allowing me to use his amazing shot of Julien Taboulet in free fall, as my cover image. It was taken at the 2013 Red Bull Storm Chase, in Brandon Bay, Ireland—where Nick windsurfs, in chapter 22.

Another thank-you to my cover designer, Sylvia Frost (http://sfrostcovers.com) for translating my vague ideas into such a cool cover.

Anyone who leaves a review on Amazon please feel acknowledged here.

Finally to my wife, Nikki, with whom I've shared more than half my life, and without whom this novel would not have been written ... for her many roles: plot consultant, developmental editor, alpha reader, beta reader, line editor, and for enduring my endless ramblings.

ABOUT THE AUTHOR

RICHARD ATTREE always wanted to be a writer but was diverted into writing music rather than books.

Growing up in London in the 1960s Richard studied, experimented with sex, drugs, rock 'n roll, and grew his hair. By the mid-1970s he had a degree in philosophy, his hair had reached its zenith, and he was playing keyboards in jazz, rock, and soul bands.

For the next thirty years, he composed music for TV, working at the BBC's renowned Radiophonic Workshop, before going freelance.

In 2007 he retired from the media music business and down-shifted to El Médano—a sunny, windy, surfy town in the Canary Islands, off the coast of Africa. This gave him the opportunity to get to grips with writing while pursuing his other passion: windsurfing, combining them in a series of articles for 'Boards' magazine: 'Life on the Reef'.

Richard has been a windsurfer for most of his life. Like Nick (the main character in his novel: 'Too Close to the Wind') he sometimes jokes that it's his 'religion'. It's certainly an obsession that has taken him around the world searching for wind, waves, and adventure.

These days there's not much hair left and he focusses on writing (when it's not windy). His motto is: 'Keep Scribbling!'

He's published two books co-authored with his wife, Nikki: 'Nobody's Poodle' (2013), a short novel written from the perspective of their rescue dog, and 'Somebody's Doodle' (2016), a fast-moving, heady mix of crime, humour, romance, and a few more dogs.

'Too Close to the Wind' (2019) is his debut solo novel. It's a journey of self-discovery narrated by a young Australian windsurfer. Dogs don't feature in it.

You can connect with him at www.RichardAttree.com (where there's a more revealing and entertaining version of this biog, complete with some occasionally embarrassing pics illustrating how the haircuts have reflected the zeitgeist of the decades he's lived through) and on his FaceBook page: Richard Attree - Author.

Made in United States
North Haven, CT
03 December 2024

61531577R00202